The Best
AMERICAN
MYSTERY &
SUSPENSE
2024

GUEST EDITORS OF
THE BEST AMERICAN MYSTERY AND SUSPENSE

1997 ROBERT B. PARKER
1998 SUE GRAFTON
1999 ED MCBAIN
2000 DONALD E. WESTLAKE
2001 LAWRENCE BLOCK
2002 JAMES ELLROY
2003 MICHAEL CONNELLY
2004 NELSON DEMILLE
2005 JOYCE CAROL OATES
2006 SCOTT TUROW
2007 CARL HIAASEN
2008 GEORGE PELECANOS
2009 JEFFERY DEAVER
2010 LEE CHILD
2011 HARLAN COBEN
2012 ROBERT CRAIS
2013 LISA SCOTTOLINE
2014 LAURA LIPPMAN
2015 JAMES PATTERSON
2016 ELIZABETH GEORGE
2017 JOHN SANDFORD
2018 LOUISE PENNY
2019 JONATHAN LETHEM
2020 C. J. BOX
2021 ALAFAIR BURKE
2022 JESS WALTER
2023 LISA UNGER
2024 S. A. COSBY

The Best
AMERICAN
MYSTERY &
SUSPENSE™
2024

Edited and with an Introduction
by S. A. COSBY
STEPH CHA, Series Editor

MARINER BOOKS
New York   Boston

FIRST EDITION

ISBN 978-0-06-331585-3
ISSN 1094-8384

24 25 26 27 28 LBC 5 4 3 2 1

Contents

Foreword

A FEW DAYS before Christmas, my father was home alone when he heard what sounded like pebbles hitting his bedroom window. He looked outside and saw two masked men in head-to-toe black, standing expectantly in his backyard. They'd hopped my parents' gate and were checking to see if the house was empty; they had, I assume, burglarious intentions.

We hosted a Christmas Eve party right after this happened, and I overheard my dad telling this story no fewer than three times. According to at least one version, my sixty-seven-year-old father grabbed his gun and chased the men into the street. He also concedes that they started running as soon as he came to the window.

This was one of the more dramatic happenings in my family's life in 2023. It was, anyway, our year's closest brush with crime. It was also a true nonevent in the scheme of things: a trespass, an aborted burglary, a retiree with an unloaded gun. At most, a NextDoor post. For us, though, it held a certain small significance. Everything feels meaningful when it's close to home.

This is, of course, the power of a good story. It removes distance, letting us experience other people's problems with an immediacy that is otherwise hard to access. Over the last four years, I've read thousands of crime stories for *The Best American Mystery and Suspense*. I'm familiar with the genre conventions and, at this point, I'm almost never surprised by the novelty of a plot line. On the other hand, I remain constantly moved and delighted by particulars.

It is an honor to edit this series, to find stories I love and share them with such an appreciative audience. Since its inception as *The*

Best American Mystery Stories in 1997, this anthology has published
short fiction by many of your favorite writers at different points
in their careers. It also boasts an illustrious roster of guest editors:
Robert B. Parker, Sue Grafton, Ed McBain, Donald E. Westlake,
Lawrence Block, James Ellroy, Michael Connelly, Nelson DeMille,
Joyce Carol Oates, Scott Turow, Carl Hiaasen, George Peleca-
nos, Jeffery Deaver, Lee Child, Harlan Coben, Robert Crais, Lisa
Scottoline, Laura Lippman, James Patterson, Elizabeth George,
John Sandford, Louise Penny, Jonathan Lethem, C. J. Box, Alafair
Burke, Jess Walter, and Lisa Unger.

For *Best American Mystery and Suspense 2024*, I had the pleasure
of working with Southern noir juggernaut S. A. Cosby. I'm not
even sure when Shawn and I met, but we've known each other
for years, and I'm a huge fan of his work. He's written four fantastic novels: *My Darkest Prayer, Blacktop Wasteland, Razorblade Tears,*
and *All the Sinners Bleed.* The first of these came out in 2018, but
he's already had an enormous impact on the mystery and suspense
world, with award-winning, bestselling books that have helped re-
shape the genre. He's won the Macavity, the Anthony, the Barry,
the Hammett, the International Thriller Writers award, and the
Los Angeles Times Book Prize, some of these in back-to-back years.
He's also a multiple Edgar nominee. For many readers, including
one Barack Obama, he's probably *the* defining writer of contempo-
rary crime fiction.

What many people might not know is that Shawn cut his teeth on
short stories, cranking out hundreds of them in the years leading up
to his first novel. He published many of these with Thuglit, which
also counts many *BAMS* authors among its contributors. Shawn
may write instant bestsellers now, but he spent years honing his
craft and voice in the comparatively niche world of short crime
fiction. This may account, in part, for his deep camaraderie and
continuous generosity with other writers.

He still writes tons of short stories, by the way—I'm always excited to come across them in my reading for this anthology. He
was a contributor to *The Best American Mystery and Suspense* in both
2022 and 2023. He would've been eligible for this year's, too, but
he took a year off to be my guest editor. Shawn has been an ex-
tremely game partner in this process, and I am very grateful to him
for his intelligence, enthusiasm, and willingness to work on the
unreasonable schedule I foisted on him.

I've had a wild year—I judged the National Book Awards and have been shooting a TV show in South Korea, where I am currently in a hotel room writing this overdue foreword after an all-nighter on set. As I've mentioned in past volumes, I also have two small children. My first was born less than two weeks after editor Nicole Angeloro tapped me for *Best American*. Because of all the above, I've gone five years without working on a novel. Editing this series has kept me connected to my people and my love of crime fiction. I will never get sick of reading fresh stories and working with writers like Shawn.

This is my fourth anthology, so I knew where to find eligible stories, and, helpfully, writers and editors knew where to find me. I read through every issue of *Ellery Queen* and *Alfred Hitchcock's Mystery Magazine,* as well as Akashic's collections of noir and genre stories. I tracked down crime anthologies, many of them after receiving submissions from individual authors or editors, and kept tabs on the various mystery publications, both in print and online. I also hit up editors of literary journals for crime or crime-adjacent stories. I sifted through all these stories and picked around fifty of the best (or, more accurately, my favorites), which I passed on to Shawn. He read them as fast as I could get them to him, and he chose his favorites. We had an 11:30 p.m. Zoom meeting on maybe the last possible night before selections were due and finalized the list, sharing our thoughts and gushing about these spectacular stories. Twenty of them made it into this volume, but you can find the remaining thirty candidates in the honorable mentions at the back of this book. All the writers and stories on that list are worth seeking out.

As you read this volume, I hope to be well into my reading for *The Best American Mystery and Suspense 2025.* I still worry about missing eligible stories, so authors and editors, please do send me your work. Five of the twenty this year were direct submissions by authors, and three were from sources I might otherwise not have found. To qualify, stories must be originally written in English (or translated by the original authors) by writers born or permanently residing in America or Canada. They need to be independent stories (not excerpts) published in the calendar year 2023 in American (or Canadian) publications, either print or online. I have a strong preference for web submissions, which you can send in any reasonable format to bestamericanmysterysuspense@gmail.com.

If you would like to send printed materials, you can email me for a mailing address. The submissions deadline is December 31, and when possible, several months earlier. I promise to look at every story sent to me before that deadline. After that, well, let's say it depends on my schedule.

I'm proud of all our work here, and grateful for the chance to share these outstanding stories. I hope you enjoy them as much as I did.

STEPH CHA

Introduction

THE SUMMER AFTER I graduated from high school I went to the library to get some books for the weekend. Yes, I was the kind of kid who got books for the weekend instead of being invited to parties. Anyway, as I was perusing the shelves I came across a book of short stories called *The Best American Mystery Stories*, edited by Sue Grafton.

At this time in my life, I knew I wanted to be a writer but I wasn't sure what genre was best for me. I loved horror novels and sci-fi and fantasy. However, my heart always seemed to come back to mysteries, to crime fiction. Before that day I'd never heard of the BAMS. But in that anthology, under Sue Grafton's sure hand, I found short stories that moved me, that made me laugh, that made me think. I think it was the first time I really understood the power of the short crime story. The magic that happens for a brief moment, like a shooting star streaking across the sky, when you read a story that grabs you by the hand and says, "Come with me, see what I have to show you."

It's not always pretty what we are shown but then again, we can't appreciate the light without the darkness. We can't enjoy the sweetness without a taste of the bitter. These days the market for short stories is eroding like a thin strip of beach in a hurricane and I think that's a shame. Some of the greatest crime and mystery writers of all time were masters of the form. It's a special skill that combines brevity with wit and cleverness and the hint of the existential malaise that imbues crime fiction with its gravitas.

The twenty stories in this collection are some of the finest examples of short crime fiction I've read in a long, long time. There are stories here about loss, about love, about revenge and justice. There are stories that will make you laugh; some will make you cry and some will leave you stunned by the incredible width and breadth of their ambition and the beauty of their achievements.

It was my honor to work with Steph Cha to bring these stories to you. Many of the authors here are included in this anthology for the first time. I can tell you from personal experience that being included in the main collection or being cited as a Distinguished Story can be one of your first and most important accolades as a crime writer. It's your entry into a special club, where you can find yourself alongside your idols. And that more than anything is the enduring legacy of *The Best American Mystery and Suspense* anthology. It brings you, the reader, new writers you may not have been aware of, and it allows you to read the work of writers you are intimately familiar with.

It's a place where everyone is welcomed as long as you can tell a compelling tale. It's another link in the long chain that connects all storytellers from African griots to Sophocles to your favorite authors today.

Well, enough from me, you didn't pick this book up to hear me ramble on. You came for the stories. So, sit down, get comfortable.

Here, let me show you something. Let me show you what's here waiting for us, here in the dark.

S. A. COSBY

The Best
AMERICAN
MYSTERY &
SUSPENSE
2024

Scarlet Ribbons

FROM *A Darker Shade of Noir*

ALL THE CHILDREN knew about the Hoffman House.

Penny couldn't remember a time when she didn't know about it. She had spent all of her eleven years three doors down and around the corner from it, and it had been empty her entire life.

No one had lived in the house for years, though everyone seemed to remember a time when new renters had passed through, staying a week or two and then disappearing in the night, even leaving their belongings behind, suitcases left open, boxes unpacked.

It was the neighborhood spookhouse, the Halloween dare, the stuff of all the children's nightmares, and Doctor Hoffman was the boogeyman that haunted their dreams, sharpened their taunts, fired their morbid kid fantasies.

Sometimes, high school boys threw rocks at the windows. Then, last spring, two girls in Penny's class came to school, breathless. They claimed they had snuck up to the house. The doors were all boarded shut, but they had seen things in the windows: TV trays, a dusty globe, rippled magazines, a stuffed teddy bear, its stomach chewed open. A Formica table covered with fading Christmas wrapping paper and all the trimmings, long ribbons curled into wilting bows.

By the end of the school day, they were claiming they'd seen the hammer itself, red-slathered and punched hard into the entryway floor.

That didn't seem like it could be true. *The police would have taken the weapon*, Susan Candliss insisted. *Don't you know anything?*

Besides, another girl said, *how could it be stuck in the floor? It was a ball peen, not a claw.*

And then someone insisted the Hoffmans were Jewish anyway and wouldn't have Christmas paper.

But that visit had an impact. Soon, other girls wanted to go. It was like French kissing. Soon enough, if you hadn't done it, you were good as dead.

Though it had happened many years ago, it seemed like almost everyone knew someone who was a part of it. Maybe their aunt or aunt's friend had been one of Doctor Hoffman's patients and remembered he always had such soft, dimpled hands when he placed the stethoscope over her heart. Maybe their father used to mow the Hoffmans' lawn when he was in high school and sometimes could see Mrs. Hoffman clipping her prized night-blooming jasmine, her monkey-faced orchids, her spider lilies in the glass conservatory. Maybe they'd even heard the hushed recounting from the neighbor who took in the Hoffman girl the night it happened, when she ran down the zigzag front steps and pounded on their glass door, her hair thick with blood.

The story was deceptively simple. Doctor Hoffman had been a heart doctor and his wife Agnes led the Horticulture Society and decorated their marvelous home. They had three children, sixteen-year-old Bettye and the eleven-year-old twins, Jody and Kathy.

These were the known things, the rest were heard things, passed things, behind hands at slumber parties, whispered in the kitchen at cocktail parties.

Things like this: Doctor Hoffman would sometimes have agonizing headaches that would make him nearly go blind with pain and you could hear his screams from the hill below the house.

And like this: once, in her high school English class, Bettye recited a poem she'd written herself about a merry-go-round that never stopped spinning and all the children clutched on the horses eventually grew up and grew old while the ride kept going. Their now-gray hair had grown so long it caught in the horses' pumping legs and wound around their hooves, setting sparks that caught fire and the merry-go-round went up in flames. *A fire, a fire, and they finally knew what it was that they had been running from!* she read to the rapt class, her voice shaking with feeling.

But no one could have guessed what was to come next. A December night when something snapped inside Doctor Hoffman. That was what everyone said—"Something snapped" or "He snapped," as though this could happen to anyone, as though any parent, any father, might one day take a ball-peen hammer and crush his wife's skull as she slept. Which was what Doctor Hoffman did.

Bludgeoned. That was the word people often used. It was a terrible word, Penny thought. It felt like a cold marble in your mouth, the kind that might land in the center of your throat so you couldn't breathe at all.

But Doctor Hoffman wasn't done. Bettye woke up to her mother's screams and to her father standing above her bed, the hammer raised above his head. He caught one glancing blow on her temple before she spun loose and stumbled to the floor, crawling across the thick pink carpet of her princess bedroom, then leaping to her feet, running down the zigzag steps, her father behind, chasing after her, tripping on his pajamas—patterned with painted clowns holding balloons—and stumbling, giving Bettye just enough time to escape through the front door and down the steep concrete to a neighbor's house, screaming, screaming, screaming.

The twins were climbing out their window when their father walked by their open bedroom door. He stared at them a long minute, hammer swinging at his side.

Go back to sleep, he told them calmly. *This is a nightmare.*

Go back to sleep. This is a nightmare.

Meanwhile, the neighbor opened his door to find Bettye there in her nightgown, blood pouring down her cheek and neck like a bucket of paint had tipped over on her head.

He called for his wife as Bettye kept asking, over and over, *Where are the twins? Where's Mommy?*, scratching her head with fingers red-slicked. Poking at the wound on her head until the neighbor's wife fainted right on the doorstep.

The neighbor ran to the Hoffman house and opened the front door, and he could hear this awful, ghoulish moaning. Slowly, slowly creeping upstairs, he could see Doctor Hoffman roaming the hall in his gaudy clown pajamas, the hammer loose between his fingers.

He was saying strange things, the neighbor said, and only later was it reported in all the newspapers that he'd been reciting from Dante's *Inferno,* Canto One open on his bedside table. *Midway through the journey of our life I found myself within a forest dark, for the straightforward path had been lost . . .*

By then, Doctor Hoffman had already taken a fatal combination of barbiturates.

Moments later, while tending to the children, the neighbor heard a slump and discovered Doctor Hoffman on his bedroom carpet, a swirl of his clown pajamas.

Maybe it wasn't true, at least most of it, but it felt true.

No one knew what happened to the children after. They would be grown-ups by now, maybe with children of their own. Who could guess the nightmares they had? Who could guess how they slept again?

It was rumored that Doctor Hoffman had financial difficulties. That that was what had driven him to such dark acts. He couldn't afford the grand home in which they lived, complete with ballroom and glassed-in conservatory. But others said it was "emotional." That Doctor Hoffman had struggled with melancholy before and maybe had even been in a sanitorium.

That was what Mr. Calhoun said. He was the only one on the block to remember the Hoffmans. Sometimes Penny talked to him while he was repairing radios in his garage. He gave her honey candy and butterscotch curls.

When he was sixteen, Mr. Calhoun had mowed the lawn for Mrs. Hoffman, who paid him a quarter each time.

She was a nice lady, he said. *She always said, "My husband's a heart specialist, but his heart belongs to me!"*

Once, Penny heard her mother talking in the backyard to Mrs. Candliss about it.

They were sunbathing in their new two-pieces, the only time Penny's mother took off her pantyhose because she didn't like the backs of her legs, the faint red skein Penny herself could barely see. Spider veins, her mother called them, making a face.

They were talking about Mrs. Hoffman whose head, it was said, became melon soft from the hammer blows.

I guess he got tired of her.

I guess she got fat.

And they laughed in a funny, high voices, like they didn't mean it but wanted their words to be a shield that would protect them. Protect them from whatever put Mrs. Hoffman at hazard.

Go back to sleep. That was what Doctor Hoffman told the twins. *This is a nightmare.*

That was in all the newspaper articles. It was the one detail everyone included when they told the story. That, and the hammer.

Go back to sleep. This is a nightmare.

Penny always remembered it. It was something every kid heard, all the time.

Penny knew if she ever went to the house, she would never tell her father. Certainly not her mother. But someday, she thought, she would have to go.

Everyone seemed to, eventually.

Don't go near there, her mother always said. *You'll get lockjaw.*

Lockjaw was the scariest thing you could ever get, Penny was sure. Ever since her father told her how his Great-Uncle Ernie stepped on a rusty nail and died six days later.

Don't set foot there, her father told Penny once, his face hidden behind the newspaper.

Why not?

A man went mad there, he said, shaking straight his newspaper, his fingers twitchy. *Mad as a hatter.*

Don't bother your father, Penny's mother said, watching them from the kitchen, drying dishes slowly with a long towel. *He works hard.*

You get too close to the house, her father whispered to her, his breath sweet with vermouth, *the house gets into you.*

Sometimes, four or five times a year, her father had to spend rest days in the dark bedroom, a cold towel on his face. You were never to bother him. He worked very hard selling vacuums all day. He managed the whole department and customers could be very difficult and demanding. Sometimes Penny could hear him crying softly through the door. Sometimes moaning. He had a case of the black clouds. That's what he called them. *Don't bother your father,* her mother would say. *He's very sensitive.*

But then the black clouds would pass, and he'd take Penny to the skating rink and to Schwitt's for candy and to pick any doll she wanted in the whole store. He would be grinning the entire time, grinning so hard his face might burst.

It seemed to Penny that there was a day world and a night world, and her parents' night world was so different and she only had occasional keyholes into its mysteries.

She sometimes listened to her parents talking late into the night. There was a strange, lolling rhythm to it, and she mentioned it once to her mother, who said her father talked in his sleep and sometimes sang. She said it was on account of the war. *Don't mention it,* she said. Penny never would. Her father didn't ever talk about the war except the time she heard him tell Mr. Thorpe next door that he was always the point man because he was the shortest in his platoon. Once a year, on Veterans Day, he'd go to the VA dinner and be too tight to drive home. Someone else would bring him home.

Last year, Penny thought she could hear him through her bedroom wall, singing "Scarlet Ribbons" on the sleeping porch. It was about a man who roams the town all night to find scarlet ribbons for his daughter, but all the stores are closed and shuttered. Finally, he comes home at dawn to find his daughter asleep in her bed, surrounded by mounds of scarlet ribbons *in gay profusion lying there.*

Her father's singing sounded so pretty, like a cartoon princess, crooning softly, his voice like it might crack, break, shatter as he called out the final *for her hair.*

Daddy, she said. *Daddy, are you okay?* And the singing stopped so fast, and then a *creak, creak, creak,* and he appeared in her doorway, the long shadow of him, his body swaying and only the gleam of his hair oil.

He didn't move and Penny didn't move either, and her hand, curled around her blanket, pressed against her mouth.

Go to sleep, he said, his voice low and strained. *You were dreaming.* And maybe she was.

The next day, she told her mother about it and her mother sat down at the kitchen table and cried and cried. I should never mention the night world in the day world, Penny realized. Adults never liked it and sometimes they hated you for it.

*

How could you start sixth grade never having braved the Hoffman house, zigzagging up its zigzag stairs? Suddenly that was what everyone at school wanted to know.

At first Penny could never imagine doing it. She thought it might be like all those other things you can't imagine you'd ever do, like let boys lie on top of you. And then, in the dark basement of some party, after a few passed sips of Ripple, it happens, your eyes stuck open, fixed on the dangling light bulb in the laundry room.

First, Susan Candliss did it, then Nina and Tina, the twins, together. They were still having nightmares about it. They said they saw something through the window, a dark shape on the stairs. The dark shape had followed them home and maybe was living in their closet. Their mother had to spray all the corners of their bedroom with Florida water.

Pretty soon, all the girls in Penny's class had gone, or said they had. They all had stories. Of shadows and fluttering bats, creaking shutters and a nest of crushed baby mice. One girl claimed she'd climbed through a broken window and that it was like outside had become inside, with scattering birds and rodents living in the stove and Mrs. Hoffman's spider lilies growing deep in the carpet. She said she felt like something had gotten in her throat—a spore or fungus—and how, at night, she couldn't breathe.

You don't have to do it, Susan assured Penny, but that didn't seem true either.

And maybe Penny wanted to. Wanted to have to go, so she would.

Some days, she took the long way home from school just to walk by. She was building up to it.

Maybe it would be like that boy in the basement, making her stomach wiggle in ways she never knew it could. She could almost taste the Ripple now.

Maybe it would be okay and then over.

Maybe it would be like letting her into night world at last, where all the grown-ups lingered, exploring their mysteries, feeling feelings, seeing things untold, untellable.

One night, two weeks before sixth grade, Penny decided to do it. To go.

It was late, but still before the eleven o'clock news.

Her parents were in the TV room, the anchor's voice droning and her mother's knitting needles clacking. Her father snoring, today's newspaper twitching on his lap.

They never heard the screen door, its spring loose and lazy.

Her father's service flashlight heavy in her pocket, swinging against her leg as she ran.

One house, two house, three house, turn. Kitty-corner.

And there it was, the Hoffman house.

Spanish-style and large, three stories, the house lurching high up on a hilltop, its red-tile roof jutting out like a grooved tongue.

Penny's breath caught in her throat.

But it felt right, the time, the night, warm and moon-bright.

There was so much time going up those zigzag steps, so much time to change your mind, glancing up at its long, narrow windows, especially the biggest one, through which you could see the sharp slash of a staircase. Every time Penny looked away, she thought she saw something moving up those stairs. Maybe it was the dark thing Nina and Tina had seen, the one that followed them home and, despite the Florida water, still hadn't left, crouching over them as they slept.

There were two tall windows flanking the entryway, boarded shut.

Penny peered inside both, her legs shaking.

Inside was a grand room, a drawing room, maybe, the floor swirled with sooty sheets.

The room was so alive, dust motes dancing on the Spanish tiles, the moonlight silver-streaking the spiral staircase.

No one ever said what you were really supposed to do when you got up there. Clap the front knocker, try all the door handles, tug at the window sashes, slip a hand through a broken pane. See what you can see. Put yourself in the beast's mouth. Open the forbidden box.

She placed her right hand on the heavy wooden front door. *Maybe I'll feel something*, she thought.

The wood felt warm and spongy-soft, so soft she wanted to stroke it. So soft she stroked it a bit until she felt a pinch and pulled her hands back fast.

A spider—shiny black with a red blotch shaped like an hourglass—flitted away.

The wind—hot, sparkling—lifted.

Penny could hear a shush of leaves, branches behind her.

She thought suddenly of Bettye Hoffman. How neighbors said she sounded like a wild animal shrieking as she ran from the house. How someone said the newspapers printed a picture of Bettye's monogrammed light plate smeared with blood.

Maybe I can go home now, Penny thought. She'd done it, after all. She'd braved the ascent to the Hoffman house, stood at the front door, peeked in the front windows. But the idea of going back down those steps, of going back home, the tight stillness of the house, her parents, eyes glazed, seated on opposite sides of the living room, the TV going to snow . . .

Both hands on the heavy flashlight, Penny started moving.

She decided she would walk the full perimeter of the house, she would peer in every window, half broken, glass glittering.

The full perimeter. That was a phrase her father used, from the war. How they made the infantry walk the perimeter with dowsing rods, looking for land mines or something. *Booby traps*, he called them, *and the booby was me.* Laughing, laughing so he couldn't stop, until he bent over at the dinner table, nearly crying from laughing.

Everything was as everyone said, but different.

First, the glass conservatory on the right side, fogged and moss-slimed. When Penny pressed her face against it, she could see Mrs. Hoffman's famed spider lilies still growing, impossibly growing inside.

Next, she came upon a sitting room, a pair of acid-yellow wing chairs, the cushions heavy with old rain, a draped sofa, a draped turntable, a draped Zenith, its antennae piercing through. A dark stain on the tufted wall-to-wall carpet, indeterminate and large. There was nothing in the room to be scared of. But there was a feeling she couldn't name.

It was hard not to think of Bettye, or the twins, or even poor Mrs. Hoffman, whom Penny could picture roaming the rooms in a frilly peignoir, her hair in curlers, bending over to pick up the sock, the hammer still caught in the back of her head, hovering there like a tuning rod, blood tumbling down like scarlet ribbons in her hair.

She thought of what they said about Mrs. Hoffman, how her husband had brought down the ball peen so hard, he'd split the back of her head open. How he'd left an inch-wide hole. How she had drowned in her own blood. How even the whites of her eyes had turned red.

You could never imagine that much blood, Susan Candliss said, even as they were both imagining it. Like the spin art kit Penny got for Christmas, the hum of its motor, squeezing red paint into the spinner, spattering it across the paper. Dappling it across Penny's fingers so her mother stood her over the sink, rubbing the washcloth so hard it felt like pins.

Penny went back around the other side. She was saving the rear of the house for last. It was so dark back there, a place no streetlamps or even moonlight seemed to go.

She felt something claw at her throat. *The dust,* she thought. *It must be the dust.*

First, there was the kitchen, the oven door creaked open, the metal table laden with cans curled open, a raccoon-rummaged box of Rinso soap flakes, pastel stacks of melamine bowls, a brown-sluiced bottle of Lea & Perrins, a saucer smeared with mint jelly. It made Penny's head hurt, all of it.

Next to the window, there was a door that Penny knew would open.

She knew somehow it wasn't locked, but she didn't go inside.

She remembered the pinch of the spider and didn't touch the handle.

Don't go inside, something told her. And in her head she was already upstairs, in the Hoffman bedroom, her feet soft in the deep carpet, the deep carpet spattered black with moonlit blood.

Once, Penny's neighbor caught his dog in the car door and the dog's poor head bled all over the driveway. She remembered watching from the window as her father hosed the driveway down. You could never think a dachshund had that much blood.

Next to the kitchen, there was a set of windows too high to reach.

She crawled, spiderlike, on top of a set of cellar doors.

Panting, she stepped on the damp, splintering wood. For a second, she thought her shoe might poke through, capture her. That a nail might pierce her, poisoning her with fatal lockjaw.

But the wood held her.

Her hand on the window screen, Penny knew as soon as she saw the tinsel. It was the room everyone had mentioned. The one full of wrapped Christmas presents. The gleaming silver paper and gaudy gold ribbons, scattered pom-pom bows in tinsel red, green ribbons like tendrils, crimson ones like Mrs. Hoffman's spider-lily legs.

Scarlet ribbons, scarlet ribbons. She could nearly hear her father singing.

Scarlet ribbons, scarlet ribbons, scarlet ribbons for her hair.

Penny wondered what was inside the bright wrapping: an Erector Set for Jody, a Ginny doll for Kathy, a vanity set for Bettye? A brand-new briar-wood pipe for Doctor Hoffman? She liked to imagine inside were a pair of fancy new garden shears for Mrs. Hoffman, but maybe she was like her own mother, wrapping everything—and what was under the tree for her? Her father had trouble remembering things and sometimes he'd rush out for a jumbo bottle of Evening in Paris from Woolworth's. Once he'd forgotten entirely, then cried over Rumple Minze for hours. A week later, he spent all his money on a pretty gold locket from Ahee Jewelers and Penny's mother had to return it so they could make the car payments.

But the Hoffmans were Jewish, weren't they? Maybe they were Hanukkah presents, she thought. And the store only had Santa paper. Or maybe these weren't their gifts at all but some renters' or squatters' left abandoned as they ran away in the night.

Hold still, Penny whispered to herself, her hand on her beating heart.

That was what Doctor Hoffman had told his daughter Bettye, struggling under her bedclothes, staring up at the hammer in his hand . . . how he told her, *Hold still.*

There was no avoiding it now. The rear of the house, the blackness there. She had to go. She had to, even if it felt like she had gone farther and deeper than any of her classmates, than anyone at all

since the Hoffman children bolted out of that house, bolted from
one nightmare into the next.

She wondered suddenly why Doctor Hoffman didn't kill the
twins. Had he come to his senses by then? Or had he planned to
kill them later? Or had he looked into their eyes, blinking and
scared, and lost his nerve?

Penny crept slowly, her ankles prickling with mosquitoes, maybe
with the furry stamens of the spider lilies.

One hand on the winged wall, the stucco soft in her hand, she
turned the last corner, expecting a pool of darkness.

But it was brighter than she guessed, the moon slipping from
behind the clouds.

Everything was overgrown, muzzy, two sets of patio doors clotted with sooty mold. Spores, slime, everything mossy soft under
her feet.

She felt the scratching in her throat again, like furry things had
slipped inside her. But as she moved closer, it didn't matter anymore. Because the moonlight made the green muck iridescent,
magical.

And she could see inside.

A ballroom dancing along the entire rear of the house, its doors
spilling out onto a patio of broken tiles, Penny's ankle turning on
every one as she moved closer still.

Inside were gleaming floors, a black and gold bar along one
wall and mirrors everywhere.

In one of them, Penny could see herself, her eyes wide, her
hands gripped on the window ledge. Penny could see herself,
moonlit silver.

In an instant, all the bad feeling disappeared, the smell everywhere
of night-blooming jasmine, of floor polish, of cigarette smoke.

It was like in a movie, everything sparkling, shadows flickering.
Penny imagined whirling around inside in a swirling gown.

She heard the footsteps first, then turned, squinting. But even
before she saw him, she knew. There, at the far end of the room,
was Doctor Hoffman, tall and pale, dancing alone on the herring-
bone floor in his jaunty clown pajamas.

Oh, she thought, *he's so happy. Look how happy he is.*

Inside there was music, grand and sweeping. She could hear it, tinny and muffled through the glass doors.

Doctor Hoffman turned and looked at her. *Come inside*, he seemed to say with his eyes, and Penny wanted to, she did.

It was all a terrible mistake, she realized, a gasp in her throat. He never meant to do it. He'd only wanted to dance with his wife, with his daughter, the hammer like some glittering conductor's baton.

He never meant to do it!

She knew it somehow, watching him, large and ungainly, pajamas billowing, spinning around in his scuffing slippers, a spot of dried shaving cream caught in his ear.

Come inside, he seemed to say, waving again, moving toward her as he swayed and twirled.

I will, Penny thought. *I must.*

Her hand on the patio door's knob, she tugged and she tugged but the door wouldn't give. There was something wrong with her hand, her fingers tight and a throbbing in her palm.

Daddy! the cry came. *Oh, Daddy!*

Penny looked up and saw it was Bettye.

Bettye, curled in Doctor Hoffman's gangling arms, her feet bare and her white nightgown dotted with red bows.

Father-daughter dance, Penny thought, her face aching from smiling.

Whirling her around the dance floor, Bettye's arms wrenched high enough to meet her father's, and Penny couldn't quite see her face.

Bettye, Penny wanted to cry out, and maybe she did. *Bettye, hold still! Hold still!*

But suddenly Penny had that feeling again of something scrabbling its way up her throat, and her hand hurt even more, stiff like a claw.

She knew it was time to go.

Something had closed shut, sealed itself up.

Night world was zipping its zipper shut and if you didn't want to be trapped inside its dark center forever, you better go, go, go.

The air had grown still, heavy. The tree branches hung low, and the moon slipped behind everything.

Skittering down the zigzag steps, the flashlight clunking against her leg. The streetlamps bright and garish and the sound of an airplane vrooming above.

The night quiet, the street empty and cool.

She hurried, nearly smiling.

She'd done it, she'd done it.

Her hand hurt and felt big, like the gloved hand of her Donald Duck rubber squeak toy. She had to use her other one to turn the doorknob, the swollen screen pressed against her face.

The house was still, fans humming.

Her bed was cool, her breath settling.

She'd done it, she'd done it.

She couldn't make her brain shut off.

The house was still in her, she'd taken it with her.

An aching pain in her right hand, Penny lay in bed.

Every time she closed her eyes, she saw the red Christmas curlings and the red bows in Bettye Hoffman's nightgown and the red threads on her grandfather's cheeks, and on Principal Stevens's puffy nose. The red veins on the backs of her mother's legs. The deep red of Mrs. Hoffman's spider lilies.

Spider lilies.

It was then she remembered the front door, the spongy wood, the pinch in her hand, and the shiny spider flitting away.

Her head felt hot, everything felt hot.

She looked down at her puffy hand and saw it, a red line extending from her palm up to her elbow. A red line like one of those coiling Christmas ribbons.

Oh, how it ached.

Daddy! she cried out. *Help me, Daddy!*

Scarlet ribbons, scarlet ribbons. She could hear her father singing the song.

She could nearly feel herself like the girl in the song, tucked in bed, the crinkling sound of ribbons, scarlet ribbons swirled around her, snaking around her ankles, curling around her wrists and throat. Curling so tight she couldn't breathe.

Scarlet ribbons, scarlet ribbons, scarlet ribbons for her hair . . .

*

And there he was in the doorway, his long shadow lined black.

Go back to sleep, Penny, he said. *Go back to sleep.*

His body swaying in striped pajamas and only the gleam of his hair oil.

But Daddy, you don't—

Go back to sleep, he said louder now, louder even as his voice seemed far away. And then she knew what was coming, the red encircling her, her throat closing up around her—

This is a nightmare, Penny.

Go back to sleep.

FRANKIE Y. BAILEY

Matter of Trust

FROM *School of Hard Knox*

Eudora, New York
Tuesday, November 23, 1948

ANNIE GIBSON BRUSHED away the snow melting on her windshield and plucked the folded sheet of paper from beneath the wiper. "Just a minute, sweetie," she said to her eight-month-old son who was watching her from the front seat.

She got into the car and smiled at the baby in his booster seat. "Isn't the snow pretty, Johnny-kins? See the big, fluffy flakes? But we need to hurry and finish our errands. We want to be snug at home before the streets get slippery. First, just let Mommy see who left her a note."

The paper was a page torn from the kind of ruled composition book children used. The message was in sprawling print.

Ask him what he did.

No signature. Just that one sentence.

Ask him what he did.

Annie stared at the note, then dropped it on the car seat. It slipped under Johnny's booster. She would have to remember not to leave it there.

She started the car, heard the *whoosh* of the heater, switched on the windshield wipers.

The village was busy for a Tuesday afternoon. Thanksgiving was only two days away. Everyone was trying to get errands done before the snow came.

Annie waved as she passed Miss Henderson, the librarian. She needed to pick up another knitting book.

The baby gurgled, and she reached over to touch his arm. "I'm sorry I had to bring you along with me on my errands, sweetie. Do you miss Grandma? She'll be home in time for Christmas."

Warm air was coming from the heater now, but she couldn't stop shivering.

Who would leave such a horrible note? Who would walk up and put that under someone's windshield wiper, making the person who received it wonder what it was about?

The meat loaf was ready to come out of the oven and she was mashing the potatoes when Jack came in from the garage. He stopped, foot raised, at the kitchen door.

"Oops!" he said. "Wet shoes."

She laughed as he made a show of drawing back his foot. "Thank you, darling."

He came back wearing the leather slippers she had left by the bench.

Annie said, "And tonight, husband, we're having apple turnovers."

"My turn to say 'thank you,'" he said. He kissed her on the cheek she turned toward him. "You smell nice."

"Cinnamon and allspice. Makes both cook and house smell nice."

"Do I have time to change before dinner?"

"Ten minutes. Will that do?"

"Be back in five."

"Try not to wake Johnny," she said.

"I'll be as quiet as a whisper."

Annie smiled. He always made her smile.

She brushed her bangs back from her forehead with the back of her hand. If she couldn't get into the beauty parlor soon, she'd have to take the scissors to them.

She could hear Jack whistling softly. But that was all right. Johnny sometimes fell asleep to his daddy's whistling.

She was not going to hurt her husband by showing him a silly note. The person who'd left it had probably put it on the wrong car. Or had been playing a joke that wasn't funny.

*

They were listening to "The Bing Crosby Show" when the telephone rang.

"I'll get it," Jack told her. "I know you don't want to miss Bing."

She tried not to listen any more than she usually did.

When she heard him say "looking for a contractor" and that he would give him the information tomorrow at the office, she knew he was talking to Travis. The two men, best friends, had come to Eudora from Buffalo after the war. They had been looking for a place to strike out on their own. Jack, the real estate agent, and Travis, the contractor. They had gone in together to rent, then buy, an office building on Main Street.

Jack had met and married Annie, a Eudora girl. Travis was still a carefree—and sometimes careless—bachelor. A danger to the hearts of the women who fell for a handsome war hero.

Jack had gone to war, too. But he was ready to settle down after it was over.

Except for his weekly night out with the boys. He and Travis were on the same bowling team. Beer and bowling every Thursday night.

Jack was finishing his call on the hall phone.

Annie turned her attention back to the radio and her knitting.

Friday, November 26, 1948

Annie was paying the delivery boy from the cleaners when she remembered the note.

She had put it in her purse when she got home on Tuesday afternoon. Put it there, first, not sure if she would show it to Jack. Then, reluctant to throw it away when she didn't know who had left it or why. Put it there in her purse and been so scatterbrained this morning she had forgotten it was there.

Jack had asked if she had the checkbook. She had been making his breakfast and listening to the morning news. She had called back, "Look in my purse."

Now the inner pocket of her purse where she'd put the note was unzipped.

"Thank you," she said, accepting Jack's shirts and suit from the delivery boy.

"Have a good day, Mrs. Gibson."

She carried Jack's dry cleaning into their bedroom and hung the shirts in their place and the suit with the others.

Then she went back into the living room and looked again at the unzipped inner pocket. The note was still where she had put it. Still folded.

If Jack had seen the folded piece of paper, he had probably thought it was a grocery list. There was no reason why he would have taken it out and read it.

Except last night, he had asked if something was wrong. They had been listening to the radio, and he had reached for his coffee cup and her attention had been caught by his hands. Hands that looked as if they should belong to a concert pianist.

She had blurted that out soon after they started dating; he had laughed and said he was tone-deaf.

Last night, he had turned his head and caught her staring at his hands. He had asked what was wrong. She had said she was wool-gathering. Thinking about her post-Thanksgiving errands. All the things she needed to get done tomorrow.

Maybe this morning, he had thought of that and been curious about what she planned to do today. Maybe he had taken the note out and read it.

Ask him what he did.

If he had read that ugly message, what had he thought? Why hadn't he asked her about it?

Annie had promised to work at the church bazaar that afternoon. She wanted to get Johnny dressed and ready before the sitter came. This was a new woman and she wanted to start off well. She would need the woman's help until her mother got back from visiting her brother and his family in California.

After the sitter arrived, she had a few minutes to herself. She decided to bring Jack his lunch. A turkey sandwich and some pumpkin pie. He loved Thanksgiving leftovers even more than the first day.

She was parking down the street when she saw Jack coming out of his office. She was getting out of the car, ready to call out to him, when Travis came out of his door.

She glanced at her watch. Only a little after eleven. Early to be going out to lunch. Maybe they were going to look at property. Jack had told her they wanted to buy another building as an investment.

They started to walk away. Jack, talking and gesturing. Travis, leaning on the cane he used when the leg he had been shot in during the war was acting up. He had told her, laughing, that women never minded his bum leg. They wanted to soothe his pain.

He had a crew that did the work he lined up. So, the leg wasn't as much of a hindrance as it might have been.

They got into Jack's car. Annie watched them drive away. And wondered why she hadn't called out or waved to attract her husband's attention.

There was a trash can on the corner. She dropped the brown paper bag with his lunch into it.

Sunday, November 28, 1948

The phone rang as Jo Radcliffe was wondering if God or anyone else would notice if she missed church. No one had told her when she agreed to serve as the temporary public health nurse how often she would be called out in the evening. Last night, it was a woman who had gone into labor while she was scrubbing the floor. Having delivered four children without a problem, she had decided to have this one at home. That might have been fine if her doctor hadn't been busy at the hospital and baby number five hadn't decided to present himself feet first. But they had managed.

And the phone was still ringing. Jo tumbled out of bed and grabbed her robe. She ran down the stairs, bare feet on hardwood floor, regretting she hadn't stopped for slippers.

She grabbed the receiver from the hook. Whoever it was, was determined.

"Hello," she said.

"Jo, Eli Gordon here. Sorry to bother you early on a Sunday morning."

"Oh, Chief Gordon. That's okay, I was awake. What can I do for you?"

"Would you mind coming over to the station?" He paused. "I could sure use your help with something."

"I gather this is serious." Dempsey, her aunt Meg's Maine Coon cat, paused at the top of the stairs to sit down and lick his paw. "An emergency?"

"We have it under control. But the sooner you can get here, the better."

"Okay, I'll be there in about forty-five minutes."

"Thank you, Jo. I appreciate it."

Jo hung up the receiver. The chief had obviously not wanted to share whatever it was with any curious listeners who happened to be on her party line. Whatever it was couldn't be good.

Dempsey strolled past her, plumed tail in the air, ignoring her presence.

He was still sleeping on Meg's bed. And resisting any effort by Jo to offer him comfort.

She followed the cat down the hall. Even if she wasn't going to have time for a leisurely Sunday breakfast, he expected his.

"One of my men found him sitting in his car," Chief Gordon said as he handed Jo a mug of black coffee. "The car was in the middle of the street, and he was sitting there behind the steering wheel."

"Was he already dead?"

"Dying," Chief Gordon said. He settled his bulk into his chair. "Dead by the time the ambulance got there."

Jo took a long sip of coffee strong enough to use as an oar. "What does she say about why she shot him?"

"Nothing. She's not talking."

"But you're sure she did it?"

"The two witnesses who heard the shot and looked out of their bedroom window said it came from the bar. Then they saw him come staggering out the door and get into his car. He didn't get more than four or five blocks down the street before he slammed into the curb."

"And they called the police?"

"They called. So did three other concerned citizens. Except for that bar, it's a quiet neighborhood over there."

"And no one else was in the bar? The owner?"

"Got a call from his wife who wanted him to come home. She had the flu and was throwing up. He left as soon as he'd gotten the last customer out the door. He asked the girl to lock up. When my officer went in, she was back in the office, sitting at her boss's desk. The gun was right there on the desk."

"Her gun?"

"Her boss's. He kept it in the desk drawer."

Jo took another sip of her coffee. "If you think she should have a medical evaluation, a doctor—"

"Got one if we need him. I'm hoping you can help me with her sister."

"Her sister?"

"Different last names. Different fathers. The sister is a Rossi."

"Christina Rossi?" Jo said, remembering a slender, dark-eyed teenager.

Chief Gordon nodded. "That's her. Said she met you when the library asked you to talk about having been an Army nurse."

"She came up and asked me about nursing school."

"She's here. She got someone to give her a ride as soon as she heard what had happened. Lila doesn't want to talk to her, but she won't go home. Anyway, she's just a kid—"

"Fourteen. She said she was starting high school this year."

"And they live in a trailer park out near Mulholland Road. I don't feel easy about sending her back out there by herself."

"Child welfare—"

"When I asked her if there was anybody she wanted me to call, she said you."

"She asked you to call me? We had one conversation that lasted all of ten minutes."

"Seems like you made an impression on her." Chief Gordon gave her one of his slow, thoughtful looks. "She could use somebody to help her get through this. Doesn't look good for her sister." He paused. "I hate to see her go into foster care. It's her sister that's done the crime."

"You don't expect me to—"

"I thought you might just keep her for a few days."

"What good will that do? If her sister isn't released, she'll still—"

"You never know what might happen."

Jo set her half-empty mug down on his desk. "You said Lila Tate shot a man. Are you saying it might have been self-defense?"

"I don't know what it is. She's not talking. I just think it's kind of odd, don't you?"

"Maybe they were involved with each other. A lover's quarrel."

"That's possible. With a girl from her background, it might even be likely that she'd have a male friend who would help her out now and then." Chief Gordon leaned forward. "Except her boss was surprised, couldn't believe it when I told him what happened. Now her boss, Bill Pope, is a careful man. He likes to keep his head down. That's how he's managed to keep that bar open for almost fifteen years. He wouldn't hire a girl who was likely to cause him trouble. Wouldn't leave her alone with his money or his gun.

So, I'm thinking Lila might have a story to tell. In a few days, she might be willing to talk. But in the meantime, we've got the problem of her little sister, sitting there all alone in our meeting room, crying because Lila won't see her."

It was a long speech. Jo stared at him, knowing that he knew he had her. She almost cursed out loud.

"All right. A few days. She can stay with me a few days—if we can get approval."

Chief Gordon smiled. "Just to save some time, I've already put in a call. The lady I talked to was happy to give us her approval. We just have to do a little paperwork."

"Did you ask Christina if she knows anything?"

"I couldn't get my tongue around that. I hate questioning kids about grown-up stuff." He paused. "Maybe you can ask a few questions when she's with you."

"I set myself up for that one, didn't I?"

"Should I call you Christina, or Tina?" Jo asked, glancing over at her silent passenger.

Aside from thanking Jo for coming and saying yes, she would like to stay with her, she had said almost nothing. She was almost as silent as her half-sister in her jail cell.

The two sisters had only a passing physical resemblance. Lila Tate was short and curvy, with bleached blond hair and a cynical curve to her mouth. She'd reached for another cigarette and mumbled, "Thanks," when Jo told her Christina would be with her.

"'Tina,'" the girl beside her said. "Lila calls me 'Tina.'"

She was still staring out of the window, but Jo heard the tears in her voice.

"Tina, it is," Jo said. "Why don't we go out to your place and pick up some of your things."

"Okay."

"You'll have to give me directions."

Tina directed her to six or seven trailers on a scrawny plot of land at the end of a dead-end road. There was a ranch house down the road that might belong to the person who owned the trailer park.

"How do you get to school from out here?" Jo asked. "You go to school in Eudora, right?"

Tina nodded. "A couple of other kids and I walk down to the fork of the road. The bus picks us up there. Sometimes Lila drops me off when she has to go in early for her other job."

"Her other job?"

"She works part-time at the diner on Main Street."

"I don't remember ever seeing her there."

"She works in the kitchen." Hand on the car door handle. "Do you want to come in?"

Jo wasn't sure what she should say. She wanted a look inside, but she didn't want to embarrass her. "Would you rather I wait here?"

"It's okay if you come in. Lila made me help clean up before she went to work yesterday."

The interior of the trailer was what she had expected. Cramped, with cheap fixtures. But everything was in its place. Tidy was the word that came to mind. Stale cigarette smoke balanced by two lush green plants on the counter.

"Someone has a green thumb," Jo said. "Those are beautiful plants."

"Lila," Tina said. "She's always wanted a real garden. I'll go get my things, so we can go." She looked back over her shoulder. "How long do you think I'll be gone?"

"At least a few days. If you need more, we'll come back."

"That was Mrs. Ingram who was looking out her window when we drove up. I should ask her to keep an eye on the trailer while Lila and I are gone."

"That's a good idea."

Jack was on the telephone when Annie came back from putting the baby down.

"His brother's coming in from Buffalo," he told her when he hung up the phone a few minutes later. "He says the police told him they can't release the body until there's been an autopsy."

Annie shook her head. "I can't believe this."

Jack said, an edge to his voice, "You never thought Travis's wild side would catch up to him?"

"I always hoped you would be a good influence on him."

"Well, at least, none of them would have shot him." Annie wrapped her arms around his waist. "I liked Travis. He could be funny and charming, and he deserved respect as a war hero. And, he was Johnny's godfather."

"And his dog liked him?" Jack said.

"Yes, he did. Do you think his brother will take Max?"

"If he doesn't, we will. Travis would have liked Johnny to have his dog."

"And a collie isn't so big," Annie said. "I'm going to go check on the pot roast."

"I don't have too much of an appetite."

"Do you think you might be coming down with something?"

His laughter startled her. "Annie, my best friend was shot last night. He's dead. That—"

"I only meant . . . I know how upset you are." She brushed at her bangs. "Sandwiches and coffee. How's that?"

"Fine," he said. "I'm sorry I snapped at you."

"Don't be. It was a stupid question."

"I'm going to my study for a little while."

"I'll call you when everything's ready."

She watched him leave. Then she sank down on the sofa.

Monday, November 29, 1948

On Monday evening, Jo came home to find Tina—who had been allowed to stay home from school—sitting on the sofa reading a book. She was reading the book aloud to Dempsey, who was curled up close against her, his paws on her leg.

Dempsey spared Jo a glance out of his golden eyes. His tail twitched, but he returned his attention to Tina.

Tina glanced at Jo, smiled, and went on with her lively rendition of *The Wind in the Willows*.

Fascinated, Jo sat down in an armchair and kicked off her shoes. Tucking her feet under her, she settled back to listen to the story, too. It was a long time since she had visited with Toad and company.

She would never have expected shy, retiring Tina would be such a mimic.

Perhaps it was the rhythm of the book that was holding Dempsey enthralled. Or, maybe it was the arm Tina had curled around him as she read.

Jo's eyes drifted shut. She woke with a start when she heard Tina laugh.

"We'll finish the rest of it tomorrow," she told the cat.

Jo yawned and stretched. "What shall we have for dinner?"

"I can make it," Tina said. "I make dinner for Lila when she's tired."

"Why don't we do it together? How about hamburgers? I've even got frozen French fries."

"I've never had those. But I love hamburgers."

Dempsey followed them into the kitchen. He curled up on the cushion in the bay window.

"You seem to have won Dempsey over," Jo said.

"I like him. He kept me company today."

Jo took the ground beef out of the refrigerator. "I heard from Chief Wilson that Lila was arraigned today. That means she had her first appearance in court. She has an attorney now, and he had her enter a plea of not guilty."

"But if she shot the man—"

"Her lawyer says it's still better to plead 'not guilty' for now. That will give them a chance to work on her defense—to figure out the best way to present Lila's case and explain what she did."

"Do you think if she tells them what happened, they might not send her to prison?"

"That depends on what happened. Since Lila won't talk about it—"

"But maybe she'll tell her lawyer."

"Maybe," Jo said. She broke an egg and beat it. Added it to the ground beef. "Did Lila ever mention Travis Boyd to you?"

"No."

Jo reached for a knife. "Do you like onions on your hamburger?"

"Not really. I'd rather have pickles and catsup." Tina glanced over at Dempsey. "He looks funny with one leg up in the air like that while he licks himself."

"He would rather call it 'grooming' himself. In case you haven't noticed, Dempsey is a very dignified cat."

Tina giggled. "I wanted a kitten or a puppy, but Lila said we might have to move and we might not be able to take it along."

"When did she say that?"

"A long time ago. When I was eight or nine. We were living in an apartment then. After that we moved out to the trailer park."

"Do you like it out there?"

"It's okay. Do you want me to set the table?"

"Please. Then would you feed Dempsey while I'm getting the burgers on?"

Dempsey had eaten and settled in for a nap, and they were having dinner when Tina put down her hamburger. "I think something happened. Something with Lila."

Jo picked up a French fry and took a bite. She didn't want to spook her by questioning her too closely. "Want to tell me about it?"

Tina nodded. "One night, she . . . her car broke down. Someone brought her home. I think there were two men. But it was dark, and I only saw the shape of the one who got out. She was sitting in back, and he opened the car door. I ducked down so they wouldn't see me. Then I heard Lila coming in, and the car drove away. I got up, but she told me to go back to bed. It was a long time before she came to bed." Tina paused. "I could hear the water running in the bathroom. And then when she came to bed, she was just lying there."

"Did you ask her if anything was wrong?"

"I tried to, but she told me to go to sleep."

"When did this happen?"

"In October."

"Early October? Late?"

"Early. The first week in October. I know it was Thursday because I'd been listening to 'Charade Quiz' on the radio."

"Did she say anything the next morning about what had happened?"

"She said the car wouldn't start and she got a ride home. She got a ride with Mr. Ingram back into town that day. She had to get the transmission fixed in the car, but her boss at the bar loaned her the money."

"But . . ." Jo said, choosing her words, and reminding herself she was talking to a fourteen-year-old girl. "You think Lila was upset about something when she came in that night? Maybe she was worried about paying for repairs. Could it have been that?"

Tina shook her head. "She worries about money all the time. This was different. She was . . . that morning, it was like she was dazed, and she had this bruise on her wrist." Tina looked away. "I think those men hurt her."

Jo said, "Do you think . . . if that was what happened . . . is there someone she might have told?"

Tina poked at the half-eaten hamburger on her plate. "Lila wouldn't want people to know if something like that had happened. She wouldn't want them to think . . . you know what they think about how it's the woman's fault."

"Yes. But it isn't."

"But they already think . . . when you don't have a lot of money . . ."

Jo nodded. "People have all kinds of wrong ideas. But sometimes keeping a secret can be worse than dealing with what they might think."

Tina's head came up. "How do you know that? You live here in this big house and you're a nurse and you were in the Army. How do you know how it is for Lila and me?"

"I don't. But believe it or not, I might have a secret or two."

"You do? Is it something bad?"

"Something that people might find surprising."

"What?"

"Maybe I'll tell you one day. Right now, we need to think about how to help your sister. If something did happen that night, maybe Travis Boyd was involved. That might be something that Lila's lawyer could use in her defense."

"You think so?"

"I think we should let her lawyer and Chief Gordon know so they can investigate."

Tina sighed. "Lila isn't going to like it that I told."

"She might feel humiliated and embarrassed, but she'll know that you're only trying to help."

Friday, December 3, 1948

That Friday afternoon, Jo was back in Chief Gordon's office.

He said, "We know now Travis Boyd was at the bar that evening with his bowling buddies. Pope, Lila's boss, remembers Boyd was loud and happy. Still there for last call."

"So, it's possible he was still around when Lila went out to her car and discovered it wouldn't start," Jo said. "Do you think her lawyer will be able to get her to talk? Maybe she'll talk to me now."

"That's the other reason I called you to come in. She does want to talk to you. About her little sister."

"I wish she'd see Tina."

"Well, she's willing to see you. That's a start."

Lila came out wearing the plain blue dress that was standard issue for the few women who passed through the jail. She sat down on the other side of the table and lit a cigarette.

"Hello," Jo said. "It's good to see you again."

"Forgive me for not making nice, but I'd just as soon not be seeing you again," Lila said. "I'd rather not be in this jam."

"I can understand that. You probably didn't intend to kill Travis Boyd."

"I didn't think about it one way or the other. I wanted to keep his hands off me. I pointed the gun at him and shot him." Lila took another puff of her cigarette. "I want to talk to you about Tina. How long are you going to let her stay with you?"

"It was supposed to be only a few days," Jo said. "I'm not equipped to be a foster mother to a teenage girl. So, I think you'd better work with your lawyer."

"Nothing I say is likely to get me out of this mess."

"If Travis Boyd was one of the men who gave you a ride the night your car broke down—"

Lila glared at her. "What do you know about that?"

"Tina told me something happened. If Travis Boyd did rape you—"

Lila laughed. "My sister's a kid. What's your excuse? Didn't anyone ever tell you that girls like me don't get raped? We either sell it or give it away."

Jo nodded her head. "And living in a trailer doesn't do much for your credibility either. But if there was another man . . . if you told them who—"

"And he denied it happened. Who do you think they'd believe?"

"Don't you think you owe it to your sister to at least try?"

Lila stubbed out her cigarette. "I killed him. They aren't going to let me just walk out scot-free."

"Did he come to the bar to attack you again?"

"He came to tell me to leave his best buddy alone."

"The man who was with him?"

"And who went for a walk in the woods while Travis bent me over the hood of his car." Her eyes flared. "And then his buddy, Jack, had the nerve to play the gentleman and help me out of the car when they dropped me off. He asked me if I was all right."

"What did you do to make Travis warn you?"

"I left her a note—Jack's wife. I was driving by and there he was walking her out of his office. His pretty, smug little wife pushing their baby in a stroller. He kissed her—that was how I knew who she must be. And then just before Thanksgiving I was leaving my job at the diner, and I saw her getting out of her car with the baby. And . . ." Lila smiled. "I left her a note."

"What did it say?"

"Just, to ask him what he'd done."

"Did she?"

"Nope. Afraid of what he might say, I guess. But she kept the note. He found it in her purse. Then they saw her outside his office." Lila smiled. "Travis wanted to make sure I hadn't done more than send her a note. That I hadn't spoken to her directly."

"What did you tell him?"

"Nothing I could repeat to a lady like yourself," Lila said, her smile mocking. "But he didn't care for what I said. He put his hands on me again. This time I was ready. A knee in his family jewels. He screamed and cursed and staggered about on his bad leg until he fell. That made him mad. He looked like he wanted to kill me. When he got up and started toward me, I grabbed the gun out of the drawer and told him to stay away. He kept coming. And I shot him."

Lila picked up a matchbook and put another cigarette in her mouth. Her hands were shaking.

Jo reached across the table and took the matchbook. She struck one and held it out.

"Thanks," Lila said.

Jo said, "You have to tell your lawyer what you've just told me."

"I'll think about it. About Tina . . . are you going to—"

"She can stay with me until after your hearing."

Monday, January 24, 1949

Jack Gibson was not what Jo had been expecting. He had moved to the village after she left, and she hadn't crossed paths with him and his wife since she returned.

She had expected to see some indication in his appearance, in his expression, that he was the kind of a man who was capable of walking away and leaving a woman to be raped.

But he sat upright, looking pale but composed as Lila told her story.

When he was called to the stand, he glanced at his wife, who had come in with him and sat beside him. He raised his hand and swore to tell the truth.

The courtroom was quiet, tense as everyone waited to hear what he would say.

Lila's lawyer, young and earnest, opened by asking Jack Gibson about his occupation, his family, his friendship with Travis Boyd.

"Your good friend?"

"My best friend since high school."

"And you both moved here to Eudora from Buffalo. Is that correct?"

"Yes, we both thought there were business opportunities here."

"No other reason?"

Gibson shook his head. "I had no other reason."

"What about your friend, Travis Boyd. Did he have any other reason for leaving Buffalo?"

"He was working with his brother. Travis wanted to strike out on his own."

"And in three years, you both became respected members of the Eudora business community. Involved in civic and charitable activities."

"Yes."

"And joined a bowling league."

"Yes."

"On the evening of Thursday, October 7, 1948, did you participate in a bowling tournament?"

"Yes."

"You both did?"

"Yes."

"And your team won?"

"Yes."

"And you went to the Seafarer's Bar to celebrate."

"Yes."

"How long were you there?"

"Until closing."

"Both you and Mr. Boyd."

"Yes, I was riding with him."

"And were you riding with him when he was chivalrous enough to offer Miss Tate a ride home when her car wouldn't start?"

Jack Gibson looked at his wife. Everyone in the courtroom waited. Jo wondered for a moment if he was going to refuse to answer. He hadn't been charged with anything, but still . . .

"Yes, I rode with him." He cleared his throat. "I was there when he . . . when the incident involving Miss Tate occurred."

"The incident? You mean when he raped her."

"Yes." His voice was hoarse now. "When he raped her."

"And you let it happen?"

Jack Gibson looked down, around, blurted out, "He said she liked it rough. He said . . . I thought he had . . . they had before . . ."

"And even though he offered you a turn, you were courteous enough to walk away."

"Yes, I didn't want to watch."

"Because Miss Tate had screamed, because she was struggling and trying to escape?"

"I didn't know what he was going to do. I asked him to stop the car because I needed to take . . ." Color rushed into his face. "I had been drinking a lot of beer. I needed to . . . I went farther into the woods and I got turned around finding my way back . . ."

"But then you heard Miss Tate scream and you ran to see what was happening?"

"Yes, I thought something was wrong. I—"

"You didn't think anything was wrong with what you saw happening?"

"I didn't know what to do! I didn't think he would . . . if she didn't really want to—"

Annie Gibson stood up. She said, "Excuse me," to no one in particular.

The courtroom was silent as she walked out. On the stand, Jack Gibson bowed his head.

Jo heard a small sound between a sigh and laughter. She looked at Lila. Lila smiled back. An odd twist of her lips as tears ran down her cheeks.

BARRETT BOWLIN

For I Hungered, and Ye Gave Me

FROM *TriQuarterly*

The following interview excerpts were recorded and collected by the Arkansas State Highway Patrol (Troop 5, Washington Co. Barracks), in April 1979.

[Troy Gelineau, 22, Removal Technician]

Q:—

A: Yes, sir. That's the DOT's fancy way of saying I drive around and haul away roadkill.

Q:—

A: I'd say I'm going on three, almost four years now? It's not as bad as you think. You're out in the fresh air, you make 75 cents above the minimum. On-call pay's not bad. Just you and another guy from the garage most days, driving around, looking for dead animals.

Q:—

A: Deer, mostly. Hell, you staties are the ones most likely to call us late at night for them. When's it ever not deer at night, you know? Sir, I mean?

Q:—

A: I'd have to say it gets bad when an animal's not quite dead. That's the worst of it. That's why I carry around a big hunting knife in the glove compartment instead of a gun. It's a 4-inch Buck blade with a full steel tang I picked up at the county fair one year. My girlfriend calls it my "murder knife," which is pretty damn funny if you think about it.

Q:—

A: Sir? I'd say about once or twice a week on average. We'll get a call from y'all or the Fayetteville PD, and then we'll pull up just as y'all are done taking the insurance report from the driver, and then we'll have to wait until y'all are out of there. And I'll tell you: I keep that old Buck knife in the glove compartment for two reasons. The first is for when there's something big like a deer out there, still kicking, and I'll have to slice its throat. Put it out of its misery, you know?

Q:—

A: Okay, about that? I'm gonna tell you a real quick story. It had to have been something like my sixth month on the job, and there was this huge doe that a driver had plowed over. Just mangled it. I was nearby when I got the call, and when I pulled in, right there was the state trooper and the family that had hit the deer. Except the poor thing was still thrashing over in the right lane. Traffic was down to a crawl and everything. Kids were awake in the back seat, yelling and crying and carrying on. And so the statie—excuse me, the state trooper—gets real frustrated, goes up to the doe, tries to shoot her in the head, and he misses! And I saw it, too. Clipped her right in the temple, and now she's screaming. You ever hear a deer scream?

Q:—

A: Well, I sure as hell have. So the trooper fires again, and now this time he fires too low and gets her in the jaw, and now there's blood everywhere, and that makes everything worse. Especially for me on cleanup. So then he walks back to his squad car, gets the shotgun out, walks right past the family, and then stomps on the poor doe's neck while he's taking aim. And I kid you not: I thought I was going to have to scrape up that statie's boot with his foot still attached to it. That's how close he was to blowing off his own toes. So, yeah, that Buck knife is for when I don't want to see an animal suffer on the road.

Q:—

A: I did say that, yes. The second reason I carry around that big hunting knife is because of the boy they finally caught on the highway. You've heard the stories, right? Well, the game plan was this: If he were to sneak up on me while I was out there working, then I would hope to use the blade on him if it came down to it. Figure I might have a chance that way. But if he were to capture me? Here's hoping I'd have the courage to use the Buck to slice my own throat before the kid could get to work on me.

[Crystal Frazier, 39, Dispatcher]

Q:—

A: They said I could smoke in here. Is that all right?

Q:—

A: I appreciate it. You care for one?

Q:—

A: Suit yourself.

Q:—

A: I work for the state Department of Transportation. This is about that boy they found in the interchange, isn't it?

Q:—

A: I'd bet money on it. That large of a section between on-ramps and off-ramps, and something's bound to be down there. Didn't think it'd be something like him, though.

Q:—

A: That's fine. In dispatch, it's my job to send the crews out to where they're needed. We have our long-term construction plans, our scheduled monthly repairs, our weekly maintenance, and then our immediate jobs. It's my responsibility to break those up into tasks and send out the technicians where they're needed.

Q:—

A: Immediate jobs would be reports of car crashes that we have to sweep up, bent rails or downed power lines, which we have to coordinate with Ozark Electric on, things like that.

Q:—

A: It would include roadkill calls, yes. Those make up most of the immediate detail each day, if I'm being honest. Which I am.

Q:—

A: Never. In my time working for the DOT, we've never had road-kill calls about that particular stretch of the highway and US-71. Like it's a Bermuda Triangle of incidents. That interchange has been clean as bone for as long as I've been there.

Q:—

A: I have my suspicions, yes.

Q:—

A: If I'm being honest, which I am, I'd say it's because that was the boy's main source of food. He had most everything he needed in that patch there. When the county purchased that farmland back in 1970 to build the interchange, the acreage included an apple orchard. Came with a natural spring the farmer used to irrigate the lines of trees and the berry bushes there. If you grew up here, you probably picked blueberries at the old man's orchard one time or another. At his place or the Wickham orchard up in Johnson City.

Q:—

A: The rest, I imagine, came from the roadkill there. I don't know about the boy's hunting skills, but if the lack of dead animals on that run of US-71 was any indication, he did just fine as a scavenger. As far as those parts of the stories go, that didn't worry me. That he made no distinction between the types of fresh meat he found on the road does, though.

[Martha Crandall, 43, Licensed Clinical Social Worker]

Q:—

A: Is this going to take long? Because I don't think you're actually investigating this matter. I think you're trying to dig up crimes you can charge this poor child with.

Q:—

A: Because he doesn't know any better, that's why. You've had him locked up for the last two weeks and we've barely been given any access to him, and—

Q:—

A: Excuse me. The Fayetteville police are holding him. My mistake. Like it matters.

Q:—

A: If the rumors are true, which I doubt they are, then, yes, I know why you've taken him into custody. But that boy needs hospitalization and all types of intervention, not sedatives and some locked room in Juvenile Detention. Jesus.

Q:—

A: I'm a speech pathologist and LCSW with the state hospital, but these days I'm mostly used as a social worker. I've got three degrees, but for the life of me can't remember why I've decided to return to this backwater state, and I—

Q:—

A: Fine. I've been brought up from Little Rock to intervene on this young man's behalf and to find out what happened to him and how long he's been living in that forest in the interchange. Is that what it's called?

Q:—

A: You know exactly which area I'm talking about, but since this is for the record, it's the part of US-71 North that connects to 71 Business with the flyover, the part of 71B that connects back over to US-71 North, and then the spot where US-71 South splits from the main highway and down into the underpass that rides out to 71B. I imagine it looks like one big triangle from above. I can draw you a map if you'd like; I've been out there enough times.

Q:—

A: We don't know how he came to live in that forest bordered in by the highways, but we do know that he's been there a long time. If we had to guess, he's either fifteen or sixteen. He has the language skills of a pre-kindergartner, but the funny thing is that he communicates only by yelling. Normally, talking directly with someone means you try to match their volume—it's an earnest gesture, you're trying to keep that line of communication open and flowing—but it looks like he was never conditioned to do this. If we had to guess, I'd say—

Q:—

A: Fine. His chosen mode of verbal communication suggests that he's been yelled at by others he's been in contact with, and that this is the volume by which he's been conditioned to respond. Does that fit outside the realm of speculation?

Q:—

A: Well, think about it. If you're living in the borders of a system of flyovers and underpasses, it's pretty loud there, right? And if the verbal humans you're in contact with want you to hear them— think: stranded motorists, cops pulling over speeders or DUIs— they're going to have to yell, yes? Then, there you have it. He's been trained to respond this way because of his environment.

Q:—

A: We have no evidence of that. You want to talk about speculation? Because that's speculation.

Q:—

A: We don't have proof he would ever do something like that. Or that he could do something like that. And you all jumping to conclusions that he could do something like pull DUI victims or dead travelers from their cars is dangerous. He's a teenager, not some hyena out prowling on the savanna.

Q:—

A: Fine. Here's what we do know: We know his approximate age. We know he has the speech capabilities of a four-year-old. We know he's underweight and malnourished, but we also know it's not as severe as we might expect, and that's the strange part. We know that he's going to need extensive dental work. And we're pretty sure he survived in that forest on a diet of fruit, dirty spring water, and roadkill. And probably random fast food and garbage travelers have thrown out onto the road. And that's all we know because you all won't let us have more time to talk with him. You—

Q:—

A: Listen to me and stop jumping to conclusions and just think about this for a second, would you? Which would be an easier source of protein: freshly slaughtered raccoons and deer and animals like that, or living and breathing and possibly still-kicking human beings? Jesus.

[Calvin Walker, 29, Sheriff's Deputy]

Q:—

A: Is this absolutely necessary?

Q:—

A: I'm an FTO under Sheriff Wilde. Says so right in your notes, too. Don't know why I'm having to clear that shit up.

Q:—

A: Took you long enough. That boy in jail?

Q:—

A: You'd best keep him there if you know what's good for you.

Q:—

A: We're really going to rehash this past my initial statement? Fine.

Q:—

A: This was a 10-52 out on US-71 South. An ambulance call for an overturned GMC Jimmy, right under the flyover, just shy of two years ago. I was coming back down from Johnson City and noticed the wreck. Called it in, investigated the crash site, set up the flares, and then started walking the median.

Q:—

A: Because there wasn't a driver in the damn thing. That's why.

Q:—

A: He probably got taken by the kid, and I'll tell you—

Q:—

A: Jesus Christ. Fine. The Jimmy was unoccupied. I first assumed at the time that the driver had stumbled out of the car and away from the crash site, and that he was probably bleeding out somewhere nearby.

Q:—

A: The Jimmy had overturned in the left lane and had skidded toward the grass. I remember thinking it was hard to see out there since the county hadn't put up the sodium lights yet. Just had the Maglite to go by. So I went hunting for the poor bastard who'd managed to walk away. It wasn't until I saw the other side of the wreckage later that I learned how he'd probably exited the vehicle, Superman-style.

Q:—

A: I found a damn runway of blood leading away from the passing lane once I backtracked. Like I said, the kid had probably dragged him away from the—

Q:—

A: Fuck it. What do you want me to say? That the driver had miraculously flown through the passenger-side window and survived the fall? Because that shit definitely didn't happen, and you can write it down that I said that.

Q:—

A: Good lord. Fine, I observed the broken glass. I observed a trail of what I assumed to be blood leading away from the passing lane, where the overturned vehicle was visibly wrecked. I observed a break in the grass that might have been made if someone were trying to haul away a goddamn body.

Q:—

A: And that was it. A few of the other deputies and I set up a perimeter that night, broke out the spotlights, walked the entire length of that interchange, and we didn't find a damn thing. Another team staked out the adjoining farmland on the other side of the road, and they didn't find anything, either. We waited for daylight and then did it again.

Q:—

A: The only thing we found that week was a pile of trash under a small thicket of old apple trees that had tangled up together. A few people thought it was the site of an abandoned hobo camp. But five bucks says that's where the little psycho was sheltering.

Q:—

A: You'll have to pull the medical examiner's records for that. I'm done being corrected by a goddamn statie.

Q:—

A: Off the record? I'd say you'll eventually ID the bones of the driver in that pile you found in the irrigation ditch. Him and at least three others, I imagine. Bones cleaned down until you can't find a shred of what used to be meat on them. Empty of marrow, too, if the kid was hungry enough.

[Mildred "Millie" Reach, DO, 59, County Coroner]

Q:—

A: I'm the medical examiner for Washington County. The title says "Coroner," but I'm an actual physician, thank you very much. You have to be for this job, if we're being official about it.

Q:—

A: So we are being official about it. That's fine. I'm the ME here in Washington County. Formerly with Internal Medicine at the VA hospital here in town, and, after that, with the Pathology Department up at Mercy.

Q:—

A: Because the pay is better here and because I needed five more years, apparently, for my state benefits. Anything else you'd like to know about the job?

Q:—

A: Sure, the feral kid. Absolutely. I understand.

Q:—

A: This time, you all got involved. Yeah, I get it. Heard he hauled off another drunk driver with a self-induced case of severe road rash.

Q:—

A: I mean, c'mon. It's a little funny, right? The Ozark version of Bigfoot or the wendigo, maybe? I know: We could call him the "71-Business Baba Yaga," you know? "Be still and quiet, my little darlings, on this stretch of US-71, or the Highway Baba Yaga will steal you away!"

Q:—

A: Sorry.

Q:—

A: That's fine. I know this is serious.

Q:—

A: This was last week. Wednesday. You all called me out there once you found the bones in the irrigation ditch.

Q:—

A: Oh, bits and pieces from six different human skeletons. I've tasked a few of the daytime staff with tracking down missing person reports from that part of US-71 and the adjoining farms and neighborhoods, just stuff from the last ten years, though. That's how long we think he's been out there.

Q:—

A: Well, it's either that, or you've got some very tidy coyotes living in that forest.

Q:—

A: Nothing, nothing. I'm sure the state police are doing everything they can to make sure this roaming monster of the countryside is kept safely within the confines of the—

Q:—

A: Look, would you think about it for a second? The kid's been busy as a beaver stacking those bones in the old irrigation ditch. My guess is he finally had the raw material to dam the stream and let the basin fill up. So now, instead of trying to catch water in his hands, he can just drink freely where it runs in. And did you hear me? "Busy as a beaver"? Nothing? C'mon.

Q:—

A: You seem pretty upset. Would you like a glass of water?

Q:—

A: Let me tell you about a friend of mine.

Q:—

A: No, no, I promise. This'll just take a sec.

Q:—

A: Okay. Thank you. So I had this friend named Meagan back in med school. We were two of seven women in the entire class. The other five were gunners, heads down and focused on nothing but school, and that's fine. I get it. But Meagan and I had enough time between study sessions to talk, you know?

Q:—

A: I promise this will make sense. Now, do you want to hear this or not?

Q:—

A: Okay, so it turns out that Meagan came from a family of godly homesteaders up in Michigan. Serious folks, you know? Good folks, but serious. Grew their own vegetables and fruits on a farm up there. Raised hens for the eggs. What they couldn't grow on their own, they bartered for with their neighbors. She told me it felt sometimes like she was living on a commune. Well, Meagan's folks also had a rule of only eating meat they'd killed themselves. She said their deep freeze was filled with venison and wild boar, and that every other meat was pretty rare.

Q:—

A: I'm getting to that. I promise you'll see your captured Bigfoot Jr. in a new light if you stay with me.

Q:—

A: So here's the thing: Meagan's family also drove, and when they drove their car to church or the store, they ran over the occasional animal, you know? But because they'd killed it themselves, the animal—the roadkill, mind you—was up for grabs. Meagan said she remembered that this was how they came to have turkey and the rare bit of veal sometimes if another farmer's calf had wandered out of their field.

Q:—

A: My point is this: To Meagan's family, meat was meat. Didn't matter if they'd done the killing on purpose or by accident. The good Lord had provided.

Q:—

A: And to your little highway orphan in lockup right now, it's the same damn thing. The forest and the roadways around it have provided exactly what he's needed to live. Fat squirrels in winter, juicy rabbits that'll pop out from the thickets. Apple trees and berry bushes that bear fruit for a good portion of the year, and then, lo and behold, the occasional fresh kill found on the shoulder of the highway.

Q:—

A: It just so happens that sometimes, just sometimes, the roadkill looks a little bit like him. And as someone who's had to autopsy a few of these victims before, they can look pretty unrecognizable from hamburger or shredded pork or brisket. It's kind of humbling in a way, you know? Because it reminds us . . .

Q:—

A: That meat is meat.

Just a Girl

FROM *Obsession*, Amazon Originals

TikTok

@QuarantineDream

2000 following
11.4K followers
50K likes

Just a girl, imagining what college life would have been like without Covid, all from the comfort of her childhood bedroom. ♥

Inbox
All activity ⬇️

JoshWolfPack, Dubsy, and **75 others** viewed your profile.

SoggyNoodle added your video to favorites.

Roddyriguez12 liked your video.

Roddyriguez12 liked your video.

Roddyriguez12 liked your video.

HowlsLeftEarring replied to your comment. 😵 So happy I found your page! It's kept me sane for the last couple of years.

Roddyriguez12 sent you a message.

You are such a beautiful soul. Your videos and lives have literally changed my life. My parents wanted to know what inspired me to cook more and get better grades, and I said my friend Tiana!

QuarantineDream Thank you! Happy I could help, friend!

StaceysStickerDepot sent you a message.

Hi Tiana,
I hope this isn't weird but I made stickers for your fans in my shop and was wondering if you wanted me to send you some? Do you have a P.O. Box? You can use it as your pfp if you like it!

QuarantineDream Stacey, I love this! Thank you so much! The drawing of the textbook in the rice cooker is cute af! Changing my pfp NEOW!

Courtniander commented on your video.

I know we're on break and not cooped up inside anymore, but any chance you'll be doing summer study sessions? It's lonely studying by myself. 😢

QuarantineDream Study sessions will be back soon! Along with a surprise . . .

QuarantineDream

July 7, 2021
75K views
5 saves
103 comments

[Autogenerated captions]
STOP SCROLLING! If you've followed me from the beginning, you know I got dumped back in March of 2020 because I talked about it for like three months straight. [laughter] Yeah, that was a bad month for everybody, but having my boyfriend choose another

girl to be in his quarantine bubble was a mess. Or maybe it was a blessing for me, since I used my newfound free time to build up this account, where I imagine what life would have been like if my first year of college hadn't been virtual: what outfits I would have worn to class, food I would have eaten in the dining hall, parties I would have gone to. I don't think I would have focused on this if I hadn't been dumped, so thanks boo! Anyway, I haven't been dating because I needed to do some healing or whatever, but also ain't no way I was bringing Covid home, okay? Miss Rona wasn't about to sneak in and snatch up Granny on my watch! And if any of you want to call me paranoid, you can tell me all about your personal experience of saying goodbye to a loved one through a Zoom screen. Otherwise, fuck off. [laughter] Sorry, this is supposed to be an upbeat video! You all know how strict I've been, but now we're vaxxed and Granny is out in these streets, talking to some man named Herbert who already wants her to move to his retirement community. She put that Granny punani on him, I guess. Oh here she come, here she come.

Granny: Tiana, why are you telling these people my business?

                                    Because they love you, and so do I.

Granny: I appreciate that, but my business is MY business. If you want to make a video about YOU getting on one of them apps, talk about you! Before one of my beaus starts asking me questions.

                                                        One of my?!

Granny: I'm here for a good time, not a long time, and I'm making up for lost time with you keeping me on lockdown! With a little help from my friends. Oh, there's one of them now. See you later.

          **Okay, then, okay. Make sure you take your mask with
          you! Did you see that? Granny is setting an example.
          I had to drop her off at three different fourth of July
          cookouts last weekend and she had the nerve to ask**

"didn't I have something better to do?" than drive her around! Now you see why I decided to get on a dating app. It's called ConnectMore. Has anyone tried it? I'm not getting my hopes up, and I've never used a dating app before, but we'll see what happens!

Comments

DianaSmith1974 My son is single and age-appropriate! Come be my daughter-in-law so I can get some of that tender meat loaf you make in the air fryer at family events.

NutmegFreck Get it Granny! Put it on Willie Earl and 'em.

QuarantineDream 😂

NutmegFreck We wouldn't be blessed with your presence if Granny wasn't a freak in the sheets.

QuarantineDream No! I'm screaming and throwing up omg whyyyy

Roddyriguez12 I hate to break it to you but the boys are NOT okay. I deleted my app after one week and have decided to become a bog witch with a coven of cat familiars.

QuarantineDream Oh no, I'm nervous. Is it really that bad?

Roddyriguez12 IT'S WORSE

TikTok

@QuarantineDream

2027 following
13.4K followers
800K likes

Just a girl, imagining what college life would have been like without Covid, all from the comfort of her childhood bedroom. ❤

QuarantineDream

July 16, 2021
975K views
2548 saves
675 comments

[Autogenerated closed captions]
. . . I'm going to make some comfort food, because I need it after the WILD text I just got. A simple one-pot spaghetti with meat sauce using the hot plate Waverly sent me. THANK YOU WAVERLY. More detailed recipe and ingredients in my pinned comment. Okay: story time. You all know I decided to get on the appy apps since Granny was making ME feel like the 70 year old. BIG MISTAKE. Why was the first guy I swiped right on a whole "what's your body count?" headass weirdo? A guy who, and I quote, isn't "trying to get with someone who doesn't bring anything to the table but a ran-through cooch."

Unsurprisingly, I wasn't swept off my feet, and asked if he even owned a table. He didn't like that, and he's still harassing me days later! A message from him just popped up on my phone as I was setting it up to record, and that's why I'm so hot right now. Do you want see what he wrote? It's not my usual content but it's so out of pocket and when I showed my friends they said it's normal. IT SHOULD NOT BE NORMAL.

Anyway here's the spaghetti plated up. It's so good, so easy, and the best thing to eat after dealing with a creep. Which is why . . .

Comments

MeowtherMayl OMG, THIS LOOP IS PERFECT lol

HowlsLeftEarring I can hear how upset you are. I love you, Tiana! Sorry you had to experience this.

BettyLaFeral Body count?! I was so confused, I thought this was about to be a true crime story time! 😫

QuarantineDream 😂

ToughMudderFluff Why couldn't you just tell him your body count? Let me guess.

NoToes90210 Look at her. You know it's cause there're too many to count.

QuarantineDream Both of you are gross.

Roddyriguez12 This is why you should date me instead. I don't ask creepy questions and I own a table from Ikea.

QuarantineDream LOL I appreciate you. 🖤

PattyOCrabs Share the texts. And his name. We just wanna talk.

DanceDanceEvolution This is J name behavior.

FingerUpButt Your eyes are migrating to either side of your face yet you think you can be choosy. 🙄

StaceysStickerDepot What are you talking about? Her eyes are normal . . .

SilkNeverPressed Go touch grass, weirdo.

Quarantine Dream Thanks for defending me, sis. 🍃

see all 7 comments   •

ConnectMore App Messages between Tiana_S and [REDACTED]

July 8

Hi beautiful
How r u

Hi! I like your pfp. Is hiking your thing,
or do you have other hobbies?

I'm mostly into personal development and working on
my podcast. Trying to get my money and my mental right
so I can get rich, retire early, all of that.

Nice. We support a goal-oriented king!

King, huh? I like that. You trying to be my queen?

We'll see how things go. 😊

😊
What's your body count?

. . .

Hwhat? 🤨

How many guys have you been with? Simple question. 😳

Right.

I can't give the exact amount, but the estimate is
approximately *none of your damn business*.

I'm not trying to get with someone who doesn't bring
anything to the table but a ran-through cooch.

Do you even have a table? You're acting mad weird, bro.

I'm bro now because I asked a question? Don't be mad
because I'm not simping like the betas you usually
interact with.

I'm not mad at all. I appreciate you not wasting my time
by pretending to be well-adjusted.

**Thanks for being honest.
Have the day you deserve.**

July 10

I'm bored. Wanna chill? You could cook for me. I want
steak, rare. Gotta get that protein in cause I'm hitting the
weight room tomorrow.

Humor me: why would I cook for you?

I've seen your little TikToks. Steak is way easier than what
you usually make.
My parents are on vacation and they
didn't lock up the booze.

**This is creepy. No, I don't want to chill.
Don't message me again.**

I bet if I asked you out to dinner, and offered to pay,
you'd have a different answer.

**If you'd asked that, it would be
the most normal thing you've done.
My answer would still be: don't message me again.**

Let me guess: you're a feminist?
Fuck that lol
Females always talk about equality until the check comes.
Men are trash until you need one to fix
something for you or pay your bills.
Have fun changing your flat tire by yourself.
Feminism is the worst thing that ever
happened to our species.
You have no rebuttal because you know I'm right.

**Are you aware that you're having
an argument with yourself?
"Rebuttal" LOL**

Prove me wrong.

Go join the debate club instead of messaging random girls.

July 11

So you agree that I'm correct about females? Your silence
says yes.

Boy, bye. 😂
Seriously, stop messaging me.

Typical fatherless behavior.

A few months ago my dad almost
passed from Covid. Fuck you.

Well I'm glad he survived, even if he clearly raised you
wrong.

Double fuck you.

I thought you had some class, but I can't consider being with
a female who talks like this to a man who's courting her.
You're lucky I'm even paying attention
to someone who looks like you.
I was trying to be nice, last time I do that.

Triple fuck you, and your rickety table too.

I'm above you and you need to understand that; obviously
you don't, so you ruined whatever we might've had.

Awwwww. I really missed out.

Well.
I'd give you a second chance if you learn your place.
You can start by cooking me dinner.

July 12

Hey
What u up to?
Don't be mad, I was just joking.

July 13

Hey.
U up?
So you're ghosting me now?

July 14

Happy Flag Day! If I sent a picture of my flag pole I bet
you'd respond.
::view-once media::
Whatever, I'm sure you smell like spoiled tuna with your
BV-riddled self.

July 15

Only one person can have linebacker shoulders in my
relationship, so it wouldn't have worked out anyway.

July 16

You didn't block me so that must mean you like this.
Don't you, you little slut? 😂

July 17

I saw your video. What the fuck?
You don't have my permission to share our conversation
I will sue you

I'm serious
Take that fucking video down
Answer me
Answer me!
Bitch

TikTok

@QuarantineDream

2145 following
21.4K followers
1.2M likes

Just a girl, imagining what college life would have been like without Covid, all from the comfort of her childhood bedroom. ❤️

QuarantineDream

July 17, 2021
1M views
5000 saves
675 comments

Replying to **@DanceDanceEvolution:** This is J name behavior.

[Autogenerated closed captions]
Part two. I blocked out his name but yes, DanceDanceEvolution. These are the texts from him, up behind me. Wait, I'm not used to using the greenscreen, let me move out of the way. Like, what kind of dude tells a random woman she smells like spoiled tuna?? First of all, how can he smell me through a text message? Why does he even know what BV is? Do these dudes have an insult master list and they just choose random ones to text to you? Reminder that this all happened because I didn't want to tell him, a complete stranger, how many people I'd slept with thirty seconds after we started chatting. Are y'all not understanding how bizarre this is? Like, be fucking for real, my guy: why do you care what my body count is? It's giving insecure.

I am NINETEEN and dudes are out here acting like a simple conversation to establish whether we vibe is a job interview with bonus invasive hymen check.

I do want to ask the aunties out there: were men always like this? I thought they were supposed to be evolving, but maybe they're regressing!

Comments

StaceysStickerDepot Hey, bestie, since you matched with him does that mean he lives near you? Be careful! He seems unstable.

CarolP1963 I don't know if my generation was better, but they could at least pretend to be until they got in your drawers.

PickleRickson Would you buy a pair of used tires with no tread?

BettyLaFeral Wait. Do you think that vaginas are tread lined, and that's what the grip is? Oh dear.

see all 10 comments

JoshWolfPack You claim not to like me but made this video trying to get my attention. Pathetic.

DanceDanceEvolution I knew it!!

HowlsLeftEarring Checked out your videos. You are entirely too confident, especially for a MRA podcast bro. Get a life.

ShantysandPantys @WhyAreMen another one for you!

Inbox
All activity ⬇️

JenJenBanks replied to your video.

Men are actually the ones who cause BV. Not that there's anything wrong with it, but he is literally the source if that's his experience with women.

AlphaLyfePodcast sent you a message.

Maybe we should invite you on the podcast because I'm pretty sure you're more of a man than we are. Go wax your mustache.

HowlsLeftEarring sent you a message.

I hope you're doing okay! You don't deserve this after all the joy you've brought so many of us! We've got your back.

Roddyriguez12 tagged you.

@QuarantineDream Team unite! Protect her at all costs!

JoshWolfPack sent you a message.

Delete it now, b1tch.

SmarterThanAFemale sent you a message.

Get in the kitchen and make us a sandwich, wench.

QuarantineDream

July 18, 2021
975K views
5000 saves
675 comments

Replying to **@Ohrllysure**: These are so fake. 🙄 If you wanted to get clout off of "men are trash" tok, you could have come up with more believable texts.

[Autogenerated closed captions]
Okay last video for real because too many of you are saying I did this for views. The messages are not faked using a text generator. Trust me, I wish they were! I'd love for this to be an exaggeration. Knowing there are men who just casually talk to women like this is honestly kinda scary If you need more confirmation that this is real, he outed himself in the comments of my last video.

I love my followers and wouldn't lie to them, especially not to get the attention of a bunch of people who aren't even interested in my normal content. While I appreciate all the new follows, my main content is cooking and talking about college stuff, so if you find that boring it's okay to unfollow now. I'm not giving this dude any more attention—he's not worth it.

Comments

Roddyriguez12 We believe you! Thank you for standing up to harassers!

JoshWolfPack I told you to take down your video, not make another one. Can you not follow simple instructions?

JelenasLastStan Oooo, somebody's talking tough! 😂

QuarantineDream And I said I'm done talking about this. Maybe next time you'll think twice before spamming a woman and sending 🐦 pics.

JoshWolfPack I'll decide when we're done.

JoshWolfPack If these videos are still up tomorrow, you'll regret it.

StaceysStickerDepot
Are you threatening her? **@FBI** come get your boy!

Sister Sister Chat

Chelle

                                 Tiana
             Why are you texting me from the living room?

Chelle
I told you to swipe left on that fool.

                                 Tiana
            Are you . . . victim blaming me? Damn!
                        It be your own people. 😬

Chelle
I'm sharing some sisterly advice. You out here trying
to make moves like Granny but you don't have her
ability to crush a man's soul without breaking a sweat.

Tiana
OKAY I GET IT. You aren't even old enough
to be on a dating app. Why don't you stop
minding grown folks' business?

Chelle
I AM old enough to be on TikTok, where you shared
that business. Just be careful, okay? I know you're
usually in your little happy cooking/college/clothes
algorithm bubble, but these TikTok incels are scary.

Tiana
Wow, are you worried about me? 👀

Chelle

Tiana
You're right. The drama did get me new followers,
but that wasn't what I intended and I kinda wish
I'd never shared it. I'm just gonna stick to my
normal content because the app is stressful enough
without having to deal with weirdos like Joshifer.

Chelle
Joshifer? Is that his real name?

Tiana
No, but he's a demon so that's what
he'll be called from here on out.

Chelle
LOL

AlphaLyfe Podcast

AlphaLyfe is where real men talk about real issues, a place to fight back against toxic feminism.

10 followers on iHeart Podcasts

Transcript from July 19, 2021, episode "ConnectMore App Bitches"

Jared: This episode was supposed to be about dating apps and how to avoid low-value women, but one of us has some lived experience to share.

Conner: Are you talking about how Josh let some stupid Connect-More app bitch humiliate him?

Josh: Humiliate? Bro, she didn't humiliate me. I'm good.

Conner: That's beta talk, bro. What the fuck?

Josh: She humiliated herself, not me. Showed how she'll just talk to any man and that she can't keep a real man's interest. She's showing what kind of female she is. She might be getting supported by these social media feminists and whatever, but real men see her for what she is.

Conner: Yeah. You dodged a bullet there.

Josh: That's why you ask those things immediately. To test them. If a female won't answer your questions, that's the answer itself. It tells you that she doesn't know how to listen. To submit.

Jared: Shows she doesn't know how to serve her man. This is why we need more women who are modest, who understand the natural order of things.

Conner: Yeah. If she knew her place, she wouldn't be bothered by normal and necessary questions.

Josh: But even though she is only embarrassing herself . . . a man can only take so much disrespect before he's forced to act, you know. Because these females really think that just because they have some followers on social media, they can talk without consequences. It's all "we're as good as men" until you remind them that two men would have been swinging on each other at this point. Then they bring up threats. I'm talking reality.

Jared: What should Josh do? Let us know what you think in the Discord.

TikTok

@QuarantineDream

3277 following
25.2K followers
3.4M likes

Just a girl, imagining what college life would have been like without Covid, all from the comfort of her childhood bedroom. ♥

QuarantineDream

July 19, 2021
Summer Study Session Live
115 participants

[Autogenerated closed captions]
Okay, that's twenty-five minutes! Five minute break! Did you get your work done? Let me know in the comments. Hi Courtniander! I'm glad you could make it! I'm reading this book that's on my syllabus for next semester's gender studies class. It's called *The Will to Change*, by bell hooks. Have any of you read it? Ah, Rynelle has! It's so good, right? I wonder what class discussion will be like in a real-life classroom instead of on Zoom when I can turn down the volume when someone gets on my nerves. Wait, Adir is asking, "What's happening in the background?" Granny went to a mixer at the senior center yesterday and now she's trying to teach my parents some old school dances because she thinks she can start a viral TikTok trend. I've created a monster. Stacey asked if

Granny considers herself polyamorous and you know what, I do not want to know the answer to that! Okay three minutes left, if you need water coffee or to handle your bathroom business, go now! I might spend the next pomodoro session picking up some new dance moves instead of reading. HowlsLeftEarring, is here. Hey friend! They say that they're glad things are getting back to normal. Me, too! I made this a space for people to have fun, so hopefully that other stuff is over with for good. Oop! Let me knock on wood.

Discord

The Wolf's Den
🔽 TEXT CHANNELS
#ConnectMore-App-Bitches

Josh Okay. You guys are here because you're our inner circle. This channel is closed to the other members.

NeoRedPill3000 Can this stuff be traced?

Vinny Why are you asking?

NeoRedPill3000 Because you don't take notes on a criminal fucking conspiracy.

Kyle What?

NeoRedPill3000 It's from the Wire.

Conner What's the wire

NeoRedPill3000 Jesus. I forget that most of you are fetuses.

Jared And you're ancient, bro.

Conner Trying to clown us, at your large age.

Vinny Is this guy cool? We don't need anyone uncool in here.

Kyle He's cool, bro. I wouldn't bring someone uncool in here, and we need, like, old man input sometimes. Respecting your elders and all that.

NeoRedPill3000 Yeah. I'm the only one with credit cards and no curfew. I have to go pick my kid up from school soon, so let's get on with this.

Josh We're not committing any crimes, we're just going to teach Tiana a lesson. We'll pass the video on to the right forums and they'll mobilize to mass report her videos and get them taken down.

Conner We can spam her comments with insults and shit, and then others will follow if they aren't already doing the same. Some of them will send her email and messages with porn and threats, and we can join in on that if we want, but make sure you use a burner account for all of this. The usual.

NeoRedPill3000 That's it? And what do you mean by the usual?

Jared It's pretty standard operating procedure for men's rights activists. What'd you think we were gonna do?

NeoRedPill3000 That doesn't matter. This is a good start.

reddit

r/MensEmpowerment
Posted by u/SparkleBronyVin718 July 20

Has everyone seen this video? <u>JoshWolfPack</u> is one of us and she revealed his private conversation to millions of feminists and woke-scolds on TikTok. This could happen to any of us! We need to show what happens when these females step out of line. Maybe you should stop by her page and leave a nice, respectful comment, like all her followers are doing about men like us. If you need to know where the report button is on TikTok, here's a picture:

Twitter

MasculinityCoachSir @alpharightnow | July 20
Check out this disgusting video below. It's got hundreds of thousands of likes and countless comments, all picking on a young man who knows his worth and demands the same in a partner.

MasculinityCoachSir @alpharightnow | July 20
Replying to **@alpharightnow**

The problem with feminists is that they think that they have the right to humiliate us and treat us like eunuchs and that we just have to shut up and take it. Society gives women whatever they want, so we have been just shutting up and taking it. NO MORE.

Show this thread

Tiana's Tired of Trolls @QuarantineDream | July 19
I barely come on this bird app but there are fake screenshots and edited videos circulating on here of me saying horrible things. Keywords: FAKE and EDITED. This is my account if you want to check my past tweets, and my videos are on TikTok.

Tiana's Tired of Trolls @QuarantineDream | July 19
Replying to **@QuarantineDream**

PS: taking the time to photoshop tweets and manipulate videos of a teenager because she talked about a guy being weird on a dating app does not make the case for any of y'all not being HUGE FUCKING LOSERS. Get a job, sweeties! 😈

From: <verify@twitter.com>
To: Tiana Carter <TCarter@smail.com>
Subject: 094763 is your Twitter verification code
July 19, 2021, at 11:00 p.m.

An attempt was made to log in to your account. There's one quick step you need to complete to verify that it's you. Enter this verification code when prompted.

094763

Wasn't you? Contact support.

From: Tiana Carter <TCarter@smail.com>
To: <verify@twitter.com>
Subject: FWD: 094763 is your Twitter verification code
July 19, 2021, at 11:01 p.m.

Hi,

I've reached out to you several times over the last few hours. This is like the twentieth verification email I've received. You've already said you won't stop the harassment on the TL, but can you at least put some kind of hold on my account so that the people trying to guess my password aren't able to keep triggering this?

From: <verify@twitter.com>
To: Tiana Carter <TCarter@smail.com>
Subject: Re: FWD: 094763 is your Twitter verification code
July 19, 2021, at 11:05 p.m.

This is an automated reply. Your email has been received and a ticket has been opened. We will evaluate your concern and get back to you within 24 to 72 hours.

Group Text Chat

Keeping up with the Car . . .
Mom, Dad, Chelle, Granny . . .

Tiana
Hey everyone, so this TikTok thing is getting out of control. People are trying to hack my accounts and it seems like it might be more than one person.

Chelle
I told you these weirdos were bad news.

Dad
Is this about the dating app video?

Chelle
You've seen it?

Dad
Some of my coworkers mentioned it, but
I didn't watch. What's going on?

                                                      Tiana
                        Omg your coworkers have seen it? 😳
                    Yeah it's that one. I'm worried that the people who
                    got mad about it will try to mess with you guys, too.

Granny
I wish some fool would try it. I didn't live through
Jim Crow to be scared of some little boys who cry
on the internet because they get no bitches.

Chelle
Grandma! We need to put a parental
lock on her TikTok app.

Dad
How serious is this? Do we need to call the police?

                                                      Tiana
                    I don't think the police wouldn't do anything yet. I'm
                        hoping it blows over but trying to prepare for the
                    worst. I've been really good about not taking videos
                        that show identifying features of our house, but I
                    don't know what info is floating around out there.

Chelle
I just googled your name and your Facebook page
lists me, Mom, Dad, and Granny as family. When
you search Mom and Dad's names, the address of
our house pops up on random real estate sites.

Tiana
What!?

Chelle
I'm sending take down requests. There are forms
on the sites. Why do these sites even exist? I don't
think people know your last name to find your
Facebook, but this info needs to go regardless.

Mom
I'm at work but I'm gonna ask Mary in IT if she
knows what can be done. She gave the workshop
on securing personal information online.

Tiana
Thank you! I'm sorry that I'm causing
trouble for everyone.

Chelle
It's not your fault.

TikTok

@WhyAreMen

690 following
1.3M followers
67.1M likes

Booping misbehaving male humans in the snoot with the rolled-up
newspaper of feminist justice. She/her.

WhyAreMen

July 22, 2021
900K views
7.5K saves
2.1K comments

[Autogenerated closed captions]
Have we all been paying attention to what's happening with Tiana, the sweet teenager who just wanted to find a nice guy and instead ended up with a NICE GUY (TM)? She shared some of the gross texts she got, then the guy, who she never even identified, shows up mad in her replies! It's been a shitshow ever since, with seemingly every incel on this site and others trying to get in on the action. I'm on #TeamTiana, but as of now her account has been suspended. Is this app saying that they support harassers? Because that's what it looks like. His account is still up and he's posting gloating videos and clips from his podcast—of course he has a podcast where he and his bros bash women—and he's gaining new followers. This pisses me off. How do these manbabies cry about getting censored even as they expand their platform and women are silenced?

Comments

CremedelaCum She should have never shared those private messages if she didn't want to deal with the spotlight. This is what happens when you try to embarrass a man for no reason.

HowlsLeftEarring He shouldn't have been such a creep. If women don't talk about these things, guys get away with it.

GenericAnimeAvatar Are you saying women never harass men? Because that seems sexist. This is what feminism gets you!

NoDoyLeroy They're saying that once a guy starts acting scary, he waives his right to privacy.

DannyOwens1962 Stop exaggerating. She hasn't been silenced. Yet. I'll applaud whoever does the job. Mouthy bitches get stitches.

user9936218609 She hasn't been silenced, but you're about to be. Next time you want to threaten someone, don't use the profile with your full name and link to your Instagram.

user9936218609 Your boss Carlene will be meeting with you tomorrow.

TikTok

@QuarantineDream

4300 following
64K followers
4.8M likes

Just a girl. I know how to fight. ✊

QuarantineDream

July 24, 2021
2.3M views
7900 saves
0 comments

[Autogenerated closed captions]
Oh em gee, y'all!!! Get ready with me: morning routine. I'm
not a beauty influencer, but I got sent some new calming and
hydrating serum and foundation from Glisten Cosmetics,
so I'm going to try it. Sorry I haven't updated in a couple
days, but I was suspended and didn't feel like making an alt
account. I got reported for bullying after showing what Josh
and his weirdo "alpha" friends were saying in my comments—
apparently making content about being bullied is bullying
your bullies, and that's not allowed. [laughter] This serum
feels great by the way. Much needed self-care! The foundation
is a bit thick for my taste, but good if you're looking for full
coverage.

The harassment hasn't stopped, but I'm not going to give them
the satisfaction of sharing it. This is all such a joke anyway. How
is it fair that Josh is the creep and I'm the one being targeted,
harassed, and punished?

@FeminineDivine stitch with **@QuarantineDream**: "How is it
fair that Josh is the creep and I'm the one being targeted,
harassed, and punished?"

[Autogenerated closed captions]
For my followers who are sensitive to energy, do you feel the masculine energy that girl exudes? It's like a hammer to the face. And no, this has nothing to do with her being Black, it's because she hasn't recognized how to step into her dark feminine. If she had, she would have been able to gently decline a date without reading so much into Josh's intent.

I'm not taking sides, but I think she overreacted and then liked the attention she was getting. I turn down men all the time because I don't allow just anyone into my divine temple. There's a way to do it that lets a man keep his pride, and I don't have to make videos about it for clout.

Comments

CallMeMaster41389 We need more females like you.

AyasiaPrince If you were truly spiritual, you wouldn't be using your platform to defend misogynistic demons who are tormenting a young Black girl.

TikTok

@QuarantineDream

5765 following
200K followers
7.3M likes

Just a girl, being attacked by a horde of alpha wannabe trolls. Bite me. 🖐

QuarantineDream

July 25, 2021
200K views
1200 saves
375 comments

[Autogenerated closed captions]
Hey everyone! I just want to thank you all so much for your likes, follows, duets, over the last two years and especially these last few days. I can't believe these manbabies expect me to debate whether they have the right to harass me. I won't be engaging with the alpha male crew because they embarrass themselves just fine without my help. The app won't make them stop harassing me, so let's just ignore them and let them play with themselves, which is what they're used to anyway.

Comments

StaceysStickerDepot Yaaasss! Forget those jerks. It's pathetic how they won't leave you alone. Excited that you actually get to eat real dining hall food now and can see how much better yours is LOL

BetaSmash7 Bow down and know your place.

Kindofajerk ON YOUR KNEES WENCH.

HardKnuckleAlph You think you can ignore us? Humble yourself and BOW DOWN.

user9936218609 You're twelve. I just emailed your parents. I hope you learn a lesson from this.

YouTube Transcript

The High-Value Man's Burden

Do you see how this girl goes from making trouble to acting like a victim in these videos? So quickly! [laughter] If she had just kept her mouth shut, she wouldn't be in this situation. That is the lesson here, isn't it? Keep your mouth shut and we won't do anything too bad to you. [laughter]

From: C. Stranger <concerned1@smail.com>
To: Tiana Carter <Tcarter@smail.com>
Subject: Your Online Security
July 26, 2021, at 12:46 a.m.

Dear Tiana,

I've messaged you on TikTok and Twitter and gotten no response there, so I thought I'd send this email in the chance you see it. I did a basic security check on you and you have way too much sensitive information floating around on the internet. I know this sounds like a scam (it should if you have any sense of self-preservation) but I'm not offering any services. You don't even have to write me back. I'm not sending any links (never click on links from strangers!). Below are the titles of a few articles that you can google that will help you secure your online presence. Your immediate family members should do the same.

Don't bother searching my name, this is just a burner email.

Please read the articles and follow the advice in them (starting with "How to Get Out From Under A Misogynist Dogpile" on WikiHow)

Protecting Yourself Online (Teen Vogue)

Surviving Harassment in the Digital Age (New York Magazine)

What I learned from GamerGate (Buzzfeed)

This will not just go away. You have a dog, so let me put it like this—when it finds a piece of food somewhere in the street, is it satisfied with having found it? Or does it keep dragging you back to the spot, hoping more food will appear? These goons have your scent. Erase as much of it as you can.

Best,

A concerned stranger

From: Tiana Carter <Tcarter@smail.com>
To: C. Stranger <concerned1@smail.com>
Subject: Re: Your Online Security
July 26, 2021, at 11:13 a.m.

Hi,

I'm still not sure if this is someone messing with me, or if it's smart to reply, but thank you for the advice. I went over the articles with my family, and they were really helpful.

Sincerely,

Tiana

Instagram

TianaDreaming she/her
425 posts
8072 followers
1200 following

College girl, taking on the world.

July 30, 2021
TianaDreaming Even though my account was reinstated, I've decided to take a break from TikTok for a bit, until everyone gets tired of making gross content about me. I did nothing wrong, and I won't explain myself again or deal with people who want to twist what happened to boost their interactions while accusing me of doing the same. Today I'm wearing an old Destiny's Child concert tee that I stole from my mom's closet, high-rise mom fit jeans from Target, and Reebok classic high tops in red. Mask is from MaskC. Glow is courtesy of melanin, Fenty, and being away from social media. It's been great for my mental health, which was already in the gutter after being isolated for so long. It's nice to remember that there's a world outside of socials, and there are even some guys who have hobbies other than tracking girls across platforms telling her to unalive herself.

[Image Description: Tall Black girl wearing outfit as described, looking completely unbothered, because she isn't.]

CapybarringtonIII Girl, we got you. Take as much time as you need.

StaceysStickerDepot 😍 You look amazing! I'm sorry you've been through so much all because you exposed a pest. You don't deserve any of this!

GlobalCorp23 Okay my friends I am serious I will give $5000 to the first person to reply with "Global Goodness." I am serious!

HowIsLeftEarring Love the fit!

AlchemistAlbedo You don't get to decide when this is over. We do. 😊

July 31, 2021
TianaDreaming I have some good news that I couldn't share while everything was going on—I moved on campus! I'm so excited that I'll get to see what it's all about! But that means my content will be changing. There will still be weekly live group study sessions once school starts, and dorm room recipes because meal plans are expensive af, but an emphasis on OotD and makeup looks, and what life is like for college students in these wild and weird times.

[Image Description: Black girl with knotless braids wears blue shorts and sports bra. She sits with legs crossed in front of a stack of boxes in a dorm room.]

HowIsLeftEarring OMG that's such great news! I can't wait to see how you enjoy campus life!

PlayaDelRio$ What school are you going to?

KevinSorbosMullet Don't worry, we'll find out.

Kellllllllee Oh, this is so exciting!

StaceysStickerDepot Do you have a wishlist? We can send you stuff to decorate your dorm.

Discord

The Wolf's Den
⬇ TEXT CHANNELS
#ConnectMore-App-Bitches

Vinny Guys! Been kinda quiet in here, but turns out I know some-one in her dorm.

Josh Nice. I have a cousin on her campus but he's a beta bitch who's mad because he got hurt when we were horsin' around once.

NeoRedPill3000 Who is the contact on campus?

Kyle You can invite them into the group if you want. So we can coordinate better.

Vinny I'm not sharing his name and he's not on Discord. But him and his buddies are down for the cause and said they can help.

Conner What are they gonna do?

Vinny Let her know that #WeAreAllJosh. 😒

Instagram

TianaDreaming she/her
427 posts
9465 followers
1243 following

College girl, taking on the world.

August 25, 2021
TianaDreaming Happy Hump Day! Here is my ootd for the first day of classes. Jeans: Target. Top: Shein. Shoes: I forget. Sun-glasses: Dollar General. Wearing my biggest sunglasses because I got almost no sleep. Someone was knocking on the door to my room throughout the night. I reported it to my RA but he said he

can't do anything about it. I've been having fun apart from that, and my roommate is the sweetest, so not gonna let a bad night get me down. [Image description: hot but tired Black girl sitting on bench in the quad]

Instagram Stories

August 31, 2021

TianaDreaming 2h ago
TO WHOEVER LEFT THE BOX FULL OF ROACHES IN FRONT OF MY DOOR, FUCK YOU.

This video has been deleted.

TianaDreaming 10min ago
THEY ARE EVERYWHERE! OMG, WHY WOULD SOMEONE DO SOMETHING LIKE THIS? EVERY ROOM ON THE FLOOR HAS THEM SKITTERING AROUND! 😖

This video has been deleted.

Discord

Biology 201 Autumn 2021
⬇ TEXT CHANNELS
#Exam-Prep

Tiana Hey everyone, reminder that I'm going to be holding a virtual study session tonight, September 25, where we can go over joint classification and integumentary systems before the exam tomorrow. I used to do open sessions on TikTok live but this will be a closed Zoom.

Betsy I'm down with that! Are we going to do pomodoros like last time? I liked how you alternated with going over notes and then private study time.

Amanda And the trivia questions you made were helpful and fun!

Tiana Thanks 😊

Ashaf I definitely could not wrap my mind around histology until we talked the notes through a few times, so I'll be there!

David Actually, I'm going to lead a study session. An in person one.

Tiana Oh that's great! Maybe we can stagger them so people can roll from one session to the next. What time is yours?

David Or everyone could just come to mine. I did ace the first quiz. Have you shared your grade? What makes you qualified to lead anything?

Ashaf Chill, bro. This isn't a competition, we all need to study as much as we can.

David Only one of us is here on a scholarship, and girls are naturally not good at science anyway.

Ashaf . . .

Betsy What the fuck are you talking about David?

Amanda That's a weird thing to say.

Tiana I'll be starting the session at 7:00 as planned.

David I'll be starting mine at 7 too. In the study hall at McCormick.

Tiana OK.

Tiana Well.

Tiana See you all later maybe.

David

This is the beginning of your direct message history with **@David.**

David What's the link to your study session?

David Hey

David Send me the link

David Fuck you

David Josh was right, you know. You smell. No wonder you only do virtual meet ups. Go to the student health center and get some antibiotics. LOL

Sister Sister Chat

Chelle
Wait, so this guy is a fan of their podcast or
something, and he's in your bio lab group?

Chelle
Show those messages to your professor.

Tiana
I did. He says that I should just not interact with
him outside of class, and that the discord isn't a
requirement, but he can't move him to another group.

Chelle
Why not?

Tiana
Because it would make more work for him, I guess.
Don't tell Mom and Dad, I don't want them to worry.

Chelle
Fine, I'll tell Granny and she can get her
boyfriends to come give him what for.

> **Tiana**
> LOL

Chelle
Are you sure you're okay? I'm worried about you.

> **Tiana**
> **I'm fine! Tell me some high school
> gossip to cheer me up.**

Chelle
We found out the exchange student from France
is actually a twenty-three-year-old from Iowa. I
knew that accent was giving Pepe LePew.

> **Tiana**
> **OMG!** 🌀 🌀 🌀

DoorDash Complaint Report

Issue:

My food delivered from Great Wall Chinese Takeout on 9/27 was
tampered with. Half of the order was missing, and the pork fried
rice had an unknown chemical substance poured over it.

Resolution:

We have spoken to our driver and reviewed the photo they took
verifying delivery. Any tampering/theft occurred after delivery was
completed, and the dasher was not at fault.

TikTok

@QuarantineDream

6702 following
342K followers
9.1M likes

Just a girl at college, no longer having to dream about it. 🌹

QuarantineDream

LIVE
245 participants

[Autogenerated closed captions]
Okay so it's been a while since we've had a live together, or even since I posted. We used to be on here like every night, and it's been weeks. Hi Betty! Yeah I know I look tired, I am tired. [laughter] Hi Stacey! I'm good and no we don't have to talk about that mess, trying to put it behind me. I was gonna go to a party on campus but decided to just stay in so we can catch up. My roommate went home for the weekend so I have the room to myself. Roddy asked what I'm going to make, thank you Roddy! I'm going to try the spicy cheesy ramen recipe. I have this little hot plate thingy that should work and—

Yeah so you take the ramen and, and I don't have the fancy kind, but that shouldn't be a problem—

I'm sorry, but they started with the banging again. You hear this right? Is that what people do for fun in dorms? [laughter] Makes me miss my neighbor who blasted classic 90s rock all the time.

FakeCalamari asks . . . Why don't you answer the door when we knock? Worried what we'll do to you, bitch?

Okay guys, I'm gonna end the live now because it seems like some people don't have anything better to do on a Friday night than harass me. Stacey, don't worry, I'm gonna call campus police but

I need to use my phone. I'm good, don't worry about me! These losers do not scare me, I'm just leaving so I can document this. I'll update soon. Sorry I couldn't finish our dinner together but I'll make it up to you soon!

Comments

FakeCalamari #WeAreAllJosh

FingerUpButt #WeAreAllJosh

FierceWolfCub #WeAreAllJosh

SenpaiLife #WeAreAllJosh

SpiceyIce21 #WeAreAllJosh

RebirthOfMan Die bitch

Group Text

Keeping up with the Car . . .
Mom, Dad, Chelle, Granny . . .

Tiana
The campus police said they can't do anything because they didn't find anyone on the scene and knocking on doors isn't a crime.

Mom
Isn't it disturbing the peace? Harassment? They have to be able to charge them with something! Your cousin got arrested for laughing too loud in a common area a couple years back.

Tiana
They said they can't do anything unless someone hurts me. I'm considering going to local police, but I doubt it'll be much different.

Chelle
Do they know about Josh and the harassment?

Tiana
When I told them about it they said, "This isn't TikTok, it's real life," and looked at each other like I was delusional.

Chelle
I'm so mad! This is what the budget goes to—cops saying they can't do shit.

Chelle
Sorry, Mom and Dad, I didn't mean to curse.

Tiana
I'm trying to ignore it but it's getting scary.

Mom
Do I need to come down there? Because I will take off from work tomorrow and come show them "real life."

Tiana
No I can handle it. I just wanted to let you know what's going on.

Mom
I'll call the dean—is that who I'm supposed to call? I don't know. I'll call whoever and give them an earful. I know you can take care of yourself but this is getting out of hand, Ti.

Tiana
I'm sorry that this is still causing problems. I wish I never made that video.

Chelle
It's not your fault!

Dad
I'm coming down to see you tomorrow.

Tiana
You don't have to.

Dad
I'll be there bright and early. Keep
your door locked until then.

Granny
Should I come too? You know I keep that thang on me.

Tiana

Instagram

TianaDreaming she/her
431 posts
9998 followers
1301 following

College girl, taking on the world.

October 1
TianaDreaming My daddy said shoot. 😊

[Image description: Picture of Tiana in oversize yellow tee, baggy
acid wash jeans, and white Reeboks standing back to back with her
dad, who is wearing a flannel shirt, dad jeans, and Columbia boots.
Granny is lying on the ground fake shooting into the air. The sign
behind them says "Suffolk Laser Tag"]

TellMeAboutIt Nice! I was there last week with my family!

HowIsLeftEarring Glad you're doing something fun after last night!

Phone Recording

(legal, one-party consent state)

Is this Vincent Marino?

Yeah, who's this?

My name is Sergeant C. Stranger. I'm currently heading up a harassment investigation involving a student known on TikTok as "QuarantineDream." Your name has been mentioned as a person of interest in connection with coordinated harassment on campus.

I don't know what you're talking about.

Yes, you do. The Fifth Amendment is not going to save you. Let's talk a little, or I will make your life very difficult.

Discord

The Wolf's Den
🔊 TEXT CHANNELS
#ConnectMore-App-Bitches

Kyle Did you guys hear about Vinny?

Conner Nope. Been too busy catching up with how our bros have been messing with TikTok bitch.

Jared Same lol. Props to the dude who ordered the roaches.

Kyle Apparently the reason he just disappeared is he got picked up by the police for drug trafficking.

Josh What? No man, I know Vinny, he wouldn't do that. I mean he'd use drugs, sure, but trafficking?

Kyle Apparently the cops stopped by his place because he was connected to the university harassment, and they found like enough cocaine in his car to charge him.

Josh Coke!? He doesn't do coke.

Kyle Do you know him that well?

Josh Yeah! I think I do.

Kyle Then do you know him well enough to guarantee he won't narc on us?

Jared Why would he tell the police anything about this?

NeoRedPill3000 Yeah, he probably wouldn't. But to be sure everything is cool everyone should install this. It's a VPN thingy. I may be old but I know how to avoid being found on the internet.

Conner Yeah. And we can go public and make sure we have on record that we have nothing to do with this.

From: C. Stranger <concerned1@smail.com>
To: Tiana Carter <Tcarter@smail.com>
Subject: Campus Harassment
October 2, 2021, at 1:13 a.m.

The person who has been knocking on your door and tampering with your food is Kevin Dolan. I do not think the police will do anything, but he is aware that his identity is known, and he has been strongly encouraged to stop, particularly after his family home received one of the roach bomb boxes he set off in your dorm.

From: Tiana Carter <Tcarter@smail.com>
To: C. Stranger <concerned1@smail.com>
Subject: Campus Harassment
October 2, 2021, at 3:05 a.m.

Thank you, I think? I don't know who to trust right now, but if this is real, I appreciate your help so much. I wish I could repay you.

From: C. Stranger <concerned1@smail.com>
To: Tiana Carter <Tcarter@smail.com>
Subject: Campus Harassment
October 2, 2021, at 6:24 a.m.

You already have.

AlphaLyfe Podcast Livestream

5000 followers on Twitch

October 2, 2021, episode "What If We Did It?"

Conner: So we need to address the allegations.

Josh: Fuck the allegations, bro. We didn't do anything. I didn't do anything.

Jared: Well a bunch of people think we did.

Conner: Can they really be called people?

Jared: True. A bunch of *feminists* are saying that we have something to do with the harassment of that TikTok chick who came at our bro and look, that's not true.

Jared: All we did was speak out about what really happened and some people decided to let her know they don't believe her.

[laughter]

Conner: What's wrong with that? We have the court of public opinion and we presented evidence, that's it. We even invited her to be on the podcast but she never responded.

Jared: If she knew she was right she would have come on and had a discussion.

Josh: I didn't do anything wrong. What she wanted was for me to tuck my tail between my legs and just take it, and got the surprise of her life when I didn't. That's what females like this need to understand—things are changing. We're reclaiming the masculinity you try to strip from us.

Conner: Wait, we have a troublemaker in the audience. Pull that whiny comment on screen.

MrsBucket: How did she lie when she shared a screenshot showing your exact words, and then you started publicly attacking her?

Conner: Waaaaah! What a goddamn baby. No one attacked her.

Josh: See, they say stuff like this and then get mad when we call them hysterical.

Josh: Look, they're correcting her in the comments and I bet she's gonna scurry back to her woke rat hole and tell her friends she got dogpiled and attacked. Kick her out. Bye-bye MrsBucket.

Jared: Tiana lied because she created a whole story around this when Josh was just goofing when he swiped on her to begin with. You think he wanted to actually date her? Have you seen her pictures? No, my bro has better taste than that.

[laughter]

Josh: She wishes I had been serious.

Jared: Yeah. This is what my dad warned me about. Females always twisting situations so you're wrong and they're right.

Conner: Too bad for her we see through that now.

Josh: Because it's always "men and women are equal" until you have a situation that two men would settle with a fight.

Conner: Well, are we sure she's not a man? I mean, check out this pic of her without makeup on. It's dicey.

[laughter]

Roommates Text Chat

Tiana
Hey! Are you okay? I haven't seen you the last
couple of days, just making sure you're all right.

Melody
Hey! I'm good. Just staying with a friend.

Melody
I was talking to some of the other people on the floor
and we were thinking. Maybe you should move?

Tiana
Why would I move? I haven't done anything wrong.

Melody
Well. Not technically. But you posted that video and
shook up the hornets nest, and now we're all getting
stung. I haven't had a good night's sleep in forever.

Melody
A roach crawled out of the hood of my sweatshirt while
I was taking an exam and I had a full freak out. I'm
sure I failed because I couldn't stop itching afterward.

Tiana
I'm sorry. I'm trying to get the administration
to do something but they won't help
and neither will the police.

Melody
That sucks but aren't you being kind of selfish?
We all have to suffer because of you. I think if
you really were as innocent as you say, you would
leave so we didn't all have to deal with this.

Tiana
Wow. I don't know what to say to that.

Melody
I don't mean to be rude, but it's not fair that
your drama is inconveniencing the rest of us.

Melody
Sorry, but it's what everyone is saying. You should know.

From: <RodgersFan@smail.com>
To: <Tcarter@smail.com>
Subject: My idea of a good time
October 4, 2021, at 12:30 p.m.

Hey,

Have you ever visited Isla Vista? Over in California? I went out
once to pay homage to a hero of mine. He did what needed to be
done after getting tired of disrespect from women.

Hyperlink: <u>Killer becomes men's rights hero.</u>

Your daddy won't be around to protect you all the time. See you
soon, sweetcheeks.

From: Tiana <Tcarter@smail.com>
To: C. Stranger <concerned1@smail.com>
Subject: FWD: My idea of a good time
October 4, 2021, at 2:13 p.m.

Hi,

I'm sorry to bother you but you're the only person who's given me
concrete advice on how to deal with these guys. The police won't do
anything. The people in my dorm are mad at me and want me to
leave, like I'm the one releasing roaches. Maybe they're right. You
seem to know about these kinds of attacks. What should I do? I don't
know who else to ask, and I feel bad stressing my family out more.

Sincerely,

Tiana

From: C. Stranger <concerned1@smail.com>
To: Tiana <Tcarter@smail.com>
Subject: Re: FWD: My idea of a good time
October 4, 2021, at 2:16 p.m.

So, they're still at it. For starters, don't reply to that person and don't click on that link. Sometimes people send malware that can steal your info using links like that. It's called phishing. Next: stop trusting strangers so easily. I could be Josh, or the person who sent you this email, for all you know. I have to pick up my kids but I'll look into this more when I get back from the school run.

AlphaLyfe Podcast

6600 followers on iHeart Podcasts

Transcript from October 5, 2021, episode "We Are Legion"

Josh: Just want to give a what up to all of our new subscribers. Don't forget to follow us on Twitch, too, where we'll be having podcast livestreams every now and then.

Conner: I love that Tiana thought she would embarrass you with those texts and instead she sent tons of new listeners our way.

Josh: She's learning the natural order of things, the hard way.

Jared: We are meant to dominate women; there's no need to be nice to them. A wolf doesn't compliment a sheep before ripping its intestines out.

Conner: Jesus, man. Chill out.

Jared: What, are you squeamish or something? Sorry, little girl, didn't mean to give you the vapors.

Josh: Yeah, what the fuck, Conner? A real man doesn't care about that shit. This is AlphaLyfe, not BitchLyfe.

Jared: Awooooo!

TikTok

@QuarantineDream

6761 following
353K followers
10.4M likes

Just a girl at college.

QuarantineDream

October 5, 2021

600K views
500 saves
435 comments

QuarantineDream

[Autogenerated closed captions]
Learned something in bio class that I wanted to share: did you know that the term "alpha" as applied to wolf packs is incorrect? There is no hierarchy amongst wolves. The researcher who coined the term tries to correct this, but manly men on the internet need an identity so they ignore him. Want to know the actual first such usage of "alpha" to describe animal group dynamics? Chickens. Not roosters. Chickens! The ALPHA HEN. She's at the top of the pecking order and she'll go for your eyes. All of this gender binary stuff is literally for the birds but fuck an alpha wolf. Cluck, cluck, motherfuckers.

I'm the alpha (hen) now. 😁 Stop sending me your omegaverse fan fic, I mean unaliving threats, losers.

🎵 Original sound: Cluck Cluck, Motherf*ckers

Comments

Roddyriguez12 YES YOU ARE! I would let you peck my eyes out. 😍

HowlsLeftEarring Yes! Reclaim your power! Cluck, cluck!

CarolP1963 I know that's right!

Discord

The Wolf's Den
⬇ TEXT CHANNELS
#ConnectMore-App-Bitches

Conner That video has to be taunting us. We can't let it slide.

NeoRedPill3000 I think it came out before your episode dropped.

Josh Fuck that! It still LOOKS like she's taunting us, and if we don't do something she'll think she won.

Jared Vinny is the one with the contact on campus, right? @Vinny you still in jail buddy?

Kyle He hasn't been responding to messages. I checked his socials and he hasn't updated anything for a few days.

Conner Shit. Well I guess we could go over there. To her school.

NeoRedPill3000 Now you're stalking. I mean talking, haha. What do you want to do? Hurt her?

Josh Maybe just scare her a little. Nothing that would leave a bruise.

Kyle I don't think you should risk it. We have to play this smart.

Conner None of us have to go there. It's 2021.

Josh You're right. No need to get our hands dirty.

Kyle Don't you think we should lay low?

Josh Don't be a pussy, man. It's time to show her who's in charge.

NeoRedPill3000 Are you all talking about something like what they mention in <u>this article</u>? [hyperlink: a new and dangerous game of telephone]

TikTok

@WhyAreMen

693 following
1.5M followers
69.4M likes

Booping misbehaving male humans in the snoot with the rolled-up newspaper of feminist justice. She/her.

WhyAreMen

October 9, 2021
475K views
8300 saves
1.1K comments

Don't scroll past this! As you've probably heard, the Tiana Tik-Tok drama that everyone thought had died down blew up again in a big way, and led to injury. Tiana, QuarantineDream, was swatted at her dorm yesterday. Given the way the police execute people in this country, it's not exaggerating to say that this was attempted murder. I was able to obtain the recording of Tiana's call to the police, and I'm going to play it for you now. The fear in her voice is heartbreaking, and this is beyond bad behavior online now: whoever did this should be thrown in jail. Weaponizing the police against a Black girl—she must be so traumatized. This is hard to listen to, but we need to hear exactly how far men will go to break a woman who doesn't bend over for them. Tiana, we love you.

Transcript

Suffolk College Emergency Dispatch
October 5, 2021

Dispatcher: 911, what is your emergency?

[Number redacted]: [fast, shallow breathing]

Dispatcher: Hello? Are you there?

[Number redacted]: . . . the police are here

Dispatcher: You need me to send the police? Ma'am. Are you okay? What is that banging in the background?

[Number redacted]: [background] Open the door now!

Dispatcher: Is someone breaking into your home?

[Number redacted]: I'm in my dorm. The police . . . the police are breaking down my door. Tell them to stop! I didn't do anything! I don't want to die!

Dispatcher: Okay, just calm down. Calm down. I'm looking into it now. This is at Suffolk? What dorm? And what's the room number?

[Number redacted]: I don't want to die! I don't want to die! Tell them not to shoot me!

Dispatcher: Why are they there? Ma'am?

[Number redacted]: I don't know! I—

[Number redacted]: [loud crash] Hands up! Hands up! Put your hands up! Don't move! Don't move! Don't resist!

Dispatcher: Ma'am?

[Number redacted]: Ow! My arm! My arm!

TikTok

@QuarantineDream
6765 following
421K followers
15.1M likes
Just a girl.

QuarantineDream

October 11, 2021

2.3M views
10K saves
0 comments

[Autogenerated closed captions]
Hey y'all. Yeah, I know I look like shit, but kinda hard to do your makeup when your arm is broken and you have a bit of the old PTSD. The comments won't be on for this one anyway so none of you can try to play me. This situation is getting out of control. It's been out of hand, but now it's out of control. I've tried not to give it too much attention publicly, thinking that would stop them, but no. I'm sure you've seen the viral videos going around using the recording of my swatting as a sound. They're celebrating. Oh, man. I never wanted to cry in a video! I'm crying because I'm mad, you assholes. These are rage tears, not sadness. But yeah. I got swatted. It was the scariest moment of my life. I thought I was about to be a hashtag and I haven't even gone to a frat party yet. Sorry. Humor is a coping mechanism. My school says they can't do anything because this is something that started online. They did approve my roomie's secret request to move that she put in before this happened, so I guess they can do things for other people, just not me. Campus security says they can't do anything because it's a local police issue. My RA also doesn't give a fuck and apparently led the cops to my door—the call claimed that my drug dealer boyfriend was in the room threatening me with a gun, and he didn't share that I don't have a boyfriend, of any profession. All of this to say that I'm going to be taking a mental health break. Thanks for your support, and I understand if you want to unfollow or whatever.

You didn't follow for drama, you followed for fun. I wish I could say that real-life college was going better than I ever imagined, but unfortunately it isn't. The trolls haven't won, but they've definitely ruined something I'd been looking forward to for a long time. I don't know when I'll be back.

Discord

The Wolf's Den
⬇ TEXT CHANNELS
#ConnectMore-App-Bitches

Josh LOL I have a picture of her crying as my phone wallpaper. Justice tastes sweet.

Kyle Any news from Vinny? I haven't heard from Jared either. Do you think he might turn on us because he was worried Vinny ratted us out?

Josh No. Definitely not. That's my boy. Besides, we won! He wouldn't snitch.

NeoRedPill3000 I just looked up his socials. Jared was apparently taken by police yesterday. His IG story shows him at a police station. I mean, he had to be taken right? He wouldn't go there to narc on you or anything.

Kyle People get desperate when the police are yelling in their face. The door knocking and internet harassment stuff would have been fine, but the SWATTING is a crime that makes the cops look bad. We could do time for that.

NeoRedPill3000 I told you fucks to be more careful. Who called the cops on her?

Josh It wasn't me. I mean. I don't know who did it.

Conner They can't trace that shit if you use a VPN and an internet number, right? Like the link you sent us.

NeoRedPill3000 Theoretically.

Kyle Was it you who did it, Conner?

Conner No, it was ALL OF US who did it. We all agreed to make her pay. And to the swatting. Even if I was the one who called, we're all in this neck deep.

NeoRedPill3000 I didn't agree to do anything.

Jared Then what the fuck are you doing here?

NeoRedPill3000 Observing.

Kyle You egged us on!

Josh Yeah! And you're older than us! You should have guided us or told us not to do it. We're just kids.

NeoRedPill3000 Not legally, you aren't.

Conner Wait, he just left the server. Fuck, he's gone. Do we even know who he was?

Josh Kyle, you're the one who vouched for him. Who is he?

Kyle I think it was **@Vinny** who vouched for him.

Vinny What? I didn't vouch for anyone.

Conner Vinny! What the fuck man, why haven't you checked in? Were you in jail?

Vinny Did you guys fucking block me or something?! I couldn't get into the server and my socials stopped working. Then I got a call from the police saying you were trying to pin this TikTok shit on me and not to contact you, or I'd get arrested. Now I'm getting notifications all of a sudden.

Vinny And it was Kyle who vouched for **@NeoRedPill3000**.

Conner Wait, who vouched for Kyle? How did he get invited in here?

Kyle Cluck cluck motherfuckers.

Josh He . . . just logged out of the servers.

Josh Someone is knocking at my door.

Conner Mine too.

Josh It's the . . .

Instagram

October 15
TheSuffolkEagle In a scoop by the Suffolk Eagle that published last week, we documented the saga of Tiana Carter, a student at our school who underwent harassment online and on campus, culminating in a dangerous swatting. We received a dossier containing evidence of coordinated attacks against her, as well as personal information compiled about the alleged perpetrators Josh Harwick, Conner Smith, and Jared Baker. After our story was picked up by major news outlets, leading to a social media campaign for justice, Harwick, Smith, and Baker, none of whom are students here at Suffolk, have been arrested and will face stalking and harassment charges. Our source was anonymous, but we thank them for providing our journalists with the opportunity to help justice be served, and to launch a deeper conversation on the spread of toxic masculinity and how it's affecting the college experience. Click on the link in bio for more!

[Alt text: photo of three men—Baker, Harwick, and Smith—being led into police station.]

From: Tiana Carter <TCarter@smail.com>
To: C. Stranger <concerned1@smail.com>
Subject: Thank you
October 15, 2021, at 11:19 p.m.

I don't know what you did, but I know it had to be you.

Thank you. Please, let me know if there's any way I can ever repay you.

To: Tiana Carter <TCarter@smail.com>
From: <Mailer-daemon>
Subject: Delivery status notification
October 15, 2021, at 11:20 p.m.

Message not delivered. There was a problem delivering your mail to C. Stranger <u>concerned1@smail.com</u>. See the technical details below:

User does not exist.

Gift Note in Anonymous Delivery

Sorry that you got hurt before we put a stop to their little game. Here's a present for you. They're the ones crying now. See you on TikTok.

C. Stranger

TikTok

@QuarantineDream

8783 following
525K followers
17.3M likes

A girl, dreaming. ☺

QuarantineDream

November 20, 2021
5K views
40 saves
70 comments

[Autogenerated closed captions]

Hey everyone! I've been back home for the last few weeks. I'm still recovering, and still very much not okay, but trauma be like that. I actually withdrew for the semester—the university allowed me to after you all pressured them to. My lawyer is in discussions with the Suffolk police department and campus security, but I won't talk about that here. I know things will never be the same, but the way I want to show I'm thankful is by getting back to the things you first loved about this channel—the things that bring me joy. Today we're gonna take a sneak peek at what my parents and Granny are cooking for Thanksgiving. And before you ask, no I'm not selling this sticker on my cast. [laughter] Someone sent it to me as a gift, and it's hilarious. I forgot to put the invert filter on, but in case you can't read backward, it says "Alpha Hens Do It Better." Now to see what my family is getting into in the kitchen. Like for part II!

StaceysStickerDepot Glad to see you back and smiling!

QuarantineDream ♥

KarinaPontius You mean stuffing?

additional comments

HowlsLeftEarring Cluck cluck, motherfuckers!

Quarantine Dream ♥

TANANARIVE DUE

Rumpus Room

FROM *The Wishing Pool and Other Stories*

"I BROKE MY daughter's arm."

Kat had never said the words aloud. If she'd been able to take responsibility and say to the judge, "I did this," and not, "This bad thing happened," she might be with Yvonne right now. Instead, Yvonne was with Kat's mom in Jacksonville and Kat was in a dimly lit diner off I-95 in Key Largo telling her business to the stranger who'd bought her a Corona Lite. She waited five seconds for him to accuse her of being a child abuser. Instead, he swiveled to face her. Full attention. Gentle gray eyes swept across her face like twin rescue lights.

"Was it an accident?"

Kat nodded.

Oddly, he clinked his bottle against hers. "Accident's an accident. And accidents *do* happen. Don't beat yourself up over it. Believe me, guilt buys you nothing but grief in this world. And there's enough grief to go around. Ain't that right, sister?"

Maybe the beer was going straight to her head on an empty stomach, but she thought it might be the nicest thing anyone had ever said to her. He was the first person who hadn't glared at her after they heard her story—the ER nurse, the caseworker, even her mother, who'd beaten welts into her legs with a belt and called it discipline when she was Yvonne's age. Kat had never spanked Yvonne—*never*. Kat's throat tightened with a threatening sob. She was ready to tell this stranger everything she'd tried to explain to the judge: she'd slipped on the kitchen floor as she was grabbing Yvonne's arm to tell her to *listen*, since Yvonne never listened unless you tapped her shoulder or raised your voice. It was as if her ears didn't work by themselves, as if she needed her skin to hear. So, yes, she'd grabbed her. She'd never denied that. Fine, and maybe she'd been a little irritated at the time. That was true too.

But she hadn't seen the puddle. Ice was always flying wild from the fridge's old ice maker, melting on the floor. So when Kat moved to wrap her palm around her daughter's slim pine branch of an arm, her foot slipped on the water and she fell against Yvonne, pushing her against that cursed cabinet. Then a muffled *snap*, a sound like a physical blow to her own stomach. And Yvonne's screaming. The memory of that snapping bone, that scream, kept Kat on I-95 driving to the ass end of the state talking to strangers in bars and diners—but she couldn't stop hearing her daughter's cry. The scream followed Kat wherever she drove.

This dude didn't know any of that; he probably assumed she was here selling sex. That was probably why he'd sat next to her and bought her a beer. Maybe she'd told him her secret to chase him away so she could drink her beer in peace. But her confession had the opposite effect: he'd turned to face her full-on, not just his mysterious profile beneath a Miami Dolphins baseball cap. She noticed how his pullover matched the cap's aqua-blue just as ZZ Top sang about a well-dressed man on the jukebox. He was at least fifty, the age her father would have been by now. But he looked good down to his snakeskin boots.

He might give her a couple hundred dollars for a good time, and if she weren't broke she might have given him a good time for free. She wanted to make the offer, but she wasn't sure how. She'd never done it for money. And his shiny boots made her think he might be a cop. Was two hundred too much or too little?

While she tried to work out her sales pitch, he said, "You know how to cook?"

In a wild thought, she wondered if he wanted to marry her. It happened in movies, didn't it? Her life had turned into a horror movie for the past month, so maybe it was becoming a different kind of movie now, one with a happier ending.

"I hate cooking," he went on. "But I'm sick of this diner. I've been looking for someone to cook, straighten up. Maybe get groceries once a week. Shit like that. You lookin' for a job? If you are, I'm hiring."

She stared. Somehow, his job offer seemed more bizarre than a spontaneous proposal. "I don't . . . live here. I'm just driving to Key West to—"

"Look for a job?"

He'd figured her out in a glance. She had slept in her car again last night, and she might not have enough gas money to make it to Key West, which was another two hours of driving. And unless he bought her dinner, too, she might not eat anything tonight except another package of free saltines from the diner's cracked bowl on the countertop. Maybe he *was* a cop.

He reached for his back pocket, and she was sure he was about to pull out a badge. Fuck. After his pep talk, was he going to try to railroad her for solicitation when she'd never even said it out loud? People in jail hated child abusers.

She raised her hands. "Mister—"

"Easy there," he said with a grin. "We're not all gunslingers down here, sister."

He flipped open his leather wallet, showing her a faded photograph trapped in a plastic sleeve: a man and a girl tall enough to be six or seven, at the beach, faces obscured by the powerful dusk light as they stood beside a boulder. "That's my kid. She died."

Kat had never known anyone who lost a kid. Now every part of this stranger's face—his colorless eyes, his hollowed cheeks, his silver-streaked hair—looked like residual scarring, a mask over the man he had been before his daughter died.

"Drowned a couple years back. Her name was Amber."

Kat finally started to speak, but he held up his hand: *Don't say anything*. He cleared his throat. "All I'm gonna say about that. I can see you're going through something yourself, but as long as your daughter's alive, you'll always have another chance. I've seen enough people in jams with the law to know that someone in your situation needs a job. Something to show the courts. If you need to take some time to get yourself together, save a few dollars . . . I can hire you full-time. Cleaning and cooking. I can't pay more'n a couple hundred a week, but you could live in my rumpus room, so you won't have to blow your pay on rent or food. It's got a separate entrance. Your own key."

Kat had a cosmetology certificate, so she was decent at styling hair, but she'd never been a housekeeper. She also wasn't much of a cook. She didn't even know what a rumpus room was—what kind of old-timey phrase was that, anyway?—and she didn't like the sound of it.

Again, he looked at her like he could see every thought in her head. He grabbed the thin local newspaper on the stool next to his and fanned it across the counter, pointing out the classified ads. "Here," he said. "This is me. Ben Fuller."

He showed her the ad: *HELP WANTED. FULL-TIME HOUSE-KEEPER/COOK. MAY LIVE IN.* She took out her phone and texted the number in the ad. And heard his phone ping. He grinned as if her caution pleased him. "It's not a con. And no offense, but—"

"Says anyone about to say something hella offensive."

He winked at her. "You're not my type. And it's not about race—how old are you?"

"Twenty-six."

"Yeah." He downed the last of his beer. Watching him, she ached for another and wished the ache away. She drank far too much now. "Generation Y, Z, whatever, you're not my type. I just turned sixty. I just hate cooking. And you sounded like you could use—"

"Can I move in tonight?"

That was how Kat came to live in the rumpus room.

Most of the houses on Ben's street were in *Candy Land* colors, lined on the bank of a canal with neon-green water that looked like a Caribbean vacation. The street didn't scream *rich* like on TV, but she knew enough about real estate to guess his house was worth a million dollars despite the Mustang on cement blocks in his carport and chipping brown paint on the walls. The house was tropical style, with an oversize top floor and screened-in wrap-around porch. Small solar lights made the row of scrawny palm trees lining the driveway look like a gift.

Kat stood in his gravel driveway to take it in. The sun was moving toward the shadowy end of dusk, more dark than light, and she was at a stranger's house. A one-night stand, paid or unpaid, would have felt less like she was a fool for following this man home. A job that sounded too good to be true was the perfect lure for someone truly desperate. Apparently.

For the first time, she noticed that he was more than a foot taller than she was. A giant.

Ben reached into a large flowerpot on his wood-plank porch and pulled out a key with a Minnie Mouse chain. "Here," he said, dropping the key in her palm. "Don't need you till breakfast. I eat at eight. Rumpus room's in the backyard, under the banyan tree near the canal. Four walls all to yourself. Text if you need anything. You already know the number."

He was right: she wasn't his type. Usually men stared at her chest, yet he'd barely glanced at her before he let himself into his house and closed the door. So much for wondering if he expected her to go inside to keep him company.

His backyard was enough like a jungle that it took her awhile before she saw the yellow paint of a wooden structure about a third the size of a mobile home, a tiny garden house nearly hidden by the hanging tendrils of the banyan tree. A motion light startled her when it snapped on, lighting up the walkway stones of crushed seashells. Then she was at the door, her feet on a thick mat embroidered with *Home Sweet Home* and the image of a cat curled in a ball.

Damn, she *did* like cats. It *would* be sweet to have a place to call home.

Her stomach clenched with certainty that this guy was playing her somehow, but Minnie Mouse let her inside and she flicked on a row of overhead lights. The tiled rumpus room was small and narrow, though the lighting gave it elegance, brightening the hot-pink bedspread on the daybed near the window. The fake marble countertop with a sink and microwave in the corner shined like she was in a five-star hotel. The rumpus room had been arranged with care: bed, two beanbag chairs, a newish TV mounted on the wall, kitchenette, a small table and two chairs, and a door she assumed led to the bathroom. Under the TV, a large basket overflowed with stuffed animals and games like *Jenga* and *Hungry Hungry Hippos*. Cramped but organized.

Then it hit her: a rumpus room was a *playroom*. Kat thought about the man's dead daughter, Amber. Had she played here? Kat imagined she could see Amber's face from the photo, hidden behind bright light. Yvonne would love this little *Alice in Wonderland* room, scattering *Jenga* blocks over the tiles. Kat's throat cinched with an unborn sob. She had never missed any person as much as she missed her daughter. She even missed Amber, a phantom loss nearly close enough to touch as her own.

Kat opened the bathroom door, looking for distraction from the agony of remembering Yvonne's grinning baby teeth. (And her scream when her arm snapped.) The bathroom had a tiled shower stall with a sliding door, cheap-looking toilet, and barely room to stand at the sink. The space smelled musty, even earthy, as if the closed door exiled it to the yard. Humidity clung to the tiles. *Half wild, half tame,* she thought. The rest of the rumpus room was almost enchanting; the bathroom didn't belong. That was what she thought from the very start. Kat stepped back and closed the bathroom door. She tugged on it to make sure the latch had caught so the musty smell would not creep to the back of her throat.

Her stomach growled. The smallish fridge was empty except for a half-gallon bottle of spring water. She was about to text Fuller to see if she could come over to the Big House to make a sandwich when she remembered the freezer. Jackpot! Two full stacks of microwave spaghetti meals and a bag of frozen chicken strips were nestled in old frost. She checked the expiration date on the meals: they were a full year past their best days, but she heated one up anyway and ate it with the plastic fork she found in a packet in the drawer under the sink. It tasted so good that she ate another. And a third. It had been a while since she'd had food better than a burger.

While she shoved warm pasta into her mouth, Kat flipped through the DVD collection on the shelf under the mounted TV. *Beauty and the Beast* was Yvonne's favorite, so no way she could sit through that. She found a surprise—*Hidden Figures*—and watched it for the first time. Seeing Black women brave enough to fight through the eternal whiteness of NASA in the 1960s gave her the strength to call her mother's number. When the landline phone started warbling, she realized, too late, that it was almost nine thirty. Yvonne was in bed by now.

Five rings. Six. Kat almost hung up.

"Don't you look at the time?"

"I'm sorry, Mom, I . . ." Kat stopped apologizing when she heard Buzz Lightyear's voice booming from the old console TV. "She's still up?"

"She asked for ten more minutes, that's all." Her mother had complained to the judge that Yvonne needed a stricter bedtime, dragging their private disagreements into the courtroom. The hypocrisy raked at Kat, but she didn't want to start a fight. Maybe she wouldn't have to cry herself to sleep for a change.

"Put her on, please."

"I'm tryin' to calm her down for bed. You'll just—"

"*Is that Mommy?*" she heard Yvonne squeal, saying *Mommy* with so much love and longing that Kat's eyesight brightened and dimmed all at once. Tears overflowed.

"See?" Mom said. "Now she's all excited." But Yvonne must have been grabbing for the phone because the next voice was hers.

"Mommeeeee!" To Kat's ears, it sounded like a plea for help.

"Hey, baby girl," Kat said, stripping sadness from her voice, her superpower. "Are you being good for Grandma?" *And is Grandma being good for you?*

Yvonne told her that she was going to day care—another bit of hypocrisy, since Mom had complained when Kat had to put Yvonne in day care when she had that shitty job at Walmart. Kat wondered if her mother was spanking her too. She would find a way to ask her.

"Guess what! I got my cast off today."

"You *did?*" Kat said, trying to sound excited for her even while she heard the bone snap again, could see the ugly, swollen bruise. Her face was all tears now. She knew she should tell Yvonne how great that was and *I bet that was itching a lot,* but she needed to talk about anything else. Her throat was pinching shut.

"I won't do that again, Mommy," Yvonne said. "I slipped on the floor and my arm broke."

"What's that, baby?" Kat was sure she had heard wrong.

"My foot slipped," Yvonne said. Then she laughed. "*Silly!*"

Was her mother coaching Yvonne? Had the judge called another meeting? Kat blinked and waited for her throat to release the words she had shared with the stranger in the diner: *I'm the one who slipped, not you. I broke your arm.* She was appalled at herself when she didn't.

"That's . . ." She took a breath. "That's *so great* you got your cast off, baby. Nothing like that will ever, ever happen again." That carefree giggle again, like a dream of sudden grace. *WHAT'S WRONG WITH YOU?!* Yvonne had screamed up at her from the floor, eyes wide with agony and surprise as she clutched her parts that Kat had broken. Kat had wailed how sorry she was the entire drive to the hospital, barely able to see the road for her tears, drowning in

remorse. It had only been six weeks ago. Was Yvonne burying her
inside a happier memory?

"It's late," Mom said in the background. "Go on to your room,
Yvonne." *Your room* instead of *Mom's room* sounded deliberate. That
room had been Kat's except the seven months she'd lived with Lionel.
Yvonne had slept beside Kat in her full-size bed most of her life.

Yvonne asked for one more minute, but Mom said she was out
of time. Kat noticed the predictable annoyance in her mother's
voice. If Kat weren't monitoring her, Mom might be threatening
to get her belt. Kat tried to say goodbye, though she didn't think
Yvonne heard her.

"Where are you, Katrina?" Mom used her full name, embed-
ding more disdain in each syllable. Mom had named her after
Hurricane Katrina. Mom had escaped New Orleans a few years
before she got pregnant, losing everything she owned, and as far
as Kat could figure, Mom had blamed her baby for her troubles.
Kat could barely remember a smile from her.

"I'm in Key Largo," Kat said. "I got a job assisting a senior citizen. A place to live. I'll send you money soon." Better than saying
she'd moved in with some random guy from a diner.

Mom made a surprised sound she didn't try to disguise. "That
right?"

"Yep." Kat filled her lungs and exhaled. "I'm on the right track
for the judge."

The silence came in a gale, a disruption of their peace. In silence, they could not ignore the war between them over Yvonne. If
Mom was hoping Yvonne would be hers now—a child, at last, who
would not remind her of a life destroyed—she was dead wrong.
Mom had no idea who she was fucking with. She would get her
daughter back. She would never hurt Yvonne again.

"Love you, Mom," Kat said, her voice sweet poison.

"Yeah, you too." When Mom clicked away from the call, Kat was
breathing fast, ready to curl up on this tiny new bed to sob—

But the bathroom door was open.

Kat's throat, hot before, went cold. She remembered her care
in closing it, yet the door was now wide open, as if it had been
propped. The musty odor had already crept into the room, not
quite sour enough to notice until she saw the open door.

She stood up straight, the phone forgotten. Vigilant, her eyes
went straight to her front door to make sure the bolt lock was still

in place. None of the rumpus room's old-fashioned jalousie windows looked big enough for anyone to climb through. Her skin prickled from adrenaline even as her anxious heartbeat slowed. No one else was here.

She walked to the bathroom and flicked on the light, just to check. Foliage was growing so thick against the bathroom's narrow windows that someone might need a chainsaw to get inside—which wasn't a comforting picture. The row of windows was blackened with plant life in the dark. Oddly, again, it seemed that this bathroom was an ancient structure and the rest of the rumpus room was new.

It was fine. She was fine. She swung the errant door on its silent hinge long enough to postulate a theory: *An object in motion stays in motion. An object at rest might not be at fucking rest.* Panic attacks had been dogging her since Yvonne's injury. Every new place seemed as eager to punish her as her mother, from the rain-slick roads she drove with cramping fingers to the poorly lighted gas stations she rushed away from with her keys fanned out like claws.

To conquer this room, this new life, she would need to conquer the bathroom. This would be just the first of many uncomfortable steps that would take her back to Yvonne, a long march ahead. If this job was legit—and she wouldn't know that until she asked for a fifty-dollar advance tomorrow—no way in hell would she let herself get spooked away from a free place to live, where she could stash away money fast. When she found a second job in town, a night job if she had to, she'd have enough for an apartment near her mother. She could even ask Fuller if she could take hair customers in the rumpus room. As long as she was living in her car, she'd never get Yvonne back.

Fuck this bathroom. Fuck this door. If this door opened on its own all night long, she'd let it fan her to sleep. Just like she'd get used to its primordial odor—not strong, but distinct. Noticeable. A swamp, that was it. The bathroom smelled like a swamp. So be it.

The bathroom looked worse than before, or else she hadn't noticed the soggy brown water stain in the panel of the ceiling over the shower stall. A half dozen gnats were camped out on the mirror, so she swatted them away before she stared at her road-weary face in the light's harsh fluorescent glow. Jesus—her hair was as dry as straw, pulled back into a single frizzy ponytail. The relaxer she'd gotten for her court date was long gone. Her face was spotted with acne from eating so much grease on the road. No wonder Fuller hadn't looked at her the way men usually did, sixty or not. Did she stink too? She sniffed her armpit: not terrible, but not great. She needed a shower.

The stall's grout was spiderwebbed with dark cracks and could use scrubbing, though it looked safe enough to go in barefoot until she could find some bleach. The faucet screamed when she turned it on, so unnaturally human that Kat's body tensed. It was such a perfect mimicry of Yvonne on the kitchen floor that she had to take two deep breaths to shake loose the memory. Rusty water pattered down in a weak stream, swirling brown down the drain, soon turning clear. The water was warm even if it never quite got hot, barely body temperature.

When Kat stepped into the stall and closed her eyes, the tepid water raining on her made her think of blood.

Kat rushed out to try to start Fuller's breakfast by seven, and she found him already outside fishing on the canal bank on the other side of the banyan tree—twenty yards behind the rumpus room. He tossed a bright orange lure on his fishing rod into the water. The canal was wide, more like a river, and he, like his neighbors, had a small aluminum fishing boat roped to a waterlogged wooden stake just beyond small stone steps. Kat walked through the overgrown grass overtaking his yard at the canal bank to reach him. Below, the green-brown water rippled, opaque. She made out a pale flash of a fish skimming beneath the surface.

"Thirty feet deep," he said, not looking at her. "Watch out if you don't swim. The lady next door—nice lady, eighty years old—slipped in and drowned trying to feed the damn ducks." He pointed out a mother duck with a neon-green head and a row of four downy yellow ducklings swimming in a row not far from his fishing line, their gentle wakes blending into one.

Fuller was wearing only an old Pink Floyd concert T-shirt and too-tight swimming trunks, practically a Speedo. His bare, hairy legs startled her, but she kept her eyes at a professional level, toward his face.

"What should I fix you for breakfast?"

He shrugged. "Whatever you can find. Grab some groceries later."

He gave her sixty dollars in cash, not fifty, when she asked for an advance after serving him scrambled eggs, pineapple chunks, and slightly overbrowned toast. She messed up the first batch of coffee she tried with his fancy espresso maker, but he didn't comment on the bitter smell in the house; instead, he complimented her on nailing the cream and sugar just the way he liked. He could probably tell how nervous she was, how much she didn't want to lose this new job. How much she *couldn't* lose it. She was full of nerves, half worried she would make him mad and half worried she would turn him on. She kept a careful distance from him, and she'd worn her most drab sweatshirt so he wouldn't get the wrong idea even by accident. His house, which was large for one person, still felt far too small for the two of them.

Fuller's living room TV was playing Fox News, so his attention was far from her as he answered her questions about where he kept his dish soap and what groceries she should buy him for dinner. After she washed the breakfast dishes by hand to impress him with her attention to detail, he told her to have a look around to get a feel for the house. He never took his eyes away from the lies on his TV, paying her no mind. If she'd pegged him for a Fox News type when they met, she would still be sleeping in the back seat of her car, her stomach rumbling. She would have to quit if he started talking trash about Black people, which Fox News always came around to. Had she fucked up her life so badly that she'd been flung back to 1950? Kat's fist slowly knotted around the three twenties from Fuller as she weighed whether this money might be her last. She'd cross that bridge later, she decided. She'd tell him she didn't want to hear any nonsense from him about race, and that would be that. With a plan, her fingers relaxed.

Fuller's house was more than a couple thousand square feet, well-kept for a single guy without a housekeeper. She wondered if he'd been in the military like her ex, Lionel, who was in Germany instead of with her and Yvonne. The books on Fuller's built-in shelves were in perfect descending order of height, mostly biographies and guides for science geeks. Instead of leaving his bedsheets rumpled like she had, he'd tucked the corners tight and made up his massive king-size bed after he got up. He even rolled up the toothpaste tube on his bathroom counter. For a panicked moment, she wondered how she would keep herself busy in a house that was already neater than anywhere she had lived. She was relieved to find spotted floors that needed mopping and high shelves lightly coated with dust.

She'd explored his bedroom, two bathrooms (neither of which smelled like a swamp), his library, a room that seemed solely for fishing gear and mounted fish, and even his garage before she realized there were no traces of Amber anywhere. Kat had steeled herself to open a door and find his dead little girl's bedroom frozen in time, full of stuffed animals and stolen joy, but she didn't see Amber even in a photo. Fuller didn't have any photographs on display, as if his life had never happened. But people grieved differently. Maybe he wanted to forget his old life, and how could she blame him? If Yvonne had died, she might not be able to stand her photos either. Even trying to imagine that pit of sorrow made a tear needle the corner of her eye.

"I like steaks," he said, handing her an ATM card. "Porterhouse is my go-to. If they don't have that, bring home some rib eyes. But ask the butcher, Manuel. Tell 'im it's for me. And a couple of packs of chicken wings. I like 'em fried."

"What else should go with it?"

Fuller only shrugged, his eyes back on the Fox News demons. "Surprise me."

"What's my spending limit at the store?"

He finally looked at her, eyes blank. A guy living in a million-dollar house on the water didn't have a spending limit at the grocery store. He didn't use coupons and wait for sales. Kat tried to imagine having an ATM card she would be willing to give to someone she'd just met. Or going for a free-for-all grocery shopping trip with her own worthless card.

Fuller grinned at her. "Go hog wild at Safeway, sister."

With Fox News playing, she didn't like the sound of the word *sister*. It seemed to shade more toward the N-word, and her face burned with a combination of embarrassment and resentment. But she only smiled and said, "Sounds like a plan."

Kat spent almost three hundred dollars on groceries just because she could. Nearly a quarter of what she bought at Safeway was to stock up the rumpus room, including two bottles of her favorite Chardonnay, with a *cork* bottle, price be damned. It was the least she deserved if she had to listen to Fox News all day.

The work didn't take long, even when she was more meticulous about cleaning than she ever had been, sticking her nose close to stubborn spots to make sure they were truly gone. While she was slowly dusting the top built-in bookshelf in Fuller's wood-paneled bedroom, she chuckled to herself at how amused Mom or Lionel would be to see her Mary Poppins act.

"What's funny?" he said, startling her so much that she braced her palm against the wall to keep her balance. She glanced back at him. He looked so earnest with those odd gray eyes that she felt supervised for the first time.

"Me—doing this, that's all. I'm not a neat freak." Kat noticed a bright yellow child's hair clip on the far back of the shelf, behind an old plaque for Citizen Watch. She almost reached for it, but she didn't want to surprise Fuller with a glimpse of Amber, so she kept wiping as if she hadn't seen it. So he *did* have a few memories of his daughter in the house.

His presence simmered beside her, which she might have mistaken for attraction when she was younger; but she'd learned to recognize it as wariness. Even so, she didn't like him standing behind her in his bedroom, probably staring at her ass.

"Come on down from there 'fore you hurt yourself. You don't strike me as the picture of grace." It sounded more like an order than a suggestion, so Kat stepped down once, twice, three times, until her feet were back on his shiny wood floor. She'd made it to solid ground before she realized he'd held out a genteel hand to help steady her. Lionel *never* would have done that. When she didn't take his hand, Fuller smoothed his hair back instead in a gesture that looked shy.

"Tomorrow morning at five thirty," he said, "you might learn you're great at fly-fishing."

"Oh no, I definitely won't."

"You will if you come fishing with me." Was he joking? He answered the question on her face: "Don't look at me like that. Get over yourself. It's just nice to teach someone." He didn't say it, but she guessed he'd fished with Amber too.

Still . . . nope. *Hell no,* actually. She stepped away from him, shaking her head. He shoved the hand he had offered her into his pocket as if to hide it from sight, stepping away too.

"Be ready to pan-fry some trout tomorrow, then," he said as he turned to leave the room.

"*That* I can do." After she looked up a few recipes on the internet, anyway.

She cooked him a marbled porterhouse for dinner, a sizzling heap of dead flesh as black as the cast-iron skillet. He said he liked it well done, but it looked charred to her. She only ate a small portion because she liked her steak rare. Fox News came back on after the dishwasher was running and the counters were wiped down, so she hurried to do a quick survey of the house to make sure he would have nothing to complain about before she left for the day.

Upstairs, she met celestial, dying sunlight. His wraparound bedroom blinds were open, overlooking the waterway and a tangle of palms and tropical trees. As she stood in his open bedroom doorway, she glanced downstairs to make sure he was still hypnotized by his TV. Then she slipped inside his bedroom's wash of golden light, almost like a portal in a science-fiction movie. She would claim she was there to move the little stepladder she'd left behind. Instead, she carefully climbed the three steps to the highest bookshelf.

She wanted to see the hair clip again. If he asked her what she was doing, she would have no idea what to say. Was it because she missed Yvonne? Did she only want to touch something that had belonged to a child, that might still hold a strand of her hair, even if the child was dead?

But when she looked behind the plaque, the yellow hair clip was gone.

Two nail holes in perfect vertical alignment caught Kat's eye as she turned her key in the rumpus room's doorknob. The holes were at eye level, so obvious she wondered how she hadn't noticed them before. They had been painted over, but indentations in the yellow coat were visible in dim light. She ran her fingers across the holes; her daughter wasn't the only one with a powerful sense of touch. She swept her hand left from the frame to the door and felt faint signs of even more matching holes just across the crack. And then two more three inches left again. She puzzled over this as she ran her finger back and forth, and her temples tightened as if someone had yanked a band around her head: a door latch. She could almost *see* it through her fingertips: the nails on the door supporting the panel for a bolt lock clear across to the doorframe.

But long gone. Painted over. She stood on the *Home Sweet Home* doormat to mull it over. She took a step away, surveying the door.

Her conclusions weren't pretty, just like the image the aligned holes conjured: once upon a time, Fuller had locked this door from the *outside*. Silence enveloped the spot where she stood. No sounds came from leaping catfish in the nearby canal or hungry mosquitoes sniffing her blood.

Kat's heart thrummed. She slipped her hand into her pocket to feel the three neatly folded twenties again, enough gas money to get back on the road. She imagined alternate possibilities for the six mysterious holes, each one slowing her heart a bit more: Christmas wreath. Mezuzah. Some kind of posted sign. Woodpeckers. The holes didn't *have* to be from a lock.

Still, she stayed riveted because she pictured the lock best of all—a bolt pulled across from the outside, shutting in . . . who? Would a parent lock a child inside the playroom? Was it to keep Amber from wandering to the canal, something any responsible parent might do? Or was it a hint of something she should be very worried about?

"Fuck, fuck, *fuck*."

She would have to ask him. She would have to bring him outside and show him the holes and ask him why they were there.

"And then he might fire you . . . or murder you."

Her whispered worst fear sounded ludicrous. Hilarious, even. Maybe the firing was more likely, but still not great motivation to question her new boss about painted-over holes—which, if she were honest with herself, might not be as perfectly aligned as she first thought, given the places obscured by paint. *Get out of your own goddamn way, Kat*, her mother always said. Was she trying to sabotage her job? Was this like Walmart all over again, where she'd clung to grievances her coworkers didn't notice until she convinced herself the money wasn't worth it? That she should just put up with Mom and live with her until she came up with a better plan for her and Yvonne?

And now look. If she'd kept that job, she might have been promoted by now. And she'd already have an apartment, or at least enough to share an apartment, instead of having to cook and clean for a stranger she wanted to trust but couldn't. Not quite. Maybe not at all.

But Kat let herself back into the rumpus room, latching the lock she suspected might once have been on the other side. She'd closed the bathroom door, but of course it was wide open again, so the smell was more unpleasant now, tickling her nostrils and down into her throat.

A swarm of two dozen gnats circled near the bathroom's jalousie windows, though they were locked tight with no clear holes. And the gnats were everywhere, it turned out, not just near the windows: In the shower stall. On the mirror. The gnats knew it too: the bathroom smelled more like a *bog*, a quiet rot carrying the promise of a feast for creatures who dined on death. Yet the bathroom's rot was active, more alive than dead, as if she might find a hidden heartbeat if she followed the trails of gnats.

But the gnats led nowhere. Maybe they were coming up from the shower drain. Maybe they smelled something in the toilet. Even after a day of cleaning, Kat couldn't rest until she went to work with her newly purchased bleach, scrubbing the shower tiles, the sink, the bathroom floor. Perspiration stung her eyes as she scrubbed in the muggy room. She hated the smell of bleach almost as much as the rot, but even inside the thick chemical scent, the boggy odor crept through. She plunged the toilet brush into the toilet water, irritated, trying to erase the scent at its origins. Where was it coming from?

The answer skittered into sight with a flash of yellow across the rear of the toilet's drain. She fished it out with her gloved hand: a child's hair clip. It was just like the one she'd seen on the bookshelf. Was it Amber's?

Kat was so startled that she dropped it. She pulled it out again and scrubbed it in the sink. The clip was shiny plastic and didn't look at all like it had been stuck in a toilet drain, with no signs of waste or wear. It was identical to the one in the house, a hair clip in the shape of an ice cream cone, pitted to look like a waffle cone. But how was it in the toilet? She had flushed that toilet three or four times since she'd arrived.

With the toilet brush, Kat probed the rear of the drain, poking to dislodge whatever else might be hidden. She felt a tug of resistance when she tried to pull the brush out. It wouldn't budge. What the . . . ?

She yanked, and the brush moved, trailing strings of hair clinging like a squid. Another yank and it came entirely free, the clumped hair limp, dripping across the floor, snakelike.

Kat's arm vibrated with the weight of the hair. The illusion of movement made her let out a strangled yell and drop the toilet brush to the floor. She jumped away from the tangled heap, her knees buckling from the memory of how the hair had *seemed* to move. But there it lay, regular hair after all. Set against the white tiles, the strands spread apart retained a golden hue, only darker where it clumped. Blond hair as silky and thin as a spider's web. (*Good hair*, Mom would say. She was forever praising Yvonne's hair, crediting Lionel's genes.)

The growing army of gnats wheeled above the damp hair on the floor.

Kat was so unnerved that she felt winded, so she leaned on the doorway's frame and laughed at herself. So a hair clip and some hair had come out of the toilet: big fucking deal. Except it *was* a big deal, and she couldn't laugh her way out of knowing it to her marrow. Her laughter was manic, not amused.

She closed the bathroom door, shutting the gnats inside.

Small things had never weighed so heavily on her: The holes outside of her door. The hair. Gnats. She didn't know what they added up to, though she knew she wouldn't be able to get to sleep if she didn't say something to Fuller while looking him straight in the eye.

Solar lights tracked Kat across the walkway, her shadow marching alongside her, a glimpse of how she would look if she were taller than five three and bigger than 130 pounds, closer to Fuller's height and weight. She knocked on Fuller's door without rehearsing. Anything she said aloud to herself would have sounded wrong, so she might as well sound wrong spontaneously. Her hand wound a fist around the hair clip.

Fuller was in shadow from the porch light when he opened his door.

"Can I come in and talk to you for a second? It's about the rumpus room."

"What about it? That's the deal. That's where you sleep."

"I know," she said. "But . . . we have to talk about something."

It was a bold opening, and she had no idea how to follow it up. And why had she just invited herself in instead of insisting that *he* come out? She should have rehearsed. She shouldn't have let her imagination run wild. He turned on his foyer light and made room for her to come in, but she stayed fixed in the doorway so he could not close the door behind her. His face was in full view now, down to the gray hairs in his razor stubble.

"You gonna let all the mosquitoes in?" For the first time, he sounded annoyed.

"I'm sorry. I just . . ." She hadn't planned to give him the hair clip, or even show it to him, but now it was her only reasonable play. Her hand trembled slightly as she displayed it to Fuller under his light.

He didn't hide his surprise. "Where'd you get that?"

"The rumpus room." She stopped short of admitting it had been in the toilet, and she thought better of bringing up the hair. She studied his eyes as he stared.

"That was Amber's," he said quietly. She expected him to reach for it, but he didn't. "Guess she must have dropped it playing out there. I built it for her, you know. That room."

"I figured." She waited for more of the story, though he didn't offer it. "Where's her mom?"

"You tell me," Fuller said, eyes narrowing. He moved closer suddenly, leaning over her to spit outside, over her shoulder. The sharp cinnamon of his chewing gum was in her face, intimate. She also noticed his height again. "Maybe Hollywood? That was the kind of bullshit she always talked about. Big surprise it didn't work out." So close to her ear, the anger in his voice felt more directed at her.

Kat's heart didn't start drumming until he pulled away again, as if she'd only realized in retrospect that he'd moved toward her so unexpectedly. She hadn't even noticed that he was chewing gum. She took a small step back, her heartbeat shaking her ribs.

"So . . ." Was she actually going to ask? "Did that room used to lock from the outside?"

He moved quickly again, this time to lean closer to peer into her eyes, the way she'd won his full attention when she confessed the worst thing she had ever done. "Why?"

"I saw some holes in the wood. They line up like a lock."

"Door's old. Sure. Used to be a shed with a padlock."

"Oh!" She faked a smile, as if backyard sheds and home improvement were her hobby. "So you added the bathroom?"

"Built most of that bathroom myself."

Of course he had. *What did you build it out of, compost and human hair?* But Kat kept that question to herself. Fuller's eyes waited, patient. He still hadn't touched the hair clip; he noticed her noticing.

"Where'd you find that, by the way?" he said. "Exactly?"

Kat hadn't planned to lie, but she did: "Under the bed."

"Oh." He sighed in a shuddery wave, perhaps imagining Amber in the bed Kat was sleeping in now. "Yeah, must've missed it when I cleaned up." His gray eyes misted. "It's hard for me to look at, you know? Would you mind . . . ?" He waved it away from his sight.

Kat slipped the hair clip into her pocket. She wanted to ask about the other one she'd seen in his bedroom—high on a shelf, seemingly hidden—but she couldn't think of a way to make it her business. "I'm sorry to ask, but can I see her picture one more time? Since I found this . . . I just . . . I want to see her better. Does that make sense?"

It *didn't* make sense, not even to her. But Fuller nodded, although he didn't move at first. She watched him thinking it over. Then he sighed and walked away, toward the stairs. She'd expected him to complain or demand a better explanation for prying into his greatest tragedy. The instant he was gone, she wished she could take back her request. What was the point? The longer he was gone, the worse she felt. And the more she wondered if he would come back at all. Or what he was doing out of her sight.

Fuller came back downstairs holding the wallet up high like a prize, his gaze cutting: *You happy now?* He tapped on the banister to keep steady as he swayed down the steps.

He gave her his worn folded leather wallet, and she held the photo close to her face, the way she had stared at the stains on his floor. Even a longer look couldn't make the photo much more coherent because of the bright shroud of backlight, reducing their faces to a duel between radiance and shadow. She barely recognized Fuller in the glare because he had a sparse beard in the photo, and he was so much thinner now. The tattooed tip of a large wing peeked out of his open shirt, probably an eagle like Lionel would get.

She could see a bit more of Amber. Half a smile. An elbow jutting out from her hip with attitude. And long strands of blond hair listing across her shoulders, clamped at the end by a yellow clip. Her hair was the point, Kat realized. She'd wanted to see if it was the same hair . . . *and it was.* The memory of the clump of hair slithered across her arm, leaving goose bumps. The yellow hair clip felt like it was glowing warm in her back pocket.

Kat snapped the wallet shut and handed it back to Fuller. He was looking at the floor, arms folded. "You done?" He sounded more like the tired old man she had painted for Mom.

"Yeah, thanks. Sorry if I upset you."

And, damn it to hell, she actually *was* sorry. Kat felt like a paranoid asshole as she walked back toward the rumpus room and heard Fuller's door close behind her with slightly pointed force—but unease still jittered across her pores. She hesitated when she came face-to-face with the holes on the rumpus room's doorframe again. A breeze whispering through the banyan tree's leaves made her glance toward the canal.

The glow from the neighbor's deck lamp was so strong that she saw the green-headed mama duck skimming across the water in the halo of light. But she was alone. Kat waited to see if the ducklings would come. If the ducklings were gone, that was a bad omen for sure.

Two of the ducklings finally followed, paddling furiously to catch up to their mother.

Thankfully, the bathroom door was still closed.

When she opened it, the air inside was so damp that it breathed rankness across her face, making her blink to clear her eyes. And the linoleum floor was bare. The hair was gone.

Kat might have lost her shit entirely if she hadn't heard so many stories from her grandfather when she was young. Grandpa had grown up in North Florida, in a place called Gracetown, and he'd warned Kat that Gracetown blood ran through her veins, so she could expect unusual events in her life. Kat had taken him at his word, waiting twenty years for dreams that felt like premonitions, or the ability to know other people's thoughts, or conversations with ghosts—but so far, all she had was Amber's missing hair.

And the hair wasn't even missing, it turned out. She followed the hum of the gnats and realized the clump of damp hair was now in the corner behind the door, bunched up. But it was the same hair: it had left a trail of water on the floor.

Kat let out a yell when her phone buzzed in her pocket opposite the hair clip. She closed the bathroom door and leaned against it, not letting herself fully grasp that she was bracing the door so the hair would not get out.

MOM, the caller ID said.

"Yvonne?" Kat said. Often, Mom put Yvonne on the line without speaking first.

But Mom's voice came this time, heavy with disappointment: "It's me, Katrina."

Mom's most common trigger was to call her by the hurricane's name instead of the nickname she preferred, but Kat had bigger problems tonight. "Mom, did Grandpa ever—"

"I wanted you to hear it from me," Mom interrupted, her voice as rote as a recording. "I've decided to petition for permanent custody of Yvonne."

Kat's ears were plugged by a sound like a test pattern squalling inside her head, the first time she had ever felt any of her senses shut down by a surge of emotion. When her ears popped to allow sound in again, Mom was still talking.

". . . not doing this to hurt you. That's the main thing I want you to know. I'm doing this because we both know it's best for Yvonne."

Kat had stopped leaning against the closed door, pacing while she tried to avoid saying anything that might incite her mother. She pinned her lips together so tightly that they hurt.

"You've got nothin' to say?"

Kat's verbal dam broke. "You're not doing this to hurt me? Since when, Mom? You know this would hurt me more than anything in the world. Didn't you hurt me enough? The belt wasn't enough?"

"But I never broke any bones, did I?" she said. "Only one of us can say that."

"Is that why you can't believe it was an accident? You think I'm like you—that I *like* hurting people. You had your chance to be a mom, and you're really bad at it."

"That's funny coming from you. Pot, meet kettle."

If her mother had been standing in the room with her, Kat might have hit her with a pot or a kettle, or both at once. God help her, maybe the rage Mom had planted was too close to the surface sometimes, yet how many times had Mom criticized Kat for "coddling" Yvonne instead of using a belt when she talked back?

Yes, she had messed up—that one time. She'd been mad when she tried to grab Yvonne's arm and she'd tugged so hard that she had thrown herself off-balance. She never would have slipped if not for the water on the floor, so it wasn't a lie to call it an accident.

But if she hadn't been irritated, if she hadn't made an explosive movement, it would not have happened.

It was her fault. And Mom knew it.

"Just so you understand?" Kat said, breathing out her rage at both herself and her mother. "Trying to take someone's child away after one mistake—your own daughter's child—is not a normal thing to do. You know who does that? A psychopath does that. I will *never* let her grow up with you."

"If I was so bad, why'd you move back in? Why'd you bring her into my house, Kat?"

The sudden gentleness in Mom's voice, so sincere rather than triumphant as she poked at the ugly truth, scorched Kat's insides. Her mother's last jab laid bare the essence of this betrayal: *You're my mother, that's why. You were all I had.*

"I didn't know the real you until now, Mom."

"Guess I can say the same thing."

Kat ended the call before her mother could hear her wail. On her knees. On the floor. Exactly where Mom wanted her. Or exactly where she belonged. Either her mother was a monster—or she was. Or neither. Or both.

Kat hardly recognized the world enough anymore to judge.

She cried her throat raw, curled on the rumpus room's cold floor. She was lying there when she saw a shadow move from the crack underneath the bathroom door, from one side of the room to the other, toward the shower. The rapid motion made her gasp and sit upright.

Whatever had moved was too big to be the clump of hair, so Kat wasn't surprised to find it where it had been before, still scrunched behind the door. The cloud of gnats circling it had grown to a swarm of thirty or forty, unbothered by Kat's intrusion. But the hair was only hair.

Kat felt an urgent need to touch the hair clip, so she pulled it from her pocket and ran her finger across the dimpled cone. Yes, Yvonne was like her in that way: sometimes she needed to touch or be touched to understand a lesson. Maybe that was what Grandpa had meant about her inheritance. Kat squeezed the hair clip, and her own voice whispered in her ear: *Was it really Bob Fuller in that picture?*

The thought was a blow, knocking her back on her heels. Fuller had looked more different than similar in the photo—she'd only believed it was him because he'd claimed it was, so she'd excused the mismatches, more interested in studying Amber. Did he even have a chest tattoo? She tried to remember seeing him bare-chested, but she didn't think she had. She couldn't compare height, and under that beard the man in the photo might have a very different facial structure. Their body types didn't match at all. Why hadn't she let herself see it?

"What if it isn't him?" she whispered. "What if he stole that picture from you? What if your name isn't even Amber?"

The toilet gurgled.

Kat had already decided she wouldn't spend another night in this rumpus room, and the bathroom was the first place she wanted to leave behind. But her neck moved of its own accord, turning to face the toilet with its lid beckoning, open wide. A few flies buzzed out, joining the horde of gnats.

A thick gray-brown snake was floating in the toilet water, coiled around the drain, a sight so shocking that she sucked in a long breath before she realized it *wasn't* a snake, it was a rope—the braids fraying at the end. Still not good, but at least it might not leap out at her. She breathed motion back into her muscles and took a step closer to the toilet, peering from directly above, almost daring the rope to move.

Fraying strands waved in the water, though it seemed like an ordinary rope—except that nothing was ordinary about a rope crawling through her plumbing when it would have clogged every flush. The rope had not always been there. Maybe, like the hair clip in Fuller's bedroom, it would disappear if she turned her back.

"Why is this here?" she whispered to herself, or probably to Amber.

The rope's thickness seemed familiar, and it took her an instant to remember why: this looked identical to the waterlogged rope tying Fuller's rowboat to the wooden stake beside his steps to the canal.

Every instinct screamed at Kat to leave the bathroom, but through the semitransparent shower door, she glimpsed a large dark spot in the corner of the stall that did not belong. Whatever it was had not been there while she was cleaning. More hair? Frigid dread held her in place for another few breaths before she slid open the shower's door.

The stall still stank of bleach, but in the corner under the faucet a fungus was growing out of a dark crack at the tile's base, as bold as if it had been there all along. *But it hadn't been.* The fungus was at least eight inches tall, the color of caramel, with several thin branches fanned across the shower tiles from the trunk poking out of the hole.

It was impossible. Explanations for the other things she'd seen—including the hair that seemed to have moved—were improbable. But a fungus that grew to that size in only a few minutes could not have happened. Yet, here it was preening for her. Her feet tingled with the memory of standing in the shower stall with naked toes, only inches from this impossible fungus. (At least she *thought* it was a fungus, but how the hell would she know?)

"Son of a bitch," Kat whispered. She wished Grandpa were still alive so she could consult with him on the meaning of such a thing. Kat raked through her memories and landed on his lesson on the difference between a "haint" and an "Abomination," the latter being his word for pure Evil. He'd said she would know if she ever stumbled across a true Abomination because it would turn her hair white and make her bones ache. It would want to hurt her with single-minded purpose, and only incantations and offerings could tear it away from her. Her very soul would tremble, etcetera. (Grandpa had been most prone to talking about haints and Abominations when he'd had a drink, and when he'd been drinking he talked a *lot*. And he went wild with his hickory switch, Mom said, so at least Kat knew where Mom had gotten that tendency from.)

Despite the bathroom's rotten smell, Kat didn't think whatever was nesting here was trying to hurt her. Something was choosing her, that was all. Something wanted to be seen. Grandpa had told her that most haints, unlike Abominations, only craved to be a part of living memory. *Like the way a barking dog only wants you to look out the window too,* he'd said.

Kat took a closer look at the fungus. It looked like a hand. The "thumb" was stubby and short, but the shape hugging the wall looked far too much like a child's hand. Amber's hand? Or was she just seeing what she believed might make sense of it? A hand? A tree? The fungus never moved, though its form was an ever-changing Rorschach to her eyes.

A fat droplet of brown water fell from the showerhead, splattering a mess on the white tile. Then another. Then the faucet screamed and opened up a spray of water with a tinge of green gleaming in the brown—like the canal water. The tepid water soaked her hair, dousing her with the bog smell. Yelling curses, Kat slammed the shower door shut and rushed to scrub her hair with her bath towel. Gnats buzzed around her ears, flitting against her face. Diving into her nose's deep, tender parts. She rubbed her nostrils with both fists to stop their crawling.

What if it *was* an Abomination?

Kat's limbs wobbled from panic as she closed the bathroom door and raced to grab her duffel bag, throwing in the few clothes she'd taken out. She left the two bottles of expensive Chardonnay on the counter, still corked. She might have forgotten a pair of shoes, but she was in such a hurry that she didn't check before she scooped up her handbag and fled the rumpus room.

Outside, she was breathing in gasps as she ran to her car, which was parked alongside Fuller's pickup truck in the wide gravel driveway. She tried to walk lightly across the crushed stones, but the motion lights betrayed her, the next one snapping on with each few steps. *Shit.* She looked up at Fuller's bedroom picture windows, where she could see the light was still on beyond the closed shutters. The shutters didn't move, so she hurried the rest of the way to her car, which was parked closest to the rumpus room.

As soon as she was sitting in her old Accord with the soothing *click* of her electronic locks, her panic ebbed. Her fingers were still shaky as she rooted in her handbag for her car keys, praying for them, really, and they answered with their familiar music.

She slid the key into her ignition, but she didn't turn it. Not yet. She didn't want to make a sound. The less panicky she was, without gnats in her nose, the more this felt like she was reliving her last argument with Mom, racing out to her car with her life stuffed in a duffel bag. Running away. As much as she wanted to get away from Bob Fuller and whatever he had birthed in his rumpus room, the sense of unfinished business held her rooted. Her breathing was already fogging her windows, but she saw his upstairs light go off, his house now in darkness. Maybe he was going to bed, so she might not have to worry about him confronting her.

The rumpus room was pale and glowering in the darkness. Kat sat for long minutes waiting to see if the door might open on its own the way the bathroom door had. The hot air inside the car felt charged with anticipation of a dramatic event, though nothing so grand helped guide her. The rhythm of the breeze or the rising and falling chorus of crickets might be trying to tell her something, but what?

The night's excitement had made her abnormally tired, and she hated driving when she was tired. Sixty dollars wouldn't get her gas and a motel room, even a cheap one. Her Accord was twenty years old and the chassis trembled above sixty miles per hour, but the spacious back seat was a decent bed, still lined with her thick pallet of blankets.

"Fuck it," Kat whispered.

Doors still locked, key in her hand, she maneuvered into her back seat to try to go to sleep, curled with her knees to her chest. Her mind rocked from the strange things she had seen, and her questions as she contemplated the photograph that might or might not be Bob Fuller. And a girl who might or might not be named Amber. The only thing she felt for certain was that something had happened to a girl in that rumpus room, probably in that bathroom.

The ghostly clues from the haint, if that's what she was, would not be enough. Where could she find out more about her? She could check a database of missing children in the area for the past few years—maybe there had been an Amber Alert.

Amber Alert.

Amber. Fucking. Alert.

Fuckity fuck fuck. Kat's adrenaline surged, chattering her teeth. Had Fuller chosen that name and shown Kat the photo of a man who looked nothing like him as a sick game, toying with her until he decided to kill her? She'd been so stupid to knock on his door. So stupid to still be here. Every new thought made her more certain that she should drive away.

But it felt too much like leaving another child behind.

The crickets' swell grew louder, and throaty rumbles from bullfrogs rattled the car windows. Kat woke up confused about why she was outside. Her blankets, and the mound of fast-food wrappers and empty beer cans on the floor, helped her remember she was in her car again.

And a man was reclined in the front passenger seat.

The seat was angled directly in front of her, with only a foot separating the man's statue-like, shadowed profile from her shocked open mouth. Kat patted the blankets for her keys, her only weapon, and could not find them. Panic swamped her until she noticed the sharp jut of the man's chin, and skin that wasn't just made dark from the night.

It wasn't Fuller. The man sitting in her front seat was Grandpa.

This is a dream, she told herself, until it was obvious. No frog was loud enough to shake a car: that should have been the first clue. And she was wearing footie pajamas from childhood, not the sweatshirt she'd had on when she fell asleep.

Yet, everything about Grandpa looked so real: white hair shaved close to his scalp, his cauliflower battered earlobe, the thin white beard powdering his face. In her dream, Kat could see in the dark, true to her feline namesake, down to the patterns of wrinkles in his blue shirt from the Gracetown Mill where he'd worked. She hadn't dreamed about him since she was thirteen, the night he died. (Now that she thought about it, he'd told her he was dead in her dream before she woke up to learn the news.)

I conjured him, she realized. She had asked for his help—probably for the first time—and he had come. How many other times might he have come to her with answers if she had asked him? In her dream, the rumpus room felt a world away. What mattered more was that she finally had the chance to talk to her grandfather.

"Grandpa," she whispered, but he did not turn to look at her. She didn't want to tug any harder at the dream, so she satisfied herself talking to his unblinking profile. "Why did you hurt Mom so much? Didn't you see she was bleeding from that switch? You hurt her. And she hurt me. And I hurt Yvonne." Speaking the truth came more easily in her dreamworld too.

Grandpa seemed to grow taller, but he was only inhaling for a long sigh, weary and heartsick. "My papa punched me in my ear so hard I lost my hearing," he said. She'd known Grandpa had hearing in only one ear, though she'd never known why. "His daddy got lynched for mouthing off at a white man and Papa wanted to make damn sure I knew my place. I didn't know how to be different, pumpkin."

In the waking world, she would have expected an apology, but hearing him call her *pumpkin* soothed part of that ache. And now he was here to help her learn.

"I think a gator killed that girl, Grandpa." She was talking about Bob Fuller, but somehow her words came out wrong in dream language. "Maybe drowned her in the toilet."

"Unnnh-hnnh," Grandpa said in quiet affirmation. He was smoking his pipe now, the smell of his tobacco filling the car. But his pipe didn't bother her, for once. "They run faster'n people think they do. Gotta always keep your eye on a gator, on land or in the water."

He had given her this same advice when she was a child Amber's age. Maybe a dream was mostly remembering and part wishing. But this dream, like the one she'd had when she was thirteen, felt more like a visit.

"What happened to her? Where is she?" Kat asked.

It seemed for a while that he might not answer. He exhaled a cloud of pipe smoke so thick that it obscured his profile. "You were s'posed to touch the rope," Grandpa said. "You had to touch it to see. That's why she sent it to you."

"Who?"

Grandpa pointed toward the windshield.

The haze parted long enough for her to see a young girl standing at the bank of the canal, beneath the sprawling branches of the banyan tree. She was only a silhouette in the dark, but it was Amber! Kat gasped, yet the surprise was coming from her waking self, not her dreaming self, and the cloud draped everything in white. She couldn't even see Grandpa anymore.

But she heard his voice, crisp and loud and somehow real in her ear: "*Eyes open, Kat.*"

She woke up in time to see Bob Fuller quietly close his front door and check the lock before he walked down his porch steps with a fishing pole. It was still night but closer to dawn, the sky turning gray. She watched through her window propped on her elbows until his motion light clicked on, illuminating her. She dipped low to stay out of his sight as he walked toward his pickup truck. She heard him toss his fishing pole into the other side of the truck's bed.

Her heartbeat rained stones across her head and chest as his footsteps fell on his gravel driveway, closer and closer to the truck's door, three steps, four steps, five. She was parked so close to him, barely a nose or two short of his truck, that if he peeked over his shoulder he might see her. She couldn't risk rattling her beer cans to climb down to the floor, so froze where she was and counted on luck. Seven steps. Eight.

Shouldn't he have reached his door by now?

But his footsteps were moving *away* from his truck. She ventured a peek between the front headrests. He was well lighted as he walked toward the rumpus room, and she took in details about him between ferocious thumps of her heart. He was shirtless, only wearing cargo shorts, holding his key ring ready. His back was to her as he walked toward her front door—the door that had once locked from the outside—so she could not see if he had a tattoo of any kind on his chest. But his back was bare and wiry and looked nothing like the photo once more.

And he had something strapped to his shorts. A holster? No, a sheath for a large knife—a hunting knife. The handle's wooden finish shined. (*We're not all gunslingers down here, sister.*)

Why was he going to her room? Fresh from her dream, she *knew* he was the gator who wanted to eat her, but she tried to tell herself he only wanted to invite her to come fishing again. This seemed less likely the longer he stood in front of her front door in deep contemplation. He swung his hand holding the keys slowly to and fro, though he must've had his fingers clutched around them, because the keys were silent.

Jesus, he was thinking about it. He was considering whether or not he should kill her.

Kat tried to slow her frightened breathing so the fog wouldn't tell him she was in the car. She inhaled for a count of four, held it for four, exhaled a long, slow count of eight, the way she'd learned in her court-ordered anger-management sessions. She did the exercise twice while Fuller did not move, staring at her door like a freak. Her heart stopped punishing her in its fright, its blows less painful. She reminded herself of her advantages: She was in her car, her doors locked. She could move quickly to the front seat and start her engine.

But you didn't test it. What if it won't start?

The horrid thought shattered Kat's false serenity just as Fuller turned around, and she hoped the headrest disguised her as she pressed her head against it for cover. Like Yvonne, she closed her eyes as if she could make him not see her, until she forced them open for a peek: his chest was passing her windshield, in perfect view with a triangle of hair between his nipples.

No tattoo like a wing. No tattoo of any kind.

Now his keys jingled loudly, almost literally in her ear. He climbed on the running board to the pickup's door, and the large

wooden knife handle was displayed in her window. Kat kept still
and silent by promising herself that she could outrun him if she
had to, consoling herself that at least it wasn't a gun. She counted
her breaths until he opened his truck's door, and counted them
again as his engine came to life, loud as a dragon, and the pickup
started rolling out of the driveway. He was looking up at his rearview mirror instead of to his left, or he would have seen her as
clearly as she could see him. She watched him roll past her window, not blinking, memorizing his sharp-featured profile to the
tip of his nose.

She had gone home with this man.

She had lived in his torture room.

She had run away from Yvonne.

Tears of self-reproach drowned Kat. She was still trembling
from anguish and her brush with Fuller when she finally climbed
out of the car. Her engine went on fine, she'd learned, so she left
it running with the door open as she walked to the canal bank to
stand approximately where she had seen Amber in her dream.

The fledgling daylight was mostly gray, but more pinkish bands
were emerging, a glimpse of a new morning. The neighbor's solar
lamp illuminated the gently rippling waters below, where Fuller's
rowboat bobbed. Kat switched on her phone's flashlight for a better look at the rope, which was the same thickness and color as the
one floating in the rumpus room's toilet.

You were s'posed to touch the rope, Grandpa had said. But hell no,
she would not go back to the rumpus room. The buzzing was so
loud from the rear bathroom window that the room must be thick
with gnats and flies. The ornery insects bumped against the thin
jalousie panes so loudly that she heard pinging and slapping across
the glass even from twenty paces. The insects sounded bigger too.

Kat steadied herself with the wooden railing as she climbed
down the stone steps toward the aluminum rowboat, which was
conspicuously empty. No clues there. But a two-lane bridge beside
Fuller's property created a dark nook at the edge of his yard, with
a coral ledge wide enough to walk on. She shined her flashlight
there and noticed another identical rope tied to a stake pounded
into the coral wall, barely visible above the waterline. If the canal
water was sometimes higher and sometimes lower, the rope would
not always be visible. She was looking at just the right time, maybe.
Like Amber wanted her to.

Kat moved gingerly from the steps to the ledge, inching into the darkness. The hair clip still in her back pocket was burning so much that her ass itched (a sign, she supposed, albeit an annoying one), so she kept up her cautious progress despite pebbles scraping beneath her shoes and her fear of falling into the water. She could swim, but not very well.

When she was close enough to the mysterious, slimy rope, she pulled on it—and it only gave slightly. Something heavy was tied to it below. Shining her phone's flashlight into the murky water did no good.

Kat wiped sweat from her eyes with her forearm and checked her phone: 5:48 a.m. Mom would kill her for calling this early, but she pressed *1* in speed dial. Her mother's phone rang.

"Kat?" Mom sounded alarmed. "What is it?"

"I'm all right. Sorry to call so early. I . . ." Where should she even begin?

Mom's concern vanished. "Do you ever look at a clock?"

"Mom, I'm sorry. I'm sorry I ran off. I'm sorry I scared you and Yvonne. I'm sorry I hurt her. I'm sorry about everything."

"It takes more than *sorry* to raise a kid, Katrina. Are you drunk?"

"No. I've stopped drinking." True, she'd just bought two bottles of wine, but she hadn't thought about opening them. "Not for long—but I'll get in a program. I'll get therapy. I'll get another job closer to home. You won't have to take my word for it—you'll see it."

Mom didn't believe her. Her silence made this plain.

"Just please give me one month. Thirty days. Please don't file with the judge."

"I knew saying that would get your attention," Mom said.

"You did, and I completely understand. I didn't give you any choice. I'll do better."

Mom sighed into the phone. "I sure hope so, Kat . . . I . . ." The pause was so long that Kat wondered if she'd been cut off. "I wish I'd done better too."

Kat wanted to tell her about her visit with Grandpa, what he'd revealed about their family curse, but she would save that for later. "I'll drive all day so I can get there. Can I see Yvonne?"

"Of course you can. As long as it's before nine."

Jacksonville was only about a six-hour drive, so she might be able to make it before lunchtime, if she didn't stop. She might have enough for gas. Nothing would keep her from getting home to her daughter. Nothing—not even her own Abomination—could scare her away.

Kat hadn't realized that she'd nestled her phone between her ear and shoulder so she could grip the rope two-handed. It was heavy and slippery, but not impossibly so. She was slowly raising whatever the rope held, still hidden in the murky pool below.

"I have to go, Mom," Kat whispered, near tears again at the grimness of her task.

"Stop calling me at all hours, hear? I still say you're drunk—"

Kat barely noticed her phone slip loose and clatter to the ledge behind her. She discovered that if she braced her feet against the coral wall, she gained more strength for her pulling, one hand over the other, slowly bringing up whatever Fuller had weighted down in his backyard canal, hidden in plain sight. Another private game.

Through the salty perspiration stinging her eyes, Kat saw the green head of the mama duck swimming just beyond Fuller's boat, webbed feet flurrying to propel her sure motion. Kat took a gasp of air and bunched up the rope to lift it higher, hand over hand. Her palms were scraped raw as she held tight to the waterlogged rope, and something tied to it bumped against the bank beneath her. But she was pulling it out. It was working. Kat gritted her teeth and heaved again. She watched the duck so she would not think about what she might find at the other end, so she would not lose her nerve, so she would not scream from the pain of her burden.

The mama duck swam on, unbothered.

Her ducklings were nowhere in sight.

The Body Farm

FROM *Epoch*

IT BEGAN WITH a letter. At least, that's when it began for me. I worked the night shift and came home weary. The house was dark and silent when I pulled up in front. The sun rose bloody that morning, as though it knew what was coming. Heavy clouds soaked up the crimson light like a bandage over an injury.

I entered the house on tiptoe, listening for movement. You weren't awake yet, my beautiful boys, four years old then. Yesterday's mail lay scattered around my feet, pushed through the slot in the door sometime after I left for work. I gathered it all up, noting absently that among the bills and catalogs was an electric blue envelope of thick card stock, addressed to Beatrice. A yowl signaled the arrival of the cats, the only ones awake, three night-black silhouettes twining around my ankles. I stacked the mail on the kitchen counter with the blue envelope on top. I didn't give it another thought as I went upstairs.

Beatrice was sound asleep in our king-size bed in her usual pose, flat on her belly with her knees bent and shins lifted in the air. I have never seen anyone else sleep like that. Once I took pictures to show the friends who did not believe me, but Beatrice made me delete them.

I went to check on you. Technically you had separate rooms, but you always slept together. That morning you were tangled in a heap of sand-brown limbs in Theo's bed. I lingered in the doorway, watching you dream, Lucas's feet twitching, Theo snoring delicately. The sky brightened by the second. Soon your eyes would open at precisely the same moment, and at once you would both be talking, updating one another on your dreams, wondering what to have for breakfast, and continuing your ongoing, interminable debate about which one of you the cats loved more. There is no foggy transition between states of mind for children that age: one minute out cold, the next entirely awake.

As I stood in the doorway, the exhaustion of my long night fell over me. I staggered back down the hall and collapsed into bed beside my wife, dozing off as the house woke around me.

You did not know much about my work then. This was fine by me. If asked, you would both report that I did "science"—Lucas thickening the esses with his adorable lisp. The specifics of my job were not important to you. You were scarcely out of your toddlerhood, sapling-skinny boys with identical crooked grins. Your existence revolved around the central hub of our house, our yard, your toys, and the cats. You knew that Beatrice (Mommy) stayed home with you, reading books about dinosaurs, making play dough from scratch, and kissing away your "boo-boos," real or imagined. You knew that I (Mama) went to work and then came back again. What I did out there in the world, away from you, was inconsequential and vague. Your biggest concern about my job was that I always smelled like antiseptic when I returned. You both refused to get in my lap until I'd been home for a few hours, enough time to accrue the odor of cats and curry from dinner and a residue of Beatrice's perfume.

At that time, I had worked at the Body Farm for nearly ten years. The official name is the Anthropological Research Center, but nobody ever calls it that. From the outside, the place is intentionally anonymous. A flat concrete building. A bland, unspecific name. There's nothing else nearby—no offices, certainly nothing residential, just a blank strip of highway forty miles north of Lyle, Iowa, our hometown.

Visitors to the Body Farm are limited to the occasional police detective or forensic anthropologist. Sometimes teenagers from Lyle sneak over at night to see if the stories are true, but these would-be oglers inevitably find themselves stymied by the high concrete walls and motion-activated lights. Honestly, the smell alone is usually enough to deter them.

Behind the walls, the Body Farm comprises forty acres. The area was chosen for its variety: a stretch of forest, a stream, a meadow, zones of unbroken sunshine and perpetual shadow, a wetland, and a dry, high slope—as great a range of types of terrain as can conceivably be found in a single biome.

During that fateful winter, this idyllic stretch of midwestern greenery was inhabited by 127 dead people.

The purpose of the Anthropological Research Center is simple. Within its walls, corpses decay in every conceivable way, and my colleagues and I observe and record it all. How will a body deteriorate if we bury it in a shallow grave on a windy hillside? Will the data change if the corpse is nude, half-dressed, wrapped in plastic, or slathered in sunscreen? What is the exact, mathematical progression of larval growth? What happens to the internal organs after four days, seven days, two weeks? What happens to the bones?

New corpses are always coming in. Thousands of people have signed up to donate their bodies to the Anthropological Research Center after death. (My own will stipulates the same.) Whenever a new cadaver arrives, the other researchers and I debate where to place it. Our aim is to study decomposition in every possible locale: riverbank, direct sun, partial shade, tall weeds, swamp. Each season of the year brings new information. Corpses are different from day to night, winter to summer—there's always more research to be done. Should the cadaver be stripped naked this time? Should it be injected with heroin or oxycontin? Should it be hanged from a tree? What kind of data will be most beneficial? What gaps currently exist in our research? Once the corpse has been laid to rest—perhaps buried in sand, perhaps floating in the creek—its decay will be charted until nothing remains.

I'm one of seven on the team. Georgina is our botanist. Hyo specializes in fungi and bacteria—"the slime lady," she calls herself. Kenneth trains law enforcement officers in the science of decomposition; they come from all over the world to learn at his feet. Luis focuses on microbes, a new and fascinating field, with groundbreaking applications for antibacterial medicines and anticancer chemotherapeutics. Jackson and Cal, both MDs, share the study of the corpses themselves. They dissect and photograph festering skin, weigh liquefied organs, slice up bones, and keep samples of blood at every stage of putrefaction. Then there's LaTanya, who has the most difficult job of all: she serves as liaison, publicist, spokesperson, and official witness, testifying in court cases on behalf of us all and translating our data into digestible, user-friendly language.

I am the Body Farm's entomologist. I spend my days among beetles and blowflies. I know the life cycles of pyralid moths and cheese skippers. In cold weather, I check for winter gnats and coffin flies. At a glance, I can tell the difference between species of insect eggs. The shelves in my office contain preserved larvae at every stage of maturation, lovingly coated in chemicals that won't dehydrate the samples or change their color. My drawers hold trays of beetles, bright as pennies, and velvety moths arranged by size.

It's disgusting work. But the grotesqueness of the Body Farm stands in direct proportion to its worth. Months, sometimes years after a corpse has been found, my colleagues and I can pinpoint the time of death, cause of death, manner and likely location of death, and more, offering a cornucopia of distasteful but salient facts. Killers have been convicted on the strength of our research.

The dead can't speak for themselves. The story of how someone died—and, even more important, what happened to their body afterward—has fallen to me and the other researchers to uncover. I help put away "bad guys," as you would call them. I name the nameless. Too many children die at the hands of a parent. The number one cause of death for pregnant women is homicide, usually by an intimate partner. How can a person walk around knowing these things and not participate in a solution? I get answers for the bereaved. I reunite the dead with their loved ones, bringing anonymous bodies, badly decomposed, home to the family who declared them missing months earlier. The dead can't speak, but insect activity communicates loud and clear.

Still, I do not talk about my work with most people, and certainly not with my children. I have never told you anything about the Body Farm, my beloved twins—not until now, writing this letter, my confession.

On the day the blue envelope came, I woke with a foul taste in my mouth. Working the night shift always leaves me disoriented and bad-tempered. My colleagues and I take turns handling this unpleasant but vital task.

I climbed out of bed and washed my face in the bathroom sink. There was a bang, and one of you—I could not immediately tell which—dashed through the door and slammed into my legs. I let myself be climbed like a tree, then taken by the hand and led downstairs, where a glorious mess greeted me.

Given the bitter wind howling among the rafters, Beatrice had decided that this was a good day to make bread from scratch. She always spends the winter baking, chasing away the midwestern chill with the warmth of the oven and the comforting aroma of yeast and sugar. Flour coated the kitchen floor and hung in the air in a fine mist. Both of you were covered in it, too, your curls powdered like the wigs of British lords. Music jangled from the radio. Scuffling around in the snowfall of flour, you two were playing the mirror game, imitating one another so closely that I could not tell who was leading and who was following.

At the counter, Beatrice kneaded a sticky lump of dough. A smear of flour painted one cheek. I leaned in for a kiss and realized that her eyes were bloodshot and swollen. She had been crying.

She and I did not have a chance to talk until your nap time. You were on the verge of giving up this relic from your toddler years. When Beatrice was on her own with you, she often let you skip it rather than risk a dual tantrum. I, however, intended to maintain nap time for as long as possible, until you were in college, hopefully.

I set you both in my lap in the rocking chair in Theo's room and read the dullest, most repetitive nursery rhymes I could find. Against your will, you yawned, your heads drooping and rising again, each blink slower and more prolonged than the last. I nestled your precious bodies, limp in my arms, beneath Theo's blanket. Your faces inches apart. Each of you breathing in the air the other had just exhaled.

Then I went downstairs and found Beatrice at the dining room table, her head in her hands, staring at the electric blue envelope.

I sat beside her. I rubbed her back. She was crying again, no sobs, just a wellspring of tears that seemed to ooze from somewhere deep down.

"I don't know what to do," she whispered.

I picked up the envelope and pulled out the note inside—the same color and weight, azure card stock. Two words had been scrawled in ballpoint pen.

FOUND YOU

Beatrice wiped the tears away with her palm. "What are we going to do?" she asked, still in that throaty whisper. "What can we possibly do?"

I thought about burning the note or running it through the shredder in the office. But instead I put it carefully back in the envelope, preserving the evidence.

And now I must go further back. At the age of four, you were not particularly interested in how your parents had come to be together. You knew that having two mommies was slightly unusual, but not unheard of. Domingo, a boy in your class at the preschool you attended a few mornings a week, had two daddies, and another girl lived with her grandparents, no mom or dad in the picture. Your teacher made sure to read books that highlighted all the different shapes a family can take.

For my part, I'm a gold star lesbian and proud of it—no boyfriends ever, not even in my own childhood, when all it took to become affianced to a classmate was a shove on the playground. I like the term *sexual orientation* (as opposed to *sexual preference,* the problematic phrase used in my youth) because it so closely mirrors my own experience. I was born with a compass in my chest that points truth north. There was never any question about which way the needle would lead me.

Beatrice, however, identifies as bisexual and primarily dated men before we met. That's fine, nothing wrong with men, they just aren't my personal cup of tea. But among her sensitive poets and tattooed drummers, Beatrice happened upon a sociopath. Or maybe that's the wrong diagnosis—I don't know, I'd never met the guy, not then, anyway. A bad egg, a ticking time bomb, pick your metaphor.

They dated in college, long before Beatrice and I found one another. I've seen pictures of Emerson: a corn-fed white boy, strapping and tall, with a receding chin. Beatrice never loved him. She was young, sowing her wild oats and reveling in being out of her parents' house. After one single evening together, this man told her he planned to marry her. He told her he'd been waiting for her all his life.

She has never disclosed very much about that time. Even now, it's hard for her to talk about. Emerson consumed her college years—I do know that. She stayed with him because he made it clear he'd kill himself if she left him. No more wild oats. Four years of Emerson walking her to every class and panicking if she didn't text him back within minutes. He bought her necklaces and bracelets and pouted if she didn't wear them, which made her feel, she told me, like a pet with a collar. He pleaded with her to leave her dorm and move in with him off-campus. She was only able to hold him off by blaming her parents, claiming they'd revoke her tuition if she did such a thing, though truthfully they wouldn't have cared either way. In photographs, Emerson is always touching Beatrice, one arm snaked around her waist, sometimes holding her braid in his fist, while she flashes a fixed, panicked smile that does not reach her eyes.

After graduation she found the wherewithal to end it. She took a job in the Colorado mountains, miles from their New England campus. She did not tell Emerson a thing about it until the day of her flight. Then he wept, pleaded, and threatened suicide. He outlined all the plans he'd made for her life—marriage, dogs, babies, nothing she'd ever consented to. When Beatrice held firm, Emerson opened the window of her third-floor dorm room, now bare, all her things packed and shipped already. He flung one leg over the sill, yelling that he'd throw himself out if she left him.

This time, however, she was prepared. She called 9-1-1, and Emerson spent the night in a hospital on an involuntary psychiatric hold while Beatrice flew across the country, believing she was finally free.

We had a security system installed at the house the next day. You were both ecstatic to have workmen clomping up and down the stairs and looming on ladders outside the windows. Nothing this exciting had happened to you since a fire truck came down the street the previous afternoon. Shrieking and pointing, you shadowed the workmen all morning while Beatrice attempted to nap—it had been a sleepless night for her—and I guarded the bedroom door, keeping you out.

At nap time I tried to sedate you with fairy tales, but my plan backfired. You are growing, always growing up before my eyes. Suddenly you could follow the plot, whereas only a few weeks earlier you would've been interrupting me constantly to ask unrelated questions about the nature of time or farts. Now, however, the story caught your attention, and you sat up straighter in my lap. Your eyes shone. "And then what happened?" you each whispered at intervals. I ended up reading fairy tale after fairy tale right through what should've been your nap time, all damsels in distress and armor-clad knights and a happy ending, maybe with a moral thrown in.

My shift started at three that day. I did not feel right abandoning my family in this moment of crisis, but Beatrice rose from our bed and said she'd be fine, you'd all be fine. The alarm system was armed now, and she had let a few friends know what was going on. They'd be dropping by and checking in throughout the day. She promised to keep you both at home. She promised to text me instantly if anything untoward happened.

In the parking lot behind the Body Farm, I took my vial of peppermint oil from the glove compartment and dabbed a few drops, as always, beneath my nose. Over the course of the workday, I would become inured to the stench of decay, but the first wave was invariably overwhelming.

I passed LaTanya's office on the way to my own. She was on the phone, leaning back in her chair and speaking in her most soothing customer service voice: "I understand, but that's not information we have. I can't help you. I'm happy to share what we do know at this point. However . . ."

She caught my eye, made her fingers into a gun, and shot herself in the head. I laughed and moved on down the hall. I did not envy LaTanya, always on the phone, on the go, consulting with overworked police officers and blustering district attorneys. Every murder case is an emergency, while our work remains gradual and complex and painstaking. Death can't be rushed.

Stepping onto the grounds of the Body Farm was like teleporting to some echelon of the underworld. An elderly woman lay swaddled in a heavy tarp, only one hand visible, curling limply upward, not yet touched by maggots. A teenage boy had been rolled in a pile of leaves, naked from the waist down, his limbs smeared with mud. Corpses in direct sunlight. Corpses on the riverbank. Some were fresh, still recognizably human. Others had decomposed to the point of genetic regression, returning to an amoebic state, pink and gelatinous, perfuming the air.

The afternoon was icy, the sky frosted over with pale clouds. Leafless trees surged in a stiff breeze. I wore my usual uniform— latex gloves, a surgical mask, and cotton clothes that did not retain odors as much as polyester. On the hill lay my first stop of the day: a twenty-two-year-old woman, dressed in jeans and a neon green T-shirt, half-buried in soil. She had been there for six days, and her organs had melted into soup. Her torso appeared sunken, the ground beneath her stained and damp. Her brain, I knew, was already gone. The bacteria in the mouth worked quickly after death, devouring the palate, then everything else.

I opened my tool kit and took out my forceps. There were several maggot masses. I collected a few samples from each area, then checked the temperature of the flesh; the insects' bustling generated its own heat. I plucked up the wriggling bodies with a practiced motion, dropping each one into a separate jar. As always, I kept half alive and killed half immediately, preserving them for later inspection.

Next I studied the area around the body. Since the corpse lay on a slope, some of its fluids had seeped downhill. Maggots always follow fluids. I dug through the leaf litter with a sterile tool. Insect activity is a fairly reliable measure of time of death, though many things can alter the data: if the body has been moved, kept in extreme cold or heat, or covered with fabric or plastic. Part of my job is to think of every possible factor that could alter the timeline, study each one, and keep records.

Not long ago, I discovered that cocaine in the bloodstream of a corpse will supercharge the maggots, accelerating their growth and maturation, whereas barbiturates have the opposite effect, lulling them into lethargy. A serial killer was convicted on the strength of my data. That's right—a *serial* killer. LaTanya testified on behalf of our team, as she always does, offering glossy photographs and her patented brand of wry humor to put the jury at ease. The result: multiple life sentences without the possibility of parole.

Emerson began stalking Beatrice the moment her plane touched down in Colorado. That was not the word she would have used then, however. It was a less enlightened time, lacking the language to describe the many kinds of mental and physical violence people can inflict on one another. If your boyfriend followed you everywhere you went and never let you out of his sight, that was puppy love. If an ex called you long-distance hundreds of times and bombarded you with bizarre gifts and death threats, that was just the natural expression of his heartbreak.

Beatrice stayed in Colorado for two years. She was content there, working at a coffee shop and daydreaming idly about getting an MFA in visual art or theatre, something creative. She liked the clear mountain air, the hiking trails, and the breathtaking vista outside her living room window.

Emerson remained in Massachusetts on the campus where they'd been happy together, at least in his mind. Most days he called Beatrice dozens of times, leaving ragged, rambling voicemails. He sent presents at least once a week—a teddy bear with a heart on its chest, a charm bracelet, nothing that suited her taste at all. She figured that eventually he'd wear himself out. Surely he would find a new object for his affections. Every now and then, she decided it was time to reason with him and answered the phone, leading to hour-long arguments that left her raw and shaken.

She has a good heart, your mother. She did not realize that each time she gave in, she was training Emerson to be persistent. Not that I'm blaming the victim, you understand—he should have stopped the first time she said no. Always remember that. And Beatrice meant well; she had compassion for Emerson, no matter how much he hurt her. But if he called fifty times in a row before she answered the phone, he learned that it took fifty-one attempts to force her to submit. If he sent her ten cutesy stuffed animals without reply, then received a text saying *Please don't give me any more gifts*, he learned that eleven unwanted presents would trigger a response.

Back then, Beatrice still believed she could set boundaries if she just explained herself well enough. Perhaps she hadn't yet been clear, she thought. This is the danger of being a decent person in this complicated world, someone with a functioning conscience. She could not imagine the malevolent mentality of a brute like Emerson. All he wanted was contact, and every time he got it— even if it was "No" or "Stop" or "You're scaring me"—his desire was met and his resolve strengthened.

Beatrice probably would have stayed in Colorado, and she and I might never have met, and you two would never have been born, if Emerson had not turned up on her doorstep one evening, sweaty and disheveled, suitcase in hand.

I wasn't there, of course, but I can picture it clearly. Beatrice has told me the story many times. He tried to push past her into the house. He told her he was sick of "doing long distance" and it was time for them to try living together. Her "little independent phase" was getting him down.

Beatrice was almost too stunned to respond. She managed to bar the door with her foot, keeping him on the porch. He was acting as though they'd never broken up, as though the events of the past two years had slipped his mind. She could not tell if it was a performance or if he really believed they were still together and imagined that she would let him into her home, into her bed.

"Let's order pizza," he said. "The plane food was awful."

"You have to leave," she gasped out. She did not even know how to argue with him—he was so far from reality as she understood it that there was no common ground on which to stand.

There followed an incoherent shouting match, him declaring that she was acting childish and crazy, her sobbing that he wasn't her boyfriend anymore. Eventually one of her neighbors called the police. Beatrice felt a swoop of hope when she saw the red and blue lights dancing off the buildings. She still imagined then that the law could help in situations like this.

Two officers clomped onto the porch, both men. Emerson spoke first, explaining that he'd flown across the country to see his girlfriend of six years and for some reason she wasn't letting him in. The men looked at Beatrice with their eyebrows raised. This would prove to be a tactic of Emerson's: if he could establish his own version of events with enough confidence right off the bat, anything Beatrice said to contradict him, no matter how true, seemed dubious to their audience. Faltering, she mumbled that she and Emerson broke up years ago. He shouldn't be here, she said.

"I brought you this." He reached into his suitcase and handed her a wrapped package. "Open it."

"I don't want it," she said. "I don't want anything from you. You need to leave."

Emerson threw a glance at the officers, who nodded back sympathetically. He tore open the wrapping himself, revealing a lacquered plaque with *Home Sweet Home* etched into the wood. Beatrice has always hated that kind of schmaltz, of course. Anything in the vicinity of *Live, Laugh, Love* leaves her cold. She believes that people who need placards on the wall to remind themselves about affection or comfort or joy are deeply unhappy. In the past, she had said as much to Emerson. Did he listen to her? Ever?

"You have no idea who I am," she said, with dawning horror.

"I think it's nice," one of the officers said, bristling on Emerson's behalf.

Eventually Beatrice made it clear to everyone that Emerson wasn't going to enter her house that night. The policemen offered to drive him to a hotel a few blocks away. It wasn't technically allowed, but they obviously felt such sympathy for this poor jilted Romeo that they broke procedure to give him a ride.

In the morning, Emerson showed up at the coffee shop where Beatrice worked. He followed her to the grocery store on her lunch break and critiqued her purchases. He introduced himself to her coworkers as her long-distance boyfriend. They were all surprised they'd never heard of him, accosting Beatrice in the break room to ask for details. Hadn't she been dating the clerk from the Taco Bell a few months back? Was she cheating on Emerson? Or did they have an open relationship?

Two weeks later, Beatrice moved to Maine.

After Emerson's letter came, things were fraught for all of us. Beatrice flinched every time her phone rang. One of the cats tripped our new alarm system in the middle of the night and Beatrice seemed to forget how to breathe, wheezing and choking beside me as I threw off the blankets and ran to investigate.

The two of you were affected as well. Four-year-olds are as sensitive as tuning forks, picking up and echoing the vibrations of their parents. You each responded differently—Lucas by sobbing at imaginary injuries and ending each day with dozens of colorful Band-Aids on every limb, Theo by charging around the house with a plastic spear and cardboard armor, fighting pillows and shadows and the poor cats, who took to crouching on top of the tallest furniture.

And I was angry. I don't know that I've ever felt such sustained, slow-burning rage. Teeth gnashing. Fists clenched. Even my dreams were fiery and bloodstained.

Our friends rallied around us, offering to babysit or spend the night on the couch. Several of them made noises about involving the police, but Beatrice, with the weary resignation of painful experience, explained that the electric blue note wasn't signed, and anyway it didn't contain a threat or anything actionable. All her previous restraining orders against Emerson—one in Maine, one in Virginia, and one in Texas—had lapsed.

So there was nothing we could do but wait, all of us, Beatrice terrified, me furious, and both of you keyed up. Tender Lucas. Warlike Theo. We did not know what would come next. It was like waiting for a meteor to fall to earth without having a clue when or where it would land.

In the past, Emerson had sent texts, selfies, hand-written sonnets with improper scansion, and an engagement ring in a velvet box. Whenever Beatrice changed her phone number, he eventually discovered the new one. He lurked outside her previous apartments in his car, smiling up at her window. He sent flowers to each of her workplaces. Once he slashed her tires. He no longer claimed to be suicidal, not since she'd had him involuntarily committed. Sometimes he threatened her, but never in any way she could substantiate to others. He might send an anonymous note saying he'd kill her if she didn't stop sleeping with that trashy line cook from the diner. He might leave a knife on her porch steps. He stayed just on the legal side of things. She couldn't prove he'd been the one to slash her tires. She couldn't explain to the officer behind the desk why it was so alarming that he'd sent her a diamond ring.

Each time she moved to a new town, a new state, there would be a grace period before Emerson caught up. Beatrice could breathe again. She could begin to hope that the last time might have been the last time. Maybe he wouldn't discover her new locale. Maybe she had finally proven to be too much trouble for him to pursue. She would find a job and rent an apartment. She might tumble into a crush, into bed with someone new. She even dated men, which to me seems rather like visiting grizzly territory after having been mauled by a bear. As time passed, she would relax, sleeping through the night again, not looking over her shoulder every time she turned a corner.

And then the call, the knock on the door, the bouquet sent to her desk at work. Can you imagine her fear and dismay? I couldn't, not until it happened under my roof.

At the Body Farm, I sat at my desk with the lights off, spinning in circles in my wheelie chair. Would the meteor strike today, while I was out of the house? Armando and Joe—longtime friends of ours, a dear married couple in their sixties—were spending the morning with you and Beatrice, teaching you to grow herbs in pots, which could then be transferred to the garden when spring came. But I wasn't sure this was sufficient protection. Joe was frail, requiring a cane to walk more than a few feet, and I didn't like the bulbous appearance of Armando's nose lately, the distinct thickening and reddening caused by alcohol overuse. Sometimes it's hard for me not to look for a cause of death in the making.

A knock at my office door startled me. Hyo stepped into the room, holding a canister of specimen jars. Her expression was quizzical, her eyes as bright as a bird's.

"Let's go," she said. "It's a perfect morning."

"What?"

She leaned over and flipped on the light. "How long have you been sitting here? Come on, there's work to be done."

"Right."

"You okay?"

"Yes. Fine. It's nothing."

We strolled down the hill, both of us in down coats and latex gloves and surgical masks, muffling our voices as we chatted. We had worked together for years, and our small talk was as comfortable as breathing: slime, larvae, mildew, blowflies. Hyo sported a sunflower-yellow shower cap, incongruous in the wintry air. In theory, this would keep the smell of death out of her dark mane. I wore my own hair pixie-short. Easier to scrub clean at the end of the day.

As we walked, I was surprised by my ability to perform normalcy. My mind was not there, on the grounds; it was back home, hovering around my family like an avenging angel. And yet, I made notes on my clipboard and conversed casually with Hyo about the humidity, the cloud cover, and the corpse lying in the grass: a man in his thirties, his face melted like candle wax. Despite the cold, phorid flies droned around his torso. Hyo leaned over him and began gathering specimens. I watched her label each jar in her tiny scribble before dropping it into her bag. Beneath her mask, her cheeks were pink from the chill.

"Remember when we first started?" she said. "You always used to put the bodies on their bellies. You didn't like to see their faces."

"That was a long time ago."

She brushed a stray lock of hair off her cheek with her forearm. We were all conditioned never to touch our faces with our gloved hands out in the field.

"I was worse than you," she said. "I couldn't use the word 'murder.' Remember? I'd say 'dispatched' like we were in a Jane Austen novel."

I put on an upper-crust British accent. "This fellow was dispatched a week ago. The bloat is quite severe. His testicles have swollen to the size of a cricket ball."

Hyo laughed. "God, how things change. I've got no problem with it now. Murder, murder, murder."

She moved up the hill, toward the next corpse on her list. I stood still, the word echoing in my mind.

At three in the morning, Beatrice's cell phone rang. I heard her turn over in bed and fumble around on the nightstand, knocking the lampshade against the wall.

"Hello?" she muttered into the pillow.

With a lurch, she sat bolt upright. I did the same. Even in the dark bedroom I could see that her pupils were ringed with white all the way around.

"How did you get this number?" she asked. Then, quickly, she placed the phone on the blanket between us and put it on speaker.

"—always do," a man's voice was saying. A reedy tenor. Clipped consonants. I reached for Beatrice's hand and laced her fingers through mine.

"Did you get my letter?" Emerson asked.

"I did. How long have you been in the area?" She gripped my hand so tightly that I felt my bones scrape together.

"Just got here," he said lazily. "You know, I've come to really enjoy this game we play. The thrill of the chase never gets old."

"It's not a game," Beatrice said. "I thought this time—"

"You thought I wouldn't find you? I'll always find you, honey."

She shuddered convulsively at the endearment. I moved closer, laying my cheek against her shoulder.

"You got *married*," he said. "You changed your *name*. I liked your old name better."

There was an unsettling singsong quality to his speech. I wondered if his voice was always pitched so high or if emotion had altered it.

"I'm going to hang up now," he said. "I'd rather talk to you when you're alone."

"Are you saying—" she began, but he was gone. She checked that the call had ended, then turned her phone off. She tucked it under a pillow, shook her head as though disagreeing with herself, got to her feet, and paced. Finally she carried her phone into the bathroom, holding it between two fingers like a grimy scrap of garbage, and shoved it into a cabinet among the hand towels. Only then, it seemed, could she be sure that no part of Emerson was present.

"Is he watching us somehow?" she murmured to me, climbing back into bed, her eyes darting everywhere. "Is that what he meant? 'When you're alone,' he said. How did he know?"

I stroked her hair out of her face. "He made an educated guess. He assumed I'd be in bed with you. Where else would I be? He's just trying to scare you."

Privately, however, I vowed to check and recheck all our new security cameras. Maybe I'd get one of those bug sweepers I'd seen on spy shows. Who knew what this madman was capable of? The rage burned in my chest like a coal.

"It's never going to stop." Beatrice buried her face in my throat, wetting my skin with her tears.

Ours was a whirlwind courtship. Fleeing Texas and Emerson, Beatrice moved to Iowa. We met at a summer barbecue hosted by one of her new coworkers. Within the week we were engaged. My queer friends teased me for hitching the U-Haul to the Subaru with such stereotypical swiftness, but nothing about this love felt ordinary to me.

I'd always maintained a distance in relationships before. My work made romance tricky. I would wait a reasonable period of time before telling each new girlfriend about my job, hoping first to enchant them with my wiles and sexual prowess. Usually they broke it off as soon as they learned the truth. Other times they stuck around for a short while but urged me constantly to get into another field, something normal, not quite so horrifying.

It has always been difficult for me to explain why I enjoy this work. Initially I took the job because full-time gigs for entomologists are few and far between, and I have no taste for academia. I figured I would see what the Body Farm was all about, help close a few cold cases, and leave for greener pastures as soon as I got an opportunity for fieldwork, ideally in a rain forest where I could make my name discovering a new species of beetle. There are always more beetles to be found.

Most researchers stay at the Body Farm for either a couple of hours or their entire lives. There was, of course, an adjustment period for me. In my introductory meeting, LaTanya informed me casually that if I needed to throw up or faint, that was fine, as long as I didn't do it on the corpses themselves. And yes, I vomited once or twice at the start, I admit. But soon it turned out that I had the right mindset. I could focus on the trees instead of the forest. I learned to turn my attention to the details (the timeline of pupation, the movement of larvae through rotting tissue, or the metallic sheen of healthy adult blowflies) while ignoring the bigger picture entirely (existential dread, gut-wrenching repulsion, and my own fear of inescapable death).

I didn't stay just for the bugs, however. My work matters. I sleep well at night knowing that I'm helping to balance the scales of justice. Even as a child I was a righteous soul, beating up other people's bullies on the playground and shattering a neighbor boy's magnifying glass when he used it to fry ants. Now I take on the work that few others are capable of. I look death in the face every day and analyze how it moves, what it wants. I do it for the good of us all.

"I think your work is amazing," Beatrice told me the night I proposed. No one had ever said anything like this to me before. She even enjoyed my interesting insect facts—or pretended to, anyway, well enough that I never knew the difference.

God, I was smitten—I still am, honestly, all these years later. Your mother is a rare creature. The way she listens with her whole body. The way she radiates calm in a palpable forcefield, softening the mood of an entire room. The way she reacts viscerally and audibly to whatever she's reading—laughing and nodding and saying "Oh!" alone on the porch swing, as though the author could hear. Her hopefulness is like a kite rising on the wind, carried irresistibly upward. As a grouchy pessimist, I stand in awe of her innate buoyancy. Nothing else could have seen her through Emerson's madness. Each time she escaped him, she was able to hope, sincerely and completely, that it would finally end.

We married. She took my name. By that point Emerson had been silent for over a year, the longest stretch since college.

He did not make contact when we traveled to Paris for our honeymoon. He did not make contact when we bought our house. He did not make contact when you were born, first Theo, then Lucas, a vaginal delivery, brave Beatrice laboring for thirty-seven hours. You looked like her even then, my angels, with your identical tufts of black fuzz and crumpled faces. Her nose went to Lucas. Her chin went to Theo. Both of you got her perfect tawny skin.

Seven years of peace punctured by a bright blue envelope. I thought Emerson was gone, I really did. To be honest, I figured he was dead.

A second electric blue envelope showed up a few days after Emerson's late-night phone call. You two found it, rushing to the door at the sound of letters sliding through the mail slot. I'm sorry that I shouted at you. The world dissolved into a crimson haze the moment I glimpsed my babies holding something that monster had touched. I yelled, and then the envelope was in my hands and you both were staring wide-eyed at me from the safety of Beatrice's embrace on the other side of the room.

"Don't take it out on them," she said.

"I'm sorry," I said. I went to you, kneeling down to your eye level. "Mama's so sorry. Mama was being a jerk."

"Mama was being a jerk!" you chorused.

"A-plus parenting, babe," Beatrice said, plucking the blue envelope from my grasp. She gave me a nudge to take the sting out of her words, then slipped from the room.

He had written her a poem, that son of a bitch. I won't repeat his maudlin little stanzas here. Suffice it to say that after reading it, Beatrice went to bed and cried for the rest of the day.

I know a lot about murder. I've spent years considering motive, means, and opportunity. There are five classifications of death: homicide, suicide, accidental, natural, and unknown. Though the cadavers we study at the Body Farm usually fall into the "natural" column, our research applies to all the other kinds too. Part of our job is to beat killers at their own game, to think like they do, to think better than they do. The police are fond of saying there's no such thing as a perfect murder, but I don't agree. There are flaws in any system. I helped design this particular system, so I'm aware of its flaws.

Toxicology reports, for instance, are far from comprehensive. During an autopsy, the medical examiner studies the victim's blood. She looks for illegal substances (like heroin and cocaine), and prescription medications (like opiates and amphetamines). But it simply isn't possible to screen for everything. Nobody checks for jellyfish venom or deadly nightshade, for example—not unless there's a specific reason to do so. Other poisons melt away upon ingestion, leaving no trace in the body. Cyanide does not linger in the blood; the only indication is a faint smell of almonds, and even that varies. Ricin, too, kills within days and leaves no sign of its presence.

Then there are the everyday poisons, so ordinary that they fly beneath the radar in a different way. Large amounts of potassium can be lethal, but it also occurs naturally in the body and is always found in the blood. Why would anyone bother to test for a substance that's definitely going to be there? Toxicology reports focus on a couple hundred possible poisons, but there are thousands more in the world. In truth, almost anything can be fatal in sufficient quantities. Too much nutmeg. Too much salt. Too much water.

Even air can be a problem. Once a cadaver came to the Body Farm, a woman who'd died of cardiac arrest. But given her comparative youth, Jackson and Cal, our MDs, were not satisfied with this verdict. Cardiac arrest means only that the heart has stopped beating. It is a symptom of death, rather than the cause.

So Jackson did a thorough autopsy. He scanned for surface and subcutaneous trauma. He examined the seven locations in which a needle can be inserted without being noticed by most medical examiners. At last, he found an incision beneath the woman's tongue. Someone had injected her with a syringe full of empty air, which formed an embolism and stopped her heart.

And, of course, there are accidents—or deaths that appear to be accidental. The world is a dangerous place. People fall down the stairs and slip in the shower. They get drunk and crash their cars. They leave cigarettes lit and burn their houses down. With a little help, life can be fatal. A loose wire. A stove left on. A push at the wrong moment. An unseen, guiding hand. Even if the police suspect foul play, they can't act without corroboration. Innocent until proven guilty, after all.

Corpses are like postcards, written unknowingly by the killer, full of unintended clues. Fingerprints. Hair. Droplets of saliva or

tears. Without meaning to, the murderer might record whether
they were right- or left-handed. They might hint at whether
they had done this before. (An inexperienced, nervous attacker
leaves different marks from one who is confident and assured.)
They might indicate their height and weight. (A blow struck by a
short, skinny woman is quite unlike a punch from a six-foot, three-
hundred-pound man.) At the Body Farm, my colleagues and I can
read these things printed on the flesh in the killer's unique script.

To get away with murder, it's best to dispose of the corpse al-
together. A wood chipper and an eight-foot grave. A deep lake,
a length of chain, and a cinder block. A concoction of lye and
bleach, melting the flesh like warm ice. No evidence at all. No trail
for the police to follow. No message for the medical examiner to
decode. No body, no crime.

What was the tipping point for me? Not Emerson's first letter, or
the late-night phone call, or the pathetic poem. Not the nights I
lay awake in bed, tossing and turning, finally getting up to verify
for the tenth time that every door and window was locked and
that you were safe and dreaming in your shared bed. Not the second call, which came one morning while you ate breakfast and Beatrice sat beside you at the table, smiling cheerfully at you with the
phone to her ear so you wouldn't be alarmed. Only heavy breathing, she said later, but that was bad enough. Not even Emerson's
third letter, in which he described me as an "androgynous nothing
person."

He had always treated Beatrice's lovers that way, as though they
couldn't possibly live up to his example or offer any real threat. He
would graciously forgive her each time, too, clucking his tongue
and reveling in his own magnanimity.

His assault on our family went on for weeks. Another letter on
blue card stock, which the two of you avoided like it was radioactive. You collected the rest of the mail and left that envelope
in the front hall for me to find on my way to work. More heavy
breathing down the phone. A single rose tucked beneath the windshield wiper of Beatrice's car. How did he know which one was
hers? I went to the police then, but the officer said exactly what
Beatrice told me he'd say. Emerson hadn't done anything illegal.
Was I even sure it was him? The car was parked on the street; anyone could have put the flower there. If the guy became violent or

trespassed on our property, I should file a police report for sure. Then it would be too late, I said, and the officer raised his hands, palms up, in a gesture of helplessness or supplication.

I fervently hope that you don't remember that brief, terrible phase of your young lives. Beatrice's nerves tautened like a guitar string pulled too far, ready to snap. I subsisted on coffee and energy pills. A bracelet in a velvet box left on the porch. Another electric blue letter covered in drawings of hearts. A dead bird in the grass of our backyard—had it fallen from a nest in the pine tree, or had a Machiavellian maniac tossed it over the fence as a warning? A midnight call, consisting only of kissy noises and sexual groans.

But the tipping point came when I saw Emerson with my own eyes.

I'm still not sure what woke me. I'd been sleeping lightly for weeks, startling at every sound, but there was no creak of floorboards or tap of branches on the window that night. I slipped out of bed, listening to the ringing silence, the carpet cold beneath my bare feet. Beatrice lay on her belly with her feet in the air. My ridiculous, wonderful wife.

I padded down the hall to check on you both. You were in Lucas's bed this time, sleeping head to foot. I wondered if you'd started out the night that way or if you began with both heads on one pillow and one of you migrated. You were wild sleepers at that age, kicking and rolling in frantic motions that never woke either of you.

I went to the window to make sure it was locked. And there he was, standing on the sidewalk, staring up at the house. At your room.

My heart jolted violently enough to knock the wind out of me. I don't know if Emerson saw me through the curtains. He did not react to my appearance, at any rate. The street lamp turned him into a copper statue, dressed in a puffy coat, hands folded behind his back, blond hair glittering. He was taller than I'd expected. His stance suggested he'd been out there a long while, despite the cold. An unnerving stillness. Endless patience. As my eyes adjusted to the watery glow, I saw the expression on his face: chin lifted, a small smile.

I read once that geckos can hold a pose for hours, exerting no energy while remaining perfectly alert, ready to launch their tongues at the first appearance of prey with the speed and lethality of a bullet. They are harmless to humans but vicious predators of insects. There was something of the lizard about Emerson as he lurked there on our street, motionless, vigilant, waiting.

I watched him watching us. I stayed where I was for god knows how long. The two of you mumbled in your sleep, smacking your lips and rustling amid the blankets. My leg began to cramp and I needed to pee, but I didn't move from my post at the window until Emerson pivoted on his heel and strode away. I kept my gaze on him until he turned the corner and disappeared into the darkness.

Once I make up my mind about something, I act quickly and decisively. I have always been like that. I wanted to buy our house the moment we stepped inside, and we made an offer that same day. Beatrice longed for babies before I did, but the instant I knew I was ready, too, we went hand in hand to the sperm bank.

I decided to murder Emerson the night I saw him.

The idea had been bubbling away at the back of my mind for some time, but I had not taken it seriously. We all think crazy things in the privacy of our weird little brains. To blow off steam, I'd considered means and opportunity. Motive I already had in plentiful supply. It had become a game to play during sleepless nights or quiet moments at the Body Farm. A reverse whodunit, figuring out how, in theory, I might get away with it.

Female killers are not caught as often as male. It skews the statistics. In fact, no one really knows how many women have committed murder. The records track only those homicides that result in arrest and conviction. It's impossible to count the successful killers—the ones who are never found out, never suspected at all.

The evidence of women's prowess in this area is anecdotal but compelling. Cal, one of the MDs at the Body Farm, worked at a hospice facility for years before coming to Lyle. He was shocked, he said, by the number of sweet old ladies who confessed on their deathbeds that they'd poisoned or suffocated somebody decades ago. None of their relatives or friends ever dreamed of such a thing, Cal said. These women made it to old age, to the point of their own demise, with their crimes undiscovered.

In the break room, my colleagues and I debated the gender disparity of murder. Everyone had a different theory to explain it. Luis believed that social conditioning was the root cause. At a young age, boys were encouraged to lash out, to dominate, whereas girls were taught to contain and control their anger. As grown women, this ability allowed them to act with premeditation and cool heads, which accounted for their success and secrecy.

Hyo thought it was a matter of cleanup. Men couldn't properly scrub a toilet or discern when the carpet needed vacuuming. How could they ever hope to leave behind a sterile crime scene? In addition, most women had decades of experience scrubbing bloodstains out of their underwear. Men wouldn't know to soak the fabric first and wash in cold water, since hot would induce the stains to set.

Kenneth, who had more experience with the law enforcement side of things, believed it had to do with ego. Men overestimated their own intelligence and made mistakes as a result, while women often underestimated themselves, leading them to plan more thoroughly and take greater precautions.

Georgina felt it all came down to motive. Women held grudges, she said. They could wait years before taking action, long after any apparent motive had faded from everyone else's minds. Men didn't tend to let things fester that way. They either acted at once or moved on.

And LaTanya said that women were simply the smarter sex, more capable of doing everything under the sun, including homicide.

Now that I have become a murderer myself, I believe all of them were right, more or less.

Do you remember the fairy tale that obsessed you during that time? I hope so, since I read it aloud to you daily for weeks on end. You'd found it on one of your shelves, a hand-me-down picture book with no cover, the pages soft from use. I still don't know the title. The spine, like the cover, had been torn away by some other child's hands.

The heroine was a "golden-hearted woman." No other personality traits were mentioned, but perhaps they weren't needed. She caught the eye of an evil wizard, who cursed her, transforming her into a bee. That was the part I liked. Any story with an insect in it gets my vote. She flew unhappily from flower to flower, growing weary, so lonely, until a kind farmer held out his hand and gave her a place to rest. His touch transformed her back into her human shape. They married and lived happily ever after. Heteronormative but sweet.

"What happened to the evil wizard?" you asked every single time I closed the book.

"It doesn't say," I told you.

"Did he die? Did he go to jail?"

"I don't know."

You were never satisfied with this answer. Eventually you would climb off my lap to finish the story on your own, drawing crayon illustrations of the wizard boiling to death in a pot or falling off a cliff. You killed him a hundred bloodthirsty ways and cheered his demise, then asked me to read the book aloud again.

I've heard people say that children can't fully understand death. That's why they crave such cutthroat stories and playact such barbaric things. (Once the evil wizard had his arms and legs ripped off by elephants; another time he got kicked into a volcano.) But I think children are perfectly capable of understanding what death is. They're not naive and guileless; they're clear-eyed about the limits of justice. They know that the world of fairy tales is better than ours.

Real life isn't fair. In my work, I've seen the full measure of what human beings can do to one another, and I've seen the limits of our justice system too. But in a fairy tale, there's no need for cops or courts, since the story itself brings balance. Murderers have their eyes plucked out by doves or drown in the sea, while good people are guaranteed to live happily ever after. The Body Farm wouldn't exist in a fairy tale. Why would anyone study death and decay in a world where magical retribution is a fundamental law of nature?

That's the reality I want.

The book with no title became your obsession because it broke the most essential rule of fairy tales: it wasn't fair. You wanted to hear the story over and over because it bothered you, not because you liked it. Yes, the golden-hearted woman and the kind farmer were rewarded by fate, as they should be, but what about the evil wizard? You kept hoping that he might finally be punished this time. And then, when the ending let you down again, you wrote a better one yourselves.

My plan was simple. The best plans always are. I bought a burner phone on my way to work, taking a leaf out of Emerson's own playbook. He used disposable cell phones so that he could harass

Beatrice and threaten her without leaving a paper trail. She would go to the police and show them a string of terrifying text messages, and they'd tell her there was no way to be sure of the source.

One night, as Beatrice slept, I scrolled through her phone. (To be clear, I usually respected her privacy. This was a one-time breach of my moral code, done only in exigent and extreme circumstances.) As I suspected, Emerson had been bombarding her with texts for weeks, from a slew of different numbers—messages she hadn't told me about, not wanting to worry me. Beatrice never replied, but that didn't stop him.

Using my new flip phone, I texted his most recent number, posing as Beatrice. Emerson believed she would do that—contact him of her own volition, after all this time. Can you imagine? I asked to meet him in an isolated spot, late at night. He agreed. We worked out the details of our rendezvous, him and me.

Now I wonder: Was he really so arrogant, or was he delusional? Did he actually believe that one day it would be him and Beatrice, a perfect match, destined for one another? Did he buy the story he kept selling? Or did he see the situation clearly—predator and prey, psychopath and victim—and the poems and diamond rings were simply weapons in his vast arsenal? How much was gaslighting with the intent of causing harm, and how much did he regard as true?

I guess it doesn't matter. Actions are important, not motives. That's what LaTanya always tries to explain on the stand. The jury wants to know *why* the victim was killed, *why* the murderer did it, but the only thing science can reveal, at the end of the day, is *how*.

I met Emerson at midnight, in a place of my own choosing. I wore a hat and scarf and he didn't know it was me until it was too late. I won't go into the details. That is not my purpose, and I don't want you to be burdened with those images.

When he was dead, I wrapped his corpse in a tarp, laid it in my trunk, and drove to the Body Farm. It was my turn to take the graveyard shift. We all hate doing it, so we follow a rotating schedule. Temperature, insect activity, fungal growth, humidity—these things don't stay constant after nightfall, and it is essential that we observe our subjects around the clock. But the Body Farm is creepy after dark, even for us. The trees rustle menacingly. Darkness erases the visual markers of death—liquefied eyeballs, putrefied flesh—that we normally count on to remind ourselves that these

are corpses, not people. At night, the Body Farm seems to be inhabited by a watchful, unmoving crowd.

In addition, the dead are not always silent. Fresh cadavers sometimes sigh or groan. I've heard them pass gas. I've seen them twitch
their fingers or blink. As they move further through the process
of decay, the sounds don't stop; they merely change. Sometimes
month-old corpses bubble or belch. In rare cases, they explode,
their torsos ripped apart from within by a profusion of volcanic
gases.

That night, I parked by the back door, where there are no security cameras. Why would there be? We only ever use that entrance
to receive the dead or throw away hazardous waste. To get that close
to the building, we have to pass through two locked gates with key-
pads. The cameras face outward along the walls, keeping teens and
miscreants away, rather than monitoring the researchers inside.

I fetched a gurney and wheeled Emerson's corpse through the
halls. I did think briefly about keeping him there, on the grounds.
I could mock up the paperwork of a new admission. I could smash
his face and snip off his fingertips, rendering him unidentifiable.
I could find an appropriate resting place for him and watch him
molder away until there was nothing left but bones.

There was an odd symmetry to the idea. I imagined counting
the maggots that devoured him and measuring the life cycle of
the coffin flies that made their homes in his flesh. In life he had
been a pernicious soul, causing only harm, but in death he could
be useful. His body would provide data and aid the noble cause of
science, and I would be able to savor my revenge.

I blame the graveyard shift for that particular line of thought. I
am not normally such a ghoul, but the Body Farm is eerie in the
wee small hours.

I cremated him. We have our own incinerator, for obvious reasons. I needed to use it that night anyway, since we'd amassed more
skeletons than we could use, picked absolutely clean by insects and
bacteria, nothing left to learn. I burned four skeletons and Emerson, then went out onto the grounds to do my work.

I wish I could tell you that it upset me to take his life. That's what
I'm supposed to say, isn't it? That it left me nauseated and shaken.
That I could scarcely look at myself in the mirror afterward. That
it haunts me to this day.

But the truth is quite different. Years at the Body Farm have reshaped my reaction to death. Emerson was a problem for me to solve. At work, I solve objectively disturbing and disgusting problems all the time. What's the most efficient method of removing blowfly eggs from the mouth of a corpse? Use a child's paintbrush. What's the ideal preservative for beetle larvae? Alcohol or naphtha. What's the best way to change Emerson's body from alive to dead? That was the problem before me: a man who ought to be a corpse. I found an ideal solution. Doing so was no more repugnant or upsetting than any old shift at the Anthropological Research Center.

The next few months were difficult. I knew Emerson was gone, but I could not tell Beatrice, who continued to wake up screaming from nightmares and startle every time her phone rang. With the two of you, at least, I could be myself again. Fun Mama. Science-y Mama. When the weather warmed, I took you to the zoo. I hung a tire swing from our oak tree. We worked in the backyard, transferring the herbs Armando and Joe had helped you grow in indoor pots to a vegetable garden by the fence.

"It's been a while since I've heard from you-know-who," Beatrice said on a rainy day in spring. "I'm getting antsy waiting for the other shoe to drop."

"Maybe it won't," I said. "Maybe he's finally moved on."

She smiled at me. Her hopefulness is amazing. I will never stop admiring it.

Flowers bloomed. You splashed in puddles. One morning you found caterpillars, seven of them, crawling around on the parsley we'd planted in the garden. They were black swallowtails—I could tell from the coloration and their choice of host plant. We carried them inside, safe from predators, and raised them by hand. I have never seen such smiles. You named them, loved them. When they melted and solidified into chrysalises, you mourned. When they hatched into miraculous, dewy creatures with midnight-black wings, you laughed. When we released them into our garden, you danced, watching them flit and circle and finally rise, vanishing into the blue.

On the one hand, homicide is objectively wrong. On the other hand, is it? I don't think I'm deranged. I hope you don't think so either, my darlings. I believe you see me as I truly am: a doting mother, a loving wife, and an affectionate friend to my friends. A good provider. A well-balanced person. A conscientious member of society.

The Emersons of this world are a dying breed. That's my hope, anyway. I want it to stop with your generation. It comes down to you, my beautiful boys. You are growing up every moment, and one day, all too soon, you will no longer be interested in fairy tales. You will shed the wild sweetness of these early years. It's hard to imagine you as preteens, high schoolers, adults, but I know it's coming.

You will be good men. That isn't hopefulness on my part—it's decision, intention. Despite our years together, none of Beatrice's optimism has rubbed off on me. I know you'll be good men because I will see to it. Lucas, with your tender heart, so like your mother's. Theo, with your righteous spirit, so much like mine.

"Can Emerson be gone?" Beatrice asked when summer came. "He isn't gone, is he? I'm afraid to let my guard down."

"I think he gave up," I said, pouring her a glass of wine. "Maybe he finally saw how happy you are. How happy we are."

She laughed the way she used to, a cascading waterfall. I hadn't heard that unfettered laugh since the first blue envelope arrived.

When I began writing this letter to you, I thought I understood my purpose. I believe I was setting down my confession in case the truth ever came to light. I wanted you to know why I did what I did. At the Body Farm, we only care about *how*, but you, my children, would want to know *why*. And so I have tried to explain. I intended to hide the letter somewhere secret, to be opened in the event of my conviction. Not arrest, you understand—*conviction*. That was my plan at the start, anyway.

But now that I have written it all down, I can see that I will never be caught. It was indeed a perfect murder. I even incinerated Emerson's burner phone, and mine, along with his body—the only extant things in the universe that could possibly connect him to me.

It has been a year since I killed him. Winter has settled in once more, and Beatrice seems at ease in her own skin again. I've seen her shoveling snow without glancing up every time someone walks by. She forgets to turn on the security alarm some nights. The doorbell rang the other day and she ran, excited for the package she'd ordered, throwing open the door without looking through the peephole first. I took her out for a night on the town and she did herself up, highlighter on her cheeks, a slinky red dress I'd never seen before. She wouldn't have been so bold and colorful if Emerson was on her mind. Our lovemaking—well, I'm sure you don't want to hear about it, so I will only say that Emerson had a stifling influence on both of us that has since vanished entirely.

Even now, the police don't realize he's missing. They probably never will. Beatrice mentioned once that Emerson didn't have any family. I'm sure there are no friends to report his loss either. A loner. An oddball. The only person who will notice his absence is Beatrice, and for her it has been a balm, a delicious silence, the cessation of persistent pain.

What, then, have I written here? Not a confession—there would be no point. I will take the truth to my grave. I will let time prove to Beatrice that Emerson is gone, and I will say nothing, not to her, not to you, not to anyone.

And yet, even if no one will ever read this letter, it may still serve a purpose. It could be a blueprint of sorts—a battle plan. Not that I anticipate ever needing to take such drastic action again, you understand. I killed Emerson because I had to. There was no other solution to the particular problem of his aliveness.

But if I were to take the lessons I learned from his death and turn my attention to someone else, another "bad guy," a stranger to me . . . I will admit that during one of my recent graveyard shifts, in the ghoulish lull of the witching hour, the thought did cross my mind. The only tricky part of Emerson's murder was the connection between us, however tangential. There was the slimmest chance that a search of motives could lead back to me.

A stranger, however—someone with no link to me at all—well, what could be easier? Yes, the thought has crossed my mind. There's that neighbor who screams such vile things at his wife after a few drinks. There's the principal of the local elementary school, who has kept his job for a decade despite persistent rumors that he sexually harasses his teachers. There's the woman Hyo told me about, a dear friend of hers from college, trapped in an abusive relationship, too afraid to leave him even after he beat her badly enough to put her in the hospital. Hyo mentioned the man's name to me as she wiped away her tears. I did just happen to jot it down.

And a couple of weeks ago, there was a news story about a serial rapist right here in Lyle, convicted of assaulting eight different women and sentenced to a paltry two years in prison. I did just happen to make a note of his release date as well. God, it would be so easy. No affiliation between any of these men and me. No apparent motive. My rotation on the night watch comes back around like clockwork, and the skeletons are always piling up again, ready to be incinerated.

So maybe what I have written here is a cautionary tale. Maybe it was never intended for you or me. Maybe, all along, I meant it for men like that rapist or the principal or the neighbor—men like Emerson. The fact that none of those despicable souls will read it is irrelevant. A story like mine has power in the mere fact of its existence. A warning. A tremor in the fabric. A new kind of ending.

I don't have to decide yet what I will do. I have all the time in the world to see what kind of person I am becoming. We are all in a process of constant evolution, larvae metamorphosing into blowflies. That's what I love most about insects: their capacity for transformation. A tiny translucent egg sac becomes a half-blind, slow-moving grub, which mutates into a cocoon filled with mush that lies motionless in the soil for days as though dead, then erupts into its final form, a fierce winged creature with a panoramic field of vision and an accelerated perception of time, with feet that can taste the ground. It's the closest thing to magic to be found in this life.

And insects transfigure more than themselves. Without bees, there would be no flowers or fruits. Without bone beetles and coffin flies, the dead would not decay, and the cycle of life would be broken. The work of insects, like mine, is both grotesque and vital. They transmute flesh and bone into mulch and nutrients. They change the dead into the raw materials for new life. There are no plants as green as the ones on the Body Farm, feeding from the richest, most blood-soaked soil on earth.

What happened to Emerson was not legal, but it was right. It was fairy tale justice. And I suppose, in the end, that's what this story is: a fairy tale. Once upon a time, there was golden-hearted woman, pursued over hill and dale by an evil ogre. She met a gallant knight—me, of course—and bore two fine sons. They lived peacefully for a time, hoping the ogre was gone, but he came back, as wicked things so often do. Bravely, cleverly, the knight slew the ogre and burned him up. The golden-hearted woman rejoiced. Together they raised their sons to be better men than the men who came before them. And they all lived happily ever after.

NILS GILBERTSON

Lovely and Useless Things

FROM *Prohibition Peepers*

> The harsh, useful things of the world, from pulling teeth to dig-
> ging potatoes, are best done by men who are as starkly sober as
> so many convicts in the death-house, but the lovely and useless
> things, the charming and exhilarating things, are best done by
> men with, as the phrase is, a few sheets in the wind.
> —H. L. Mencken

THE STRIKE OF a match lit the alleyway, casting a long, pistol-
wielding shadow. Pat Boyle paused before raising it to the cigarette
on his lips. The flame danced and the shadow turned from darkness on brick to dimly lit flesh and steel, then back again. Boyle
drew from the cigarette and tossed the match to the gutter.

"You mind stepping into the light?"

The trembling pistol came first, then the young man wielding
it. Boyle waited until he could see the whites of his eyes, ignoring
the chatter of the men at the dock behind him as they unloaded
cases from the Potomac.

"Can I help you, son?"

"Don't *son* me, mister."

"We're all someone's son." Boyle took a long inhale and looked
back to the dock.

The young man thrust the pistol toward him. "Why don't you
take your eyes off the booze for a change."

Boyle's stare drifted back. "Either shoot or tell me why you're
pointing that thing at me."

The young man glanced down his arm to the pistol as though
he'd forgotten he was holding it. "My father's name is—was—

Willard Reynolds. He used to frequent the speakeasy—Sixteenth Street spot—that you work at."

Boyle nodded. "I'm sorry, son."

"Don't call me—" He squeezed his eyes shut for a moment, as though frustrated by the dim alley light. "Sorry for what?"

"Sorry you sprung from the seed of Willard Reynolds."

Before the young man had the chance to process the indignity, another man emerged from the shadows. Boyle asked, "How long we got?"

"'Bout ten minutes and we'll be good to go."

"We're square with our friends?"

"All paid up."

"All right. Get out of here."

"But—"

"I said get out of here."

The figure retreated to the shadows and made its way back to the dock.

"What's your name?" Boyle asked, turning back to the man with the gun.

He swallowed and his forearm quivered, tired, unaccustomed to the pistol. "Willard Jr."

"Willard Jr.," Boyle said, shaking his head. "Give me one guess."

"Guess at what?"

"Guess at what reduced you to this. See, I knew your old man. Used to be a decent fella. Drank now and then but held a steady job. Paid lip service to the Anti-Saloon League but lamented their stubbornness in private. But once they got their way—once the political tides shifted—he didn't speak out. No, that takes courage. Instead, he started frequenting our place. Why? The continental clubs reserved for the congressmen and their cronies stopped allowing nobodies like him. The casual imbibing turned heavier." Boyle snuffed out the cigarette and lit another. "I had a front row seat from there. It's funny you coming here, Willard Jr. Your old man died with a hell of an unpaid tab." He took a step toward the trembling arm. "But I couldn't bear calling in that debt. I see the debt in your eyes—the debt of being the seed of that man, dead from choking on his own sick in a gutter."

"But I—but you—"

"What, it's *my* fault? Your father never drank like that before Prohibition, correct?"

He paused. "It's not right what you and Johnny Dunn are doing at that place. It's nothing but a refuge for skanks and sinners."

Boyle chuckled. "You want to talk about sin? Let's talk about the sons of bitches down the street who voted this madness into law but got bootleggers hand-delivering Canadian booze to the Capitol for briefcases of cash. Let's talk about the clubs for the politicians and industry men that stocked up on a decade's worth of hooch before the law kicked in. They take kickbacks and send people like me to jail on a whim, but *we're* the sinners." Boyle continued toward the retreating young man. "Meanwhile, they turn fellas like your old man from ordinary, flawed men to devils. I'm not the devil, son. The devil and his cronies live at the big domed building on First Street. If you want to kill someone over your father's death you better—"

Before finishing the sentence, Boyle leaped forward, grabbed the barrel of the pistol, and slammed the grip into the bridge of Willard Jr.'s nose. He crumpled and Boyle watched blood paint the road crimson black. He flicked his cigarette and said to the figures he felt behind him, "Bring him back to the club."

Pat Boyle followed the truck through downtown Washington, DC, reflecting on his mortality. Never once did he think the boy would shoot before he got to him, but the throb in his chest told him he didn't know a damn thing about the boy. Hell, he didn't know anything at all. He didn't know about right versus wrong or good versus evil or moral versus immoral—same as the boy—same as everyone. But at least he knew he didn't know, and at least he knew he didn't need to. The best men, he thought, didn't command their fellow man from a giant domed building. The best men disregarded the commands of those who sought power and control and instead basked in the plenitude of life and the abundance that this world offered, in all its forms. He felt his heart in his chest and smiled.

The Moonlight Club sat on the third floor of a narrow building squeezed between two luxury hotels a few blocks north of the White House. Upon arrival, patrons entered on the desolate floor level and would be stopped by a fella dressed as a security guard, who informed them it was private property, and they ought to leave. If they shared the password—any sentence incorporating the phrase *lovely and useless things*—the guard would direct them to a concealed staircase.

The truck pulled into the lot at the back of the building, surrounded by tall fences. Boyle followed it in. He parked and watched as fellas started unloading the cases. Two men dragged Willard Jr. from the truck to the back entrance.

The club was brimming with drunken regulars. Men sat at the bar trading slurred ramblings and downing cocktails concocted by Leroy, the bartender. Thick smoke hung like fog above the tables before the small stage, where a man crooned along with a jazz ensemble. The Moonlight Club wasn't the sort of spot you'd find the congressmen and other bigwigs toasting to their reckless use of government power, nor was it one of the hundreds of gin joints that dotted the back alleys where, upon entrance, there was a serious risk of taking a knife between the ribs or going blind from bad hooch. The clientele was made up of regular folks. Everyone from schoolteachers to shopkeepers to lawyers and everything in between. It was also the drinking spot of the local authorities. And when it came to enforcing the Volstead Act and its accompanying laws, if the clubs paid off the cops and DC government, there was little concern the feds would bother interfering. Even the mayor stopped by the Moonlight Club for a rollicking good time now and again. Not to mention, Johnny Dunn, the fella who ran the place, made for damn sure every cop on every corner in a two-mile radius of the joint was getting a generous monthly cut.

Boyle found his usual spot at the corner of the bar and flagged down Leroy.

"Hey, Leroy. I'll take a rye, neat."

"I'll make it a double for ya, sir. Considering the night you've had." He pulled a glass and popped the cork from a bottle and poured generously.

"Word gets around that fast?"

"You know how it is 'round here, Mr. Boyle. Word travels faster than influenza."

"Only question is if it travels accurately." Boyle took a long gulp of his drink and Leroy filled it back up. The bartender was a middle-aged Black man who, before Prohibition, had worked as a porter at The Stinson, a hotel that Johnny Dunn had frequented on business trips to Richmond and that Boyle had once visited—at

Dunn's recommendation—while tracking a congressional aide's runaway wife. Dunn and Leroy had gotten close enough for Leroy to share some cocktail recipes. When Prohibition hit and Dunn got into bootlegging, he invited Leroy up to DC as head bartender at the Moonlight Club.

Leroy leaned forward on the mahogany bar. "I hear it was the boy of Willard Reynolds—the fella who died in the gutter after drinking here. That true?"

Before Boyle could answer, he felt a hand on his shoulder and turned to see Mick, one of the fellas who ran errands for Johnny. "Mr. Dunn wants to see you in his office."

Johnny Dunn was taking laps around his desk, mumbling numbers under his breath.

"Hi, Johnny," Boyle said. "I—"

But the short, balding man raised a stubby finger in his direction and continued with his routine. Boyle stood and waited.

When he finished a few minutes later, Johnny Dunn nodded toward the solitary leather chair sitting atop a spotless hardwood floor at the center of the office. Once Boyle sat down, Johnny Dunn said, "Do you know what makes me successful in this business?"

Boyle shrugged. "By the time we were fifteen, you might as well have been selling earplugs to the deaf, Johnny. You got a knack for it."

His boss shook his head. "Not even close. It's because I'm *careful*. Because I imagine everything that could go wrong with the operation before it happens, and I plan for it. But I don't *react*. No. I see where our competitors or government busybodies will strike next, and I *act*. I act in a way that *max*imizes profit and thus, by necessity, *min*imizes violence." He paused. "Do you know me to be a violent man, Boyle?"

"C'mon, Johnny," he said. "We both know the answer to that. *Nine times out of ten, violence is bad for business,* that's what you say. Anyway, can we skip the spiel tonight? I got a date with a bottle that I hope is strong enough to spin me to sleep."

"Postpone it. We got this Willard Jr. issue to deal with. What concerns me is that a sniveling little shit like him can get that close to my number two man, sticking a pistol in his face while he's overseeing a supply pickup."

"Number two, huh?" Boyle still carried his PI ticket, but since the beginning of Prohibition, his client list had dwindled to one.

As long as the Moonlight Club was in business, he didn't need surveillance jobs for suspicious spouses to pay the bills.

Johnny Dunn ignored the quip, instead licking his finger and
rubbing out a smudge at the corner of his desk. "Irv's in there now
with Willard Jr. I don't like it, but sometimes what's hard is necessary,
like pulling teeth."

"You talking literally or figuratively? 'Sides, shouldn't I be the
one working on the kid after he stuck that piece in my face?"

Johnny Dunn shook his head. "Irv has a taste for that sort of
thing. I want you to find out who's behind this. In my experience,
beating it out of them doesn't work as well as you expect."

"What's there to figure out?" Boyle asked. "Willard Jr. and his
old man were close. The boy went nuts when his pa drank himself
dead in our joint. He said it himself."

Johnny Dunn sighed. "One thing I've learned in this business is
that it's rarely that simple. There are powerful interests out there
who would like to see this place reduced to rubble with us inside.
I know you have some contacts who can help you find out if this
was petty revenge or something worse. I see something bigger in
the works." Johnny Dunn closed his eyes and inhaled through his
thick, red nose. "I can *feel* it."

Before Boyle could respond, Irv Redding stumbled through the
office door. Panting, he looked at Johnny Dunn, then Boyle, then
back to the boss. "You better come see this, Johnny."

"This ought to be good," Johnny Dunn said.

"It's Willard Jr., sir. He's dead."

Swollen, purple veins bulged in Willard Jr.'s pallid neck like worms
burrowed beneath the skin. The whites of his eyes were now red,
drained of life, and his cheeks were puffy and criss-crossed with
a maze of burst capillaries. His hands were tied behind his back
and his head tilted backward, Adam's apple prodding cold flesh,
threatening to pierce through.

"The hell happened?" Johnny Dunn asked.

"I ran out for a second to get some supplies," said Irv. "I come
back and find the son of a bitch dead as his old man."

"And looking like his old man, too," Boyle said, examining
the body. "I remember Willard Sr. had the same discoloration of
the skin, swollen veins, red eyes."

"That's bull," Irv said. "The old man died choking on his vomit. He was a drunk, it happens. Willard Jr. hasn't had a drop of booze since he's been here." He paused. "My best guess is Willard Jr. had something on him to take in case things went sideways. He knew what we'd try to get out of him, and he knew he'd squeal."

"Suicide is your theory?" Boyle asked.

"Yeah. I was the last one with him and it's the only possibility that makes sense."

Boyle leaned toward the young corpse. "Making sense can be a wonderful thing," he said. He turned his gaze to Johnny, then to Irv. "But, sometimes, aren't things more interesting when nothing makes sense at all?"

A few silent moments later, Mick joined the three men in the windowless room deep in the belly of the building. "Christ," he said, examining the body. "Looks same as those dead folks at the joint over in Dupont where they had a batch of booze cut with wood alcohol."

"The Rooster Room poisonings?" Boyle asked. "You sure this looks the same?"

Mick nodded. "Sure. I was meeting a gal there and watched half the place stumble out confused, veins bulging, struggling to breathe."

Boyle turned to Johnny. "That stuff's no joke. Any reason to shut down tonight?"

Johnny Dunn closed his eyes and recited numbers in his head with subtle, noiseless movements of his lips. It was as though he were calculating every variable in all of history that had led to that single moment. Then he said, "No reason to think someone spoiled our hooch. We know our sources and there's no indication that Willard Jr. had a drink here. Irv, clean up this mess. Boyle, find out what the hell's going on."

The night was dwindling and, despite the free-flowing drinks and raucous jazz ensemble, the clock on the wall suggested that soon the place would empty and all that would be left were those who ached at the notion of being alone.

Boyle sat at the corner of the bar sipping rye whiskey. "You plan to perch yourself on that stool all night, Mr. Boyle?" Leroy asked with a grin.

"What, I'm not good company?"

"Company got nothin' to do with it. I get to rest all day before I'm back at it tomorrow night. My guess is Johnny's got you running 'round town solving problems."

"Bartenders know all, don't they?"

He topped off Boyle's drink and said, "Ain't a damn secret in this joint that folks can keep from me for more than an hour."

"I don't doubt it." Boyle lit a cigarette and waited for the distinguished lines of the bartender's face to crease from a smile to a portrait of regret.

"It's about the Willard fella and his boy, ain't it?"

Boyle nodded.

Leroy glanced over each shoulder. "I remember the night Willard Sr. died. I was the one serving him. Sure, he came in with whiskey on his breath already, but he only had a few drinks here. For a fella like him, last thing I expected to hear the next morning was that he'd died from too much booze. I'd seen that man drunker than a sailor every Friday and Saturday for half a year." He lowered his head. "But then I think, ain't that only a way for me to make amends for the role I played in his death? I don't know, Mr. Boyle. Way things are these days, it's like any decision we make can lead to a man's downfall. How do you carry on in a world like that?"

Boyle took a drink. "What do you think has existed longer, Leroy, guilt or alcohol?"

"Excuse me, sir?"

"I'm no sir. Which one?"

The bartender pondered the question before answering. "Booze has been around awful long, but I imagine guilt has been there since the start of man. Bible times. It's inherent in us."

"Wrong," Boyle said. The flickering candlelight set his eyes aflame. "The intentional fermentation of alcohol for purposes of ingestion dates back to the Stone Age. Tens of thousands of years ago. The invention of guilt—by weak men who sought to order society as they saw fit but lacked the strength to do it by force—occurred much later."

Silence filled the club as the jazz ensemble finished their final set, the wail of the trumpet evaporating into the smoky, windowless room. "I'm afraid I don't follow," said Leroy.

"As you reflect on the choices you make, I want to remind you which plays a more fundamental role in our civilization. When guilt wins, *they* win. When alcohol wins—when liberty wins—*we* win." He lifted his whiskey glass. "I can feel it, Leroy. I can feel life in all its wonder when this elixir burns my belly. It isn't sin; it's life itself."

At that, both men turned and saw a woman with a narrow nose, thin lips, and bobbed dark hair fill the doorway. The pin affixed to her dress signified membership in the Woman's Christian Temperance Movement, but he had met her years earlier when she hired him to tail her wayward husband.

Boyle waved her over.

She took the seat and said, "Leroy, darling, be a doll and fetch me a Corpse Reviver."

"Yes, Miss Rebecca," he said, already prepping the glass.

"Thanks for coming," Boyle said without looking up.

"Oh, it's not like I have anything better to do at this hour."

They sat in silence until Leroy served the drink. She had a sip and relented to a smile that she couldn't have fought off with every ounce of will in her.

"What's the latest with your teetotaling friends?" asked Boyle.

"That's it? Right to business?"

"Business is all you get at four in the morning."

She stuck out her lower lip, imitating a pout. "But we agreed, didn't we, that this was the safest time for me to stop by? So that my teetotaling friends, as you call them, don't catch wind of our meetings?" Her drink was half gone, and she signaled with a dimpled smile for Leroy to start fixing another. "They're not wrong on everything you know," she continued. "If their husbands weren't such brutes coming home drunk and doing Lord knows what to them every Saturday night, they wouldn't have it out for you and your spirits."

"Plenty of blame to go around for the ills of the world," Boyle said.

"I must say, my life has improved since my husband died."

"I'm sure he's in a better place."

"Hell?" She shrugged. "It might give this desolate rock a run for its money."

Leroy lifted the rye bottle to Boyle, and he shook his head and pushed the empty glass forward, as though betraying an old friend. "I'm tired, Rebecca. I spent part of my evening with a pistol in my face and I'm trying to figure out why. What do you got for me?"

"There's no question that the Anti-Saloon League is hiring undercover agents to get involved with some of the saloons and speakeasies. It's their thinking that the feds aren't enforcing anything so it's their holy duty to act by any means necessary. I'm not privy to the details nor have I heard anything specific about your establishment."

"That connected to the Rooster Room poisoning?"

"Can't say for certain but I'll keep my ear to the ground."

"What about Willard Reynolds?" Boyle asked.

"The dead one?"

"I mean his son, Willard Jr."

Rebecca started on her second drink and slid a generous bill across the bar toward Leroy. "I've observed him with some of the others, part of the groups of young men who want to join the ranks. He seems to be quite involved."

"With anything in particular?"

She shrugged. "I can look into it. Why? Would you like me to speak with him?"

"Sure," Boyle said. He stood and adjusted his hat and nodded to Leroy. "You can check in with your husband while you're at it."

As he walked home, Boyle watched the orange glow of dawn rise above the Tidal Basin and saturate the waning night sky. The majestic monuments reminded him of man's obsession with legacy, but the apathetic manner with which night traded shifts with day assured him that no stone structure could memorialize the fleeting nature of existence. We were meant to disappear, he thought. Only once we accepted and embraced that fundamental truth could we truly live.

When he returned to his cramped apartment, he fried an egg and drank a warm glass of milk and slept for a few hours. He dreamed vigorously. As though his subconscious was alarmed by the listless manner with which he carried himself by day and sought to shake him from his waking slumber by presenting its vilest concoctions of the mind. That night, his subconscious shunned the strictures of reality and Willard Jr.'s bullet pierced Boyle's brow. At once, he was a boy again, his mother at the Sunday night dinner table trying to wipe the wound from his forehead, insisting he was making a fool of himself showing his face to their church friends like that. Boyle tried to sit still like a good boy, but he couldn't

help but squirm as his mother's finger excavated the shards of
skull and rubbery brain matter beneath.

He woke to the midmorning sun and scratched his forehead
and, after the customary internal quarrel, rose to face the day.

The only person in the bar that morning was Gordie, Mick's
eighteen-year-old cousin whom Johnny paid two bucks a day to
do chores. Boyle found the young man, built like a lineman and
already balding, emptying cases of liquor behind the bar.

"Hey, Gordie."

"Mr. Boyle," he said with a wayward smile.

Boyle pulled a cigarette from his pocket and lit a match. "You
were around last night, yeah?"

"Sure was."

"You help out with the Willard boy?"

"Dragged his ass upstairs and tied him up."

"How'd he seem to you?"

"How do you figure?"

"Drunk? Acting funny?"

Gordie shook his head. "Sort of dazed, but sober." He paused.
"Irv was acting funny about it."

"How so?"

Gordie scanned the room before responding. "Made sure he
was in there alone with him. I stood outside and waited. Didn't
hear much. Then Irv came out and said no one in besides for
him."

"Then what?" Boyle asked.

"He came back about twenty minutes later. Went in and came
out white as a sheet. Said Willard Jr. was dead."

Boyle nodded. "He seemed surprised?"

Gordie shrugged. "Far as I could tell."

Boyle smoked his cigarette and Gordie wiped his sweat-
dampened brow and grabbed a soda pop. Boyle closed his eyes
and felt the hot smoke in his throat and keyed in on the unique
creaks, like fingerprints, signaling the descent down the stairs
from the offices above. He took one last drag—resisting the allure
of the clinking bottles—before opening his eyes to find Mick
staring at him.

"Thank God you're here, Boyle," he said. "Johnny's losing his
shit. You better get up there."

Before following, Boyle turned back to the bar. "Hey Gordie, you ever seen a snake shed its skin?"

"Say what?"

"It's a hell of a thing. They leave the dead part behind but come out just the same."

Irv was already there. He stood in the corner and watched Johnny Dunn, on his hands and knees, scrub the crevices of his desk with a toothbrush.

"Shoes," he hollered as Boyle opened the door. "Take off the damn shoes."

Boyle slid them off and approached the chair before the desk. "What's the problem, Johnny?" he asked. "Besides for dust build-up."

Moments passed with no response but for vigorous brushing and Johnny's quickening breaths. When he emerged, he was beet red and sweating. "Got the message this morning—there's a blown still out at our source near Leesburg."

Boyle shrugged. "Pain in the ass, but we've got other sources."

Johnny shook his head. "That's just the start. An hour later, word comes through that a truck expected in this afternoon had an axle snap and the whole shipment's busted. We don't even have enough supply to get us through the night."

"Hell of a coincidence," Irv offered from the corner.

Boyle turned to him. "Mark Twain was born and died in the years Halley's Comet appeared seventy-five years apart."

"Shut up, Boyle," Johnny said. "There's no question the Anti-Saloon League is behind this. Word is out that the mayor's stopping by tonight—the perfect time to target us. And you know Congressman Buckner, one of our few allies on the Hill? He was an old fraternity man with Willard Reynolds. I already got a call from him saying we need to stop bringing attention to the joint—and that if he finds out there's any funny business behind Willard's death, we're dealing with the teetotalers alone." He paused to catch his breath. "You learn anything last night?"

Boyle still had his eye on Irv. "Nothing. Those pious types are a crafty bunch. Lotta hours of the day with unsullied minds. No surprise they come up with a clever idea or two."

"I can handle the supply problem, boss," Irv said.

Johnny glared at him. "Yeah? How's that?"

"You know Geary, the fella in Baltimore who we get a shipment from every few weeks?"

"Yeah."

"He keeps a stash on hand and uses it in situations like these to strengthen connections. Jacks up the price for short notice but nothing crazy."

"How do you know this?" Johnny asked. "And why haven't I heard it before?"

Irv shrugged. "Never had this issue before."

Johnny grumbled as though half-satisfied with the answer.

"It's never smart to pay up for a last-minute batch," Boyle said. "You know what those bootleggers will do to the stuff to make some extra bucks."

"He's trustworthy," Irv said. "Besides, we already buy from him."

Both men turned to face their boss. After a heavy breath, Johnny said, "Irv, set it up. We can't afford to go dry this weekend."

"It'll be here," Irv said. He headed for the door.

Once he was gone, Johnny turned to Boyle. "You got something to say, smart guy?"

Boyle lit a cigarette and shrugged. "Can't be right without risking being wrong."

A note waited for Boyle at the bar. "You see who left this?" he asked Gordie.

"Some kid," he said. "Said it was for your eyes only."

Boyle cracked the seal. It read: *Prescott's at noon. You're expected. RB.*

The thick heat made the midday walk to Logan Circle a pilgrimage. As he walked, sweat dampening his linen suit, Boyle considered that his livelihood had turned him into a man of the night. A creature who emerged only to poison and be poisoned in the wee hours under cover of darkness. The sun's glare an enemy, he yearned for the comfort of the shadows.

Prescott's was a speakeasy housed underneath a pharmacy that served a high-end clientele. Inside, Rebecca sat at a lonesome table drinking champagne and nibbling on crab cakes.

Boyle joined her and the barman greeted him with a whiskey. "Anything to eat?" he asked.

Boyle shook his head. "Hope I'm not picking up the bill," he said as Rebecca slurped an oyster with as much grace as possible.

She tilted her head and cleared her throat, and, in her soft features, Boyle recognized her shameful delight in knowing something he didn't. "I've caught wind of a plan tonight at your spot. I take it you've had issues with your regular supplier?"

Boyle took some drink.

"Of course, you have," she said. "I know Johnny's careful, but the replacement booze will be adulterated. Same MO as the Rooster Room. You have to shut down tonight."

Boyle chuckled.

"Is this funny to you?"

"They say in the midst of suffering is when men prove their worth."

She leaned forward. "What are *you* worth, Mr. Boyle? Far as I can tell, nothing is worth much to you."

"I have an acute fascination with lovely and useless things."

"Well fascinate yourself with this—there's a plot to target the poisonings to particular patrons at your joint tonight."

He pondered for a moment. "How could they target the poisoning without help from the bartender?"

Rebecca shrugged. "Men are creatures of habit—they drink what they drink. A marking perhaps? Otherwise, it seems it would require direction."

"Men drink what they drink," Boyle repeated. He downed the last of the whiskey and rose. "Thank you, Rebecca."

"I'll hear from you tomorrow?" she asked.

"I hope so."

Boyle returned to the Moonlight Club at seven that evening—an hour before it opened. As expected, he found the barroom empty but for Johnny and Irv at a table, Mick and Gordie unloading the new shipment, and Leroy tending bar.

"All whiskey and gin?" Boyle asked Irv.

"You bet."

"Well done," he said. "Plenty to get us through the weekend."

"My pleasure."

Boyle selected a couple of new bottles and took them to the bar. "Shall we see if it's any good? Leroy, fix us a round. What'll you have, Irv? Johnny?"

"I'll pass," said Irv.

"Nonsense," said Johnny Dunn. "Boyle's right, you earned it. Let's have a round."

Irv dabbed the sweat in the valleys on his forehead with his handkerchief. "All right. Gin martini."

They watched in silence as Leroy fixed the drink, the only sound the clink of ice against glassware. "You fellas joining me?" Irv asked as Leroy served it up.

"Sure," said Johnny. "But only if you break out the special reserve you were bragging about. You know, the good stuff for the mayor?"

Irv chewed his lip like it was steak fat, forehead scrunched as though he was pondering every decision he'd ever made.

"Special reserve?" Boyle asked.

"Uh-huh."

Boyle returned to the cases and went through the inventory. He noticed that several of the whiskey bottles had a small diamond-shaped marking on the neck.

"Ones with the diamond?" Boyle asked.

Irv's face was still. In the background, Boyle saw that Leroy's wasn't.

"Can I see that?" the bartender asked.

Boyle brought it over and Leroy examined the bottle like a precious artifact. His worn face reflected a keen familiarity with evil, but a simultaneous exasperation with its ubiquity.

"The mark," he said, eyes on Irv. "It's the same as the one on the bottle for Willard Reynolds Sr. the night he died." Leroy's gaze shifted to Boyle. "He said the same thing then—that it was a special reserve bottle for old man Reynolds."

"You watch your mouth, boy," Irv spat, rising from the table. "You watch your mouth spreading nonsense like that."

"Sit down, Irv," Johnny belted. "*Now.*"

Irv shot one more look at Leroy and complied. He took a breath. "Look, Johnny, I don't know anything about whatever's going on here. Leroy's lying through his crooked teeth, and I can't say why." He turned to Boyle. "Unless *you* put him up to it."

"Tell me," Boyle asked, "why is it that the truth is often so hideous?"

Irv didn't respond.

"Because the truth reflects reality and, in reality, people do hideous things. And they do the *most* hideous things in the name of good." He picked up the bottle and pointed to the small diamond. "Does this mean anything to you, Irv?"

"Not a thing."

Boyle retrieved a glass, uncorked the bottle, and poured two fingers of the golden liquor. "Care for a taste?"

Irv shook his head. "I can't stand whiskey. The damn stuff makes me sick."

Boyle swirled the liquor in the tumbler, eyeing it with wonder. "I'm sorry, Johnny," he said. "We better shut things down tonight."

"Why's that?"

"Irv's with the Anti-Saloon League. He's a member of their undercover army trying to bring joints down from within."

Irv's mouth fell open but, by then, Mick and Gordie hovered behind his chair.

"You can thank Leroy's keen eye for confirming it," Boyle continued. "See, the mark signifies bottles poisoned with wood alcohol. Irv's first victim was Willard Sr. He instructed Leroy to give him the so-called special reserve—a targeted killing. Irv knew that Congressman Buckner might go sour on us if his old college buddy croaked here. But that wasn't the only reason he did it. Willard Jr. was already involved with the Anti-Saloon adolescent army, and it was a way to turn an eager young man into a devoted fanatic. A mad dog to sic on their enemies. That way, when Willard Jr. came for me, it would look like vengeance—a crime of passion—not a choreographed political killing."

"But Willard Jr. botched the job," Johnny Dunn said.

"He sure did, poor kid. And after we dragged him back here, Irv knew he wouldn't stand up to our questioning. So, he slipped him the same medicine his old man got so he wouldn't spill."

"This is all horseshit," Irv said, hunched in his chair, voice shaking.

Boyle ignored him. "Next step wasn't as original: blowing up stills and jacking trucks. See, Irv needed a way to substitute the shipment with one he had control over. Can you imagine the shit storm if—on top of the congressman's buddy dying—the *mayor* did? Or a few of DC's finest? We'd be finished. We'd crumble and they'd move on to the next target in their holy war, God knows how many bodies in their wake."

At that, Irv's face contorted to a smirk which turned into a jubilant howl. "That's all you got, is it? No proof at all? Only wild accusations from a freak like Boyle?" He turned to Johnny Dunn. "Johnny, you can't be buying this. How long have we known each other? You wouldn't do me in without a shred of evidence, would you?"

Johnny eyed the bottle with the mark before turning to Boyle. "How do you know all this?"

"Tips from friends in convenient places." Boyle had lots of friends in convenient places, all relationships he'd cultivated during the years he'd gumshoed for anyone willing to pony up a retainer. "I'd be happy to bring them in to corroborate. Some of them are right here—Leroy, Gordie." Johnny glanced at each, and they gave their boss a solemn nod.

Irv took a long inhale, as though unsure of how many he had left. "If this is all true, Boyle, you know who my friends are. The most powerful men in the world down the street. If you kill me, they'll come for you."

Boyle lifted the tumbler and swirled the whiskey in his palm. "Who said anything about killing?" He presented the glass to Irv. "All I ask is that you take a drink."

DIANA GOULD

Possessory Credit

FROM *Entertainment to Die For*

DAVID MICHAEL MENDELSOHN had written many murders, so he didn't think it would be hard to commit one. If it's true that "a coward dies a thousand deaths; a hero dies but one," it was equally true that a writer kills every time he puts himself in the mindset of a killer. And once he murdered Andrew Lovekin, David Michael Mendelsohn was sure he'd never have to kill again.

The idea came as most of his ideas did: a tug in the gut; embryonic, inchoate. He was having lunch with his agent at Estrusco, a trendy Italian restaurant in Brentwood. At every table, men and women dressed in their best "business casual" schmoozed and networked over delicious expense account meals. The room thrummed with a mixture of adrenaline, bluster, hope, and fear.

Over *insalata carciofi*, his agent told him the good news. *Sins of the Angels*, a movie David had written, would be showcased at Cannes. Not opening night, but still. David was elated. Writing that script was one of the hardest things he'd ever done. He felt it was his best, most personal work yet. Going with it to Cannes would finally be the recognition he'd longed for.

But with the *spaghetti alle vongole* came the rest of the news. The studio was sending the director and the star but would not spend money to send the writer.

"But I wrote the movie! It was completely original! They wouldn't have had anything to work on without me!"

"I know. 'In the beginning was the word.' Believe me, I sympathize," said his agent. "But in the end, it's a director's medium." The director, Andrew Lovekin, would represent the film, and of course, Mariana Winters, its star. Nobody really cares who wrote the movie.

David sat in his car, parked on Sunset, staring at the billboard promoting "Andrew Lovekin's *Sins of the Angels*." The ad featured a close-up of Mariana Winters, staring out to sea, wind whipping the hair around her beautiful face. Her expression was haunted yet radiant, fragile yet fierce. Bold letters bigger than the title proclaimed, "An Andrew Lovekin Film. Starring Mariana Winters." On the bottom, "written by David Michael Mendelsohn" was barely readable in letters squished together to accommodate the names of the other actors, producers, editor, composer, music supervisor, production designer, and director of photography.

David and Andy had gone to film school and made their first film together, written by David, directed by Andy. A horror movie on a film school budget, it became a cult classic, and launched both their careers. Each got an agent, each got jobs. Andy was the studio's bold choice to direct a film that was greenlit and ready to go; David was given a crack at adapting a novel the studio had bought. Andy brought his movie in on time and under budget; it made back its investment, so was considered a success. David's contracted "three drafts and a polish" took almost three years. Not because he was a slow writer, although he was. But by the time he got his notes on each draft from each producing partner and studio executive, there was a lot of downtime. His agent suggested he take other work between drafts and got him an uncredited rewrite on another writer's script. After his last contracted polish was complete, the studio gave his script to another writer. Still not happy, they gave it to two more writers before shelving the project, determining that period pieces would not sell overseas.

 And so it went. David worked constantly and made a good living. He added his middle name to his credit, thinking it would give him more gravitas, and it did. He became a well-respected screenwriter, to whom producers turned when they couldn't make a script work. It's not unusual for a studio to go through many writers to get a draft that gets the go-ahead. Guild rules allowed credit to be granted only to two. While David was caught in the treadmill of "development hell," working on films that didn't get made, or not receiving credit on ones that did, Andy made one film after another and his reputation grew. Whatever was good in a movie was attributed to him; critics pointed to moments that were "pure Lovekin." Finally, he acquired enough clout to get the prized "possessory credit," a contractual guarantee that any film he directed would be billed as "Andrew Lovekin's . . . [title.]"

The idea that had begun as a tug in the gut twisted into a knot as David remembered the night Andy called, saying he had an idea for a movie. They hadn't worked together since film school.

"It's for Mariana Winters." They were having dinner together at Kaiseki, another expensive restaurant where the elite of show business could go without being bothered by anyone except each other. By this time, Andy had a development deal at the studio and could pick up the tab.

Mariana Winters had been one of those young actresses whose train-wreck lives provide a running drama unfolding on the covers of tabloid magazines—the twenty-first-century equivalent of the nineteenth-century serial novel. Each weekly installment—falling in love, gaining weight, breaking up, losing weight—bulimic?—car crash, rehab, relapse—had been headline news.

"Is she still alive?"

"And how." His sly smile made David think he must be sleeping with her. "She's got this incredible quality. Sexy, vulnerable, tempestuous, kind of a gutter-tramp sensuality wrapped up in a hungry little girl . . ."

David was sure Andy was sleeping with her. He usually made conquests of the women he directed.

"She had to leave the business for a while to get clean, but she's back. I want to develop a story for her. Something where she can be wild and angry; smart, sexy . . ."

"Like what?"

Andy held up his thumb and index fingers, creating an imaginary frame. "It's the beach at dawn." He moved his hands, simulating a camera panning. "A woman stumbles down to the water's edge. She's in evening dress—plunging neckline, expensive jewels . . . her shoes in her hand . . . she seems haunted, desperate . . . she takes a few steps in . . . foam swirls at her feet . . . she turns to look behind her, we move in close . . . she's terrified . . ."

David could hardly wait to hear what happened next. "Yes . . . ?"

Andy shrugged. "You're the writer." He signaled for the check. "See if you can take it from there."

Andy suggested David get to know Mariana, with the goal of creating a story that captured her essence. He was sure he could get funding if they had the right script.

David met with Mariana a few times, sometimes with Andy, sometimes alone. He did find her all the things that Andy had suggested: vulnerable, sexy, fragile, tempestuous—and insufferable. The years she'd spent on magazine covers had given her a sense of her own importance that David found hard to share. He spent hours listening to operatic arias of self-involvement. She fed on excitement like a vampire on blood; being stuck in traffic was tantamount to being detained at Guantanamo.

Wildly jealous, she found ways to monitor Andy's texts and emails. When she was with David, she badgered him with questions about what Andy did when he was away from her. David often found himself lying to cover for Andy, to avoid the tearful tirades that came with the truth.

Andy felt that being a director required arrogance. He broke dates and told lies with abandon, tantalizing Mariana with his mixture of ardor and indifference. He enraged her, knowing that their reconciliations would be all the more torrid. He was unfaithful every chance he got. A director with a studio deal and possessory credit, he got a lot of chances.

David soon grew weary of their fights. But watching them together did give him a sense of the character he thought she could best play.

He came up with the notion of a gambling addiction, as a metaphor for her insatiable hunger, and decided that the beach Andy had pictured was Monte Carlo, the morning after she'd lost everything and more. He had her character sell her necklace to pay off her debts, becoming entangled with an international crime ring and a jewel thief who was really an Interpol agent. But her gambling addiction caused her to sabotage herself at the worst possible moment, and this layer added depth to what was otherwise a nifty little thriller.

Andy and Mariana loved the idea. David went off to write it.

Responding to an ad in the Writers Guild newsletter, he rented a cabin in Arrowhead, surrounded by woods. The landlady lived down the road and was used to renting to writers. The rent included a daily delivery of supplies and a guarantee of being left alone.

He began the painstaking work of constructing a story. He wrote detailed biographies of all his characters, until he knew them as a mother knows her child. He wrote ideas for scenes on index cards, and put them up all around the cabin, so he could rearrange and cut them as needed. He spent days coming up with plot points that would turn the action in surprising ways.

Writing had always been hard for David, and this one with its intricate plot lines and intersecting stories was particularly challenging. Sometimes he'd get so stuck, he could only lie in bed, knowing in his heart of hearts that he hadn't the talent to pull it off. His stomach hurt; his head ached. He imagined he had cancer. He hoped he had cancer; it was his only way out.

Then he'd wake up, with a glimmer of an idea, which he knew was stupid, but he'd write it down anyway, and as he did, he could see where it could lead. He'd massage it, nurture it, and then he saw how this idea could be a bridge to the climax, but he'd need a scene to justify it, and that's what he could put in the place he'd been stuck.

He suffered and struggled in solitary battle, working forward and backward, in anguish as intense as labor pains.

Miraculously—no other word would do—what came forth was not only a screenplay that was as well-constructed as the cabin he'd written it in, but a reflection of his truest self, expressing in ways he could only marvel at, his most deeply held views about life. Commercial, yes, but idiosyncratic; nobody could have written it but him.

He delivered it, like giving birth to a child.

Which, as this was Hollywood, was wrenched from his arms, to become "Andrew Lovekin's *Sins of the Angels*, a film by Andrew Lovekin."

He'd need an alibi.

Because, he thought, as the idea to kill Andy took malignant hold of him, among the things he meant to accomplish, not getting caught was first on the list.

He went to work.

He approached the project as he would a screenplay, but this time, instead of being blocked, he was fueled; animated by hatred he found strangely exhilarating. He put notes on index cards, knowing he would destroy them later. He did all his work on computers in public libraries, running searches that could not be traced back to him. He developed a list of possible suspects, writing backstories on each, as he did for the characters in his scripts. He spitballed alternative narratives, determining evidence he could plant that would suggest them. He wasn't planning to frame anyone. He had too much of a conscience to want anyone to go to jail for his crime. He just needed to confuse the police, leading them down wrong paths, away from him.

He contacted a source he'd used for a script about street gangs, and asked how he could get false ID. It was surprisingly easy; for eight hundred dollars, he was able to get a driver's license with his picture and someone else's name. He used that to open a bank account and get a credit card.

With his new identity, he rented a car and drove to Vegas. Stopping in a Western wear store, he shed his screenwriter uniform of jeans, sneakers, and T-shirt, buying instead work boots, tougher jeans, an engraved silver belt buckle, a fringed vest to go over a Jack Daniel's T-shirt, and a wool felt Stetson. As he'd hoped, he blended with the crowd at a gun show, where he bought a gun and silencer. He went to a shooting range and took lessons, becoming confident in his ability to use his weapon.

When he returned, he examined his evil plan from every angle, searching out and fixing its flaws. When it worked like a Rubik's Cube, he destroyed his notes, called Andy, and suggested lunch.

Over seafood salads at Mersea at the Shore, David pitched an idea for a movie they could do together. A few years back, a beautiful "actress/model/whatever" had been found shot to death, in her Mercedes, on Mulholland Drive. The case had made big headlines. Her name was Jaycee Peyton, but because of a religious icon on her dashboard, she'd been dubbed "The Mulholland Madonna." The police had pursued various avenues of investigation, but nobody was ever charged. Why not do a film about her?

"What's the angle?" Andy's eyes darted around the room. It was a habit David found exasperating, as if Andy was always looking to see who might have more value to him than the person he was talking to.

"It's *Laura* meets *L.A. Confidential*," said David, knowing those were two of Andy's favorite films. "Good cop, investigating the crime, vs. bad cop—maybe he was sleeping with her, using her to find out dirt about her other johns, and shaking them down for hush money."

Andy's interest was piqued.

"Was there really such a cop?"

David shrugged. "Who knows? There could have been. She's a high-priced call girl, right? The guys she's sleeping with have secrets to protect. Like, let's say there's one who's pulling some financial shenanigans, and she finds out about it."

Andy mulled it over, no longer scanning the room, thoughtful. "Did they ever find out who killed her?"

"No. Maybe we could actually solve the case. Wouldn't that make a great story. But in any case, there's great material to work with. Wait till you read some of this stuff." He patted his pockets. "Do you have your phone? I must have left mine at home."

Andy handed David his iPhone, and David used it to pull up stories about the case, knowing there'd now be a record of Andy's interest. Andy read and was intrigued.

"It would be great for Mariana," Andy said, clicking on one link after another.

"That's what I thought too."

This time, David insisted on picking up the check.

David suggested developing the story together, and asked if they could meet at Andy's house, rather than the studio. Andy was surprised; having his own production company with offices and assistants were perks he was proud to have negotiated. But David said the studio made him nervous, and this would be more like their days at film school.

That way, David made sure that all the research on suspects in the unsolved murder was done on Andy's computer, all the calls placed from Andy's phones.

"I called Detective Childs, the lead investigator, but my name means nothing. Maybe if the call came from you?" suggested David. Andy left a message that Andrew Lovekin wanted to speak with Detective Childs and got an immediate callback. But when Andy explained the project, Detective Childs said he could not discuss a case that was still open.

David pretended disappointment, but all that really mattered to him was that there was a record of Andy's interest. He suggested Andy put out word through his publicist that he was researching the case, urging anyone with information to come forward. David said they would fictionalize what they found, but they'd get better material from the true details.

People came forward, and one person led to another. Jaycee Peyton had cut a swath through the upper echelons of Hollywood, as well as its seamy underside. Her clients included businessmen, actors, agents, and executives. She was distributing drugs; had a pimp boyfriend who beat her. Her roommate said Jaycee had found out something incriminating about one of her johns, but she wasn't sure which one. The roommate had told this to the police, but to her knowledge, they hadn't followed up.

"The crooked cop!" said David. "Life imitating art!"

Between them, David and Andy compiled a list of over a dozen people who might have motives to kill her.

"Who do you think really did it?" asked Andy. "The corrupt cop? One of the guys she slept with? The dealer she was fronting for?"

"My money's on the john she got the goods on. The financial shenanigans guy. And the bad cop wouldn't follow up on it, because he was getting a cut. I don't know if that's what happened, but that would make the best story."

All David really cared about was making it appear that one of the people suspected in the old case might have killed Andy for getting too close to the truth.

Once, when they were working together, David ventured, "I wonder . . ." but then changed his mind about saying what he'd been thinking.

"What?" asked Andy.

"Nothing," said David. "Only that . . . never mind."

"Come on."

"Mariana. Do you think she might be too . . ."

Andy waited.

". . . old?"

"She's thirty-three!"

"Exactly. Jaycee Peyton was twenty-four. Our girl should be young and hot."

"Mariana is young and hot."

"Right." And after a pause, "You're the director."

He changed the subject, feigning a desire for a certain kind of cheese that could only be gotten at a specialty cheese shop in

Beverly Hills. He borrowed Andy's car and keys to make a run for it—and made a duplicate house key on his way back. He asked Andy for the alarm code, so he could let himself back in.

When he got back, Andy was poring over an online casting directory, checking photos and resumes of younger actresses.

"What about Hilary Wilde?" said David, suggesting an actress he knew from his gym, and showing Andy her headshot online.

Andy wasn't familiar with her work, so David introduced them. They met at a trendy new club. David knew Andy well enough to be pretty sure, when he left them at the end of the evening, where it would go from there.

It did.

The next time David saw Hilary at the gym, she was excited at Andrew Lovekin's interest in her, and the possibility she might be in his new film. David warned her that Andy could be unreliable; he urged her to barrage him with gifts, phone calls, and funny, sexy emails, to keep herself in the forefront of his consciousness.

Then he took Mariana to dinner, and bemoaned Andy's interest in a younger actress to play the part he was writing specifically for her. Mariana wanted to know who the younger woman was. David made a show of regretting that he'd said anything, but in trying to take it back, he let slip Hilary's name.

The next time he saw Hilary, he went back with her to her apartment. While there, he managed to filch a toothbrush, and one of her nightgowns hanging on the bathroom door.

A few days before he planned to commit the murder, David put the last piece of the puzzle in place. He told Andy that a friend was in town from England, selling antique jewelry. Incredible pieces, from estate sales all over the English countryside; he could buy one for Mariana, and it might mollify her about Hilary. Only thing is, he'd have to pay cash. His friend would not accept checks or credit cards.

The meeting with the imaginary friend was postponed. But there was now a record of Andy withdrawing twenty-five thousand dollars from one of his accounts.

Satisfied that he had completed the setup, David went off to Arrowhead, renting the same cabin he'd had before.

He drove out early in the morning, but instead of going straight to the cabin, he drove to a dealership in town for an oil change. From the dealer, he called a rental car company, and asked to be picked up. Wearing his vest and Stetson, he used his false ID to rent a car, drove it back to the dealership, and parked a block away. Then, having taken off the vest and hat, he walked back, picked up his own car, and drove it to the cabin.

He met the landlady to get the keys. He told her he'd be holed up writing; he'd prefer not to be disturbed.

"Oh, I always know, when I see your car there, that you're in there working away. I don't know how you do it."

He took the keys and moved in.

He spent the day putting up index cards and timelines all around the cabin walls, for the bogus project he was pretending to write. He made his dinner, burning his steak, filling the house with the aroma of food, and built a fire in the fireplace. He put on a pot of coffee, and turned on his computer, just as he would to pull an all-nighter. He opened his laptop, and left it on, making an adjustment that the screen would stay lit and not go to sleep.

Shortly after dark, with his computer and work light on and his car parked in the driveway, he went out the back window and walked through the woods back to town. He picked up the rental car and drove two hours back to L.A.

It was a little after one when he got to Andy's house. To his dismay, Andy's car was not in the driveway. He'd hoped to enter by stealth, shoot Andy in his sleep, plant the evidence, and drive back to Arrowhead. But Andy wasn't home.

Quelling his rising panic, he decided to enter anyway. He parked a block away. He was dressed all in black, including his sneakers, gloves, and balaclava ski mask which covered his face completely. He carried a satchel. Instead of going through the front door, where the surveillance cameras would have seen him, he went to the back of the property, breast stroked his way through the protective hedge. Out of range of the camera, he scurried to the side of the house where the pool equipment and electric panels were kept. He tripped the fuse that governed the surveillance cameras and eased his way to the side of the house where outdoor steps led to the lower level. He entered through the back, using his spare key and knowledge of the alarm code.

First, he went upstairs to Andy's office. He put research on the Mulholland Madonna on Andy's desk, with detailed files on each one of the suspects.

And a note, pasted together from cut-out letters, "Twenty-five thousand or I tell—or you die."

Making his way to Andy's bedroom, he took Hilary's toothbrush and nightgown from his satchel. He put the toothbrush in the bathroom, the nightgown under a pillow. He put an assortment of illegal drugs in the nightstand by the bed. He took out the gun and silencer, attached one to the other, and stepped into the closet to wait.

It wasn't long before he heard a car pull into the driveway. He heard the front door open, footsteps come upstairs. He heard someone enter the bedroom, but then—nothing. He was expecting to hear Andy emptying his pockets, or turning on the TV, or going into the bathroom. Taking off his clothes, coming into the closet, where David would be waiting for him. Instead, he heard nothing, except the sound of his own heart pounding, and someone else, breathing.

Whoever else was in the room was opening and closing drawers; it sounded like they were ransacking the room. David held his breath. What if they opened the closet? He was sure it wasn't Andy. Who could it be? He wanted to peer through a crack in the closet door, but he dared not move. The next sound he heard was unmistakable: the safety on a gun being released.

Suddenly, David Michael Mendelsohn realized why he had become a writer. He liked to imagine things, not actually do them. He must have been crazy to think he could go through with this. So Andy had taken credit for the work he had done. So someone else got the glory while he did all the work. Was that really so terrible?

Yes! He conjured the image of the poster for "Andrew Lovekin's *Sins of the Angels*," and felt the familiar knot in his gut, grown large and twisted by his rage. He touched the gun at his waist. He took deep, slow, quiet breaths to bring his blood pressure down.

Finally, there was the sound of a car pulling into the driveway. The front door opened, and this time, the footsteps that sauntered up the stairs toward the bedroom were Andy's.

He heard the sharp intake of breath, as Andy took in whoever else was in the room. There was a long silence.

Andy spoke first, in a voice weary and patronizing.

"Okay. You've made your point. Very dramatic. It's no accident you're a great actress. Now, put it down. Better yet, give it to me."

"Where is she? Isn't she with you?" The voice was vulnerable, sexy, fragile, tempestuous: Mariana.

"Who?"

"The one who left this!"

In the closet, David gulped. He'd meant for the police to find the nightgown and suspect Mariana; not for Mariana to find it and actually shoot Andy.

And yet . . . if the end result was the same, where was the harm?

"Where did you find this?" asked Andy, genuinely puzzled.

"Where were you tonight?" Mariana's voice was trembling.

"With David." Then wearily, "Put that down. Better yet, give it to me."

"Liar! You were with her!"

"Who?"

"You mean there's more than one? Does Hilary know you're cheating on her too?"

David could hear Andy take a step forward and stop. He imagined that Mariana must have raised the gun and was holding it on him. That's certainly how he would have written the scene.

"Baby, think it through. What is shooting me going to accomplish? Is it worth spending the rest of your life in jail?"

"Yes! It will be worth it to see you suffer. To watch you die, like I've been dying. I'm dying! I'm already dead; you killed me. Lies do that you know, they kill people, just like bullets . . ." Her voice was starting to break, and with it, David imagined, her resolve. "I could shoot you in the heart and it would make no difference; you have no heart!"

He'd bet anything that the hand that held the gun was trembling along with her voice.

"Baby . . ."

"Don't touch me!"

David heard a door slam closed and lock, and then there was silence.

David listened to the sound of his own breathing. He surmised that Mariana had gone into the bathroom, taking the gun with her.

David imagined Mariana locked in the bathroom with a gun. Would she kill herself? Where was Andy? He should be pounding on the door, begging her to come out. David considered coming out of his hiding place and confessing all he had done. He knew he couldn't bear to have Mariana's suicide on his conscience.

He put a hand on the closet door, opening it just the tiniest crack, to allow him a view of the room. Empty. The bathroom door was closed; Andy had walked out onto the balcony, his back to the room.

Cool, detached, arrogant. Typical!

David took the gun from his waist. He had a clean line of sight. He could shoot Andy now, from the closet. And yet, Mariana was in the bathroom. If she heard the shot and discovered him, all his planning would be in vain.

Suddenly, a shot rang out. He looked at his gun. He had only thought to pull the trigger; he hadn't really done it—had he? No. And yet, Andy fell backward, into the bedroom, blood pouring from his chest. David watched in horror as a man clad in black climbed into the room from the balcony, stood over the bleeding Andy, held a gun to his head at close range, and pulled the trigger; then just as quickly strode back.

The bathroom door opened, and Mariana came out, still holding the gun. She saw Andy and shrieked. The man turned toward her, raising his gun. David heard a shot, much louder than the first two, and the man crumpled.

David stood frozen on the spot. Mariana went to the phone, and quickly dialed 911. Her voice was hysterical as she sobbed into the phone.

"Come quickly! Andrew Lovekin's been shot. A man came in and shot him, I saw him and I . . . I killed him . . ." She broke into sobs. She managed to give the address. "Yes, yes, hurry, please!"

She left the room.

David peered through the crack. Except for the two dead men, the room was empty. As quietly as he could, he came out of the closet, put the gun in the empty satchel, and tiptoed with it back out through the sliding glass doors onto the deck, from which the intruder had come.

He walked quietly down the back stairs to the street and hurried up the block to his rental car. As he drove away, he heard the sirens, and passed the ambulance and police that were arriving at the scene.

He was back in Arrowhead before morning. He parked the rental car and crept through the woods back to his cabin, entering, as he had left, through the window in the rear.

*

It was late afternoon when the police arrived, interrupting David at his desk. With no phone or internet connection in the cabin, David had not yet heard of the death of Andrew Lovekin. He was shocked, devastated by the news. The police asked him about the Mulholland Madonna project. David said that Andy had done research into the case, but so far as David knew, had never found a way to tell the story. They had discussed it from time to time, but David had been spending his time working on something else. He showed them the index cards around the cabin, describing the musical he was working on.

Had Andy told David that he had been one of the men that the Mulholland Madonna had been sleeping with?

"What?" David did not have to feign his astonishment.

"Did you know he was paying Detective Childs to keep his name out of the files?"

"What??" David was almost too flabbergasted to speak.

"We found twenty-five thousand dollars in cash at his house. When we looked into it, we noticed that every time Andrew Lovekin had withdrawn twenty-five thousand dollars, twenty-five thousand dollars showed up in Detective Childs's account. Starting just after the murder of Jaycee Peyton."

"But Andy didn't kill the Mulholland Madonna." David's mind was reeling. "Did he?"

"No. He was only one of the men paying off Childs to make evidence disappear. He's a real piece of work, Detective Childs. We've suspected for years that he was disposing of evidence in exchange for payoffs, but it took Lovekin's murder to prove it."

"Is that who killed Andy? Detective Childs?"

"No. Turns out, Detective Childs was using Jaycee Peyton to shake down her other johns." The look of astonishment on David's face caused the cop to add, "I know. It's like something out of an Andrew Lovekin film."

David bristled. "But you said he wasn't the one who killed Andy."

"No. The man who shot Lovekin, whom Mariana Winters shot, was Harold Rosenbach."

"Who?" The name was unfamiliar to David.

"Another one of Jaycee Peyton's johns. A business manager. He'd been pulling all sorts of financial shenanigans with his clients' money. Peyton found out and threatened to go public. Rosenbach killed her. But his name never appeared in the files, because Childs had been shaking him down, so they both had something to hide. But Lovekin discovered the truth. Evidently, he was obsessed with finding the killer. We found files of research in his office, and his phone logs show calls to everyone involved. When Childs found out Lovekin was doing the film, he must have tipped off Rosenbach. Rosenbach killed Lovekin, with the gun he'd used on the Mulholland Madonna. If Mariana Winters hadn't been in the bathroom and seen it, he'd have gotten away with it."

David blinked, trying to absorb all that he was being told.

"Good thing you were here the whole time. We went to your apartment, and it was tossed. If you hadn't been here writing, you might have gotten killed too."

"No," David stammered. "I never left . . ."

"We know. Your landlady said your car's been here all night. Well, Lovekin's obsession paid off. He solved the crime and got killed in the process. Amazing story, isn't it? Pure Lovekin."

A short time later, David's agent again took him to lunch at Estrusco. He waited until the *bistecca fiorentina* to broach the delicate subject. The death of Andrew Lovekin would make a sensational movie; he felt sure he could interest at least one studio in the project, if David would agree to write it. He had known Andy the longest and had written two of his films; also, the case was so complex and intricate, it would take a David Michael Mendelsohn to tell the story. David demurred. Andy had been his friend. Writing a film based on his death would feel exploitive.

"Even for two five plus points? I'll bet we could get that."

David shook his head. The material was too close, too personal. Writing it would open wounds that had not yet healed. It would take more than money for it to be worth his while.

"More than money? Like what?"

He smiled, as the knot in his gut finally unraveled.

"Possessory credit."

My Savage Year

FROM *Southwest Review*

WHEN I WAS a senior in high school, my biology teacher murdered his entire family and got away with it. I'm going to lie to you
about it now, but first I need you to understand this much: He did
it. He killed them all, and in the end they let him go.

I've been trying to tell this story ever since. Trying to find the
right lies I need to tell the truth.

See me back then, on that Monday morning near the start of
1995. How I sat in my car in a strip mall parking lot down the
street from my high school, waiting for the bell to ring. My hair
long on the top, shaved on the sides. Four earrings in my left ear
and three in my right. Wearing flannel and Doc Martens. Tapes
scattered on the floor, band names like Ween and Butthole Surfers
and Nine Inch Nails and My Life with the Thrill Kill Kult and the
Dead Milkmen and the Flaming Lips and Suicidal Tendencies and
Ministry and Black Flag. Under the driver's seat hid a sawed-off
shotgun that I carried in my car that whole crazy savage year. We'll
talk about the shotgun later.

See the dirty cotton sky. An Ozarks winter storm clicked sleet
against the windows. I sat in the cold, ate a sausage biscuit from
the McDonald's drive-in, watched my classmates heading to class
across the street. The school parking lot full of old beaters and
a few rich-kid Mustangs and SUVs. Neil Young was on the tape
deck, telling me that I was like a hurricane. I did not think I was
like a hurricane. I thought I was like an iceberg floating deep in
a black ocean, with just the tip breaking the water. Like a lot of

teenage thoughts, this one was overwrought and dramatic and also true.

The last of the students filed into the school. I turned down the music so I could hear the tardy bell ring. I turned the music back up. This dread at the heart of me—not some premonition, nothing like that, just the deep dread that high school plants in you, especially if you have ever been one of the picked-last, the weirdos. The fear that this is all life is or can be, that all the doors marked EXIT only open onto brick walls.

My parents and my teachers always told me I wasn't living up to my potential. My biggest fear was that maybe I was.

I fished out the second sausage biscuit. I chewed without tasting and looked out blindly into the ice.

That is how I missed the announcement of the murders.

Before the novels or the TV shows, before even my early-twenties stint as a music journalist, the first thing I ever got paid to write was in my hometown newspaper. The year before the murders, I'd written a column for the school paper about why I hated my hometown. The opinion-section editor of the local paper called my journalism teacher, Mrs. Ray, and offered to pay me to print the article on their opinion page. I had written about the blandness, the whiteness. The protests outside the movie theater when they showed *The Last Temptation of Christ.* The people angry over teaching evolution in the schools, who called the whole idea from goo to you, via the zoo.

I talked about the boring surface. I didn't talk about the things that boiled underneath. I didn't talk about the Nazi skinheads who lurked in the city square, or the people sizzling their insides with meth like they were cauterizing some wound inside them. I didn't talk about the way the town gnawed on anything different, tried to chew it off you.

I wrote that even though it was bland it was my home, and that even though I'd leave as soon as I could, I'd come back someday.

That last part was bullshit. All I ever wanted to do was leave.

The school was cave-warm against the winter storm when I came inside an hour later. Kids clotted the hall. The bell had rung; they should have been rushing to their next class. But they didn't. Every eye wide open. The babble of their voices had a strange new note to it. Gooseflesh bloomed on my arms, the way they say it does just before a lightning strike. I heard the words *all dead.* I heard the words *just a baby.*

Something is happening. Something is wrong.

I passed Amy C. standing in the center of a ring of girls, weeping so that her friends had to hold her up. Her legs buckled, this great hand of grief pressing down on her.

A freshman in her cheerleader uniform came moving through the halls like a deer running from wildfire. I kept moving down the hall, faster now. My blood like shook soda in my veins.

Something is happening. Something is wrong.

I headed toward the journalism classroom at the T intersection at the center of the school, passing by the principal's office. Mrs. Davis stood with a man in a yellow sports coat, a ruff of fat above his collar. I had seen him before, talking on the news when that banker murdered his wife and got away with it the year before.

I walked into journalism class, the desks askew as always, the yearbook girls and the newspaper kids all clumped together, Mrs. Ray at the center of it, everyone whispering. And they all looked at me at once, and I guess they could see by my face that I didn't know, and the circle opened to let me in, and I kept my face from smiling as I joined it, as they told me what the principal had said. My hands tingled, my skin slid against my flesh, like sitting by the fire at the end of a cold day.

Something is happening, something is wrong.

Finally.

Every school has a Mr. Simmons—I mean, the way we all thought of him before the killings. An animal perfectly suited to his environment of the science classroom. He was a teacher you liked, who talked to the kids like they were people. He was goofy looking. He was funny. He wore his weirdness comfortably. To us, all the teachers were weird, but most of them didn't know it. He knew it. He wasn't a poser, he wasn't pretending he was something he wasn't. That's what we thought about him.

That's how good he was.

Later on, after the charges were filed, my mom heard a story from one of her friends who taught English at a different school, a story about being out at a bar with other women teachers, and my mom's friend had wanted to call it an early night. The other

women said no, you have to wait for Jim Simmons. She told my
mom how the other teachers had been giggling and laughing and
trading secret glances. And my mom's friend ordered another
drink and waited, expecting Brad Pitt to walk through the door.
But it was just this pasty guy with a gut and glasses and a Beatles
mop top. She glued on a smile and tried to finish her drink quick
and bail. Five minutes later she was blushing and touching his
forearm and ordering another round.

That's how good he was.

You couldn't help but notice, in the papers and news reports after the killings, that Cindy Simmons was beautiful. I'm not telling
you that to make the death seem more tragic or anything. Maybe
you had to look at her in those pictures because to look at their
four-year-old son and their baby daughter was just too much to
bear. And when I tell you that in the photos in the paper and the
news you couldn't help but notice her breasts, so high and outsize
on her body so that even modest flower dresses couldn't hide it,
I'm not saying it just to be lurid. I promise you it will matter later.

You'll see. You won't like it, but you'll see.

The teachers taught us the best they could over those next few
days, even though we were all electrified, all of us together in
this storm cloud of mystery and fear and something else, something that we wouldn't dare name. I remember Mrs. Capistrano
the math teacher, who was married to Mr. Capistrano the other
math teacher, trying to teach us algebra, x and y and the quadratic
equation. But nobody could hear her over the sounds of our own
blood. The lub-dub of our heartbeats chanting *all-dead all-dead all-
dead.*

We put the story together like dinosaur bones:

Mr. Simmons had been at a teachers' conference up at the lake,
ninety miles north of town. Sunday morning one of Cindy's friends
was supposed to ride with Cindy to church. She called and called,
got nervous when she never heard from her, and drove over to
the Simmons house to check on them. Maybe she was scared, or
maybe just annoyed in a way that must have ate at her later. She
saw how the garage door hung open, with Cindy's car parked inside. She let herself in the house through the garage.

She must have called out as she walked into the house. How
loud her voice must have seemed to her. In the right kind of quiet

your skull becomes a megaphone. She saw a footprint on the living room carpet in dried paint. The words DIE BITCH and SATAN
painted on the walls.

What was there in the back of her brain as she walked through
the silence? The things I want to know about her are things she
probably doesn't know about herself.

She went into the master bedroom and saw the red-black spatter on the wall above the bed, saw the unmoving lump of Cindy
Simmons underneath it. She ran for help before even checking on
the children, and she is lucky for that. It was the police who found
their four-year-old son and infant daughter in their own beds, with
their own spatter.

I don't know much about that friend, but I am sure that sometimes she blinks and the corpse is still there behind her eyes.
That's how it works; I know that now. Some things you see burn
so hot they brand themselves into your eyelids. Some things don't
leave until you do.

It's so hard to write about this. I've been trying for decades. I've
tried twice to write it as a novel, first before I got my first novel
published, and the second time a few years later. That version
ended up mutating into a whole other book about teenage criminals in the desert. So I tried to sell this story as a TV show last year.
The first line of my pitch was the same as the first line of this story.
The executives liked it but then the network decided they didn't
want to do a crime story with teenagers in the lead. So now I'm
trying it like this, to get the story out hard and fast. But it does not
want to come.

Maybe it's because it feels wrong to lie about these things. To
change the names but keep the corpses. I've never been interested
in telling the story as true crime, even though maybe you'd like
that version better. Maybe you want to feel it in your bones that
this is the way it happened. You want to see the killer's face. You
want a rope of reality between you and the crimes. It makes you
feel alive, doesn't it?

So maybe the lies are just for me.

That Friday night after the murders, the crew—me and Matt and
Chael and Zach and Joe—drove up into the hills. The air acrid with
bad weed smoke. Higher than giraffe pussy, Matt always said. On

old roads in the Ozark hills, up and down so fast that when we crested the hills the wheels lifted off the shocks and I felt in my belly what the birds must feel, just for a second before crashing down. It would knock loose the shotgun so that I had to kick it back under the seat.

We might as well talk about the shotgun.

The shotgun was real, it's not one of the lies I'm telling you. Matt had gotten it in trade for a car stereo he'd stolen from a neighbor's car. The barrels had been sawed-off a half-inch past the stock, poorly, so the mouths of the barrels wore jagged teeth of twisted metal. It looked as evil as it was. It was loaded. I know it was crazy that I drove around with it under my seat for so long. If you'd asked me why it was there, I would have said something like where else would it be? Like it was all a joke. Most of the time I even forgot it was there, at least with the front of my mind.

The front of my mind was focused on the murders. Death had never been so close to me before. I read everything I could about the killings. I watched the evening news. I talked about it until I worried that people could see the dark thrill at the heart of me. In those early weeks, though, everyone wanted to talk about it. In those first weeks the killings still felt like a mystery. Who would kill Mr. Simmons's family?

That night in the hills, Matt said it first. "Shit, ain't no mystery. Who kills women? Men do. Who kills wives? Husbands do."

We might as well talk about Matt.

We'd been friends since second grade, when I learned about the boy who couldn't have candy and had to give himself shots every day. I guess nowadays he'd have an insulin pump. He was a wonder to me, this boy who jabbed himself every day, who would let the hypodermic needle dangle loose from his side just to make the girls scream.

Matt's mom worked third shift at the GE plant. She was shaped like she lived on Jupiter, like the gravity of this planet was heavier for her than everybody else. Matt had her genes. He was short in a way that made it hard for him with girls, which is why he clung to Donella so fiercely. A girl from the Holler with cutoff jeans and sky-blue eyes who covered her acne with foundation that made her cheeks look like stucco. The two of them matched well together because for both of them love was a knife fight. They would laugh and curse and fuck and cut each other up real good for a little while, until the bleeding got to be too much for one of them. And then they'd quit for a while and then they'd run the cycle again.

Matt was short in a way that surprised the men of the Holler when Matt came for them for hitting on Donella, came for them with his fists or a bat or a fold-out knife. With a violence behind the eyes that he came to honestly.

Our senior year, as the rest of us made our college plans or other escape routes, Matt split his time between us and Curtis. Curtis was this white trash Frankenstein's Monster sewn together with prison ink and homebrew chemicals. He'd seen something in Matt that he could use, shape toward his own ends. Curtis scared me. Later on, I used his name in the book about teenage criminals. I made him a more honorable outlaw than the real one ever was. He's dead now anyway.

I met Matt's dad only once, by accident. We were at a restaurant and a man and a woman walked by on their way out the door. The man said, "Hello, Matt," and Matt said, "Hi, Dad." The man didn't even break his stride. So I understood why Matt went out to Curtis's place, the way you understand shipwrecked people turning to cannibalism.

The stealing was something else. Matt stole everything from everyone. He stole every lighter that was ever handed to him, and his mom's prized Camaro, and I think he stole my car stereo once. He sat at Curtis's feet, and Curtis shaped him—but the clay was already there for him to mold. In those days after the murder, Matt was stealing more, dealing more, fighting more. I can see now how for Matt high school was a plank he was walking, that once he reached the end of it there was nothing left but the fall and the splash.

Anyway, that's what I try to tell myself.

"Men are funny," Aurora said to me when I told her what Matt had said about Mr. Simmons. "I don't mean ha-ha funny."

I met her in a mosh pit. The most beautiful girl I'd ever seen, holding on to the front of the stage at a punk show while the big mooks slam-danced behind us. She had the same haircut I had, long on the top and shaved on the sides. She was funny and weird and she didn't belong and didn't want to. She was a first-generation Filipina American in the whitest city in America. She was a piano prodigy who sang in a punk band. We talked about everything except how she was going off to Yale next fall and I wasn't.

Her father was the city medical examiner. I know that sounds like something I'd make up for the story, but it's true. So we knew things about the killings that the other kids never knew. She and I talked about the murders late into the night, on the phone in the dark. Or in back seats of cars or in our bedrooms when our parents were away, sweat-damp. Her little hands always cold against my neck. We loved each other enough to show each other the worst of us. To let each other see how much the killings thrilled us.

One long Saturday night we talked it out step by step. If it was him, how would he have done it? How would he have driven back from the lake in the middle of the night, the ninety miles on the highway? Did he play the radio? Did some song come on that chilled him, caught him by surprise, made him laugh with the irony of it all? We sat there and imagined him; we talked it through in real time. How he would not park in front of the house. Three a.m., that evil hour, nobody stirring, a dog or two barking as he walked down the street. How he would walk up to his front door quickly, that one moment of pure risk when a nosy neighbor could see him.

"Maybe he hesitated just inside the door," Aurora said, a catch in her throat, fear and shame and something electric. Her eyes closed. She talked faster. "Maybe he stood there in the dark, like when I sneak out at night, trying to stay quiet, how the dark has a texture, how air in your lungs feels ticklish, and maybe he stood there, hearing his heart in his throat, blood-thump in his ears. And maybe he stood there like that and it felt like forever."

Her eyes opened and they were wet.

"And maybe he thought, 'I could turn around now.' But he didn't."

And we talked through the killing, step by step. He'd go to Cindy first. The only one who could fight back. Maybe she'd woken up, murmured his name in sleep-talk at the familiar sound of his steps. And then he'd brought the hammer down. And then he moved to the next bedroom. And the next.

"But why?" I asked her. "Why would he kill his whole family?"

She smiled through the tears.

"Men are funny," she said again. "I don't mean ha-ha funny."

We sat in a thick silence.

"My dad has the photos in his office," she said. "The crime scene and the autopsy."

Maybe she wanted me to say no, to be the one who turned away. Or maybe she needed someone else there with her, to see these things that no one should see.

"I'll look," I said. "I'll look with you."

Even though the photos felt unreal, the blood too dark, the skin too white, everything grainy and lurid in the flashbulb pop of a police photographer, they were also the realest thing I'd ever seen. Too real to be believed.

I looked at those photos for only a few minutes. I'll never stop seeing them. Aurora's face was in her hands, peeking through her fingers. And I realized I was doing the same thing. Something ancient at the base of my brain said there is death here, look away. But there was another part of me that needed to see. That needed to know. To see the shining red divots on a woman's head, a head that had been shaved to make the wounds easier to see. To see how death takes everything from you. It takes your pulse, your heat, and it takes the million thoughts and illusions that make up a human being.

I can tell you these things, but I cannot make you see them. I can't make you see the blankness of the eyes, the purple stains on skin where the cold blood pooled. The children, and the horror that was done to them. I can say those autopsy words to you, contusions and exsanguination and blunt force trauma. These are just the facts. Facts are dry.

But the truth is wet.

I drove for hours that night, my eyes coated with what I'd seen. Shapes from the crime-scene photos re-created themselves in the shadows, in the shape of snow drifts. I got lost, let the stranger inside me steer. I turned onto Glen Oaks Street without even knowing it. But of course, that's where I was heading the entire time. The address from the police files we'd just read. The place of the murders. I pulled to a stop across the street from the house.

Fingers of gray light flickered from between the blinds of a front window in what had been the Simmons house.

Someone was home. It couldn't be Mr. Simmons. There was no way he'd live in the house where his family died. Even a killer wouldn't do that.

Would he?

I opened the door.

I crept to the window. The venetian blinds were half closed. Through the gaps I could see slices of a woman, nude. The video was homemade, the image brined with static. I saw a mouth, a cock. I heard a distorted moan.

Something shifted on the other side of the glass. A man's head on the other side of the glass, inches from me. That familiar Beatles mop top gently bobbing against the couch. I realized what he was doing, doing in the house where his family died, where specks of death still floated.

I moved away from the window, slipped, fell into the sharp coldness of frozen grass. The sky dead above me. Something radioactive at the core of me, invisible and sickening and hotter than the sun.

I was pitching a TV show once, a supernatural crime story about a drug that is also an alien that takes over a town in the California high desert, and an executive at a studio asked me what the difference is between terror and horror.

"Terror's what you feel when you're running from the wolf," I told her. "Horror's what you feel while you watch the wolf feeding on your guts. Showing you what you're really made of."

I didn't sell the show.

As winter turned to spring, after the snow but before the thunderstorms, my friend Zach and I went to an all-night house party. We pulled the old sleepover trick, telling our parents that I was spending the night at his place and he was spending the night at mine. Our old friend Courtney's parents were out of town. We had been closer with her in junior high, before the great sorting had put us in one camp and her in another. So the party was mostly the pretty people, the soccer guys and cheerleaders. Some older brother had bought the party kiddie booze, Boone's Farm and peach schnapps and watery beer.

I never drank—although I'd put any other chemical inside my body that I could get hold of, alcoholism ran in my family and I feared booze like a lycanthrope fears a full moon. So I watched the others get sloppy and wild.

Amy C., queen of the dance squad, was there, drunk as I'd ever seen anyone to that point. She got sick, and after she emptied herself in the bathroom, Zach and I helped Courtney get her to Courtney's bedroom so she could lie down. But she didn't want to, and she fell on the floor laughing. She peeled off her shirt and used it to wipe her face. She sat on the carpet in her bra and jean shorts. Her laughs turned to sobs. Her eyes muddy with smeared mascara, her eyes alive and weeping. I turned away, trying not to look at her, half-hard in my pants and ashamed of it. Zach, whose face looked like mine felt, tried to give her his shirt but she slapped it away.

"I'm so worried about him," she said. "He must be so sad, he must be so scared."

"Amy—" Courtney said, real fear in her voice.

"Who are you worried about?" Zach asked.

"Jim. Poor Jimmy."

Some deeper part of me put it together before I did. It coughed up the memory of the day of the murder, Amy keening in the hallway after the news broke.

"Is she . . . ?" I asked Courtney.

"She's talking about Mr. Simmons," Courtney said.

"He's so sweet," Amy sobbed. "So sweet."

"Why the hell is she calling him Jimmy?" Zach asked.

"They're in love," Courtney said.

"Her and Mr. Simmons?"

"You can't say anything," Courtney said. "Promise you won't."

And I didn't. But somebody else did. Amy's parents sent her away. They took her out of school and sent her to an aunt in Waterloo, Iowa. And she never came back and she never said out loud what had been between her and Mr. Simmons.

Turns out it didn't matter. Turns out the thing Mr. Simmons had was lots and lots of love.

Secrets have an inertia all their own. Once a few get free, others follow. Faster and faster.

The detective in the yellow sports coat set up shop again in the principal's office, where we could see the girls coming in from across the hall in journalism class.

We saw Becky Polk go in and come out crying. We saw Sarah Gelson go in and come out crying. So many others. Too many to name.

As the girls talked to the police, word spread all over. It was the same week the rains came, came hard and like thunder, like they do every spring in the Ozarks.

I heard he bought Jennifer beer.

I heard Rachel and Annette went out with him and his friends to the Coral Courts Motel.

I heard there's a house on Lone Pine, a house that's just for partying. A fuck pad.

I heard it's the house with the overgrown shrubs. The one with the brick chimney.

I found the house. I couldn't have been the only one who looked. I drove to it late one night. Wind gusts creaking the trees. Flashes of faraway lightning.

The only dark house on the block.

The house stank of a million cigarettes, smoke baked deep into the walls and carpet. The air was ticklish against my skin. There were couches and beanbags everywhere. The sort of posters college kids hang on the walls. A TV set and a VCR. And there were rows of video tapes, all of them blank, a few of them labeled with tape and marker across the top. No names, just dates. I grabbed one and fed it into the VCR. It swallowed it down with whirring noises. The TV came alive with a loud blast of static. I killed the volume and taught myself how to breathe again.

The image bent and distorted, like the tape had been played many times. The colors were lurid and too real, like the murder-scene photos. Bodies in the night, darkness behind them. Mrs. Capistrano the math teacher, who was married to Mr. Capistrano the math teacher, naked on her hands and knees in a pontoon boat down on some lake. Men with their swimsuits pooled at their feet, one in front of her and one behind. The camera swayed, bands of light and static bent across the screen. My face warm in the gray light. I turned the volume up just enough to hear the splash of water, the grunts.

"Fill her up," the cameraman's voice said. "Open her up and fill her."

The voice sounded choked, like his throat was swollen shut by desire. But I still knew Mr. Simmons's voice when I heard it. The video bent and the images flecked with static, the way tapes got when you watched them too many times.

I almost didn't hear the footsteps on the front walk. I killed the TV and ran back through the house, feet shushing against shag carpet, static sparks dancing, purple ghost lights blinding me in the dark. And I ran out into the night. Summer lightning flashed. The crash came a breath later. The storm so close.

They burned the house down that night. Maybe they saw me or heard me as I ran. But I don't think so. I think whoever did it, Mr. Simmons or one of his friends, did it because too many people were talking, too many secrets were bleeding out.

I drove by it the next day to see. The house in the daylight, the front windows broken by the firemen. Water from fire hoses had shattered the front windows on either side of the front door, so the smoke poured out and left dark stains, like the smeared mascara of a crying woman.

Police tape across the door. Cops carrying out boxes of tapes, melted and black.

They arrested Mr. Simmons the next day.

He hired the same lawyer who got off the banker who killed his wife the year before. The lawyer called Mr. Simmons the fourth victim of a killer on the loose. A lot of people believed him. A lot of people still do.

Rumors swirled. They came from the adults now. About men trading wives, about men and young girls. About how it wasn't just teachers.

People talked. About how Mr. Simmons had talked Cindy into getting breast implants, and how she hated them. How he'd talked a lot of other women into doing things, things they wanted to do and things they weren't sure about.

The murders themselves began to fade, even for me. Mr. Simmons had been arrested, and for all my punk rock posing I still believed back then that the cops were there to do their job and that job was getting murderers off the street.

Sometimes time gushes like blood from a wound. Days passed in spurts. We graduated from high school. I started making plans for going up to the big state school. Joe was going to be my roommate. Chael was looking at the army, and Zach was looking to move to San Francisco. Aurora was planning her move east. All we talked about was what was about to begin. We didn't talk about what was ending.

We didn't talk about Matt, and what was happening to him.

One evening that summer, the two of us drove around, smoking ditch-weed joints on country roads, the double yellow line chipped on old Route 66. The way the light smeared in the dusk. Those ancient hills.

Angry guitars on the stereo. Matt's knuckles were scraped, one eye clotted with blood. He caught me looking at it. He said, "Curtis has got these problems, some guy fresh out of jail who thinks he runs the Holler. And we're showing him the hard facts of things."

A patrol car came up behind us at speed on the old country road. Fear chemicals filled me up. I was stoned hard on a country road with a cop car right behind us, headlights in the rearview. I gripped the steering wheel to hide how my hands shook. Matt's eyes were flat in the dark as he looked me over.

"Do you have the shotgun?" he asked me. Not like he was scared the cops would find it. Like he wanted me to get it out.

I said, "Fuck that." But he could hear the tremble in my voice.

"Get ready," he said.

The cop's cherries switched on in my rearview. Cold air came in through cracked windows to flush the pot smell. The sawed-off shotgun under the driver's seat. Those moments when your life balances on the edge of something, two whole and completely different lives you could have lived depending on which way the coin tumbled. All I could think about was getting out. How close escape was for me. Maybe not for Matt, but for me.

I pulled the car over. Matt unbuckled his seat belt.

The cop car slid past us up the country road, roaring as it accelerated.

"You know what your fucking problem is?" Matt asked me, but his voice had deepened, gotten more of a Holler twang, so I knew that Curtis had asked him this same question in this same way. "Your problem is you think you've got something to lose."

I came home that night still stoned, still scared, and I could hear my parents watching the news in the living room, calling to me. I didn't want to go to them because I didn't want them to see my bloodshot eyes, and I didn't want them to see the fear. But they called to me again, like it was important, so I went into the living room, ready to be caught. My parents barely glanced at me. Their eyes were on the television. The local news. A floating chyron with the words CHARGES DROPPED. A photo of Mr. Simmons's face.

*

It fell apart so quickly.

Mr. Simmons's lawyer had noticed that the autopsy photos, the ones Aurora and I had seen, were numbered out of order. That there were photos missing. And so he hunted down the negatives, or somebody did, and they found the missing photos. Mrs. Simmons on the autopsy table, naked, with the detective in the yellow sports coat with his hands on her body, on her breasts. Later he'd say he'd never seen fake breasts before. That he didn't mean anything by cupping them. He couldn't explain why the junior medical examiner needed to take photos. Why they'd hidden them from Aurora's dad. Why he'd had a smile on his face.

The lawyer took the photos to the prosecutors, who talked to whoever it was who could make those kinds of decisions. And they decided to keep it quiet. Which meant dropping the charges. Which meant keeping it quiet about Mr. Simmons and all those women, and all those girls, and they kept it quiet about all those other men who were a part of it, too, whoever they were.

And maybe it really was the lawyer who figured it all out on his own, but I wonder about that. I wonder if maybe somebody didn't give him a nudge. Either way the charges were dropped; the secrets were safe. A few had leaked out, sure, but that always happens. It wasn't enough to hurt anybody or change anything. Just a little bit floating inside us, not doing anything. Like the lead in our blood.

Aurora sobbed on her bed. It was a week before she was leaving for Yale. Her suitcases were already on the floor, waiting to be filled. She sobbed for Cindy Simmons. For what they did to her. I reached out for her, and she pulled away from me. Like I was poison.

"It's never enough for you men, is it? We're never enough. It doesn't even stop when we die. Our deaths aren't enough for you. Nothing is ever enough."

And I wanted to say not me and I wanted to say I'm different but I was at least smart enough to shut up. And anyway, I wasn't so sure how different I really was. And so I sat there and I watched her cry, and when she stopped I watched her breathe. After a while I got up and I said goodbye to her. I said I was sorry, and even if I don't know what I was apologizing for, I know that I meant it.

*

I sat parked on Glen Oaks Street. It was dusk and the light was beautiful. Summer had come. My escape was at hand.

The shotgun sat on my lap. I pressed my thumb into the splinters, wanting the pain of it, letting it crawl up my shoulder, pressing harder, like maybe I could get the pain of it all the way into my heart, lance it, let it bleed out the bad things that filled me. I pressed until blood wept.

Mr. Simmons pulled into his driveway. He got out of his car and walked up the drive with a bag of hamburgers and fries.

He walked to the door. I thought about what he deserved.

Our deaths aren't enough for you, she'd told me. Nothing is ever enough.

I could see him torn in half there on the driveway. I knew it would only be justice.

I want to lie to you just a little more now, tell you I put my hand on the door handle, tell you that I almost got out of the car. But I didn't. I sat there and I watched him walk into the house. After a while the sun set. I sat in the dark. I started the car and I drove home.

I thought about that life I could see just outside my grasp. The one where I would be free and whole and away from there. The one where I reached my potential. I thought that maybe I did have something to lose.

But I thought about other things too.

The next day Matt and I got a pizza and some grape soda to play Street Fighter on my Nintendo.

While we were bringing the pizza into the house, I grabbed the shotgun from under the seat, stuffed it under my shirt.

"I'm tired of driving around with it," I told him. "Like what the fuck, right? We could have got busted the other night. Not like I'm looking to shoot anyone."

"Yeah, that's a good move," Matt said, "what with you being a pussy and all."

When we got to my room I put the shotgun in my closet, under a pile of clothes. I did it with the door open, where Matt could see me. We played for a while. The pizza roiled in my guts. I liked to play Blanka, the monster from Brazil. Matt played Ryu, the hero. I lost more than usual. I tried to find the right moment.

I paused the game. I told him I had something to tell him. I could feel my pulse in my eyeballs.

"I saw Donella coming out of the principal's office. When the cops were there. I didn't want to tell anybody."

I wouldn't have used her name if she wasn't on a float trip with her family down in Arkansas. I wouldn't have done it this way if she had been in town. I swear.

"Bullshit."

"I saw the list," I told him. "I saw the list, from Aurora's dad. Of all the girls Mr. Simmons had been with. Donella's name was on it, Matt."

Matt looked into my eyes to see if I was lying. I held that gaze. I let him see something true inside me, even if it wasn't what he thought it was. He broke off the stare. He unpaused the game. We sat there in this storm of silence. I beat him three rounds in a row. Matt studied his fingers, watched them turn into fists. He got up and went into my closet. Maybe he muttered an excuse. I pretended I didn't hear him rustling in the back. I pretended I didn't see the lump under his shirt, clamping something down with his armpit as he mumbled his goodbyes.

After he left, I went downstairs and tuned the TV to a local station. Some endless car auction. I sat and I watched, waiting for the interruption I knew was coming. When they cut away to the newsroom I knew what they were going to say before they said it. I knew they'd throw up a picture of Mr. Simmons's face. And then they did. And now I look back and I wonder what I was feeling, and maybe I've forgotten. But what I worry is, I wasn't feeling anything at all.

I drove to Aurora's place that night, late, after the story of Mr. Simmons's death and Matt's arrest had played itself out on television and in phone calls. You can see it, can't you? How Matt had parked right where I had parked the day before, with the same shotgun in his lap. Waiting the way I had waited. But of course Matt got out of the car when he saw Mr. Simmons. He knew from Curtis how to get close, how to get that shotgun right up against Mr. Simmons's back and pull the trigger.

I told myself that Matt was still a minor, and I wasn't. I told myself that I didn't make him do anything, that he made his choice. I told myself that even if Matt didn't know it, everyone else could see the thing building in him, that it was going to come out, and all I had done was make sure it was pointed in a direction that did the world some good.

Isn't it crazy how you don't need to believe a lie for it to have power?

I drove to Aurora's house that night. Sometimes when you sit on a dark street where no one is awake it feels like a cage. Sometimes it feels like you could do anything at all. I walked through the dark. I thought about Matt someplace in a cell. I could smell honeysuckle on the air and summer thunder coming. I went around the side of the house to Aurora's bedroom window. I knocked on the glass, softly, our secret knock. She sat up in her bed. First scared and then smiling. I tried to look at that smile, burn it into my mind forever like all the terrible things I had seen, but mostly what I saw was my own reflection looking back at me. I wondered what she saw. If she could see me at all. If anyone ever had.

I told you I would lie to you, and I did. And now I will tell you the truth.

The story about the breast implants and the detective violating the corpse of a murdered woman really did happen, but it was in the case of the banker who killed his wife and got away with it the year before Mr. Simmons killed his wife and got away with it. Mr. Simmons got set free because of a witness who maybe lied or maybe got confused. It's not as good a story. So I used the terrible detail, scavenged it from the dead. Because that is what I do.

Aurora and I tried to stay together, but of course it fell apart that first semester of college. But listen: everything ends, every fruit fly and every blue whale and every diamond and every star, and if it all falls then nothing does.

Curtis really is dead. He died in a hotel room meth-lab shootout with the cops. Like something I'd write in one of my books. I've tried to use his death in a few different stories, but it hasn't quite worked yet. Someday.

Matt is dead too. He died in his thirties of complications brought on by neglected diabetes and heavy drinking. Donella, who watched over him in those last days when he didn't have anyone left to stand for him, called me the day before he died. She told me he wanted to talk to me. And I didn't call him, even though I knew it was the last day. Maybe I was angry, maybe I was scared, but either way he tried to end with us in peace and I didn't call him back. And I have to live with that.

You get older and the thing between you and the world gets thicker, stained, harder to see through. But there's plenty I can still see. I can see I was right about a lot of things back then when I was an angry punk kid who wanted to burn the world down because adults are selfish and cruel and scared. And the fact that I'm one of them now only proves the point.

I left, and I never moved back. I took my love of the darkness and I shaped it into something I could live off of, something I could sell. Like I'm doing right now. Because that's the best thing I can figure to do in this world we've made.

I don't know if I ever reached my potential, or if maybe I'd already reached it back in that savage year. What I do know is, the thing I left my hometown to find, I never found, and the thing I left to run away from has stuck to me the entire time. The only peace I have found is to see that it will never leave me, and learn to live with that, and that helps me.

Sometimes.

KAREN HARRINGTON

The Mysterious Disappearance of Jason Whetstone

FROM *Reckless in Texas*

IN 2015, A talented mediator disappeared on his way to work. Months later, his remains were found inside the childhood home of one of his clients. Those responsible now sit in prison, one maintaining innocence. To this day, there are lingering questions. Reporters from *The Garlandian* look back on the chilling case.

This article is the second of an eight-part series about strange crimes in Garland, Texas.

Despite the calendar inching toward Valentine's Day, Christmas lights still outlined a few houses in Jason Whetstone's tree-lined Richardson neighborhood. With Whetstone's portfolio, he could have afforded an updated Tudor near his office in upscale University Park. But his associates said the humble, compact, detail-oriented man liked to be underestimated. And that he was the last person to be involved in any kind of crime.

This made his disappearance all the more baffling.

The day he vanished was like any other day for the fifty-five-year-old. He left his house in his usual go-to-work uniform: bespoke vest over button-down shirt with a tumbler of black coffee in hand. His calendar revealed that he had an early-morning appointment as the fundraising chair for a foster-based dog-rescue group. He slid into the leather seat of his Lexus sedan. The doorbell camera across the street from Whetstone's home recorded him backing out and driving away around 5:30. He never made it to his destination.

In the weeks leading up to his disappearance, Whetstone's newest clients—two sisters—had become embroiled in a growing social-media spectacle. Whetstone was a senior partner at the Remedy Clinic, a cottage business aimed at helping Dallasites discreetly settle odd disputes before they entered the court system or drained their bank accounts—or both. Its founder, Dr. Erik Kellog, hired skilled mediators like Whetstone to act as part legal gymnast, part therapist.

"Our range of services and remedies are sometimes unusual, but then, so are the client issues," Kellog said. "Whetstone occasionally added a rescue animal to a prescribed remedy. He was that kind of guy. Very caring."

The Stratham sisters had the kind of knotty, petty issue Whetstone was skilled at untangling. The dispute centered on a family memory and who was telling the truth about it. While this kind of debate might be hashed out at a family Thanksgiving gathering, the Stratham sisters' feud was uniquely public. Both sisters were novelists. And each had written her version of the truth.

What the sisters did agree on was this: twenty-five years earlier, when the girls were sixteen and fourteen, there was an argument with their mother about why her portion of spaghetti meat sauce was smaller than everyone else's. After a furious debate erupted at the dinner table, Mother Stratham grabbed her car keys and her youngest, Michael, and stormed out of the house. Years later, each writer cast herself as responsible for the consequential family event—and then wrote about it. It was Whetstone's job to listen to both sides and determine if there was memory overlap or a whiff of plagiarism, as one sister claimed.

The older sister's editor pointed them to the clinic after reading about a Whetstone case that made national news. It involved two neighbors' annual autumn conflict over falling leaves (the wind blew a voluminous number of dead leaves from Client A's yard into Client B's yard).

"Everyone can relate to this kind of situation, this unjust chore of someone else's leaves literally falling at your feet. For these men, it was leaves. But it wasn't really about the falling leaves," Whetstone once told a reporter. "It never is."

Whetstone let the neighbors thrash out their dispute before issuing a remedy: hire the same landscaping company to collect the leaves from both properties on one assigned day. The collection of leaves, Whetstone said, removed the need for conflict. The remedy drew ire from some as too simplistic or too unjust. But his clients accepted it and moved on. They'd each garnered support on social-networking app Nextdoor from hundreds of neighbors dealing with similar petty domestic issues.

"Whetstone had been smart enough to recognize that sympathy for a problem was a dose of medicine in itself," remarked Kellog.

Like the falling-leaves dispute, the case about gatekeeping a memory promised to be about more than meat sauce for Laura Stratham and Mona Stratham (who used the pen name Mona Moore).

Laura Stratham had left home at age eighteen to marry her blue-eyed high school sweetheart, Dave Fogel. The pair had an on-again, off-again relationship, but friends recalled that Dave's easy smile and charm constantly wooed Laura back. Noted for her long thick dark locks, Laura cut her hair to a pixie when the duo married, selling her healthy strands for money. While Dave finished trade school and Laura worked odd jobs, the newlyweds lived a hand-to-mouth kind of existence. Laura filled stacks of black-and-white composition books, always ready to capture a piece of dialogue. In Laura's memoir, she claimed Dave had a snarky way of introducing her to friends:

"He'd say, 'Be careful what you say. Laura might include it in her little stories.' He put the words *little stories* in air quotes. He called my scribbles a hobby, but that made me want to work harder. I'd gotten married, in part, to just get out. I never knew which version of Mother I'd find at home."

Dave was also captured on the pages of her fiction, following their affair-fueled breakup and tenuous legal battle over their only child, a daughter. Inside those early pages, there's a scene where the Dave-like character, Earl, packs his things and prepares to leave his crying wife, Lola. On their mantel, there's a wooden heart, each of their names carved into one side. The names interlocked like two puzzle pieces. Lola broke it apart and threw half the heart at Earl.

"That really happened," Dave said. "She wanted me to take my piece, and I wanted her to keep it together. I was a jerk for having an affair, okay, but she did still love me. She did."

Laura adjusted to a new life as a single parent. "I was either working or writing in the library with my daughter. She read books and I wrote. The mac-and-cheese days."

Years later, Laura's mac-and-cheese days were behind her. She not only enjoyed bestseller status, she also became a hit on the writers-conference circuit. She found herself reciting entertaining vignettes about her childhood and early marriage.

"There was a market for her rags-to-riches journey," said her longtime editor, Soozi Finkels. "She was intrigued by the project and dove in, pen first."

The memoir, a rambling portrait of the Stratham family, gave praise to a dysfunctional childhood for toughening Laura. The opening pages showed her father, a high school science teacher, taking the family for a ride on a Sunday afternoon only to be left stranded hours later in a small town because he hadn't bothered to check the gas gauge. Worse, he didn't have any money so he asked the kids to panhandle on the side of the road while their mother napped in the car.

Laura wrote that it was the first time she learned that her family didn't always have her best interests at heart. "Part of writing the memoir was making sense of the past, which is why I included the meat-sauce story. When my mother got angry at me that night, it adversely impacted our entire family. I was just sixteen. Mother flew into a rage after surveying the entire dining table and decreeing that she'd been shorted meat sauce. She left with our ten-year-old brother, Michael, and lived in a motel for a month."

It didn't take long for news of Laura's memoir to reach her sister Mona. Inside Jason Whetstone's mediation-interview records, obtained exclusively by *The Garlandian*, Mona stated, "I've avoided reading Laura's work. Some people might like it, but it felt so crafted to me. Just not my thing. I guess there's a market for stories like that."

Whetstone replied, "Stories like what?"

"Her writing is to literature what fast food is to a gourmet meal. Digestible and forgettable."

"But you read it and that's how you formed this opinion?"

"I didn't need to read everything to know. And, besides, many of my friends and readers filled me in."

Years earlier, Mona had penned *Downward*, a novel that included a family argument at the dinner table. The fictional uproar led to the death of the matriarch, who fled the table in tears, grabbed her car keys, and soon after was involved in a fatal accident. Though Mona hadn't risen to the acclaim of her sister, her eagle-eyed readers noted the striking similarities in *Downward* and parts of Laura's memoir.

"The scene where the mama gets angry over meat sauce, blames the daughter, and leaves the family? It's the same in each book," one reviewer wrote.

Mona was puzzled. Why would Laura falsely write that she was the one who'd angered their mother that night? And since *Downward* was published five years before Laura's memoir, was this more than stealing a memory—was this also plagiarism?

"It was me who angered our mother and set her off," Mona said. Whetstone questioned her. "And you want to own the fact that you alone angered your mother? Slighted her dinner plate?"

"I own it because it's the truth," Mona answered. "You can't claim someone else's childhood trauma as your own. And that's what Laura has done. Though my fictional mother died, it was like the death of our family after that night."

Both sisters' works described a home in which the matriarch was unpredictable and eccentric. She refused to buy living room furniture. She painted all the time. The Stratham family of Laura's memoir and the characters in Mona's novel sit in white-and-green lawn chairs facing a huge wooden television set. There was also a modern black-and-white mural in various stages of completion. Laura wrote, "Our mother was always painting on small canvases, but the mural that dominated the dining room wall was a never-ending geometric work in progress."

Like Laura, Mona dreamed of a way out and up. A red-headed beauty with hazel eyes, Mona was famished for attention and validation, friends said. Where Laura chased after a youthful romance to escape a dysfunctional home, Mona saw herself in Paris cafés, writing and observing. She got as far as Iowa, earning a prized spot at the Iowa Writers' Workshop. Associates remember her as kind, teacherly, ever ready for a public reading or critique session. She loved hosting late-night happy hours. Members of the writing community called her "Queen" because of the way she loved to hold court.

"There was a book that outlined the inspirations of something like fifty famous writers," a former classmate recalled. "She knew all of those origin stories and would orate them again and again. It was over-the-top, but she'd look into your face and compare your writing to a legend, pulling out a pearl of a sentence and praising its beauty. How could you not like that kind of adulation? It was a little like taking a drug while knowing it's bad for you."

After the term at the Iowa workshop ended, Mona's options were thin. She took a job in Southeast Oklahoma as an insurance adjuster. She held nighttime critique groups, helping others workshop their stories while getting feedback on her own. When *Downward* was published, she sent copies to all of her family members.

"They had the book, and they didn't respond," Mona wrote on her blog. "Maybe it was because I'd pulled a lot from my life, our life, and put it on the page. It was healing for me. If they wanted to keep their distance, fine."

But it wasn't really fine. When Laura sold her debut in a splashy two-book deal two years later, Mona reached out with congratulations and an offer to do book events together. (By then, Mona had self-published a new book of linked short stories about Oklahoma tornado survivors.) Laura took a while to reply to Mona's offer. "I think my publicist is working all that out. I hope you'll come to an event! Would be great to see you," Laura wrote in a short text to Mona.

Mona responded, "Why don't you want to see me? Why don't you want to get together? All my friends have solid relationships with their sisters. I don't understand. What have I done, Laura?"

Her questions went unanswered.

Laura's debut released to praise, her sophomore follow-up garnered even more fans, and then came her popular memoir. Soon after the memoir hit the shelves, Mona launched a series of Facebook posts devoted to the stolen meat-sauce story. Her fans took her side and began pummeling review sites with scathing one-star reviews of Laura's books.

In one of Mona's Facebook posts, she wrote:

"My dear friends know that there was a period in my life that devastated me. I've written about it privately most of my life. And to find out that it had been written about so publicly and without my knowledge in the pages of Laura Stratham's book. Is there any civility anymore? I mean, what would you do if someone took your precious memories and monetized them for personal gain? We've sought a professional referee to help us with this issue, but I fear the truth will never see the light unless all parties are accountable."

Laura seemed to have taken the bait of her sister's social-media provocation. A short while later, she stated in an interview, "It's ridiculous to say I plagiarized anything from Mona. Some of our experiences overlap. She doesn't get to gatekeep our childhood memories."

This is when Laura's editor, who'd read about the falling-leaves saga, persuaded her to take the issue to Whetstone at the Remedy Clinic.

"I hoped it might quickly settle things," Finkels said. "I'd read his book, too, and it seemed like its wisdom applied."

Whetstone had penned a pithy, pocket-size book on his tips for settling disagreements with chapters including:

What Is Your End Goal?

What Does Winning Mean to You?

Prioritize Peace over Being Right

It was recommended reading for his clients.

"The Strathams couldn't be bothered to read the book," said Dean Ray Vanderbilt, the Remedy Clinic's attorney. "Jason was fond of saying that people don't want an apology or money. They want a time machine. And once they realize that's not possible, Jason often led them to a peaceful resolution. But it took time to get there."

A month before Whetstone's disappearance, the Stratham sisters' dispute stalled. Vanderbilt hinted that Whetstone had presented three options to the embattled sisters, one capitalizing on the increased notoriety and book sales both authors had enjoyed since the case went public.

"One of the sisters was incredulous that this might be seen as a remedy," Vanderbilt said.

Mona wrote in a post that nothing short of a full public admission of memory stealing was acceptable. Her followers on Twitter started a *#tellthetruthlaura* hashtag campaign. Laura confided in friends that she was annoyed by her sister's online antics.

Mona fired off a rapid succession of emails and texts, accusing Laura of purposely dragging out the mediation for dramatic effect. Most of them went unanswered by Laura. Interview records captured Mona's complaints to Whetstone about being ignored. "The nice thing to do would have been to let me sit on one of those author panels and discuss it with the public. Let the sunshine disinfect. Others could learn from our unique dynamic."

"Is that what you would like from this experience? To teach others?" Whetstone asked.

"It's lemonade from lemons now," Mona replied. "That's what Ike says, anyway."

At this point, the eldest Stratham sibling was drawn into the fray.

Ike Stratham is a tall good-natured man. A former Marine, he's now a physician assistant who often works with Doctors Without Borders. He had also been in charge of his father's estate. (Mother Stratham, who'd moved to nearby Plano following the divorce, preceded her former husband in death.) When his father died in 2005, Ike, fresh off a divorce, moved into the childhood home in Garland, dubbed the Submarine because of its bright-yellow brick and squat ranch-style architecture. Ike paid each of his siblings a share of its worth and sent them one of the old folding green-and-white lawn chairs.

Weeks after Mona and Laura engaged Whetstone's services, Mona visited Ike at the Submarine.

"Mona read both passages from both books out loud," Ike remembered. "Yes, they were very similar, I had to admit. But I'm no reader, and so I felt, one is nonfiction, one is fiction, what does it matter? Then Dave showed up, looking for a beer, and Mona asked him the same question."

Fogel, hit by financial downturn, had moved back to his parents' Garland house, a block from the Submarine, and was still friendly with most of the Strathams.

"He was on her side," Ike said. "You should have seen Mona. She was thrilled."

Soon after, Mona moved her diary of the meat-sauce issue to an exclusive blog, called *My Beef*. She led it off with a summation of the case and a quasi-interview with Dave about his experiences with Laura. It rehashed his resentment about being cast as disloyal, dimwitted fictional Earl, giving readers of the *#tellthetruth-laura* hashtag the chance to see that "Laura wasn't afraid to use or trash her family to get ahead."

"Mona got Dave to side with her because they were both upset with Laura," Ike said. "But the book stuff was ridiculous, and I believed this Whetstone guy could referee it quickly. But when he didn't, I invited them to the Sub to talk."

Ultimately, the sisters' dispute could not be solved at the oak dining table inside the Submarine, where the contested event occurred so long ago. "And it all blew up, anyway, because we found out that Laura was recording our conversation."

This fact found its way onto Mona's blog.

Looking back, Vanderbilt remembered how Mona pleaded with him for permission to post the full transcript of her private sessions with Whetstone. When he refused, she wrote her own version.

"It was difficult to understand why Mona believed this cast her in a positive light," said Vanderbilt. "Unless we consider that it kept the drama going and provided additional fodder for her readership."

Blog Entry, March 28

Dear Readers, I'm sharing insights into my mediation with my sister at the Remedy Clinic. See for yourself what it's like to be interviewed by Jason Whetstone. We're still praying he's found safe and we can resume our discussions.

MONA (STRATHAM) MOORE, INTERVIEW 1

MONA: I'm hoping this will be a swift mediation, because I think the press has wind of it or soon will. I desperately want to show a united front should we have to talk to a reporter, you know? I only want justice.

WHETSTONE: Justice?

MONA: The fact is, Laura's been usurping from our family for some time. I'm utterly crushed.

WHETSTONE: How do you mean?

MONA: She lifts from everyone's life.

WHETSTONE: Arguably, the work of all writers.

MONA: This is much different.

WHETSTONE: How so?

MONA: My friends read her stuff, and they have questions
for ME. Can you imagine? Anyone related to a writer,
take heed. Have you spoken to Dave, her ex?

WHETSTONE: No.

MONA: Well, you should. But the fact is that she misused
MY story. My parents' vicious fight started over the lack
of meat sauce, specifically on my mother's plate. She
believed I'd purposely cheated her. I hadn't noticed, that
I remember. Why would I short her on meat sauce? My
own beloved mother. She had a tremendous outburst.
She often had flare-ups with me. We had the worst
relationship, but I keep that private, except from my
closest friends. That night, my dad jumped in to quell
the argument. Suddenly forks were flying. Before I knew
it, she moved out with Michael. All because of what I did.
My action helped end our happy family. And Michael?
His life was irretrievably broken by it. Destroyed. I
think back and wonder, did I do that on purpose? But I
wouldn't do that. Perhaps the best way to illustrate this is
by reading the scene from my book.

WHETSTONE: There's no need. I already reviewed both
books.

MONA: But I really feel . . .

WHETSTONE: No, that won't be necessary.

MONA: I see.

WHETSTONE: I'm curious about one thing, Mona. You
have four siblings. Michael, Ike, Laura, and Claire. No
mention of Claire in this memory?

MONA: Well, I don't know. I don't know why that is. But I
need you to understand what I wrote.

WHETSTONE: Let's shift gears a bit. Laura wrote a scene where the kids had to panhandle for gas money. Do you recall that day?

MONA: Laura sat on the curb and let Ike do most of the work.

WHETSTONE: But that vignette, that memory, she remembered and recorded it correctly.

MONA: I guess.

WHETSTONE: You see where I'm going here?

MONA: Just because she got some things right doesn't validate her entire account.

With the help of Vanderbilt, *The Garlandian* accessed the actual mediation transcript from this interview. They are identical, suggesting that Mona had secretly recorded her session. She would never confirm or deny this action.

Throughout the years, Laura and Mona had little contact with their other sister, Claire. Claire moved a lot, and her whereabouts were difficult to track. Now a chef for a posh Las Vegas eatery, Claire had responded to an email from Whetstone, saying, "I'm the middle child. That's all you need to know about why they haven't talked much about me. My brothers either. As much as it might be fun to watch them continue paying you hefty fees, which I pray they are, this will all be solved if you ask them about Brenda."

Here, Whetstone might have ended the conflict between the two sisters by inviting them to consider what happened with the mysterious Brenda. But why didn't he?

Vanderbilt speculated that Whetstone was determined to let Mona and Laura reach an epiphany. "He loved seeing people round that corner independently, though I can't say if that was his plan," Vanderbilt offered. "I encouraged him to verify Brenda's existence and settle the case. It's fair to say that at this point in the mediation, Jason and I didn't know about Mona's numerous posts or the anti-Laura Twitter hashtag. He would have called foul on that, I'm certain."

As it turned out, Brenda was real.

She was a childhood neighbor. If the Strathams were scraping by, Brenda's family was poorer still. Her father sold her cat for a carton of cigarettes. She was often seen drinking water from the outdoor hose. Whatever eccentricities Mother Stratham exhibited, she made it known that Brenda could come in and out of the Submarine whenever she pleased. What no one but Claire had observed was Brenda sneaking in, helping herself to a few bites from one of the bowls on the day of the infamous meat-sauce argument, then slinking out just as quickly. The story of Brenda's easy access to the kitchen was corroborated by Ike Stratham.

"Oh, yes, Brenda," Ike told Whetstone in a phone call the week before he disappeared. "She was a slip of a girl."

Whetstone probed a little further, asking Ike if he thought the revelation of Brenda's visit would help end his sisters' quarrel over the meat-sauce tale.

"Honestly? No, I think they are going to push this to the bitter end."

Indeed, Ike was prescient.

The sisters would ramp up their efforts to continue the battle on their respective social-media sites.

When news that Mona had published an excerpt of one of her Whetstone sessions reached Laura, she shot back with a post on her website.

Dear Readers,

I'm unhappily drawn into this public spectacle with my sister. If you want to learn my version of events as related to Mona and this particular incident, you can find those details in my memoir within the chapter titled "Mother Takes Michael."

Recently *The Garlandian* wrote to younger brother Michael at his address at a Texas correctional facility to get his perspective on the family drama. His only response to the meat-sauce night was this:

"My parents fought at dinner all the time. My mother required an audience. My sisters are nuts. My mother packed up and left the Submarine and took me with her. That this was all about meat sauce is crazy. People do shit and break up. I think they have lost the plot. Even if I was free, I wouldn't set foot at a Thanksgiving table with those two. One day I'd had too much to drink and was a jerk at my father's birthday party. I left on foot. Laura chased me down an alley, and I told her, I said, 'All you want is material for your novel.' That's probably true, but she was also trying to give me a ride home. You never know with writers. They are always stealing."

Michael Stratham is serving a two-year sentence for theft.

In one of Whetstone's last notes in the Stratham file, he mused in the margins. "Interesting that Mother Stratham easily shared food with Brenda but made a family fight out of it as well. Proof of falling-leaves theory?"

Thinking back on the events, Vanderbilt remembered having growing concern about the Remedy Clinic's reputation getting tarnished by the drawn-out drama. Hoping to put the case to rest and focus on Whetstone's disappearance, he arranged and recorded a Skype call with the sisters to discuss Brenda.

Transcript of final minutes of Skype call between Mona and Laura.

LAURA: Brenda. Do you remember her? I guess that's that.

MONA: What do you mean?

LAURA: It means that Brenda probably ate some of the meat sauce.

MONA: I doubt it very much.

LAURA: Well, you got what you wanted. We went for a remedy and now it's done. We know what must have really happened.

MONA: I don't accept that. You stole my story. Tell the truth, Laura!

LAURA: Oh, yes, your fancy little hashtag.

MONA: I can't help what my fans do.

LAURA: Fans?

VANDERBILT: Authorities will be reaching out if they
have more questions about Jason.

SKYPE CALL ENDS.

From this point, Mona's serialized journey from starving artist
to justice seeker took on a new component. She promised to tell
more of the family secrets and concluded each post with an admo-
nition to her readers to read both of the sister-writers' works and
provided links to stores from which signed copies of her novel,
Downward, could be ordered. Each post teased readers that the
conclusion of the mediation would be forthcoming "as soon as our
mediator, Jason Whetstone, is found safe and resumes his work."
She began monetizing her blog, adding a link to a Patreon account
to fund her artistic works. She never updated her readers with the
revelation about Brenda.

Laura quietly went back to work on a new novel. She attended a
writers' conference where she dodged questions about her sister's
serialized story. "I'm much more interested in the serious concern
of where our adviser and friend, Jason Whetstone, is and if he is
safe."

As April rains descended upon North Texas, the case broke open.

Laura received a panicked call from her daughter. "Mom, Mom,
check the news. Something to do with that missing guy. He's dead."

Laura did a quick search on her phone and pulled up a disturbing
article.

MISSING RICHARDSON MAN FOUND DEAD

Noted mediator and Richardson resident Jason Whetstone,
who went missing earlier this year, was found dead Monday
afternoon, said a spokesman from the Garland Police Department.

Around 1 p.m., GPD officers were dispatched to a home in
the 4500 block of Clairmont Drive after a body was found.
The body was later identified as Whetstone, officials said. His
cause of death is unknown.

"The homeowner, Ike Stratham, returned from an extended
trip and discovered the grisly scene. He did not immediately
know the identity of the victim," police said.

Stratham told police he'd hired a neighbor, David Fogel, 41,
as a house sitter. A subsequent search of Fogel's house and
garage led to the recovery of Whetstone's car.
"Fogel admitted he abducted Whetstone at gunpoint three
months prior and drove him to Stratham's house," police said.
Fogel was arrested on kidnapping charges, with other charges
pending. An autopsy will be conducted, and the death remains
under investigation.

After three months, the long search for Whetstone was over.

Laura texted Ike, "What's going on?"

She got no answer. She texted Dave and Mona. All her texts and
calls went unanswered.

Mona was silent and for good reason. She'd known the location
of Jason Whetstone from day one. And she'd been having an affair
with his kidnapper, Dave Fogel.

A man torn between two novelists, Fogel quickly became an
open book.

Fogel told police that when the affair started, he was between
jobs and had loads of time on his hands. He drove up to Durant,
Oklahoma, to visit Mona. What began as a supportive friendship
quickly spiraled into a passionate tryst. Dave spent days with
Mona, doing odd jobs around her house, visiting the local casino
in the evenings. He was about to head to Hochatown, Oklahoma,
to do repair work on cabins when he half joked to Mona that for
the right price, he'd take Whetstone along with him and pressure
him to side in her favor, vindicating her original claim of owner-
ship to the childhood drama and "to get back at Laura." Mona
"liked the idea instantly," Fogel said. He canceled plans to head
to Hochatown, because Mona suggested they hide Whetstone at
the Submarine.

"Ike was out of town for a volunteer gig in Honduras," Fogel
told police. "He'd asked me to keep an eye on the house. All I had
to do was get Whetstone there."

Days after Fogel returned to Garland, he was busy casing Whetstone's neighborhood, aiming to find an ideal spot to overtake the
mediator at gunpoint. His planning worked. That fateful February
morning, Fogel took an Uber to Whetstone's neighborhood. At
a stop sign, Fogel demanded entry to Whetstone's car. Then he
instructed Whetstone to power off his phone and drive to Garland.

They parked inside the Submarine's garage. Fogel then locked and barricaded Whetstone inside a bedroom, but not before giving him a sedative.

Later, he received a text from Mona.

MONA: Do you have him?

DAVE: Yes.

MONA: Laura's gonna freak out, and I'm here for it.

DAVE: What next?

MONA: I'll take care of it.

Fogel was unsure how to interpret that, only that he thought Mona would be the next person to visit the Submarine.

"I'd done my part. I moved his car to my house. Mona was going to, you know, interview him or something. After another week had passed, she wouldn't tell me how she'd taken care of Whetstone, only that I shouldn't worry about him," Fogel said.

For better or worse, Fogel's internet search history revealed that he was still thinking of it. On day eight, he'd searched: *how long can someone survive without food.*

It would be the early return of Ike Stratham that unveiled the truth about Whetstone.

"I came home to a horror. A horrible smell came from the back room. A sense I wasn't alone." He entered the hallway, found a locked door, and kicked it in. Ike rang the police, then Fogel. Fogel, he said, issued several expletives and broke down on the phone, saying he needed to talk to Mona. Mona, he cried out to Ike, knew all about it.

Fogel walked from his own house to the Submarine. He was arrested on the porch, where he had once come to pick up Laura for dates.

"I didn't think this would happen," he said to officers. "I didn't think anyone would get hurt. Mona said she'd take care of it."

While investigators collected evidence at the Submarine, Ike sent Mona more than thirty texts filled with questions and accusations.

As her phone blew up, Mona spent three hours typing up a final chapter for her blog and scheduled it to post automatically at a future date. Then she texted Ike that she was on her way and was aghast at what Dave had done.

Ike recalls that she wrote in all caps, "I'M COMPLETELY SHOCKED!"

Next, she drove to the house where Ike, Laura, local police, and Vanderbilt had gathered.

"I wanted to see her face," Vanderbilt said. "To look her in the eye for Jason. She was stone cold."

A long night unraveled for the Stratham family. Ike, whose bag was still packed from his trip, hunkered down across town with Laura.

"We mourn the loss of this talented man and will pray he didn't suffer and his killers will be brought to justice," Kellog said to a TV news reporter.

The investigation moved swiftly, though Mona remained silent.

"She wouldn't talk to anyone but her attorney," Ike said. "She stared at the floor when I asked her if she was sorry that she'd ruined Dave's life and caused Whetstone's death. And, not inconsequentially, the fact that my house was ruined."

Ike had already begun to think of having the Submarine razed.

"All Mona would say was that she couldn't help who fell in love with her and what they'd do for love," Ike said.

According to the medical examiner, Whetstone had been dead for months when Ike found him. Authorities wouldn't immediately comment on the contents of the deadly drug cocktail. However, court records would later reveal that Fogel administered a fatal dose of his parents' prescription medications.

Whetstone was quietly laid to rest, surrounded by friends from his dog-rescue group and several of his former clients, including the men from the falling-leaves case.

"He didn't deserve this," one of the men told *The Garlandian*. "What's wrong with people?"

While Fogel and Mona awaited their days in court, one final twist in the meat-sauce story surfaced.

Exactly a month after Mona's arrest, her *My Beef* blog spit out a new entry.

Dear Readers, by now, you may know about recent events and accusations in the case of Jason Whetstone's disappearance and David Fogel's involvement. Follow the steps below to read the full, untold account.

Readers were directed to a paywall, behind which they could read the latest entry in her ongoing blog series. One commenter said the long-form entry read "like an unintentionally comic romance." It expanded on her family and the tortured relationship with Fogel, on whom she laid full blame for Jason Whetstone's tragic death.

Readers swarmed the page, paying to read one of the last chapters of the Stratham family drama.

Mona was convicted of criminal conspiracy and felony murder. Fogel was convicted of felony kidnapping and felony murder. Mona's attorneys are working on an appeal.

The Garlandian questioned everyone in the case about why a writer would go to these unlawful lengths.

Vanderbilt puzzled it out. "I think Mona got what she wanted. Fame and a lot of sympathy. But it's her failure to accept any responsibility or show remorse that's troubling. There's no remedy for a person like that. Jason was right, you know. He would have said it was never really about the meat sauce."

With the Right Bait

FROM *Playing Games*

REGGIE NEVER GAVE a damn about games. Life was not a fucking game. Life was about winning and losing, yes, but the stakes were a lot higher than a $46 pissant pot in poker or bragging rights to a silver trophy. When Reggie Lymon went up against somebody, it was only with the goal of busting them in the teeth and leaving them gasping for breath, not gleefully shouting "Bingo!" when his numbers were called before some other guy's. Games were for losers.

But Reggie was in Huntington Memorial Hospital, had been for two days now waiting for part of his colon to be removed, and what the hell else was there to do for a seventy-two-year-old man imprisoned in a hospital but starve, play games, and watch television?

Of course, playing a game had been Brenda's idea—"I know what we can do! Let's play a game!"—because showing childlike enthusiasm for the dumbest shit imaginable was his wife's greatest talent. He tried to decline in the most polite way possible, which was to say no so many times he nearly slapped her across the face with his dinner tray just to get her to shut up, but she was relentless. No matter how many options he declined, she found another to offer him.

Cards? *No thank you.*

Chess? *Get serious.*

Trivia? *Not a chance.*

By the time she got around to naming board games, his will to deny her was all but exhausted. *Monopoly, Life, Clue, Scrabble . . .*

"Mouse Trap," he said, surprising even himself. "Do they have Mouse Trap?"

The kid's game had been his favorite growing up, something he and his older sister Emily had played nonstop. He hadn't thought about it in decades. But what he remembered now was how stupidly simple it was, a metaphor for life itself: build a trap, catch a rat.

And oh yes, Reggie knew all about rats. Dirty, filthy vermin skulking around in the dark, making plans to slip into a man's home and rob him blind. Reggie had a big rat needing extermination right now, and he was going to see the job done before he got rolled into an operating room in this godforsaken dump and came out with a sheet over his face.

His wife was the rat in question.

Besides being a lightweight intellectually, Brenda was also a gold digger. Reggie had known this for years. Maybe she was kinder and more selfless than most, and maybe whatever sleeping around she was doing behind his back was being done so discreetly, he'd yet to see any concrete evidence of it, but she was a gold digger just the same. What kind of idiot would Reggie have been had he married this woman eight years ago, seventeen years his junior and magazine cover beautiful, and not understood that his money was all she was really after?

Not that Reggie himself hadn't benefitted from the marriage. Up until his body started giving out on him three years ago, the devil's bargain he had made with Brenda had been paying off nicely. Service, companionship, and all the sex an old man could handle. He had little reason to complain. But underneath it all, for all the good stuff on the surface, he knew what motives were being hidden from him, the betrayal of trust that was coming. It was inevitable.

So as his doctor visits and medical bills piled up, as his physical ability to be a vibrant and active partner to his wife dwindled away, he began to pay closer attention to her, to watch and listen for the telltale signs of a woman looking past her current husband to her next one. And yeah, it wasn't his imagination, those signs were there now. The uptick in spending, in preparation for the free rein she'd have with his money once it was all hers; the lunches and dinners with "girlfriends" that had become more frequent and of longer duration; the weight she was losing to fit into clothes she never felt the need to fit into before.

If she wasn't already banging somebody on the side, it was just a matter of time.

His analyst would say this was all in his mind, a byproduct of his lifelong inclinations toward paranoia combined with the stress that went along with his declining health. But Reggie's analyst was full of shit. This was real. Brenda was counting the days until his death.

While she was waiting for him to die, however, secretly laying the groundwork for her next and better life without him, she was continuing to play the loving and devoted wife to the hilt. Sitting in on every meeting with his doctors, monitoring his diet and medications, encouraging him to stay positive and think only good thoughts. She prepared his meals personally, careful to avoid his numerous food allergies (shellfish, nuts, eggs—the list seemed endless), as if his life was as important to her as her own. Anyone other than Reggie would have thought Brenda was an angel.

But she wasn't an angel. She was a rat.

And soon she would be a rat in a trap. All Reggie had to do was live long enough to build the trap, bait it, and spring it on her.

They had mouse trap down in the hospital rec room, but much to Reggie's chagrin, it wasn't quite the game he remembered as a kid. At some point in the last sixty years, some genius had decided to change it, add "cheese pieces" for players to collect and dumb down the Rube Goldberg–like machine that dropped a net over the losing player's plastic mouse at the end. The changes weren't fundamental, but just significant enough to make playing the game more of a challenge for Reggie than he'd been prepared for.

That first night, they set up the board and played for about twenty minutes. Brenda wanted to go a whole round but Reggie begged off, claiming to be tired but actually just acting on an inspired thought. He would stretch this thing out. Make the game last for three days, right up until his scheduled operation, so that it only ended when he was ready for it to end. Reggie had a soft spot for symbolism and springing the game's plastic trap on Brenda's green plastic mouse only hours before he sprang the trap on her for real, and for good, struck him as the height of poetic justice.

So they went slow. Took turns flipping the spinner, moving their little mice (Reggie's was red) down the meandering path on the game board, one or two squares at a time, building the convoluted mouse trap, piece by piece, as they went. The lamppost, the stop sign, the boot, and so on and so forth. Reggie might have actually been having fun if he weren't so fucking hungry all the time. The diet his doctors had him on since he'd been admitted held him in a constant state of what had to be malnutrition, the food he was served as distasteful as it was insubstantial. Plus, Reggie was too intent on winning to enjoy the damn game. He had to win, or what the hell was the point of this nonsense? And winning was going to be tricky, because this was a game of chance; no amount of genius or skill could guarantee the outcome. Unless he could figure out a way to cheat, which he would be more than happy to do if such a tack proved necessary.

Brenda, on the other hand, *was* having fun. Making jokes, laughing at all the game's twists and turns. Two steps forward, three steps back, it was all the same difference to his wife; she giggled and clapped her hands with glee either way.

Reggie just let her enjoy herself. She was on the clock even more than he was, and she didn't even know it.

"Why don't you just write her out of your will or something?" Melvin had asked.

Reggie had known the question was coming. His nephew was a dim bulb, but he wasn't a total idiot.

This was a couple days before Reggie went into the hospital, in his bedroom at home while Brenda was out "at the spa," she said.

"Because I don't have time for all that. Phil would ask a million questions about my reasons and none of them would satisfy him. He'd insist I wait until after the operation to make sure I was in my right mind, and I want this shit settled before that."

"Phil" was Phillip Landsbury, Reggie's longtime attorney.

"*Are* you in your right mind?" Melvin asked, grinning.

"Look, do you want the job or not?" Reggie asked. He'd offered his nephew sixty grand in cash to arrange for Brenda's murder, and now he was starting to regret he'd ever brought the kid into his confidence.

"Sure, sure, Uncle," Melvin said. "I've got this, no problem."

Which had been spoken like the sociopathic little mobster Melvin was. A twenty-two-year-old health nut with muscles on top of muscles, he'd driven his mother, Reggie's sister Emily, to an early grave, dabbling in crimes both petty and felonious for most of his life, yet he and Reggie had always shared an odd affinity for one another. Maybe because they both recognized a fellow, conscienceless predator when they saw one. It was hard not to admire one's own mirror image, after all.

That Melvin was capable of murder, Reggie had no doubt. And Reggie knew he wouldn't much give a damn that Brenda was the one Reggie needed killed, either. Sentimentality stuck to the kid like wood to a magnet. But could his nephew be bought for a reasonable price, and counted on to do the job right? That was the great unknown.

"How will you do it?" Reggie asked.

"Don't worry about that," Melvin said, biting the end off one of his ubiquitous vegan energy bars. The crap he ate and drank in the interests of fitness and health sometimes made Reggie want to puke. Meatless breakfast sausage? As the kids today liked to ask, *WTF*? "Unless you want it done a certain way, in which case—"

"It'll cost extra. Yeah, never mind, then. Do it however you want. I'll let you know when."

Reggie decided "when" should be Friday afternoon, the day Reggie was scheduled to be operated on. Hungry and tired and in constant pain, he was feeling more and more like he wasn't going to make it out of surgery and he wanted to know with some certainty, before the anesthesia kicked in, that Brenda had been paid her due.

He remained committed to killing her but, by Wednesday morning, he was fighting off second thoughts. In Reggie's experience, doctors were wrong almost as often as they were right, but maybe this time what Daniel Greene, his analyst, would have told him—were Reggie crazy enough to consult him—would have been on the money. Maybe Brenda's bad intentions really were all in Reggie's head. Maybe Reggie was just a paranoid lunatic hopped up on pain killers and food deprivation who was seeing a "rat" where none existed. Maybe his wife really did love him and wanted nothing but the best for him.

In playing the game with her for an hour and a half over the last two nights, he kept finding himself wondering why he hadn't tried harder to enjoy the simple things with this woman. Going out to a concert or a ballgame, driving out along the coast with the top down on the convertible, sitting by the pool eating grilled burgers and dogs. What would have been the harm? Was her laughter really that annoying, her childlike innocence that great an offense?

But rather than take her for the uncomplicated soul she was and relish her company, he'd all but avoided it instead, only drawing near for a few minutes at a time to issue an instruction or lay his hands on her body as a means of foreplay. Like everyone else in Reggie's life, Brenda was only good for the bare necessities, a scratch or two where he had an itch and nothing more.

Watching her at the hospital as their rounds of Mouse Trap progressed, her brow furrowed with concentration as she struggled to put one new piece or another on the game board trap, he had a hard time maintaining the outrage he would need to go through with his plans to kill her. But he managed. His anger and suspicion were the only things keeping him alive now, and he either held on tight to both or perished.

Neither his surgery nor his cancer was supposed to kill him, if his doctors could be trusted to tell him the truth, but Reggie had already made up his mind that his life was over. There was so little current left running through the veins of his ancient body, so little desire to care what the next day would bring, he was practically dead as it was. So he was either going to die on the operating table in two days or at home in his bed six months from now, no matter what statistical arguments his physicians and wife offered him to the contrary, and he wasn't going to go without putting everything and everybody in their proper place. He'd been nobody's sucker in life and he wasn't going to be anybody's in death.

Maybe if Reggie had had someone other than Brenda to focus on, he would have directed his scorn elsewhere. But his wife was all the family he had, other than his nephew Melvin. He'd scared everyone else off: friends, partners, distant relatives. When you spent your entire life building an empire with a scythe in one hand and a bullwhip in the other, this was destined to be your reward: a cheering section of one.

And Brenda was the one. She was the one waiting to cash in on his demise, to take the fruits of his labor and squander them on God only knew what, perhaps starting as soon as the last of his ashes were poured into the urn. Even if she meant no harm, if there was no malice intended in such self-gratification at her late husband's expense, the injustice of it would have been crime enough to satisfy Reggie. Had she earned the wealth she was in line to inherit? By blowing and banging him a few times a month, keeping him fed and his home well maintained? By giving him someone to talk to when he needed to rant, helping him in and out of the bath when he was too weak to be trusted doing so alone? No. No!

And if she'd been doing all that while fucking some guy at the tennis club, or the bank, or the gym where she seemed to be spending more and more of her time lately? Even if she was just *thinking* about it?

Death was too good for her.

So Reggie's resolve held. The game went on and his plans for murder remained in effect—until an unexpected complication threatened to render them useless:

"There's no diving board," Brenda said.

"What do you mean, there's no diving board?"

"I mean, it's not here," Brenda said. "It's not in the box."

And hell if she wasn't right. The damn diving board was not in the game box. Reggie shuffled through the remaining pieces of the trap himself and couldn't find it.

"Shit!"

What the hell was he supposed to do now? The game had to end tomorrow night, only hours before Melvin was scheduled to earn his sixty grand by murdering Brenda in whatever fashion he had devised, and there was no way to end the game without a goddamn diving board. A diving board from which the diver could jump, into the wading pool, triggering the net that would drop like a feather onto Brenda's little green mouse, foreshadowing with perfect precision her own fatal downfall the next day.

"It's okay, baby," Brenda said, trying to head off one of Reggie's signature tantrums before she had to call a nurse. "We can play something else."

"Bullshit! We're damn near finished, we can't stop now!"

"But what can we do? If we don't have all the pieces—"

"Go buy another copy of the game. And don't come back here without one."

"Are you serious? You really want me to buy another copy of Mouse Trap just to get the diving board?"

"Tell me: Do I look serious? Or do I look like I'm joking?"

It was a question his wife might have once been dumb enough to actually answer, but tonight, she just let out a big sigh, kissed him on the forehead, and left, nearly colliding with her step-nephew Melvin as they passed each other at the door.

"Did I miss something?" Melvin asked, taking a seat at his uncle's bedside.

"The fucking game's incomplete," Reggie said, nodding at the game board and the partial Rube Goldberg machine spread out across his lap.

"What the hell is this?" Melvin couldn't help but grin, tickled by all the colored plastic. "Is that—"

"Yeah. So what?"

"Mouse Trap, right? You guys have been playin' Mouse Trap? For real?"

"I've got my reasons. Did you come here just to piss me off, or was there something else?"

Melvin started peeling a banana he'd taken from his jacket pocket. The sonofabitch was always eating something. Reggie hated bananas but his mouth watered, all the same. "We've got a business deal to close, Uncle. Remember?"

"You'll get your money, Melvin. Don't worry."

"Uh-huh. And when would that be, exactly? Before your surgery or after you die in the middle of it? Come on, Uncle." Melvin took a bite out of the banana. Reggie watched his jaws work with an envy that almost had him sobbing. "I don't mean to be a downer or anything, but we both know you may not be around after Friday."

"And I'll tell you something else we both know, asshole: that I'd be a complete idiot to pay you sixty grand now for a job you may never actually do if, as you say, I'm not around after Friday."

"Okay. Point taken. So how about this." He bit off another two inches of banana. "You can get your hands on fifteen thou by tomorrow, can't you? As a retainer?"

Of course Reggie could. It would be complicated, but it was doable, and there wasn't much point in Reggie denying it. Still . . .

"No," Reggie said.

"No? Seriously?"

"You heard me."

Melvin nodded and finished off the banana, tossing the peel into a nearby trash can. "Okay. No problem. To be honest, I thought this might happen, so it's all good."

"What? You thought *what* might happen?"

"That you'd lose your nerve and back out. I mean, it's understandable." He stood up to leave. "This was a very big adventure we were about to embark on, you and me, and not everybody's got the stomach for it."

"You think I've lost my nerve? Fuck you!" Reggie said, gasping for air. "Nothing scares me, you little punk! Nothing!"

"Then we're still on for Friday?"

"You're damn right we are."

"And you'll have fifteen grand here, waiting for me to pick up, by tomorrow afternoon at three?"

Reggie realized immediately what had just happened: his nephew had played him. Used Reggie's pride as a lure and drawn him into a mouse trap of his own, *snap!*

"Yeah, sure. Fifteen grand, by three tomorrow. Now get the hell out of here before I call for security."

Brenda arrived at the hospital Thursday morning with fifteen thousand dollars in cash and a new copy of the Mouse Trap game. Reggie told her the money was to pay off an old gambling debt and a man would be coming by later to collect it. Her husband liked to bet on sports from time to time, always seeming to lose more than he won, so Brenda didn't question his explanation. She gave him a big kiss and promised to come back in several hours for their last evening round of Mouse Trap before his operation the next day.

And how would she be spending her time in the interim? Reggie asked.

At the tanning salon, she said.

It was another mark against her, this feeble addition to all her other sorry alibies (the gym, the spa, the tennis club, etc., etc.), and Reggie had spent the last eleven hours doing a final tally: Should he kill the woman or not? He wasn't losing his nerve, as his nephew suggested the night before, he was simply making sure. Testing his suspicions against his perceived evidence. Lying flat on a gurney tomorrow at 4 p.m., watching a parade of fluorescent ceiling lights march past his fading vision as they wheeled him into surgery, he wanted all his doubts erased. If he was going to have a change of heart where his wife was concerned, now was the time.

But no—there would be no reprieve for Mrs. Brenda Lymon. Given the choice between having an innocent woman murdered in error and letting a guilty one go free, Reggie would take the former every time.

So it was with almost no regrets whatsoever that he gave Melvin his retainer when his nephew came looking for it that afternoon. He was doing the right thing. A man had to trust his instincts, right up to his last breath.

"I tell you what, Uncle," Melvin said, biting into the sandwich he'd brought with him today. A goddamn *sandwich*, the sonofabitch! Reggie's last meal had been a limp green salad and a bowl of chicken-less chicken soup. "I'm gonna give you a few more hours to think about this. Just to make absolutely certain this is what you want."

"I don't need any more time to think about it. I just paid you, didn't I?"

"All the same. If you want me to go through with it, you're gonna have to give me a call. Say, around eight. Leave a message if I don't answer."

"A message? What kind of message?"

"Make it simple." He took another bite of his sandwich, which from where Reggie was sitting and salivating, looked like ham and cheese, no doubt on some kind of gluten-free excuse for sourdough. "Something like, 'The eagle has landed.'"

"Are you *shitting me?*"

"Of course I'm shitting you," Melvin guffawed, crumbs flying out of his mouth in all directions. "Just say, 'We're on for Friday.' As if you're talking about your surgery tomorrow. Okay?"

"Okay."

"Nothing happens if I don't get that call. Are we clear?"

"We're clear. But—"

"Yeah?"

"Do me one last favor before you go, will you, kid? Please."

When Reggie got a good look at Brenda's left hand that night, as they were setting up the board for their final round of Mouse Trap, he knew he could make the call his nephew was waiting for with a totally clear conscience. Because what married woman who wasn't cheating on her husband went around without wearing her $38,000 wedding ring?

"Are you okay, baby? You aren't worried about tomorrow, are you?"

Brenda had picked up on his sense of distraction. Of course he was worried about tomorrow; for all he knew, Friday was going to be his last day on earth. There was no avoiding the fact. But that wasn't what was most on his mind at this moment. The game was. For three nights now, he'd engaged in this idiotic throwback to his childhood for one reason and one reason only—to put a fitting exclamation mark on his wife's impending murder, to exit the world (if that was to be his fate) on one last, fiendishly clever act of sticking it to anyone who had the audacity to cross him—and it was all for nothing if he didn't end the exercise by winning. When all was said and done, he had to drop a red plastic net over a green plastic mouse to symbolize the justice he was about to mete out against his wife. This liar, this adulterer, this *rat* sitting before him now.

He had to win. He had to.

And finally, relying on the strength of his intellect and the power of his luck, he did it. He got Brenda's fucking mouse on the space of death, right where he wanted it, and he pulled the trigger. Down went the little silver ball along the winding blue staircase, around the red chute and into the yellow bucket; up the ball went from there, propelled on the arm of a blue, broomstick catapult, to take another red chute ride into a similarly colored bathtub, where it fell down the tub's oversize drain onto the previously missing diving board below. At the other end of the board, a green diver was kicked into a yellow washtub, which upset the delicate balance of a red net perching at the top of a connected yellow pole. The net fell, inching down the pole's serrated surface, and landed as soft as a feather, Brenda's mouse trapped hopelessly in its clutches.

Game over.

Reggie laughed like a kid at the circus. He couldn't remember the last time anything had felt this good to him.

And Brenda, God bless her clueless ass, laughed right along with him, until she realized laughing wasn't all her husband was doing.

"Reggie, what's that you're eating?"

He took another celebratory bite, a big grin on his face. "It's a sandwich. What's it look like?"

His first guess had been right: ham and cheese, though the bread wasn't sourdough, or gluten-free. It was just a stale, garden variety white. His nephew's palate was beginning to show signs of normalizing.

"You can't be eating a sandwich! Are you crazy? Where did you get that?"

Brenda stood and reached for what remained of the half-sandwich in his hand, but he pulled away, laughing again, and stuffed the last of it in his mouth. After eight days of hospital slop, ham and cheese tasted like a Porterhouse steak on his tongue.

"Oh, my God," Brenda said, near tears. "What have you done? Nurse!" She snatched up the call button on Reggie's bed. "*Nurse!*"

Reggie just went on laughing, enjoying the show. His wife's final performance of "The Loving Partner" before he made the call to Melvin that would end her acting career forever. In the several minutes that followed, chaos reigned. The nurse rushed in and together with Brenda, began peppering Reggie with questions. They found the plastic wrap he had peeled off Melvin's sandwich and took turns sniffing it for clues.

It was hysterical, and Reggie would have laughed through it all had he not been preoccupied with the suddenly arduous task of breathing. Out of nowhere, he was having a lot of trouble getting air into his lungs. And swallowing. Two things he had never had trouble doing before. Something was happening to him and it wasn't good.

Recognizing his distress, Brenda began to scream, sending the hospital staff into overdrive. A doctor appeared and two other nurses. It could have been an army of medical personnel and it wouldn't have made any difference. They couldn't clear his airway in time to save him.

With the last few minutes of life he had left, Reggie did the math and came to a few conclusions. The first was that he very possibly owed his wife an apology, because they always made you take your jewelry off at tanning salons and Brenda might have simply forgotten to put her wedding ring back on after today's session in the booth. Maybe it was fortunate that Reggie would never be able to make that phone call his nephew was waiting for.

His second conclusion was that a man with as many food allergies as Reggie should have known better than to eat anything Melvin considered edible, no matter how ordinary it appeared. Meat was never just meat with Melvin and dairy was never just dairy. If a nut could be used as the basis for something instead of the milk from a cow—almonds, for instance—you could bet Melvin had it in his refrigerator.

And finally, just as his lights were about to go out for good, Reggie's last cogent thought was that, of all the things you could bait a mouse trap with, one old standby was still the most reliable. Got the little bastard almost every time.

Cheese.

Baby Trap

FROM *School of Hard Knox*

Posted on Reddit in r/JustNoMIL:

I need advice. My husband died two months ago, and I've got an eight-month-old baby and no job. There's some life insurance money, but it won't last long, and no place that would hire me would pay enough to support us. I don't have family to help me—my parents and my husband's father died years ago, and we were only children. Plus we moved here when I was pregnant, so I haven't had a chance to make friends.

But yesterday I got a letter from a lawyer. My husband's uncle died last year, but it took a while for the lawyer to track us down. The uncle left his house to my husband, and with him gone, that house belongs to me. It's in the town down south where my husband grew up, and the cost of living down there is so low that the insurance payout should last long enough for me to figure out what to do next. There's just one snag: my mother-in-law. I'll call her the Harridan, which means a bossy old woman. (Three years of liberal arts education weren't wasted on me!) I only saw her once, and that was plenty.

My husband and I met in college and started dating when I was a freshman and he was a sophomore. Near the end of his senior year, I got pregnant. Yes, we used birth control, but it happened. He already had a great job lined up, and we decided to get married right after he graduated. Then I'd take a year or two to tend to the baby, and eventually go back to get my degree.

I wanted him to tell his mother right away, especially since she and I had never even met, but he wanted to wait until graduation. She and I sat together for the ceremony, but I could tell she wasn't happy about it, and she made a face when he said we were all going out afterward. On the way, she whispered to him that she thought the celebration should be "only family."

After we got to the restaurant and ordered, he sprang it on her: the job, the wedding plans, and the baby.

She freaked!

She said she'd never let him marry some tramp who'd baby-trapped him, and since he clearly couldn't make good decisions, he had to give up his dream job to go back home with her. As for the baby, she said either I could abort it—IT!—or give it to her to raise.

That was enough for me. I got up and walked out. And after the longest five minutes of my life, he came running after me and apologized. He said his mother wasn't going to be in our lives, and he never spoke to her again.

So why is the Harridan an issue now? Because she lives in the town where the house is. Should I risk moving there? And if I do, how can I protect myself and my baby?

IT TOOK ME a month and a half to make the arrangements to move to that inherited house in Rocky Shoals, North Carolina, and I hadn't been there twenty-four hours when I spotted the red Cadillac Escalade for the first time. It was parked along the dirt road that ran parallel to the property line, and since it was outside the fence, technically it wasn't my business, but it was a weird place to park.

The house was on a dinky two-lane road with no other houses in eyeshot, so the car didn't belong to anybody visiting a neighbor. It wasn't a bus stop, scenic vista, or roadside shrine to a traffic accident victim, and nobody went hunting in a shiny late-model Escalade.

There was absolutely no good reason for the SUV to be there.

When I stepped off the screened-in front porch and looked in that direction, the Escalade's engine started up and the car left dust trails in the field as it curved around to get back onto the road, moving so fast that I couldn't get a good look at the driver.

That hadn't been suspicious at all.

I went back inside, making sure the door was locked behind me, and armed the state-of-the-art security system I'd had installed before moving in. The folks on Reddit had been firm that the house needed the best cameras and tech available, and I agreed completely.

I also turned on a few lights throughout the house, including the back bedroom, trying to make it look as if there were multiple people in residence. Then I went to the kitchen to make a grilled cheese sandwich and warm up some tomato soup for dinner. Afterward, I put Barney in his crib and spent the rest of the evening crocheting and watching TV.

Just before bedtime, I looked out the window to see if the SUV had returned, but I didn't see it.

The next morning, I dressed Barney in a crocheted hat and jacket and put him in the wicker rocking chair on the porch to take pictures. When I had enough, I carried him to the car and posed him in the car seat for more photos.

That's when I saw the red Escalade, parked in the same place as before. And again, as soon as I looked toward it, it drove away.

Leaving Barney where he was, I went back inside just long enough to make sure the alarm was set, and then headed off on errands: curbside pickup of groceries I'd ordered online, drop off of a couple of postage-paid padded envelopes at a FedEx box, a gas stop for the car, and finally, a trip through a McDonald's drive-through for lunch.

I spotted the SUV, or one just like it, three times. Rocky Shoals isn't a big town, so seeing it again could have been a coincidence, but I didn't believe it.

As soon as I returned to the house and had Barney and the groceries squared away, I followed Reddit's advice again and created a file of incidents, which so far was just the times and locations where I'd seen the Escalade. I thought about calling the cops, but what would I say? "I saw a car three or four times, maybe five. No, nobody threatened me." So I went back to my crocheting.

The Escalade showed up in the late afternoon and stayed until well after dark.

For the next week, the Escalade was nearby every day, parking at a safe distance, and appearing in town whenever Barney and I left the house, but it stayed far enough away that I couldn't see the driver or license plate, let alone get a picture. I carefully documented every time I spotted it, but I didn't think there was anything else I could do as long as they kept their distance. I didn't even know if it was the Harridan herself following or if somebody was working for her.

Eight days after I'd moved in, my stalker took it up a notch. The security system included an obvious camera over the front door, and she had enough sense to avoid it, but she didn't know that there were hidden cameras and motion sensors that covered the entire perimeter of the house. I knew precisely when she came onto the property that night and made her way around the house until she got to the window of Barney's room, where the glow from the nightlight showed through a gap in the curtains.

Part of me wanted to charge out to confront her, but I had to stick to the plan. That meant I just watched and videoed as she spent a good five minutes peering inside the room before creeping back to the SUV. Unfortunately, she'd worn a COVID-style face mask and a scarf to cover her hair, so I wouldn't have been able to pick her out of a lineup. Still, I could tell that she was white, with a thin build and no trace of athleticism in her movements. Just like the Harridan.

The next morning, I considered next steps. Some Reddit advisers suggested I call the police as soon as anything illegal happened, and trespassing and peeping certainly qualified, but others warned that bringing them in too soon could make me look paranoid or crazy. And though I was sure it was the Harridan, I had no proof. Finally I decided to wait another night, hoping she'd show her face to the camera.

I stuck to my usual routine. Dressing Barney in a new hat and jacket, taking photos, dropping off packages, and TV and crocheting in the evening. At bedtime, I did "accidentally" enlarge the gap in the curtains in Barney's room, hoping to tempt the Harridan to come closer and stay longer. Then I retreated to my bedroom to keep watch on my phone, sitting in the dark so she'd think I'd gone to bed after putting Barney down for the night.

She was so sure of herself that she only waited fifteen minutes after I turned off the lights. She started out wearing the mask again, but she must have had a runny nose from wandering around at all hours of the night, because she pulled the mask down to wipe it with a wadded tissue. When she didn't pull the mask up again, I got a perfect shot of her face.

It was, without a doubt, the Harridan.

My cell phone was already in my hand to dial 911. "Hello? My name is Runa Darlow, and there's a prowler outside my house. Can you send somebody right away?"

The Rocky Shoals cops had enough sense not to use their siren, but either the Harridan heard their car, or got spooked, or had had her fill of voyeurism because she was already driving off by the time the patrol car pulled into the driveway.

I met the two uniformed officers on the front porch while wearing a loose T-shirt and flannel pajama pants to show I was so shaken I hadn't taken time to dress.

The older cop was a man with a sturdy build and reddish-brown hair cut short, and he was followed by a blond with hair braided and coiled behind her head and a slightly pointed nose.

"She just left!" I said breathlessly.

"Just calm down and tell us what happened," the male cop said using a tone that he probably meant to be reassuring.

I took a deep breath. "I'd just gone to bed and I heard something outside the window. So I called up the app—"

"The what, now?"

"The app? On my phone? It's tied into the security system."

"Oh, like one of them Ring doorbells."

I resisted the urge to roll my eyes. "Yeah, only it shows all around the house. Anyway, I saw a woman sneaking around, looking in the window! Here!"

I shoved the phone at them and let the man fumble with it before the woman reached over and pushed the right buttons to start the video showing the Harridan's face.

"Isn't that—?" the woman started to say, but the man interrupted with, "Hold on, Addalyn. Let me take a look." He watched the clip three more times before saying, "Well, this could be anyone."

"Seriously?" I said. "She's perfectly recognizable."

"Not to me. Now show me where this unknown person was."

I wanted to accuse the Harridan right then and there, but instead I dutifully led them to the side of the house to show them where she'd been standing. The man barely examined the scene, and he didn't even try to take pictures of the footprints under the window.

He said, "It doesn't look to me like he or she was doing anything but looking—no attempt to break in or anything like that. No signs of a weapon."

Addalyn didn't speak, but her expression said she was wondering the same thing I was. How could the guy be so sure she was unarmed when he wouldn't even admit to her presenting as female?

"You think she was some kind of pervert?" I said.

He waved away the suggestion. "Let's not rush to conclusions. It could be completely innocent. Maybe he or she had car trouble and was looking for help. This place is pretty remote."

"She drove away just fine," I retorted, "and leaving that aside, why didn't she come to the front door?"

"Well . . ." I could tell he was thinking as fast as he could. "Were your front lights on?"

"No."

"There's your answer then. He or she went to see if anybody was awake but when he or she didn't see you, he or she left and got his or her car working." All too casually, he asked, "I don't suppose you got a look at the vehicle?"

"Not tonight," I said, "but there's been a red Cadillac Escalade parked near here several times the past few days."

He swallowed visibly. "Lots of those around. It probably had nothing to do with the person with car trouble."

I wanted to argue with him, but he struck me as the kind who'd have dug his heels in if I tried to critique his stellar investigative technique, and Addalyn wouldn't meet my gaze. So I pretended to be grateful for their rushing out there, added in a hint of embarrassment for having made a fuss over nothing, and after getting their names, let them go.

As soon as I got inside, I microwaved some coffee and set my laptop up on the kitchen table to do some research. The male cop was Theodore Fry, and I spent quite a while checking him out, but didn't find anything particularly significant. He'd been on the job for six years and seemed to have had moderate success apprehending shoplifters and teenaged joyriders, but nothing seemed shady.

His partner, Addalyn Cooper, had less time on the force, but better arrest statistics, and nothing in her background set off any alarm bells, either.

I kept digging for dirt about the Rocky Shoals police, but if anything crooked was happening, it hadn't made it into the news or onto social media. I'd originally ignored the department's own website, figuring there'd be nothing useful there, but that's where I caught what I'd missed when I planned the move.

Nolan McIntyre, the Rocky Shoals police chief, had been elected the previous year, and most of the campaign coverage focused on his many ties to the community. Apparently he was related to a large percentage of the town's population, which likely helped him win the election. There was an election night photo of him and his proud family: wife, children, parents, siblings, in-laws, and beyond. Right in the middle of the photo, standing next to Chief McIntyre, with a smug smile on her face, was his mother's oldest sister. The caption identified her as Josephine Kemp, but she'd always be the Harridan to me.

I couldn't believe I'd missed it. More importantly, I didn't believe that Fry and Cooper hadn't recognized their boss's aunt. I didn't know if they hadn't admitted it because they were corrupt, or were afraid of their boss, or wanted to allow him to handle it himself. I was betting on it being one of the first two, but I decided to give Chief McIntyre some time to do the right thing.

The next day I called the department to see if any progress had been made, but the woman answering the phone didn't seem to know anything about the case, which led me to believe that no report had been filed. Though I left messages for Fry and Cooper, neither returned my calls. Most telling of all, the red Escalade didn't show up.

I waited another week, making more appearances in town, leaving the curtains half-open, doing everything I could to bait the Harridan into showing herself again. Nothing.

It could have meant that Chief McIntyre had warned her off, but given what I knew of her parenting style, I very much doubted that she was giving up. I had to do something before she did, and I couldn't rely on the Rocky Shoals police for support.

The next morning I checked out the town's three women's clothing shops. The first one was stocked with go-to-church dresses and the second aimed at women the Harridan's age, but the third had what I needed for an outfit that said "available but not slutty." That ended up being jeans a bit tighter than I usually wear them, a low-cut sweater that brought out the blue in my eyes, dangling earrings, and a pair of high heel booties. I already had enough makeup to finish the look.

I didn't see the Escalade, but was hoping somebody in town would report what I'd bought to the Harridan.

That night, after making sure that Barney was secure, I headed for Crossroads Bar and Grille, which was several miles away from Rocky Shoals. It was fairly busy, but not packed, and I found a table where I could nurse my drink and check out the other patrons, looking for a likely target. At seven-thirty or so, a trim man with the beginnings of a bald spot and neither a companion nor a wedding band came in and got a Bud at the bar. There was something about him that made me think he was what I needed, but I did some fast Googling on my phone to confirm it.

By then he'd gone to one of the two pool tables and was lining up shots, so I edged in his direction and watched admiringly. He actually was decent, so my admiration wasn't entirely feigned. He noticed me watching, but pretended not to until I said, "Hey, you're really good."

He thanked me, we introduced ourselves, and he invited me to play. His name was Ike, and fortunately I didn't have to work overly hard to let him win. After a couple hours of pool, conversation, and beer, I'd made it plain that I was interested in continuing our interaction at my place, and he was gratified by my interest. Ike confirmed that we were both sober enough to drive —which I definitely was because I'd dumped most of the alcohol I'd ordered—and followed me back to the house in his car.

I waited for him on the porch before unlocking the front door and going inside. The lights were on in the living room. "That's funny," I said. "I could have sworn I left them off. Anyway, would you like a nightcap?"

He answered by putting his arms around me and I was impressed that he hesitated long enough to ensure that I was willing before leaning in for a kiss.

He had skills, and must have eaten a mint on the way home to make sure his breath didn't smell of stale beer, which I appreciated. Under other circumstances, I'd have been happy to continue on to the bedroom, but before that could happen, Ike and I heard noise coming from the back of the house.

"Is there somebody else here?" Ike said, probably worried that I had a lurking husband or boyfriend. Instead, the Harridan burst out of the hall.

"Where is the baby!" she demanded.

And I looked her right in the eyes and said, "What baby?"

She blinked and froze for a second before saying, "My baby! Where is my baby?"

Even in the heat of the moment, I noticed the pronoun change. "I don't know who you think you are, but if you're not out of my house in ten seconds, I'm calling the cops."

"I'm not leaving without my baby!"

"There's no baby here!"

"You're lying!"

She started toward me, but Ike stepped in front of her. "Ma'am," he said, "you need to calm down."

She actually shoved him aside. *"Where is he?"*

"I don't know what you're talking about. I don't have a baby."

"Lying slut!" Only when she'd lifted it over her head did I realize she was holding a tire iron.

I fell back against the wall and threw my arms over my head to protect myself, but there was no need. I heard an electrical buzz, a scream, and a heavy thud as the Harridan fell to the floor twitching and moaning. Ike had tased her.

As she tried to writhe toward me, Ike blocked her and said, "Stay where you are unless you want me to shock you again."

She used an excellent selection of profanity, but she stopped moving.

"Call 911," Ike said to me.

I nodded shakily and found my purse and cell phone, but dialed the Rocky Shoals department instead. When the desk clerk sounded reluctant to send somebody, Ike took the phone and said, "This is Ike Everett of the Catawba County Police, and I require backup immediately. Or should I call *my* department?" Unsurprisingly, the clerk promised a swift response.

"You're a cop?" I tried to sound surprised, though I'd known he was a cop right away. Among the basket of facts I'd discovered doing research was that Crossroads Bar and Grille was owned by a disabled county cop, and many of his former colleagues hung out there. It hadn't been hard to pick out Ike as a cop, even in civilian clothes. There was something about his haircut, the way he spoke to the owner, and how he carried himself. I hadn't been sure that he'd bring a weapon, but I had hoped. "Ike, this woman is crazy or on something. I do not have a baby."

He nodded, but I could tell he didn't know what to believe. To be fair, it was a bizarre situation. Instead of getting laid, he was having to deal with a home invader and an alleged missing baby. He was obviously relieved when the trio of Rocky Shoals cops swarmed in the door.

Chief McIntyre was a lot scrawnier in person than in his pictures, and had apparently come in such a hurry that his uniform shirt was misbuttoned. He was followed by my friends Fry and Cooper.

McIntyre took in the scene, and if I'd had any doubts about his relationship to the Harridan, they were erased when he said, "Aunt Jo, are you all right?" He turned to glare at Ike. "What the hell is going on here?"

Ike went cold and formal. "The resident and I arrived here at approximately ten p.m. and upon entering, were confronted by that woman. Your aunt?" He raised an eyebrow at McIntyre, who nodded stiffly. "Your aunt accused the resident of hiding a baby, though whose baby she was referring to is unclear. When she tried to attack the resident, I was forced to discharge my Taser to subdue her."

McIntyre sighed. "Addalyn, help my aunt up off the floor." Once the Harridan was settled on the couch, he turned to me with a look that was meant to be intimidating. "Can I have your name?"

"Runa Darlow."

The Harridan snapped, "Her married name is Kemp!"

"She told me her name was Darlow," Ike said.

"Darlow or Kemp, which is it?" McIntyre said.

"For heaven's sake, I think I know my own name."

"Can I see some identification?"

"My driver's license is in my purse." The cops actually tensed when I reached for my purse, as if afraid I were going to pull out a bazooka instead of my wallet. I handed my license to McIntyre.

He squinted from the license to me. I couldn't blame him—the photo was a couple of years old. Then he handed it to Fry, who took it out onto the porch, no doubt intending to see what he could find out about me.

"All right, Miss Darlow . . . It is Miss? Not Mrs.?"

"Ms."

"Ms. Darlow, can you tell me how you know Mrs. Kemp?"

"I *don't* know her!"

"She knows exactly who I am, and I know exactly what she is!" the Harridan snapped. "She's the one who baby-trapped your cousin. I knew she was trouble the second I met her! She probably had something to do with his death, and now she's done something with his child. When she went out tonight without him, I realized she'd left him alone like the trashy excuse for a mother she is, but I couldn't find him. She's abandoned him, or given him away, or who knows what!"

I tried to look baffled. "Do you know what baby she's talking about?"

"That baby is my grandchild! I've seen him with you."

"You've seen . . . ? You mean Barney?" I asked.

"She admits it!" she said triumphantly.

McIntyre shushed her. "And where is Barney?"

"He's in the trunk of my car, but—"

"In the trunk!" Had she been wearing pearls, she'd have clutched them. "Sweet Jesus, she killed my baby!" She broke into loud sobs that I was 85 percent sure were sincere.

McIntyre barked, "Keys?"

"They're in my purse, but I should tell you—" I started to say but McIntyre grabbed it, dumped out the contents, found the keys, and ran outside with Cooper and Ike following. Fry stayed behind with me and the wailing Harridan. While it was good procedure to keep the two of us under observation, from the way his face turned pale green, I suspect it was really to keep from seeing what he thought the others were seeing.

Neither he nor the Harridan was expecting the sudden whoop of laughter from outside.

A moment later, McIntyre came in carrying a baby doll wearing a crocheted hat and jacket. Cooper was trying to hide a grin, but Ike wasn't even making the attempt.

"What the hell is this for?" McIntyre asked.

I wanted to point out that it was perfectly legal to own a baby doll, even if I kept it in my trunk, but I opted for discretion. "I make crocheted baby clothes and blankets to sell on Etsy, and I have Barney to model the merchandise. I've got a crib set up in the back bedroom too. It makes for better pictures." I looked at the Harridan with feigned sympathy. "It never occurred to me that she was talking about Barney. I mean, he doesn't look like a real baby."

It was as if all the air had gone out of the Harridan. "But I saw him, clear as anything," she said in confusion. "He was so much like my son that he could have been his twin. And you! I remember your hair and your eyes."

"I don't know who you met, but it wasn't me. This is a new haircut and I'm wearing colored contacts." I'd lightened my hair color, too, but didn't bring it up.

"Aunt Jo, her license does show her with longer hair and it says her eyes are brown, not blue," McIntyre said.

"Then why is she in this house?" the Harridan asked. "It was left to my son. How did she get it if she's not *her*?"

"I rented it," I said. "I don't know who owns it—I dealt with a property management company."

"But . . ." She was trying to come up with some other way to prove that I was somebody I was not.

I said, "Is that why you've been playing Peeping Tom, to find a baby?"

"She was doing what?" Ike asked.

"I called the cops last week because she was looking in my windows, and I caught her on the video, too, but the officers *said* they didn't know who she was." I didn't have to fake my anger.

McIntyre said, "I was told about that incident, but it was my understanding that the video was unclear."

"It's perfectly clear, and I've still got the file so you can use it for the trial."

"Trial?" the Harridan gasped. "I've done nothing wrong."

"Are you serious? You trespassed, you broke into my home, and you attacked me!"

McIntyre muttered something about his aunt being distraught by the recent loss of her son and started asking questions. Why had I moved to Rocky Shoals? How had I learned about the vacant house? Could he see my lease? What kind of business was crocheting baby blankets? On and on, trying to find some explanation that didn't make his aunt look like a maniac and him look like an idiot. He even asked why I'd decided to change my hair.

When McIntyre reached that far, Ike pulled him aside and after a short discussion, the chief finally took his aunt into custody and the Rocky Shoals crew left.

Ike kindly helped me temporarily cover the kitchen window the Harridan had bashed in to get into the house, but romance was off the table. Unlike Chief McIntyre, Ike was no fool, and he knew something was off, even if he couldn't put his finger on what. He did accept a kiss as a thank you for saving my life, but I didn't expect him to come calling.

It was just as well. I wouldn't be in Rocky Shoals much longer anyway. Now that the Harridan had been arrested for breaking into the house of an innocent woman and claiming that a cheap baby doll was her grandchild, she'd be too busy with legal complications to go looking for my client, who was her real daughter-in-law. I'd sought out the young widow after seeing her Reddit post.

With my help, the client had been safely relocated to a town where she had friends who could help her with the baby, in a state that didn't have grandparent's rights laws. She hadn't run out of money yet, and the management company—which was owned by a grateful former client—would put the house on the market to make sure she had enough to pay the bills for some time to come. The baby, who was actually a girl and who was certainly not named Barney, was reportedly doing very well.

The next day I sent a barrage of anonymous tips to local TV stations and newspapers and took great pleasure in seeing the story go viral.

For the sake of maintaining my cover, I kept crocheting in the evening even though I was awful at it. The items I'd been selling were made by another former client, while a third had set up my Etsy shop to look as if I'd been in business for a while. My line of work, helping women in trouble, makes for very loyal former clients.

I did stop wearing the colored contacts—they were uncomfortable and I no longer needed to look like my client's twin.

After a week, I called the Rocky Shoals police to tell them that I was breaking my lease because I felt unsafe living there. Unsurprisingly, they didn't try to convince me to stay, though they took my contact info so they could be in touch if the case went to trial. Cooper confided that she thought the Harridan was going to take a plea instead and then take a rest cure in a private facility, so I probably wouldn't be needed.

Baby Trap 261

It only took a couple of days to pack up the house. The item that I took the most care with had been hidden behind a wall in the attic: the real Barney.

Of course the baby doll the police had found in my car hadn't actually been Barney. Though it had been advertised as having lifelike features, it wouldn't have fooled anybody as smart as the Harridan. No, the real Barney was an insanely expensive Reborn doll, one of the ultra-realistic baby reproductions designed to help women through infertility, miscarriage, loss of a child, and so on. Barney was so accurate that I half expected him to breathe.

It was no wonder the Harridan had believed it was her grandson. To make him even more convincing, I'd paid extra for a custom job. The client had some of her husband's baby pictures so I'd had the doll maker use them as a model.

Normally I get rid of the props I use for a job, and I certainly had no intention of keeping the crib or crocheting equipment, but I decided to keep Barney. There was no telling when I might need to catch somebody else in a baby trap.

Scorpions

FROM *Dark Yonder*

FROM THE CAMERA'S upward angle, the tear gas canisters streaked brightly against the darkening sky, arcing toward a roaring mass of protestors. The newscaster, in voiceover, yelled his excitement at society coming apart at the seams. As Joan stared at the television, she couldn't help but think the newscaster had been waiting for this night his whole life.

She stank of smoke. Her T-shirt, recently pressed beneath a bullet-resistant vest, was stiff with dried sweat. She'd last showered Tuesday, maybe Wednesday. It was hard to keep track of the days when they blended into a nonstop blur of fire and chanting and the eye-watering stink of pepper spray. She'd entered the bar with her backup piece strapped to her ankle and one of her favorite knives tucked into the pocket of her jeans, having left her badge and sidearm and phone at home.

She had business to discuss—the most serious business—but Reynolds made her wait at the bar for fifteen minutes while he finished his game of pool. Reynolds acting nonchalant in the middle of the biggest protests to hit the city in thirty years, slugging down beers and chalking up his cue before taking yet another winning shot. She remembered when he was a young punk with the ambition to build an empire he could never really define—one day he would rant endlessly about becoming the next Tony Hawk, despite having never ridden a skateboard in his life, and two days later he would be plotting his future as the East Coast's biggest weed kingpin.

The drug dealing had worked out beyond his wildest dreams, affording Reynolds all the shiny toys a man-child could desire.

That he insisted on holding court in a rundown bar was an odd quirk, but one Joan now appreciated: no security cameras, no windows, no upstanding citizens, and a minimum of lights. The air conditioning whined and spat as it struggled to cool the room's humid muck.

The bartender poured her a free beer. She resisted the urge to ask for a shot or two of whiskey. Too much alcohol too fast might knock her out completely. When was the last time she'd slept? Tuesday, maybe Monday.

"Hey, lady."

Reynolds stood behind her, the pool cue in his left hand, smiling without exposing his teeth, his pupils reflecting the television's flames.

"Hey," she said. "Good to see you."

That was a lie and Reynolds seemed to know it. Cocking his head, he studied her. "Let's go to my office," he said, before telling the bartender to bring a pitcher.

They retired to a booth beyond the pool table. The overhead bulb had burned out years ago, and Reynolds looked devilish in the red glow of the old-style jukebox nearby. "You been out in that shit?" he asked, meaning the protests.

"Yeah, I've been on the line all week." The torn booth cushions felt like the world's softest, most comfortable mattress on her aching bones. She settled in. "It's awful."

"You still believe in it?"

"Believe in what?"

"Your job. The protestors, they're out there for the right reasons, you know. Maybe if your colleagues didn't keep cracking heads, people wouldn't feel the need to take to the streets."

She shrugged. "I don't think you're wrong."

"Yet you stay on the job."

"Yes."

"Why? The pension that good?"

"How many times I told you, I think I can help change things?"

"Yeah. Your care packages." He snorted. "Remember how well that went over."

A year before, Joan had approached her superiors with an idea: care packages of clean T-shirts, socks, energy bars, water, toothbrushes and toothpaste, and a list of numbers you could dial for help—food banks, social services. Produced at scale, those packages would have cost a few dollars apiece. She imagined officers handing them out to the homeless and other marginalized folks. Community policing at its finest.

Her boss shot down the idea—politely, but with a smirk tugging at the corners of his mouth. Her fellow officers spent twelve months mocking her mercilessly about it.

"Nothing will work unless you try," she said, trying to harden her exhausted voice.

"And I applaud that. Truly. Why are you here, Joan? Surely you didn't take a break in firing off rubber bullets just to say howdy to me."

"I haven't fired anything at anybody."

"You know what I mean."

The bartender arrived, a pitcher of lager in one hand and two clean glasses in the other. Once he left, Reynolds poured fresh pints. Joan used the time to rehearse what she would say. A fresh dose of fear crackled her nerves, sweat prickling her forehead.

"Last night, our place got robbed," she said, so quietly that Reynolds had to lean forward to hear her.

"I'm sorry to hear that," he said, sounding like he meant it. "Anything get taken?"

"Yeah." She fought the urge to clench her hands in a ball, as she often did when nervous. Instead, she tightened her fingers around the cold glass. "It wasn't protestors. These professional crews, they've been using the chaos as cover to hit stores, offices, places they've had their eye on. Eric, he bought that stupid used Porsche and it must have made someone think we have more money than we do, because . . ."

"They took the car?"

"No. They tried. It has an anti-theft system that makes it impossible for dumbasses to steal. I wasn't there. They came in the house, maybe to get the keys from Eric, maybe to see what else was there . . ." She paused again, tears threatening in the corners of her eyes.

"Is Eric okay?"

"He's alive." That much was true, at least. "I wasn't there. He dialed nine-eleven after they left. And some officers from another precinct, ah, they came by, and took him to the hospital, and evaluated the scene . . ."

"They know who did it?"

"No. Three guys, wearing masks. One of them had a T-shirt on, and Eric got a glimpse of a tattoo, a big dragon or something on the guy's upper arm, shoulder. That's it."

"What'd they take?"

"Eric's wallet and one of his laptops. Also, some of my jewelry. My mother gave me this pendant before she passed, it's a gold heart, cheesy, probably not worth all that much, but it had sentimental value . . ."

"I'm sorry to hear this shit happened to you," Reynolds said, laying his left hand on the table. Close enough for her to take, if she wanted to. Close enough to the table's edge to make it seem like he was only resting it there, if she declined to make a move. "What can I do?"

"See, that's it." She glanced around. Three men playing pool, almost certainly not close enough to hear them. Four others at the bar, lost in their drinks and the screen blaring mayhem. Reynold's main man, Edmund, sat on a stool where he could watch all doors simultaneously.

Reynolds nodded at Edmund, who rose and walked over to the jukebox, fishing in his pocket for quarters. Pumping five songs' worth of silver into the machine, he queued up some old-school country, starting things off with Johnny Cash. One of the pool players began to complain, but Edmund, six-foot-four and two hundred pounds of muscle, shut him up with a look.

With Cash's growl providing more sonic cover, Reynolds gestured for Joan to continue. She opened her mouth and nothing came out. Instead, one of those traitorous tears swelled up and rolled down her cheek. Now Reynolds extended his hand, brushing her fingers on the glass. She looked in his eyes and wondered what he was thinking. Was he remembering when they were kids, stealing bikes and setting dumpsters on fire? That one hot night when they were nineteen, possibly a mistake and never mentioned or repeated?

"Eric was assaulted," she finally said. "Not beaten up. Worse. Raped. Two of the guys did it."

He stared at her for the rest of the Cash song. When it settled into silence, he said: "I'm so sorry."

She nodded, wiping her nose. "Hospital tested him for HIV. I brought it up with a Detective Scalise, he's overseeing this one, and you know what he did? He laughed. He tried not to, but I could tell he was holding it back. It's not my precinct so I don't have any juice there, can't get someone else assigned to it."

He took her hand, squeezed. "I'm so sorry."

"Nobody cares."

"I care."

"I know." She swallowed. "I need a favor. A big one."

He nodded. "I can guess what it is."

"Okay." She swallowed again. "Permanent, okay?"

"Permanent as I can make it."

She made it home two hours later, after taking the back streets to stay clear of the protests. The fucking Porsche was still parked in the driveway, its shattered windows glittering in the harsh street-lights. Her house dark except for an eldritch glow flickering from the bedroom window.

She cut her cruiser's engine and leaned forward so her forehead rested against the steering wheel's pebbled leather and took one deep breath after another. *Permanent as I can make it.* The smooth-ness of Reynold's palm against hers. God, that was the wrong thing to do, wasn't it? You just did a bad, bad thing. The worst thing.

No. It was the right thing.

She believed in the law. Believed in it with all her heart, de-spite everything she'd seen as a cop. But the law wasn't going to deliver justice for her husband. Sometimes the law couldn't get everything right.

She climbed out of the cruiser and locked it. Coughed, spat, and patted her body to make sure her equipment was accounted for. She entered her darkened house and walked upstairs to the bedroom, where she found Eric sitting on the edge of the bed, a video-game controller clutched in his sweaty hands. His face bruised, his bottom lip cut open in two places. His attention locked on the giant screen on the opposite wall, where a sleek car zoomed down a futuristic highway beneath a nuclear-orange sky.

"Hey," she said.

Eric kept playing the game. The car bounced off the highway and slid down a gray embankment, bursting into flames at the bot-tom. Game over. She sat beside him on the bed and placed her cheek on his shoulder and tried to ignore how he tensed at her touch. He restarted the game.

I did the right thing, she told herself. I did the right thing.

*

Reynolds called her two days later. "We should meet," he said.

"Where?"

"Half-pipe."

When they were kids, they wasted too many hours hanging out at a giant half-pipe on the edge of Atticus Park, watching the skateboarders risk life and limb. The structure was abandoned now, its concrete cracked and sprayed with colorful graffiti, and it was far away from any buildings or roads. No clear sight lines from the nearby roofs. No chance of a surveillance van or a cruiser sneaking up on you. Edmund and another big man sat on a picnic bench, scanning the nearby trees as she walked past.

Reynolds crouched on the half-pipe's concrete ledge, resembling a crow in his black suit, two paper cups of coffee beside his left hip. She sat beside him. "Lots of cream, lots of sugar," he said, tapping the cup closest to her.

"I'm so predictable," she said, taking that cup and sipping it. Sickly sweet. Perfect.

"Yes, you are. I have news."

The sugary coffee burned her stomach. "Yeah?"

Reaching into his jacket, Reynolds pulled out his phone, flicked it awake, and tilted it so she could see the screen. A photograph of a bare arm, an elaborate dragon tattooed on the upper bicep. "We got him."

"Are you sure?"

"Yes. He confessed. Described your house, the car."

"Show me his face."

"It's a mess."

"Do it."

He flicked to the next photograph. There wasn't much face left, just a hairline above red mush.

"What about the other two?" she asked.

He flicked to the next photos. More meat, more mess. "We were thorough."

"What were their names?"

"Does it matter?"

She placed the cup on the concrete, balled her hands between her thighs. "Yes."

"The guys know. I only arrived after it was done. I'll tell you their names the next time we meet. Also," he put a hand on her hands. "These evil pricks, they sold your jewelry. A pawn shop on Tenth, they said. I sent some guys over, and they beat the shit out of the owner, but your stuff is already gone. I'm sorry."

"Thank you."

"How's Eric?"

She shrugged and squeezed his hand and stood. "Thank you," she said again, taking her coffee with her as she gingerly descended the ramp to the grass. Her eyes burned. She remembered coming home to find Eric on the kitchen floor, his pants pulled down around his ankles, his eyes swollen shut. How the sight of it was like a dagger to the heart. She could never tell him about what she'd done for him.

Is that justice?

Sometimes she wished she was one of those people without an inner voice. It must be nice to coast through life as a complete moron. She crossed the fields without nodding to Edmund and the other bodyguard. Back in her car, she dialed Detective Scalise, who picked up on the third ring.

"Yeah?" Scalise wheezed.

"It's Joan," she said.

"Who?"

"Joan Swift," she said. "I'm calling about my husband's case."

"Oh yeah, Eric Swift?" Papers rustled. "Sorry, we have nothing to share right now."

"Look . . ."

"Yeah?"

"I'm not a civilian, okay?" She pushed some steel into her voice. "Call it professional courtesy or whatever, but I need to know more."

Scalise's voice sharpened in return, ready for a fight. "Look, we're all sorry your husband got *molested*, but the city's on fire. You realize that, right? We find anything, you're my first call."

She ended the call and tossed the phone onto the seat beside her. Took a shuddery breath and held it. This shit was all too exhausting. *I understand burnout*, she thought. *I do.* Too many cases, too many people crying, too much shit to clean. It's like acid, eating away at even the hardiest cop soul. But it sucks to be on the victim side of it. Have I ever behaved like that toward someone? Nasty in their moment of grief? I hope not. God, I hope not.

A protestor crossed the road in front of her. A teenage girl in an oversize red T-shirt and tight jeans, a sign clenched in her right hand: NO JUSTICE NO PEACE. Joan offered a thumbs-up. The girl returned the gesture, but her eyes blazed with rage.

The therapist kept fiddling with her glasses in a way that made Joan want to break her fingers. Forty-five minutes every week in this morgue-cool office with its bland art and pale furniture, stuffed into an uncomfortable chair as the therapist alternated between silence and platitudes that meant nothing at all.

"I think it's because we don't keep a gun in the house," Eric said, never looking at Joan. He had chucked off his sandals and placed his bare feet on the seat, legs tucked to the side. It reminded her of how a child would sit. "If we'd had a gun in the house, I would've been able to defend myself."

"I don't think it's that at all," Joan said. "A gun in the house usually kills or injures the owner, not an intruder."

"Remember what we said," the therapist said, raising a finger. "No confrontational language."

"I wasn't trying to be confrontational," Joan said, her cheeks growing hot. "It's just stating a fact."

"I could have handled a gun," Eric said. "You just don't trust me."

"No, sweetie, I trust you."

"You don't. If you did, it wouldn't have happened."

"Look." Joan said it to the therapist, because looking at her husband would have triggered too much anger. "I'm trained in the use of firearms. It would take me a second, maybe two, to recognize a threat and react to it. A civilian, it takes you longer, maybe nine or ten seconds, and by then it's way too late."

"That's how she thinks of me," Eric yelped at the therapist. "As a civilian."

"That's what you are," Joan said. "You're my husband, and I love you, but you can't handle a gun, and I don't think it would have helped in this situation."

"Confrontational," the therapist said.

Eric crossed his arms over his chest, his lower lip trembling. "I can defend myself," he muttered. "I can, I can, I can, I can."

"I know." She looked at him now. Her hands in her lap. Clenching, unclenching, clenching, unclenching. "I know."

*

Another night on the line. Two thousand protestors sitting in the middle of the avenue, chanting and waving signs, peaceful despite their rage. Two hours before, someone set a police cruiser on fire over on Ninth, the only major violence aside from a few thrown cans and rocks. Working the line was terrible but it was better than staying home, listening to Eric machine-gun waves of digital villains.

After five hours, she stepped away to take off her riot helmet and pour water over her head and lean against a van and just breathe. There was a pawn shop across the street, its lights blazing through smeared windows. She was on Tenth, right? It must be the pawn shop that Reynolds had told her about.

"Be back," she told the other cops, none of whom raised their heads to acknowledge her. She strode across the street still in full armor, her holstered riot baton softly tapping against her leg with every step. You don't have any kind of warrant, she told herself. No probable cause. Can't hurt to ask a few questions, though, right? Just don't go over the line.

The inside of the pawn shop was dimly lit, its glass cases clogged with all kinds of junk. Watches and jewelry gleamed in a box beside the register. She paused in front of it, scanning the wedding rings and earrings and cufflinks for anything that resembled her gold heart. Nothing.

"Help you, officer?" The proprietor emerged from a doorway behind the counter. He was thin, his shoulders stooped, his skin gray as stone. Whatever was eating him from the inside, he had maybe a year or two. Maybe less.

"Yes. Did anyone recently come in, try to sell you a gold pendant, a heart?"

He stiffened. "Why do you ask?"

"It's associated with a robbery. If it was, okay, that's fine. Just tell me."

"We don't do that kind of business in here. We're not that kind of establishment."

"Did a couple of guys come in here, maybe rough you up over it? I'm sorry if they did. I guarantee they won't harm you again." She felt the heat rising in her cheeks, just like in the therapist's office. "But you need to tell me the truth, okay?"

The proprietor crossed his arms over his chest. His face and hands unmarked by bruises or cuts. "You got a warrant?" he asked.

"No."

"Then I can't help you." He jutted his chin at the door. "You better move on. Actually protect this community instead of watching it burn."

The jewelry case shattered, glass spraying across the counters. Her riot baton in her hand, its tip buried in the case's cheap wood bottom. Fuck, she did that. She was more startled than the proprietor, who only took a small step back to dodge the flying shards. Maybe this kind of thing happened to him all the time.

"Look," the proprietor said, his voice rising to a thin shriek. "This week, we got people with watches, necklaces, a couple fucking laptops, and I swear to God a stuffed fucking monkey but nothing like a stupid heart pendant, you understand me, *officer*, so unless you have a fucking warrant—"

"Fine." Her hands shook and it took a few tries to slide her baton into its holster. "I understand. Thank you."

She left without looking back, wondering if the guy would call the cops on her. The last thing she needed was IA sniffing around. Then again, the guy certainly didn't want any cops asking more questions, not when a big chunk of his business was stolen goods. He was lying to her about the pendant—*had* to be. Because otherwise . . . well, the alternative was too horrible to contemplate.

She drove home, so exhausted the road blurred in her vision and she had to grip the wheel to stop her fingers from trembling. Had Reynolds lied to her? If so, why? They'd been friends since practically birth, always there for each other. What did he have to gain here?

If you can't trust a drug lord, who can you trust?

She parked in the driveway behind the Porsche, not caring if she blocked it in. She wanted to fill a bottle with gasoline and toss it through the plastic bag taped over the shattered driver's window, set the miserable machine on fire. Except knowing her luck this week, she'd probably burn the house down in the process.

Inside, she found Eric at the kitchen counter—smiling. He had an open bottle of beer in one hand and his phone in the other.

"What's the good news?" she said, too tired to smile back.

"They got him." He held up his phone. "The detective just called. They nailed the guy trying to break into another house, maybe a mile or two from here. The asshole confessed what he did to me."

"Bullshit," she said. It just slipped out.

"No, I'm serious." His lips wavered. A tear slipped down his cheek. "His name's Trent Mitchell. He's, ah, a pretty bad dude. He gave up those other assholes too."

She stood there on numb legs, tottering.

Eric put down his beer and phone. He placed his hands over his face and his body hitched, as if he was choking up something heavy from deep in his gut. "I'm sorry," he burbled between heaving gulps of air. "I'm sorry, so sorry. I was such an asshole to you. I'm so sorry."

Her breath whistled between her clenched teeth. Her legs alive again, the blood rushing through her warm and tingly. She walked across the kitchen and placed a hand on his shoulder and squeezed, and he spun and buried his wet face in her neck, his breath hot and harsh against her collarbone.

Not as sorry as I am, she thought. *Not half as fucking sorry as I am.*

A few texts to Reynolds, followed by a sleepless night. The next morning was foggy and gray, forcing her to drive slowly to Atticus Park, her backup piece in her ankle holster and her sidearm on her hip. The traffic was light, the city exhausted.

Edmund and two bodyguards waited on the path to the half-pipe. They stepped aside to let her pass without patting her down.

Reynolds sat on the edge of the half-pipe. No coffee beside him. No gun, either. "Hey," he said as she walked up, not meeting her eyes.

"You asshole," she said.

He shrugged. "Frogs and scorpions. Remember I used to tell that old story, fable, whatever?"

"You might be a fucking scorpion, but I'm no fucking frog, and this isn't a fucking river." She wanted to draw down on him. Blasting his brains across that cracked concrete was a tantalizing idea. But what would that solve? Absolutely nothing.

"Yeah, I never really got that story, either." He raised his head. His gaze locked on her, calm, unconcerned, reminding her of that night in the bar when he seemed like the cool anchor in a fiery, swirling world. "I'm going to reach for my phone really slowly."

"Okay."

He slipped two fingers into his jacket pocket and pulled out his iPhone. Flicking the screen to life, he tapped open an app. Another flick, another tap. From the device's speakers came the click of billiard balls and beer glasses, drowned out by her voice:

"Permanent, okay?"

He swiped the app closed, slipped the phone back in his pocket. "Of course those weren't the guys who assaulted Eric. But when you mentioned that tattoo on the guy who assaulted him? It reminded me that I wanted to get rid of a guy with a tattoo just like that. And two others, as well."

Her legs numb again. Her lungs felt deflated. It took her a minute to suck down air. "I went to the pawn shop," she said, almost whispering.

He nodded. "I know. And I'm sorry for lying to you about that. I knew you'd ask, but I was hoping you wouldn't check."

"So this is blackmail, right?" She had to sit down, her feet dangling over the half-pipe's ledge. How many afternoons had they spent out here? Two thousand? How many jokes had they told?

He raised his hand to chest level and waggled it. "Kind of? No? I don't need a mole in the police. I have enough of those already. What I need—what I've always needed—is my best friend working for me. You're too good for those corrupt jackasses and you know it."

She focused on her breathing. In, out, in, out. Don't get sick. You can handle this.

"Maybe I am like the scorpion," he continued. "I am what I am. I've always known my nature. You can't say the same for the cops. They claim they're about truth and justice, but in the end it's just about cracking heads. Preserving the power. You want to be a part of that?"

The concrete made her think of gray skies, made her think of hundreds of tear gas canisters soaring in white arcs, slamming down into the crowds. How she stood on the line with her sweaty hands wrapped around a riot baton, filled not with righteousness but a growing confusion—*why the hell was she doing this?* And nobody ever seemed to have an answer for her.

"I don't know," she said.

"Well, good, because I've removed the choice for you. I love you, but I'll figure out how to use this tape and those bodies. You mean that much to me." Tapping her thigh, he stood. "Quit the force. We start next month, hey?"

She shrugged.

"There's no justice, sweets," he said and winked. "There's no peace." He made a swooping motion with his finger, like a scorpion's tail descending, before he walked into the park to meet Edmund and his crew.

BOBBY MATHEWS

The Funeral Suit

FROM *Frontier Tales*

MADGE TOOK ONE look at the old man and shook her head. Cullen Grayson wore a black broadcloth suit twenty years out of style, with a celluloid collar and black string tie. Not a speck of dust on the suit, not a hair out of place. The guns were freshly oiled as they always were, one tied down to his skinny thigh, the other set for a cross-draw on his ornately carved leather gun belt. Cullen climbed the steps into the BonTon restaurant with his customary uneven gait. People said a Shoshone bullet had ruined one of his knees in a raid down in the Nevada territory years ago, but Madge wasn't sure. They said a lot of things about Cullen Grayson. Maybe some of them were even true.

"Good morning," she said after Cullen had tottered unsteadily inside and made his way to a table in one corner. Madge regarded him with the same level of distrust one might have for a dog with a questionable reputation. With his back against the walls, the old man seemed to relax a little. He took off his hat and placed it in the chair beside him.

"Happy birthday."

Cullen nodded curtly and said thank you when she brought him a cup of scalding hot coffee. He shifted in his seat, easing his six-shooters into a more comfortable position. Madge thought of her own gun, then. The big dragoon Colt was too heavy for her. She'd probably break her wrist if she ever fired it. But the thing worked well as a club, and she'd used it to mediate several disputes between drunken cowboys and miners, dropping the heavy barrel upside the offending party's head and looking on as he was dragged from the restaurant.

Madge didn't ask Cullen how old he was. It was impossible to tell. He was the oldest man in the Basin, certainly. And today he had put on his only suit and come to town to pay for it, just as he'd been doing for the last ten years.

Cullen poured a splash of coffee into the saucer on the table and blew on it. He lifted the saucer with a liver-spotted hand that barely shook at all and sipped. He made a face, and sipped again. Outside, the sun had finally broken over the Big Horns and the day looked bright and alien, like all the days that came before and all of the ones that would come after. Cullen's pale green eyes stared out at the street. It would start any minute now. He flexed his hands, tried to keep the tremors in check. He could remember when his hands had been fine and supple, nimble and long-fingered. Before he came west. In another life—whatever and whoever he had left behind—Cullen could have been a musician, could have been something or someone else.

Wishful thinking. He had always been the man with the gun.

Cullen had never meant for it to happen, had never meant to earn his reputation as a gunfighter. It felt like something that had simply happened to him. He had stood waist-deep in the river of time and watched everyone and everything he had ever loved be carried away by invisible currents he could not control. There'd been a few scrapes, and he survived them. That was all. Five years before, some dime novel writer had come out here to this arid, remote place and found him. What was the fellow's name? Cullen couldn't remember, and maybe it didn't matter anyway. The writer asked him how many men he had killed.

Cullen had made a mistake then. He'd answered truthfully: he didn't know. However many it had been, there were five more since.

Madge watched Cullen the way she might've observed a snake dying in the street with its back broken from a passing wagon wheel. He was thin to the point of emaciation, barely more than a skeleton. What inner fire kept him on his feet, kept him coming to town in that ridiculous suit year after year, she could not know. Heat radiated off of him like a sickness. The tails of his suit coat drooped around his hips and his trousers puddled in his lap. The collar of his shirt gapped at his neck. If you could look past the lines that had grooved themselves into his face, Cullen Grayson looked like a little boy playing dress-up in his father's clothes. Only his guns looked new, and that was because he treated them like royalty.

Cullen didn't look up. He kept his eyes on the bright and dusty street just outside. From inside the restaurant, the street looked far more vivid, brighter and somehow more real than the tables covered in gingham cloth and the ghostly glowing whitewashed walls. Madge thought that Cullen—this Cullen, the one she could touch and see and hear—held himself in some kind of stasis. He came alive only when he strode to the middle of the street, with his guns tied down and his hat pulled low over his eyes.

They heard the challenger coming, boot heels chocking on the boardwalk, the jingle of spurs playing counterpoint to the percussion of the steps.

Madge tried to ignore it.

"You want some breakfast? You look like you could eat."

Cullen stared at the street. He rose, put on his hat, and nodded to Madge.

"Maybe after."

Madge pulled in all of the breath she could muster. It wasn't her business, and yet she could not help herself.

"You don't have to do this. You don't."

Cullen flashed a smile, and in that moment, Madge could see the man he had been twenty, maybe thirty years before.

"Yeah," he said in a tone that brooked no argument. "I do."

"Did you ken him?" Cullen's voice was low, filled with an almost holy wonder in the aftermath. He had survived again. He sat at the table in the corner, just as he had before. Outside, men had gathered around the lifeless body of the loser and tended to him. Soon the undertaker's hearse would come. Someone would throw fresh dirt over the blood on the ground, and the townspeople would come out again. When it was time. When it was safe.

"It looked like Tyler Garth's boy," Madge said. She brought Cullen a plate of baking powder biscuits and bacon.

"Paul?"

Madge nodded.

Cullen didn't say anything. He had known Tyler Garth since the man had moved to town, known the son since he was a boy in short pants. Paul had been a good boy, a smart boy. What in the hell had set him on the path to challenge Cullen?

There was no way to tell. He knew that. Boys—young men, Cullen supposed—were prone to deviltry. No one had forced Paul to step into the street. He could remember being that age, young and full of fire like a kerosene lamp turned as bright as it would go. The problem with that bright heat was that it would burn away. Cullen had seen it many times over the years; gunfighters, cowboys, miners, lawmen, and outlaws burning with white-hot rage. They slapped leather and died, made too slow and clumsy in their haste to raise the gun and shoot, or else they were too afraid, too fight-sick in their fear and they missed their first shot.

They often didn't get another.

Cullen was the opposite. Stalking into the street turned him cold and allowed him to peel back the layers of his humanity, leaving nothing more than the remorseless reptile of his soul. There was a nearly sexual tension he felt in those moments, a thing he would not have admitted to anyone. The gun came up and settled in his palm, walnut grips worn smooth to the contours of his hand by years of long practice. It exploded, the round surging forward toward his opponent. Sometimes in the moments after, when he stood in the sun-drenched street with the sweat ringing the arm-pits of his snowy white shirt and the dust billowing around him like a living thing and the other man lay dead or dying in the dirt, Cullen felt as spent as the shell he calmly ejected from the six-shooter's cylinder and replaced. He always felt dirty afterward, like he had when his mother had found him with his hands down his pants. There was a sensation of disgust as he put the pistol away. A hateful thing to be used only rarely.

Madge poured more coffee for the old man, steam rising from the delicate china cup. He still didn't want anything to eat, but she buttered two thick slices of sourdough bread and put them on the table in front of him. He broke the bread with long-fingered hands that used to be elegant. Now they were knotted at the knuckles and nearly skeletal in-between. His hands trembled as he ate, and crumbs fell onto the front of his fine black suit.

Rodriguez filled the doorway. He moved deliberately, so that they could see him coming. Neither fast nor slow. He wore moccasins, buckskin pants, and a homespun shirt. His dark, wavy hair fell past his shoulders, and his wide black hat hid most of his face from the sun. If he had a gun, Madge couldn't see it. Sean Rodriguez was not yet thirty years old, the only son of a Mexican horse-breaker and an Irish immigrant, with his father's dark eyes and his mother's pale skin. He took his hat off when he came inside, and Madge busied herself with sweeping at a spot on the floor she'd cleaned twice already that morning so that he wouldn't catch her looking at him. Sean had always wanted the wild life of the mountains and streams. He hunted cougars that preyed on cattle, and sometimes he hunted men too. Madge had no idea where or how he lived; she only knew that being with Sean Rodriguez had filled her with a longing that she couldn't quite explain.

Rodriguez brushed Madge's arm with the tips of his fingers, and she turned away as he approached Cullen, who lifted a hand in greeting. Neither of them offered to shake hands, but Rodriguez pulled a chair out from the table and sat opposite the old man, putting his back to the open room.

Madge brought coffee.

"There's not going to be trouble in here," she told them. It wasn't a question. She kept her voice as flat and hard as the street outside. She filled Rodriguez's cup without looking at him. Nearly jumped out of her skin when he turned his face toward her. She remembered that face in the dark, her mouth tracing the shape of his again and again until everything had become too much and crashed over them both.

"No trouble, just a conversation. Would you get me some of that bread, maybe a couple eggs?"

Madge nodded and moved off toward the kitchen.

"How you doing, Mr. Grayson?"

Cullen shrugged.

"Good days, bad days. It's my birthday, you know. Day like this, I feel like I could live forever."

"Happy birthday," Rodriguez said. The words were automatic, something to say as he studied Cullen, taking in the shirt collar that no longer fit, the sagging skin of the old man's cheeks and neck, the tremor in his hands. The snowy white shirt frayed slightly at the cuffs of his sleeves, and crumbs of bread held on to the front of Cullen's suit coat like shipwreck survivors clinging to the wreckage.

"How old are you now?"

Cullen started to answer, but then he had to give it some thought. He raised the coffee cup to his mouth while he considered. Swallowed, put the cup back down gently on the table, and wiped his nicotine-stained mustache with a shaking finger.

"Close as I can figure it, I'm seventy-eight," he said. "Mama and Daddy came into this country in the first wave, spent their nights in a covered wagon while he built a 'dobe. I was born the next year, old Tewa woman was midwife."

Rodriguez grinned at him, a flash of white, even teeth that nearly glowed in the gathering gloom of the restaurant.

"She tell your mama that you were going to live forever?"

"Nobody ever told me. But I lived this long," Cullen said. He ate the last of his bread. He wiped his hands with a linen napkin, finally noticed the crumbs on his suit, and brushed them to the floor. Sean Rodriguez put his elbows on the table and steepled his fingers together.

"Not much longer, though, huh? You got the sickness in you, I can see it. Where does it hurt, your gut?"

Cullen's face went pale underneath the permanent burn that the elements had weathered into his skin. He ran a finger along the celluloid collar of his shirt where it gapped enough that he could fit two fingers in there to touch the wattled skin.

"I don't know what you're talking about."

Rodriguez plucked a piece of dust from the knee of his buckskins and flicked it away. He didn't want to look at Cullen. The old man was in bad shape, anyone could see that. He didn't know how much hate Cullen must have salted away in his spirit, but it must have been enormous. Maybe it was some kind of Hopi medicine that kept Cullen breathing from year to year, but it was only in those moments on the street with the sun on his face and the permanent shadow of death at his back when he truly came alive.

And everyone else paid for it.

"Go home," Madge said. She'd come up to them quietly, but her voice was high with anger and fear. "You've already killed one boy today. Isn't that enough? How many more are you going to kill?"

Cullen sat quiet, closed his eyes and tilted his chair backward until he was able to lean the back of his mostly bald head against the whitewashed wall. He looked comfortable, like a man at ease and ready for an afternoon nap. But his hands never strayed far from his gunbelt.

"All of them," he said. "Every one of them who stands against me."

Madge looked at Rodriguez then. He shrugged. She went back to the counter and stayed there.

"I don't want to be the one to stop you," he said. "I've known you all my life."

Cullen grinned without opening his eyes.

"You can't stop me. It ain't my time yet."

He sounded so sure of himself, Rodriguez thought. Of course, all of those men that Cullen had killed had been sure that they would be the one standing after the guns talked loud. Everyone was sure of themselves until they weren't. And sometimes it was too late and you were lying on the ground with dirt in your mouth and blood on your clothes and your life force racing away like the sun chased from the sky by the coming night.

How long had it been since Cullen had felt fear, the real thing, the prickling in your spine and the heavy racing gallop in your heart when death was around the corner or worse yet looking you in the eye? Rodriguez, who lived out in the mountains and hunted big cats and wolves and anything else that threatened his employer's stock, had lived with fear so long that it felt like an old friend. He recognized and welcomed it, channeled it into something useful. A sign that he was still alive. And Madge . . . Rodriguez glanced at her. A woman alone on what still passed for the frontier, where the Chiricahua had raided only a short time before. She'd come West with her husband, but he had died somewhere on the mountain near Ten Sleep. Was Madge afraid? Rodriguez thought that she must be. She was a woman alone in the vastness of this high desert plateau. Her fear was probably greater—or at least different—than his own. He wished that whatever they started that night near the canyon had led to something more, but he didn't know how to say that, didn't know what words he needed to lasso her.

Everyone thought Madge was a dance-hall girl, a sportin' woman who would take a walk upstairs with anyone. Rodriguez wasn't sure about that. If it was true, did it change the way he felt about her? He didn't know. All Rodriguez had ever seen in Madge was a woman who kept her restaurant open and fought like hell to survive.

Maybe that was all any of them had. Survival.

"You so anxious to die, Sean? Lot of country left to see." Cullen opened his eyes and cut them toward Madge. "Seems a young man like you should be at home with a woman. You don't want the reputation that comes from killing me."

Madge sat a little apart from the men, trying to ignore them. She'd left the coffee pot on the table between them. She polished the restaurant's silverware and folded the white linen napkins. Her fingernails were bitten down to the quick, and every now and then she would worry at one with her small, sharp front teeth. Did Rodriguez even have a gun? Madge couldn't see it if he did, but it might be stuck in his waistband. Not every man wore a holster, let alone two of them like Cullen. She wished she knew. She wished Cullen would go home. She wished Sean had never come to town. She wished. The idea stopped her cold. Madge never wished for anything. She couldn't afford to.

Why now? Why today?

Rodriguez put his hands on the table between him and Cullen. His fingers were long with scarred and knobby knuckles, but his nails were clean and neatly trimmed. He held Cullen's gaze without flinching.

"I don't want a reputation. I don't want to kill you, and I don't want you to kill me. I want you to go home."

Cullen shook his head like a man trying to clear away a pesky gnat. He pushed forward in his seat and put his forearms on the table. Around them the restaurant was dim and cool. The warm whiff of freshly baked biscuits and honey seemed to linger in the air. It was a fine aroma, maybe the best thing Cullen had ever smelled. If they would leave him alone, he could sit here all day, drink coffee, and watch the afternoon slide by like the shadows on the wall.

"I'll go home when I'm done," he said. His voice was mild, soft in the quiet dining room, but there was no mistake. He was resolute. He would not be moved, he would not be hurried, he would not turn from his burden.

"Mr. Grayson. Cullen." Madge's face wore a look of surprise, as though she hadn't realized that she was going to speak. "Please stop this. Go home. Haven't you killed enough? Aren't you tired of it by now? Why can't you just die and leave us alone."

Cullen stared at Madge, his face bone white save for two spots of color high on his cheekbones.

"If a man spoke to me that way, I would have gunned the son of a bitch down."

"If I were a man, I'd walk out in the street and shoot you myself."

Cullen shot to his feet, tottered, and had to place his palms on the table to regain his balance. Madge rose and moved toward the counter, her long skirt whispering along the floor. Rodriguez stood too. He placed himself between the old man and the woman. Dust motes floated in a stray sunbeam and the ozone smell of anger and fear overpowered the scent of baking. Cullen started around the table, boot heels hard on the bare plank floor until he met Rodriguez's eyes.

"Move."

He tried to sidestep Rodriguez, but the younger man stayed with him.

"You can't—" Rodriguez said, and Cullen went for his gun.

They were too close. Rodriguez hit Cullen with a big, work-hardened fist, hit him hard enough to split a knuckle on one of Cullen's jagged yellow teeth. The old man went down, flat on the floor, still scrambling for a six-gun that was held in place by a leather loop around the hammer of the gun. Cullen staggered up to his knees and finally made it to his feet, though he was listing badly to one side. Blood poured from a broken lip and pattered against the rough wood floor. He stared at Rodriguez with eyes that blazed like blue fire and touched his fingertips to his lips, the blood nearly glowing in the gloom.

"I'll kill you for that." Cullen spat more blood onto the floor and walked toward the batwing doors of the restaurant. His feet were loud. "I'll see you in the street, you goddamned dog."

"I'm not heeled. I'm not fighting you in the street. Those days are over. They've been over for a long time. Everyone knows it but you."

Rodriguez flexed his fist, watching the dribble of blood flow down the back of his hand. He picked up a napkin and absently wrapped his knuckles with it. Cullen paused at the door and turned toward him.

"I don't give a goddamn. I'll be in the street. Gun, no gun, I'll kill you on sight."

"Cullen, I said I'm not armed."

"I am." Madge didn't raise her voice. She didn't have to. Cullen turned to look at her standing there behind the bar and Madge was already shooting, the big Dragoon Colt braced in both hands. She fired once and the recoil of the big revolver knocked her back against the shelving where the good white plates sat stacked and waiting for a lunch and dinner crowd that would never come tonight as long as Cullen Grayson was there. A stack of them hit the floor and shattered, but Madge didn't notice. She brought the Dragoon down once more and centered it on the thin old man silhouetted in the doorway, cocked, and fired again.

Cullen Grayson lay face up, the hot blue fire of his eyes faded to the color of worthless flawed sapphires. His boots scraped the hard wooden floor and he died looking up into the nothingness from where he could not return, with no word on his lips, no thought in his mind, and no breath in his lungs. He was dead before he knew it, the punctuation mark at the end of the long sentence of twenty or more men who had fallen by his gun.

Rodriguez approached Madge carefully, as though she were a newborn fawn. He took the gun from her hand gently, loosening her grip one slim finger at a time. He slid an arm around her waist. She looked up at him, dazed at what had happened, at what she had done. They stood there looking at the body for a long time until a young cowboy who could no longer stand the suspense sneaked up the boardwalk by crawling on his belly and eventually poked his head under the batwing doors. His eyes widened as he took in the sight of the legendary Cullen Grayson dead on the floor and Rodriguez with the gun in his hand. The cowboy yanked his head back as if he'd nearly been struck by a rattlesnake.

They could hear him yelling as he clopped away through the dusty street, screaming his fool head off for everyone to hear that Sean Rodriguez had up and killed Cullen Grayson. The old man was finally dead and they were free.

STANTON MCCAFFERY

Will I See the Birds When I Am Gone

FROM *Dark Yonder*

MARCH 1997

Dear Mom,

Grandma told me to write you a letter. She said she talked to you and you told her you would like to get a letter from me. I told Grandma that if you wanted to get a letter from me why didn't you write a letter to me first. She told me that was the kind of back talk and attitude that got me into juvee and I better just shut my mouth and write the damn letter. How are you?

Grandma told me I have a half brother. What is his name? They make me see a counselor here. The counselor said I have a lot of anger and that is why I lash out like I do. They asked me what kinds of things am I angry about. I told them one thing I am angry about is that you live with my new half brother but that you couldn't live with me and gave me to Grandma instead.

The counselor told me that it would be good for me and my future if I tried to forgive you and that is really why I decided to write this letter. Not just because Grandma told me to.

We talk in group sessions and it seems like everyone here has anger problems like I do. I guess there is a lot in the world to be angry about. Or maybe we are just people that get angry over things that don't bother normal people. We are broken and are here to be fixed.

The counselor calls that being rehabilitated. When I feel angry I feel like the inside of me is a ball of flame and I don't know if I can be rehabilitated. I think that I should be in a cage forever so I don't do to more people like I did to that boy at school.

Grandma sent me some things that she said would make me feel a little less lonely. They are mostly my old comic books. One thing that she sent was this picture of me when I was really little. I don't remember it at all. It is me standing on a boardwalk holding a stuffed dog. It looks like the kind of cheap dog that somebody won at one of those boardwalk games that hardly anybody ever wins. Grandma said it was you that took the picture.

I was so young when I went to live with Grandma that I have trouble remembering you. At night when they turn the lights out and tell us to be quiet I can close my eyes and see your face. I can hear your voice too. I am afraid that before I get out of here I won't remember you anymore. That scares me but I think it would be scarier if you couldn't remember me.

Grandma says that when I get out of here it will be a few months before I turn eighteen. She says that is good because that way they won't transfer me to an adult prison. She said adult prison is where you get so messed up you can't be repaired.

I hope that when I get out I can see you and meet my new half brother.

I have one question for you before I end this letter. Did you send me to live with Grandma because you were not ready to be a mom or because you thought there was something wrong with me and you didn't want me?

Goodbye,
Matthew

JUNE 2001

Dear Mom,

I'm released in six months. I bet you knew that without me telling you. Maybe that's something you are happy about. Some days it's hard for me to think of what life will be like once I'm out. The counselor here told me thoughts like that can get overwhelming. Like there would be too much inside my head. If I get overwhelmed I'm likely to make bad decisions. So they told me to keep myself in check and take things day-to-day.

I get excited sometimes when I think about it. I'm going to see girls again. I haven't seen a girl my own age in five years. One of the guys here has his sister visit. She's kinda cute, but I only look at her over my shoulder when she comes to visit him so I don't count that.

I think maybe I would like to see a movie in the theater. I don't know what movies are playing but that doesn't matter. I would go see anything even if it were bad. All we have in here are cartoons. They don't want us watching nothing violent. I think when I go to the movies I'm going to get some popcorn. They never have popcorn here. We watched *ET* here last week and it was fun. Except, they had to shut it off before the end because some people were fighting. I would see it in the theater if that's what was playing.

Sometimes when I think about getting out I get nervous because I don't know what I'm going to do. I've never had a job. They have me fold laundry here, but I don't think that's a real job. The counselor says I've got a better hold of my temper, but I'm still scared. What if I have a boss and they do something that upsets me?

There are times when I don't want them to let me go because I feel so sad. I feel sad because Grandma died. She was the only person that I really had. I know you are my mom and that is supposed to mean that you will always love me but I know that Grandma really cared about me because she was the one that fed me. She told me that I was so frustrating to her that I was going to put her in an early grave. Maybe that turned out to be true.

I cry at night. I think I've cried every night here for the past four years. At first I was afraid to but then I realized that everyone else was doing it too. Nobody asks anybody else what they're crying about. I think that's because we're all crying about the same thing. We're crying because we have so much more to go in life and we already ruined it.

I hope I can see you when they let me out. The state has housing for me, but from what I hear that isn't too much different from being inside.

Goodbye,
Matthew

FEBRUARY 2004

Dear Mom,

I'm writing to tell you that I am doing okay. I don't know that you wanted to know that or that you even care, but I'm living with a friend I knew in juvee. His parents own a building with a bar and on the top floor there is an apartment that I'm sharing with him and two other guys. I don't really like any of them and they always like to start beef over who ate shit out of the fridge, but it's a place to live and it's better than the street.

I'm sorry things didn't work out at your place. It was nice of you to let me stay. I guess Robert didn't like me. I know that I was wrong too and that coming and going in the middle of the night bothered him but I still got the sense from the very beginning that he didn't like me. Maybe he didn't like having the reminder of who you used to be. Or, maybe he just didn't like having a person that wasn't his kid living under his roof. I get that.

I think maybe I would have felt the same way in his position. I guess I just kinda wish you had stuck up for me a little bit more. Like when he was on my ass about making a mess in the bathroom, you coulda said the mess wasn't that bad or something. But I guess you want to keep the way you live now too. It seems like you are doing better than you were when I was little, from what I remember.

It makes sense to me that you would want to keep it that way and that you wouldn't want me ruining it, even if I am your kid. I guess what I'm trying to say is that I'm not mad. Or, I guess, I'm trying really hard not to be mad.

I did live on the street for a few months after you and Robert threw me out. I was behind this shopping plaza, up against the wall under this vent with a sleeping bag. You remember where Tops Appliances used to be? I stayed over there.

Sometimes I thought maybe I would steal something from someplace or take somebody's car so I could go to jail for a little bit and at least be warm. I broke inside an abandoned restaurant once and slept in there a few days but then I got scared when I heard police sirens and ran out. I guess I don't really want to get locked up again. At least on the street I can do what I want.

Living on the street in the middle of winter, I never thought it was possible to be so cold. Like, this cold made my teeth chatter so much I thought I was going to knock one of them out. I'd just spit and out would come a tooth. The thought makes me laugh, but really there's nothing funny about it.

It's just that sometimes you laugh to get through the things that a straight face wouldn't be able to handle, like crapping behind a dumpster when it's below zero out. Person that finds it might not even know what it is they found when it's that cold.

Being without a home or a warm place makes you feel like you're not even alive, like the experiences you're having are from some kind of sick dream. Like you don't have to worry about what you're doing because you are already living your worst life. Being cold in general makes you wish you were dead but the worst kind of cold is the cold in your hands. I swear there were times I wished they'd just fall off, like I never knew pain like that could exist. Still, I would rather have that hell pain in my hands, that feeling that they'd just come out of fire but really they were just frozen, instead of pain in my heart and in my head. That's the sort of pain I don't think I've ever not felt. I wonder sometimes, is this part of living? Like, does everybody feel this freezing in the heart like I do? Then

I realize, no. I see people when I'm walking and they're in their cars and it's like, no, of course they don't feel what I feel. How could they and look like that?

Then, when I know they don't feel this coldness, it changes to something else. It's a something that could reach out and destroy people for not feeling like I do. You know how I was saying my hands were so cold it felt like they were on fire? I swear, the inside of me starts to feel like that too.

But then I'll think about Richie and that hot-cold inside of me starts to thaw. I swear, he might be the only thing that gets me to fall asleep on the worst nights. When I think that out of two at least you raised and had one good son, I think that the world can't be all bad. I know one good thing, that boy loved me because I was his brother and didn't care what I'd done or where I'd been, and if there's one good thing then the world isn't all bad.

Can you tell Richie hi for me? Tell him I'm glad he's my brother and that I'm sorry things didn't work out with me living with you guys. Just because I'm gone doesn't mean I don't love him.

Anyway, don't worry about me. I don't like these guys I'm living with, but I'm going to figure out my own living situation where I'm by myself so there's no chance of having beef with anybody else. After all the years of being me I think it's safest for everybody if I'm by myself.

Goodbye,
Matthew

Dear Mom,

I know that what I did was terrible. At least it's what our society calls terrible. I know it carries that label and I understand that, but I don't know that I feel terrible about it. The guys in here that have been here the longest, they say that at first you might not feel terrible but that in time you do come to regret it. Then, they

say, that feeling of regret, it passes too. Soon you don't feel much
of anything and don't even remember not being inside. I think I
would like that, not feeling anything.

It's feelings that got me in here. My court-appointed attorney told
me not to write anything to anybody about the case while I'm still
waiting to go on trial, but I told them that I don't care about that. I
deserve whatever it is they decide to give me. So the attorney kind
of knows I'm going to say things in my letters. If he don't know
then he's a dummy. But I suppose you'd have to be a dummy to
agree to take my case.

They threw me out of the apartment—that shithole place I told
you about. Said I was stealing money. I didn't steal shit. A few times
I ate food out of the fridge that didn't belong to me, but that's not
the same as stealing. I didn't go into anybody's wallet or anything
like that. First time that shithead Sam accused me of going through
his shit, I punched a hole in a door. I didn't expect my hand to
go all the way through the piece of crap shitty thing. There was a
scratch off sitting on a counter one time and I scratched it. That
too that ain't stealing. I wasn't going to cash it in. Fucking thing
wasn't a winner anyway.

That son of a bitch, that Sam, you know he pulled a gun on me
when he told me to leave? He didn't even let me pack any of my
shit. And as I was leaving, when he could of left well enough alone,
he says to me—good luck back on the street, not even your family
wants you.

Why the fuck would anybody say that to somebody?

And that's what did it. When he said that I turned around and I
told him what I was going to do. Now at the time, I didn't mean it.
I wasn't thinking of really doing those things. It was just that over
time, living under a bridge and the wind burning my face, those
words started to feel like the right thing to do. I was angry at that
motherfucker. He had shit that I didn't have and he knew it and
he rubbed it in my face. Thing is, if I had even half of what he had,
I would have been a million times better than him. The people
that looked at me while I was trying to sleep under the bridge, I

know what they were thinking and they were thinking the same things—that they're so much better than me. They don't know shit. They don't know what I had to work with. If they had what I had, they'd be in the dirt already.

So what I did I did because I was angry at all of them. I wanted people to feel what I felt. I wanted to create a horror that would show the world what it was.

And it was a horror, I'll tell you that. Only to me it felt like I was watching a movie instead of being there and doing it. It was like those times on the street when I was so cold and in so much pain from the ice burning through my fingers that I didn't even feel real anymore. There's this guy here inside a few cells down from me and he sits and stares at his wall nearly all day every day and people say he's getting his mind out of his body, being in a trance. That's what I think I was like then when I did those things, I was in a trance. Thing is, what that guy a few cells down knows, and what I think I've come to know, is that getting your mind out of your body to be in that away state is the only way to get through this hell thing called life. Maybe some people can live the life they're given, but some of us have to escape some way—for some people that's by staring at a wall and for others that's bringing the pain to others and making them look at it.

How is Richie? Is he in college now? I hope he is one of those people that gets to live the life they have instead of forcing their head to be somewhere else like I was saying. I hope he doesn't know what I did, but I guess everybody knows. Just, can you please tell him that what's inside me isn't inside him? Because we share some blood, that doesn't mean we're the same.

One other thing. Can you send me some things to read? I never read too much, but there's this one guy in here I talk to across the hall and he reads all the time. Says it's the only thing that keeps him from going crazy. I don't care what it is you send me. Anything you can find would be special to me.

Goodbye,
Matthew

Dear Mom,

I am guilty and I am sentenced to death. You know that. You were there when they read it out loud. You were the only person not cheering. By that I was surprised. I got this feeling my whole life that as soon as I came out of you that you wished I was dead. Maybe you wished I was never born, which I suppose is a different thing, right?

So I am going to die. I'm going to appeal and see what can happen, but I'm not holding my breath. Whatever days I have left I think I am going to spend a lot of them thinking about how you cried when I was sentenced. When I close my eyes I see tears running down your cheeks with black in them from your eye makeup. I am going to think about how you said I wasn't bad.

But what I want you to tell me is why were you really crying? It can't be because you miss me or that you will miss me when I'm gone. When all the years in my life so far are added up, I think you were a mother to me maybe four of them. How can you cry over somebody you knew for four years twenty years ago?

The people that operate this whole system, from the people locking the cages to the people pulling the levers and pushing the needles, they think taking my life is some terrible thing. That it is the ultimate punishment. But what the hell kind of life have I had. When I go in my head over it all I think that ending it is probably one of the better things they could do. If I was to be let out, what would I do? Die under a bridge? The world isn't the kind of place I want to live in anyway. I can imagine a world where I would want to live but it's so far from the one we have.

Maybe that was what you were crying about. You know that the life I had to some degree came from the kind of mother you were. By that I mean the kind of mother that didn't want to be a mother, not to me anyway. Maybe to Richie. Maybe you were crying because you felt guilty for what I had done. Do you think that the reason that family is dead is because you birthed me? I think you feel in some way like you are the murderer. Like my guilt is on you. I saw the way you avoided looking at what was left of my old roommate's family. You looked at the ground the whole time except when you had to answer the questions the lawyer was asking you. Then you just stared at the wall like there was a fly on it.

And I have to be honest with you Mom, I think that maybe had you been a better mother that that family would still be alive.

I went in that house and I knew they cared for that girl. She had a room with toys and pictures of her family on her wall. Everything was clean. I don't think I ever owned anything as clean as what was in her room like her clothes and her bed sheets. She had a picture of her and her brother, the one that threw me out at gunpoint. There weren't even any fingerprints on it and the edges weren't bent.

I was jealous of her. When I shot her while she was crying after she'd seen what I'd done to her parents, I thought that it was as unfair as anything that she got to have love like that and I didn't. So I took it away. I took everything away.

Or were you crying because you can't handle difficult situations or difficult feelings? Like how you couldn't handle raising me. If you could have run out of that court room without people chasing you, I bet you would have. If you could have pawned that court appearance off on to Grandma, I bet you would have.

Goodbye,
Matthew

NOVEMBER 2020

Dear Mom,

They have given me my date.

I've spent lots of time in here thinking about how I would feel when I was finally given a date. Now that it is here, I think I feel some relief. I feel like the most painful part of this has been the loneliness and the waiting, the staring and the living in my own head. When it ends, I won't have to be inside my head anymore. I don't know where I will be, but I imagine I won't be surrounded by my own thoughts. At least I hope that is the case. On my darkest nights I wonder if that's what death is—just the constant barrage of thoughts. That would be hell.

Thank you for sending me all of these things to read. On most days I feel like I have lost my mind. But on the days when I feel something that could be described as sanity, I think it is because I have these written words that you have gifted me. As I have told you before, I appreciate most the books about the natural world.

I know that your friends from your new church gave you the Christian books for you to give to me, but I must be honest and say that they do not resonate with me. That is not to say I do not appreciate them, but only that they do not strike the same nerve as the nature books do. I do not believe in resurrection and I do not believe in the Holy Trinity. However, that does not mean that I do not believe that God is with us. I only believe that God is with us through the natural world.

For most of my life I felt that there was no God because it would be hard to argue that God played any role in my life. I've come to change my opinion. God has played and is playing a role.

The fact that I existed, as imperfect as I am, as awful as I am, and that I changed, to me, shows the presence of God. I do not mean that my life is some sort of plan. I do not believe that. If God planned this then God is a bastard. But I believe the fact that I have been able to change, the fact that love exists in even the most terrible places and inside the most terrible people is evidence of something greater than us, something that I think can be called God.

Mother, you have changed also. We have forgiven each other. I will go to my execution and have a needle put in my arm, poison injected in my veins, knowing that I am loved. And before I die you need to know that I love you and that I am not angry with you and I do not blame you. You are not responsible for this.

And I thank you for bringing me into this world. I do not believe that humans have gotten it right. If we did, I would not be here. But, that does not mean I think the world is a terrible place. If it were a terrible place, we would not be surrounded by the beauties I've read about in the books you've sent me.

I used to think that scientists knew everything there was to know, that the world was fully understood by people smarter than me. Reading those books, I now understand that even the smartest and most educated people have so much they do not understand. Scientists do not know how birds find seeds they've hidden or why exactly they sing. No one knows for sure why whales sing or what they are saying. No one can explain the boundless love of an albatross. And no one knows what happens when we die.

I am allowed outside in a small fenced-in cell one hour each day. I spend that hour looking up and around. I watch and I listen. As you can imagine, the prison yard does not have much in the way of wildlife. Though we are not in the middle of a safari, I do see what I think most people would consider to be pests. I see squirrels and I see starlings and doves. Occasionally I see groundhogs so fat I wonder how they've gotten through the fencing on the prison perimeter. The animal I most enjoy is the sparrow. An avid bird-watcher, like the ones who have written the books you've sent, would probably overlook this creature. I have spent most of my life in prison and there is nothing that I overlook. The sparrow is small, fragile, but still, he sings and is full of life. I like to imagine that he is singing to me. Does he know that I am trapped? Is he comforting me? That's probably not the case, but I tell myself that it is so that I am able to sleep.

Sleep can be peaceful. I think of you and the last time you visited when I sleep. I've always closed my eyes and pictured your face. When I drift to sleep I also see the sparrows. It's like I looked so hard at them while I was awake they are in me somehow. I hope that death is like sleep and that I will still be able to see the birds when I close my eyes for that final time.

I have had hours and hours to contemplate death. While the thought of it doesn't make me cry anymore, I would be lying if I said I wasn't scared. I am scared. I don't know what I will see when I close my eyes to never open them again.

Will I see the birds or will I see a constant cycle of what I have done? Will I see those parents begging that I not hurt their daughter? Will I see myself denying their final wish? Maybe death isn't a vision. Maybe it's a feeling. I hope it feels like a blanket instead of a cold night behind a dumpster. I hope it feels like being in your arms as a small child.

Mom, I am sorry. I am sorry that you have had to live with what I have done. I am sorry that this is all a part of you. I wish that I could live longer so that I could show to you that the love you gave me by bringing me into the world was not a waste.

I love you mom.

Goodbye,
Matthew

Monster

FROM *Reckless in Texas*

MY MOTHER-IN-LAW, ALBERTA Dolan, did not have an enemy in the world the night she was stabbed to death.

The next morning, a homicide investigator came to notify Robert, my husband of six years. Detective Castillo was kind but professional as she told us what Alberta's twice-weekly maid had found. Still, I was grateful that our au pair hadn't yet returned from taking my son and daughter to visit the Teddy Bear statues in Lakeside Park. At least my children, who were just three and four, wouldn't have to learn about their grandmother's death the wrong way—as if there could be a right one.

When Castillo said she wanted to ask us a few questions, Robert and I agreed, of course. His gait was stilted and his breaths ragged as he led her to the formal sitting room used for guests, but he showed no other emotion.

As for myself, I let my tears run freely. I'd loved Alberta dearly and saw no reason to be stoic about the depth of my loss.

"We understand you have a younger brother?" Castillo asked Robert as she sat on a pink Victorian bustle-back chair.

Robert nodded before easing himself onto the settee opposite her. "His name is Mark. But he wouldn't have done it."

Castillo eyed Robert pityingly. "I understand it's hard to consider—"

"No," Robert said, cutting her off. "I mean that he had no motive. My mother removed him from her will a few weeks ago." Robert huffed out, as if it were an expletive, "Drugs."

Castillo nodded, and I assumed she'd already seen Mark's arrest record. What I didn't understand was why she was asking about

Mark at all. Surely she knew that Mark had the perfect alibi? Or did she think his alibi was too perfect—perhaps prearranged?

Robert's lip curled in a sneer. "Mark would shoot up, and Mom would cut him out of her will. Mark would eventually go to rehab, and Mom would put him back in the will. This was the third time she'd written him out, but since he's yet to hit bottom and go back to rehab . . ." My husband shrugged, as if to say he didn't care one way or the other. "No money for Mark."

Castillo looked around the room. I wasn't sure if she could tell that the sideboard was an original Hepplewhite or that the inlaid table was a William Moore, but since we were in a five-thousand-square-foot house in Highland Park, it was pretty obvious we weren't destitute.

Robert must've noticed her interest, because he said, "My dad passed away ten years ago. Mom was the wealthier one, so she encouraged Dad to divide his thirty-million-dollar estate equally between Mark and me. Mark invested his share in a couple of failed start-ups, then tried to recoup his losses at the poker tables. He's a decent player when he's not high on heroin." Robert's voice got sarcastic. "Of course, you have to be pretty high—or stupid—to gamble away the last of your inheritance. He's been broke for, oh, about three years now."

I tugged on the edge of my long-sleeved shirt. Robert liked to keep the house a cool sixty-eight degrees, which was a little chilly for my tastes. Something in my movement likely caught Castillo's eye, because she turned to me.

"Alberta was a wonderful woman," I said, meaning every word of it. "She was so kind and welcoming when I married Robert." I realized I'd started wiggling my engagement ring back and forth on my finger and held up my left hand to show the investigator the three-carat oval-cut blue diamond. "This was hers, from her own grandmother. Alberta told Robert to use it to propose to me because she wanted me to know we had her blessing."

The detective nodded, but her face was expressionless.

"Was it a burglary?" Robert asked.

The detective assessed him through narrowed eyes. "We don't know yet. Her bedroom looks ransacked, but a lot of valuables were left untouched. And the house's exterior locks don't appear to have been tampered with."

"What about the alarm system?" Robert asked.

"Off," Castillo said flatly. "As for whether the intruder turned it off or it was never on . . . ?" She lifted her hands, palms up. "We're waiting to hear from the monitoring company about that."

"She was always forgetting to activate it," Robert complained. "I told her a hundred times, but she didn't listen. Elizabeth is just as bad," he said, gesturing to me with his head. "I can't tell you how many times I come home late from work and find the alarm hasn't been set."

"Whoever killed Alberta must've been a monster," I said mournfully. "That or horribly desperate."

Robert leaned back against the settee and rubbed the side of his index finger along his bottom lip for a few seconds. "Maybe it was Mark after all. If he was high enough to forget that he'd been removed from the will again . . ."

Castillo cocked her head. "Your brother was in jail last night, sir. Didn't you know?"

A thundering scowl fell across Robert's face. "How would I know a thing like that?"

My stomach knotted. "Um. He called here. From the jail. He wanted me to ask you to bail him out, but I told him . . ."

"That I never would," Robert declared. "You shouldn't have accepted the call in the first place."

I knew how angry he'd be about Mark slipping back into his addictions and getting arrested, but maybe my decision to keep quiet about the phone call had been a mistake. I looked down at the rug. From the corner of my eye, I saw that the fringe didn't lay flat, and I wished I could go over for just a second to straighten it.

My head snapped up when Castillo said, "Mr. Dolan, your mother had gray hair."

A crease appeared between Robert's brows. "Of course, she did. She was in her sixties."

Castillo said matter-of-factly, as if discussing the weather, "We found two strands of brown hair in her bedroom, each about four inches long. One was stuck in the dried blood."

Perhaps it was my imagination that she was eyeing my husband's brown hair at that moment, but all the same, I was relieved to have white-blond hair that went down to the middle of my back. Robert always said it was my hair that caught his eyes when we'd first met.

"Mark has brown hair too," I pointed out. "Maybe he got someone else to post bail and he was out last night."

"He never left police custody," Castillo assured us. "He's in the clear."

If my husband had any feelings about that, they didn't show on his face, but his expression became positively wooden when the detective politely inquired whether we were home last night.

"Yes," he said, his voice growing icicles. "Neither of us left the house from when I arrived home for dinner last night—around six—until this very moment."

Detective Castillo scribbled something on her notepad, then asked us a series of questions about people in Alberta's life, including whether there had been any repairmen in her house recently or others who might have noticed a wealthy woman living alone.

Robert and I said that we wouldn't know about repairmen, but that Alberta hadn't told us about anyone showing undue interest in her or the house. "And Alberta would have said something," I assured the detective. "To Robert if she felt it was serious, or to me if she just thought it odd."

"I see," Castillo replied, before moving on to even more questions. I was grateful when Robert answered most of those, but I began to worry that my children would come home before the detective was finished.

I suppressed a sigh of relief when Castillo rose at last, as if preparing to leave.

"Thank you for your time," the detective said. "I expect that I'll have more questions for you later."

Robert stood as well, demanding, "What about the maid? If she has a key, then—"

"Ms. Silva is in a band," Castillo said. "They were performing in a club down in Waco, so she's got a slew of witnesses for the first half of the night, and her bandmates can account for the rest. It couldn't have been her."

"Maybe she gave the key to an accomplice," Robert suggested.

"Perhaps. We can't rule it out yet. But if Ms. Silva was pretending to be shocked, she should win an Academy Award."

Two days later, when the police were finished processing my mother-in-law's house, they asked Robert to accompany them through the place to see what—if anything—was missing.

"Elizabeth should go," he said, gesturing to me. "She'd know better than me what belonged where in my mother's house."

I agreed that was true, and let Detective Castillo drive me to Alberta's house. The entire way there, she kept trying to strike up a conversation about my husband, but I only gave "yes" or "no" answers. If a question required something more specific, I let it go unanswered.

She quickly picked up on my recalcitrance. "Did your husband order you not to speak with me?"

"He didn't have to," I said quite honestly. "Robert has brown hair, and with his brother disinherited, my husband is probably the only person in Alberta's will for any substantial amount. You're a police officer. Every courtroom drama of the last fifty years would tell me not to discuss him with you."

Castillo smiled at me, and I thought I saw respect there.

We arrived at Alberta's house a few minutes later. I emerged from the car and cast my gaze to the stone path along the side of the house, wishing we could go to the back patio, where Alberta and I would often lunch while looking at the peaceful greenery of Turtle Creek and the golf course. Those were my favorite memories of her.

I don't know how long it was before Castillo politely cleared her throat to get my attention. I sighed before following her into the house.

We began with a tour of the ground floor. Everything looked just as it had when I'd taken the children to visit Alberta the week before. When we were done with those rooms, I paused at the bottom of the stairs. I didn't want to go any farther, but Castillo insisted it was necessary.

The detective was right behind me as I trudged up the stairs and made my way down the hall. When I stepped inside the bedroom and saw the bloodstain on the thick carpeting, I felt nauseated. Tears welled in my eyes. Alberta had been so very kind to me and was the most fantastic grandmother to my children. We were going to miss her terribly.

Castillo pulled a small pack of tissues from her pocket, handed it to me, then asked, "Do you see anything missing?"

"I . . . I don't know." I wiped my eyes with a tissue before looking around. My gaze landed on two matching antique dressers, and with a shaking finger, I pointed at the one on the left. "The top drawer of that one should have her jewelry box."

"We found it on the floor." Castillo pulled out her phone and tapped over to a series of photos. "I can show you pictures of the jewelry."

"Can you show me someplace else?" I begged, certain that I could somehow smell the dried blood. "Please!"

"Of course," Castillo said gently.

We went downstairs to the kitchen and she put the phone on the counter. She flipped through the images of the jewelry, giving several seconds to each photo. When she was done, I told her nervously, "It's strange which stuff they took."

"Strange?" Castillo asked, sounding confused. "How so?"

"Alberta had several lovely pieces she'd inherited from her mother and a few from her husband's family. She told me they should go to my daughter, Simone, one day. The heirlooms are . . . All the heirlooms are in the pictures." I felt my forehead wrinkling as I added, "At least, I think so."

"But some pieces are missing—non-heirlooms?"

I nodded. "She'd bought a set of rubies recently. Earrings and a matching necklace. They weren't so valuable compared to what was left behind, but I know she wore them last month to a gala at the art museum. The theme was fire and ice. And at Christmas, she wore some pearls. They're in our holiday pictures, but I didn't see them in the photos you have here."

"Anything else?" Castillo asked intently.

"I . . . I think at some point I saw her wearing a set of tanzanite earrings with a matching pendant." I shook my head to convey that I wasn't certain. "Did you contact her insurance company? They ought to have a list."

"We're working on that," Castillo assured me. "But she might not have updated it recently."

I had no idea whether Alberta would've or not. We'd never discussed such things. "Why do you think the killer left behind the heirlooms?" I asked, fiddling with the scarf at my neck.

Castillo said calmly, "For the same reason you're thinking."

"I'm not thinking anything," I lied.

Castillo slid her phone back into her pocket. "Your husband knew he'd get it all in the will. If he stole his family's heirlooms, he couldn't keep them because they'd be proof of his crime. By stealing the newer stuff, he could make it look like a robbery and not lose anything that mattered."

I looked down at the empty counter, not wanting her to see what I feared might show in my eyes.

"Would your mother-in-law have put Mark back in her will if he'd gotten sober?" Castillo asked, turning to lean against the kitchen counter and work her way into my peripheral view.

Robert had already admitted the truth of that, so I lifted my head to face her again. "Yes. I think she would. She did it before. Robert says that Alberta removed Mark each time only to push him into rehab, but I know she was also worried about what would happen to Mark once she was gone. If forcing him into rehab failed, I'm sure she'd have set up a trust so that she could leave Mark some money while somehow preventing him from spending it on drugs."

"Why didn't she do that already?"

"She asked Robert to be the trustee, but he refused. He said he wasn't willing to deal with trying to keep track of when an addict was and wasn't lying about his condition, or to handle Mark's abuse on those occasions when the money would be withheld."

"I see," Castillo said coldly as she straightened.

"We have small children to protect," I explained, certain she'd understand how important that was. "Robert said that Mark would hound the trustee, and he didn't want Mark coming around our house and the children when Mark was high or angry. Robert told his mother to hire a professional to be the trustee, but I think she hadn't found the right person yet. She must've thought there was plenty of time. After all, she was only sixty-three, and a spry sixty-three at that."

I buried my face in my hands, overcome by what my children had lost. Potential years of playing with their grandma. Having her around for all their major life events.

"Was your husband with you between midnight and three a.m. on the night Alberta died?"

My hands slid down my face as I looked up at Castillo. "Robert told you that he never left the house from six—"

"I know what he said," she interjected. "But it's just you and me here now." Her voice grew urgent. "I need you to tell me, was he really home the entire time?"

I didn't feel that I could lie. Not about a thing like this. "I take pills to sleep sometimes. And when I do . . ." I shook my head. "As far as I know, he didn't leave the house that night. But I can't swear that I would have seen him go."

Castillo patted me on the shoulder and said, "It might not be him. Maybe your brother-in-law hired someone to break in to steal things, and the murder was unintentional. Or perhaps the maid gave the key to an accomplice because she knew she'd have a perfect alibi for the robbery."

I was certain that Castillo didn't believe either of those explanations. Not after what she'd said about Robert when addressing the oddity of which items had been stolen.

"The DNA on those hairs should give us a definitive answer about your husband," Castillo promised. "Until then, if he asks what you and I discussed . . ." She heaved a sigh. "Tell him whatever he wants to hear. That'll be safest for you."

I nodded, certain that she was right.

The DNA from the crime scene must've taken longer to get tested than it does on television, because it was nearly a month before they got a warrant to force my husband to provide a saliva swab to compare to those results. His lawyer, Joseph Davis, specialized in murder cases and tried to fight the warrant. But since the brown hairs at the crime scene were a 50 percent match to Alberta's DNA, and her only other child, Mark, had already been ruled out as a suspect, it was a lost cause.

Two weeks after the swab of my husband's DNA was collected, he was charged with his mother's murder. The police had tested his sample, as well as one from Mark just to prevent any questions arising at trial. The odds of the crime-scene hairs coming from anyone but my husband were one in nineteen billion. The judge denied bail on the grounds that Robert was a flight risk given his wealth and the weight of the evidence against him.

My husband insisted on having a private lab re-run the tests, which was his right as the defendant. The private lab ran a test using additional loci, which we were told meant locations on the DNA strand. Their test put the odds of his innocence at one in thirty billion. The prosecutor said that he would press for the death penalty if my husband did not accept a plea bargain that carried a sentence of life in prison.

Mr. Davis and I went to visit Robert at the jail and were shown to a private room made available for prisoners to consult with their attorneys. As we waited for the guards to bring Robert to us, Joseph told me, "You have to get him to say yes. He can't win this."

"I . . . I think he'll listen to you more than me," I admitted as I sat on the bench that was attached to the table. "You're the expert."

Joseph straightened his gray silk tie before taking a seat next to me. I couldn't tell if he was flattered that his opinion counted more than a wife's or worried that the process of convincing Robert now fell almost entirely to him. He said, "If Robert won't accept a plea, and I have to discuss anything privileged with him, we'll need you to step out."

I nodded my understanding as the door opened.

A guard escorted Robert into the room, gave us all a hard look that implied he wasn't inclined to trust any of us, then went back outside to watch the meeting through a glass window.

Joseph quickly got to the point, which was the need for Robert to accept the plea bargain before the prosecutor could change his mind. He ended by saying, "Life in prison is the best we can do."

"Life?" Robert snarled in outrage. "I didn't kill her!" He pounded a fist on the table, then shot me a glare, as if I was at fault for the lawyer's advice.

I darted a nervous look at the guard, but he didn't seem to think anything he saw was worthy of concern, so I turned to Mr. Davis. "Robert was her *son*," I said, needing the lawyer to understand my husband's position. "I bet his hair, my hair, my children's hair, they're all somewhere in that house. She must've picked it up on her nightgown and . . ."

"The hair was on *top* of the blood," Joseph said uncompromisingly. "The prosecutor will say that the obvious explanation is that it fell when the killer leaned over her—after she was already down—so that he could stab her a few more times."

"I didn't do it!" Robert screamed, spittle flying from his mouth.

"You had the alarm code," Joseph said, keeping his tone perfectly calm. "You had a set of keys to her house. And you inherit two hundred million dollars from her death. That's double what it would've been if you'd waited for your brother to be forced into drug rehab as part of the sentencing for his possession charges. You've already admitted that the rehab would've gotten him back into the will. If you let this go to trial, you will lose. And you will get the death penalty. Texas juries don't like wealthy men who kill their mothers for money. Nobody does."

My husband fired Joseph Davis and told me to find him another attorney. I did, but the new one offered the same advice, so Robert fired him, too, and told me to try again. Eventually, we found a lawyer,

Jim Bates, who wanted the billable hours and media attention of a trial more than he wanted to give reasonable advice.

Oddly, it was hearing Mr. Bates say that Robert should fight the charges that made my husband realize how hopeless his case was. If that camera-hog was the only one to think a trial was a good idea, then it had to be a very bad idea indeed.

"Get Davis back," Robert told me.

I went straight to Mr. Davis's offices and told the receptionist that while I didn't have an appointment, I was willing to wait as long as necessary.

I think she must've heard the desperation in my voice, because she made a few clicks on her computer, then offered to squeeze me in that afternoon.

When I came back a few hours later, it was with a vase of flowers. "Thank you," I told her as I handed it over. "Truly. On behalf of my entire family, especially my children, thank you for helping us."

She looked at me as if I'd lost my mind, and I wondered how many clients spewed abuse at her for being a gatekeeper and never bothered to express appreciation for her assistance.

I was equally effusive when pleading with Mr. Davis to take my husband back as a client. "He sees that you were right. Please, won't you help us with the plea bargain?"

Mr. Davis agreed to represent my husband once more, but it turned out that Robert was a little less convinced than I'd thought. He told Mr. Davis that he would only agree to plead nolo contendere, which meant admitting there was enough evidence to convict him without actually admitting to his guilt.

I apologized to Mr. Davis for the misunderstanding, but he seemed to take it in stride and said, "I'll see what I can do."

Luckily, the prosecutor preferred to claim victory rather than to use up resources on a trial with inevitable appeals, and he accepted the deal. Things moved fast after that, perhaps out of fear that Robert might change his mind. A week later, in accordance with the plea agreement, the judge sentenced Robert to life in prison without the possibility of parole.

An hour after the judge hammered his gavel to mark the end of the ordeal, I filed for divorce.

Robert hired a different lawyer to represent him in the divorce proceedings, but it did him little good. The judge was persuaded by my attorney's argument that I needed the marital assets more than Robert, who would be getting free room and board for the rest of his life. I got twenty million dollars. Robert was left with five.

However, the judge ruled that Robert would not owe child support. Under the "slayer rule," Robert couldn't inherit from Alberta, but she'd left her estate to him *per stirpes*, which meant his descendants inherited instead. My children, Jack and Simone, each got one hundred million dollars, and I was made trustee for their funds until they turned eighteen.

Mark threatened to sue Robert in civil court for the death of their mother, but since my children were Alberta's rightful heirs and would therefore have a better claim to any award a jury might grant, no lawyer wanted to take his case. All the same, I felt that something needed to be done.

I sent Jack and Simone to a movie with their au pair and arranged to meet Mark in a very public restaurant at the Village. When I arrived, he was already seated, but he stood at my approach and didn't sit back down until after I had.

He looked clean and sober—and an awful lot like his brother.

I nervously draped a napkin across my lap. "Thank you for coming."

His voice was hoarse as he replied, "Thank you for the invitation."

A waiter came over with menus and asked for our drink orders.

"Just an ice water," I said.

"I'll have the same," Mark told him.

Once we were alone, I didn't even bother to look at my menu. Mark ignored his as well, keeping his eyes on me.

I got right to the point. "I'm prepared to offer you a million dollars—"

Mark shook his head. "No, that's what I came to tell you. I've decided not to sue."

I blinked in surprise. I'd assumed we'd have an argument about my insistence that any money he got would be put in a trust to give him regular payments and that he'd have to show he was sober to get the funds. He hadn't even let me get that far. "You're not here about the money? Then why come at all?"

He paused, and just when he leaned in, as if he was going to answer my question, the server came over with our drinks.

Mark and I sat in awkward silence as the water goblets were placed on the table. The waiter must've picked up on the tension, because he left without asking if we were ready to order.

Mark took a deep gulp from his goblet. When he lowered it, his hand shook so much that the ice cubes rattled. He stared down at the glass, then placed it on the table and looked up at me. "I'm here because of my niece and nephew. I want . . . I want to be in their lives. To still be their uncle. Jack and Simone are my only family now that Mom is gone and Robert is . . ." Mark's lips tightened, and just when I thought he was done speaking, he added softly, "Please, Elizabeth."

My children had already lost a father and grandmother, and my parents had passed away before my children were even old enough to remember them. I wasn't eager to deny them an uncle, but I still felt a need to protect them. "You need to stay clean if that's going to happen."

His eyes, so like my husband's, brightened, and his shoulders straightened with seeming resolve. "I will. I swear it!"

He certainly sounded convincing, but I heard in the back of my mind Robert's warnings to his own mother about trusting an addict. Perhaps there was a way to accomplish more than one thing with this meeting. "If you agree to waive all claims resulting from Alberta's death, I'll put five million dollars into a trust for you—"

"This isn't about money!" Mark insisted.

"Maybe not," I allowed. "But Alberta would want you to be okay financially, and after everything she did for me, Jack, and Simone, it's important to me that I honor that." My plan had been to start negotiations at one million and work up from there, but his request had changed the tenor of the meeting. "You won't have access to the principal, only the interest. I've found a trustee who'll deal with everything, including the drug testing that you'll have to pass each month to get your interest payments. We'll use those same tests to determine if you'll be permitted to see the children. As long as having you in their lives is healthy for them, I won't restrict your access."

"Thank you," Mark said fervently. "For all of it." He leaned against the back of his chair and gave a long exhale. "Do you remember, at your wedding, when I gave a toast and said you were too good for my brother?"

I'd been so nervous that day, I remembered little of it. I gave Mark a smile that I hoped conveyed some form of fond reminiscence.

Mark said firmly, "Truer words were never spoken, Elizabeth. I had no idea then just how right I was."

After the last of the legal and financial matters were finalized, I went to visit Robert in prison. I felt he should know firsthand what I'd done and why.

As it turned out, he already knew the most important thing. The one thing I couldn't send anyone else to tell him.

When I lifted the phone on the opposite side of the plexiglass barrier from him, the first words out of his mouth were, "You killed my mother."

I suspected that the prison recorded all visitor communications, and I'd wondered how to tell Robert the truth without incriminating myself in any way. I tried not to show my relief that Robert had made my carefully practiced hints unnecessary. "What are you talking about?"

"You had access to my hairbrush. You had access to my key ring. You knew the alarm code, not that Mom remembered to turn the damn thing on. But you would've been prepared if you'd needed it."

I kept my face blank and hoped any cameras watching me would record my reaction as one of shock. "Is this some sort of game to get a new trial? Because I won't lie for you, Robert."

"You had those sleeping pills you'd use when the pain kept you up at night. You must've put one in my dinner that night."

I'd had those pills on hand to cover the pain from his beatings. And I'd put several, not one, in his meal. I'd have put it in his nightly whiskey, but I'd feared it might noticeably alter the taste. "I have no idea what you're talking about."

"I told you I'd kill you if you ever tried to leave me."

He had. He'd also threatened to kill our children before he'd let me take them away. That was the night I'd decided to get out from under him. To make sure he could never follow us.

"Why did you kill my mother? Why not murder me instead?"

Because I was not an idiot. All those long-sleeved shirts to cover the bruises from when he'd grab me by the arm and twist. The collection of scarves to hide more bruises on my neck and shoulders. The spouse is always a murder suspect, and once the police looked closely at me, it wouldn't have been hard to figure out my motive. But I'd had no apparent reason to murder his mother, who'd never been anything but kind to me.

At some point after Robert's sentencing, he must've finally calmed down enough to examine the situation. I looked at him and saw that he understood that his lifetime of imprisonment had been my way to ensure I could safely divorce him. He was simply hoping to get me to admit it on tape.

"I loved Alberta," I said with complete honesty. "As for your attempt to blame me for her death . . ." I gave a shrug and watched the anger flare in his eyes on the other side of the plexiglass barrier.

But his anger could no longer hurt me. The authorities weren't going to be interested in his theories when they already had someone in prison for the crime and no evidence against me. And while my offer to Mark had been driven as much by my guilt as my desire to obtain an ally, it ensured he'd be uninterested in helping a brother who'd wanted him cut off. Overturning Robert's conviction—and thereby the legal procedures that had followed—would only serve to endanger the financial trust that I'd established for Mark.

Reminding myself that the conversation was likely being recorded, I chose my words with care as I stood, preparing to leave Robert for the last time. After everything I had said and done since Alberta's death, I had some experience telling the truth while misleading listeners. "Robert, do you remember when Detective Castillo came to tell us that Alberta was murdered?"

"What of it?" Robert demanded.

"I told her that whoever killed Alberta must've been either a monster or horribly desperate. I still believe that, Robert. I always will."

MARY THORSON

The Book of Ruth

FROM *Thicker Than Water*

Kirtland, OH. 1989

THE FIRST THING Dolly noticed about her daughter was not the hole in her tooth, but her hair. It went all the way to the tops of her thighs. She could have tucked it into her back pockets. Clementine, or Tiny, as they called her until just before she left them, stood on the front porch with her stringy, long brown hair and her khaki skirt that went down to her shoes and her white shirt that buttoned all the way up, making Dolly pull at the skin of her own neck. She hadn't seen her daughter in two years. It was not without trying. The fluorescent porch light turned her daughter's pale skin a shade of blue.

"Hello, Mother."

Tiny's voice sounded deeper. Dolly wondered if female voices did that between ages eighteen and twenty. Dolly wondered if her daughter started smoking. She stepped forward and put her daughter's face in her hands, coming very close because she couldn't help herself. Tiny went stiff but didn't pull away, and Dolly could feel her daughter's jaw clench against her palms. She found more differences. Slight changes around her daughter's eyes and mouth— her lips seemed thinner. She had more spots now, light and dark, dotting her cheeks and nose and forehead. A very dark one had developed in the middle of her chin. Dolly brought her daughter closer and buried her face into Tiny's neck. She breathed her in until she thought she would faint. She smelled different, almost antiseptic, but underneath there was something familiar. Maybe

Tiny was sweating or producing oils on her skin in order to make it easier to slip from her mother's bony hands, but Dolly knew that smell and her grip was strong.

Finally, Tiny put her hands up to her mother's arms—not moving them away, but a warning.

"Is it okay if I stay here? I don't know for how long. Is that okay?"

Dolly laughed and at that moment the wind came, blowing some of Tiny's hair into her mouth. She pulled it out. That was when Dolly saw the small black hole in her daughter's canine, eroding the edge and slowly splitting the tooth apart.

"Tiny, baby, of course it is. This is your home. We've been waiting for you to come home."

"It's Ruth, actually." Tiny let her arms fall as her mother kept holding her. Tiny attempted to back up.

"Oh, still?"

"Still, yes."

Before she left them, before the hole, she asked her parents to call her Ruth.

"I'm not a miner's daughter, I'm God's daughter," she had said at dinner. Dolly knew her daughter thought this was clever. Her father laughed, but Dolly also knew then that the fracture between them had worsened. Grown deeper while she wasn't looking.

"I think I'll stick with Clementine, Tiny," her father said. Dolly didn't say anything, trying to commit herself to not using a name at all.

"I lie at the feet of *Him*, like Ruth."

"That's enough of that talk," her father said. Dolly continued her silence and two weeks later, Ruth was gone.

"That's fine," Dolly said, smiling. She brought her daughter into the house and locked the door behind her, as if that had stopped her before. Tiny stood in the middle of the living room, surveying the things around her. Dolly wondered what had changed, if anything, since she left.

"Do you want anything to eat? Or do you want to put your things away?" It was a stupid question, Tiny didn't have anything with her, and she lifted her empty hands in demonstration.

"That's all right, everything is in your room."

"My room?"

"Of course. All your clothes, your records, books, whatever. It's all still there."

"Oh," Tiny said.

*

Tiny was their only child, and Dolly thought this was why Tiny didn't sleep in her own room until high school. When she was young, still just a toddler, it was easy to let her stay in their bed. Don pretended and put up a show of annoyance, but when he realized no one was watching, that it was just the three of them in that little house, he let her in-between them and everybody slept better. When she got older, she tried harder at sleeping alone. She would start off in her own bed, but then, sometime during the night, she would end up outside their open door, waiting in the dark to be invited.

Then, it seemed like it happened in one night, she became dog-gedly possessive of her space. The room that had been decorated the same since she was three; a pink flowered quilt, plain white walls, baskets of toys and things on shelves—transformed into something else, something older. Tiny grew in there, alone. And despite that she no longer came to their door at night, Dolly kept it open, always waiting. Dolly started having trouble sleeping.

"How about I make you a sandwich? We have some cold cuts in the fridge, and some mayo."

"Did you paint in here?" Tiny asked.

"Of course not," Dolly lied.

"I remember it different."

"I'm going to make us some sandwiches. I have some iced tea too. Would you like some?" Dolly asked but was really saying: *Please please stay, I'll keep it all the same for you, please.*

"Does it have caffeine?"

"No, I don't think so," Dolly said, but she didn't really know. After Tiny left, she kept up the things she wanted for a few months. No caffeine or booze in the house, the Bible stayed out on the coffee table. She kept working on the cross-stitch of a passage from the book of Ruth: *Do not urge me to leave you or to return from following you. For where you go I will go, and where you lodge I will lodge. Your people shall be my people, and your God my God.* She meant it as a kind of plea to her daughter, but it was not taken. After some time, her husband brought home some beer and they had it at dinner. Then the Bible was put away.

"I'll just have some water."

"Sure."

She pulled out an old cup from the cabinet. It had a kissing Donald and Daisy on it with hearts floating up that were almost scratched away. When she finished making the sandwiches she set the cup with the image facing toward her daughter, hoping to incite a comment. Tiny didn't notice. It had been her favorite cup, even in high school. The only thing she'd wash herself if it was dirty. Dolly watched her throat move as she drink, her cheeks slightly puffing in and out with each gulp. Tiny finished it all at once.

"Do you want some more?"

"Yes, please." She pushed the glass toward her mother and then left her hand out. The palm was calloused and looked much harder than it had, but then again, Dolly couldn't really remember her hands before, all she could think of was the way they were when Tiny was a baby. Of course, they had grown and hardened since then. She picked up the cup and went over to the sink. Behind her, her daughter moved. She couldn't see what she was doing, but Tiny was shifting or stirring, quietly, as if she was trying not to be heard. Dolly turned around and saw her daughter scraping the skin away from her thumbnail. She stretched it until it bled and then put her whole thumb in her mouth and sucked it like an infant—something she had never done. Tiny caught her mother staring and dropped it then wiped it against her cheek.

"Where is he?"

Dolly brought over the glass and set it in front of her daughter as she sat down across from her, again. Tiny's eyes were trained on her, peering through thin slits with her hands in her lap.

"He's still at work, should be home in about an hour." Dolly rubbed her palm against the table as she said, "Oh, he'll be so happy to see you." She wished she could have held her daughter's hand to keep her thumb out of her mouth, but she kept them to herself.

When they had gone to the Lundgren farm a few weeks after Tiny left, she was kept away, or maybe she kept herself away. They had waited because Don had said she'd come back when she realized how good she had it at home. When everything wasn't being done for her. Dolly didn't think so, and finally Don relented. Dolly went to the door alone. It was a big white farmhouse with a long, dirty porch, and she stepped around the pieces of a broken chair spread out on the floorboards. She pressed her finger down on the doorbell, but nothing happened so she knocked. She heard hard footsteps coming and she looked at Don sitting in the car in the driveway. He was watching her.

"Who's there?" The voice was low and strong on the other side of the door. If it had been any louder it might have caused a slight vibration in Dolly's chest.

"Hello?"

"Who's there?"

"This is Dolly Miller. I'm Clementine's mother."

Then the door opened and he stepped out onto the porch. Jeff Lundgren was fat and Dolly hadn't expected that. His hair was long and slicked back, showing off how it was receding away from his forehead. His skin was pockmarked and shiny, and he was tall, but very fat. He stepped forward, coming too close. She looked, again, to Don in the car and he finally got out. The man didn't even blink when the car door shut. Instead he put his hand forward, the tips of his fingers almost grazing her stomach. She sucked in deeply.

"My name's Jeff." He kept still.

She took her hand out of her glove and backed up in order to put it in his.

"Dolly Miller. Like I said, I'm Clementine's mom."

"Clementine?"

"We're here for our daughter," Don said, coming up behind Dolly.

Jeff let go of Dolly's hand and extended his to Don. Don eyed it before shaking it hard.

"That's a good grip, Mister . . ."

"Miller. You know, the same as Clementine."

"I'm sorry, as I was just about to tell your wife, I don't have anybody here by that name."

"You do, we know you do. She told us about you before she left. About this." Her voice was too high. In the house behind him she imagined many women dressed all the same. Their hair back in a single braid. And when she thought of Tiny in there, she thought of her when she was seven and had learned how to braid, braiding everything she found.

"I'm sorry, ma'am, I'm being honest."

"Ruth, what about a Ruth?" Don asked with his eyes closed.

"Ah." Jeff smiled and winked—a trick, then. "Ruth. Ruth is staying with us, me and my wife and children, and others like her who want to get closer to God."

"Sure," Don said.

"Can we see her? Can you send her out?"

"I can't make her do anything she doesn't want to."

"That's some horseshit if I ever heard. I know people like you; con artists, cheats. You can convince weaker people to do anything you want."

"Don," Dolly said.

"Get my daughter you piece of shit or I'll come in there myself." Don brustled up closer and taller, and Dolly saw he had the same gut Jeff had. She had no clue when he had gotten so big.

"Now, sir, Ruth is a strong adult. Not so weak as you think. She can leave whenever she wants. We love her and respect her here, which is something she says she was missing in her life. But, if you continue to trespass or attempt to gain entry to my home, I'm afraid I'll have to call the police."

"The police? I should be calling them on you for kidnapping!"

"Ruth came here to us in search of help and home. And, I'm sure I don't have to remind you, but she ain't no kid."

Don went forward to hit him, but Dolly grabbed onto his arm and he almost lifted her off the ground.

"Don! Stop, this isn't going to help anything."

Jeff flinched then and Don put his arm down. He stormed back to the car and Jeff watched before he turned back to Dolly, suddenly smiling, as if he had been the whole time.

"I'll let Ruth know that you all came by." He went back in the house and slammed the door.

Dolly stood alone on the porch for a moment. It was quiet even though she strained to hear behind the walls. She listened for her daughter's voice but heard nothing.

Dolly stared at her daughter across the table, willing her to smile in the little way she used to when she was trying to keep her happiness contained. But she only rolled her eyes.

"Right," Tiny said. "I'm sure he'll be."

"He will be. He's missed you so much. We both have."

Tiny looked at the ground. This was making her uncomfortable. "Are you okay? Are you tired?"

"I'm fine."

The phone rang, sounding unbearably loud. Tiny's eyes grew wide.

"I'm not here, okay? Please don't tell anyone I'm here."

"Okay, baby. I'm sure it's just a telemarketer."

Dolly thought her daughter was going to cry. Tiny started biting around the inside of her mouth. Dolly wanted to stay with her and smooth her very long hair. The phone rang at least ten times before she finally tore herself from the kitchen table and picked it up.

"Hello?"

There was a click, and then silence, and then the dial tone came. She hung up and walked back to the table.

"Who did you think it would be?" Dolly asked her daughter.

"Nobody." Tiny began picking up the crumbs around her sandwich with her index finger.

"You can tell me."

"I don't live here. I don't know who calls."

After the visit to the farm, Dolly and Don went to the police station. The officer they talked to, Dolly couldn't remember his name after he told it to her, said they'd had troubles with Jeff Lundgren before. Gunshots going off at the house, theft, trespassing. They'd talked to him several times, and he always backed down.

"Backed down from what?" Don asked.

"His threats, or whatever he calls them. His prophesizing."

"His what?"

"He says he can talk to God directly, and he gives instructions to all his followers as if he himself were Jesus Christ. Never heard of Jesus needing all that money, or all that company."

Dolly thought she might get sick.

"The women especially get sucked in by him. They're all in love with him, worship him, sleep with him, do whatever he wants. He hangs up a sheet in the woods and hides behind it while they dance naked out there in the dark," this he whispered, leaning closer to Don. "One of them, not his wife, came up and slapped one of my deputies in the face last time we went over there. They guard him like dogs. He's lucky we didn't take her in. Figured she's not exactly in her right mind, if you get me. None of them are, over there."

"What about our daughter?" Don asked through his teeth.

"Ah, my mouth, no one needs to hear that. Really, it's a shame, I'm sorry about that, but there's nothing we can do. She's over eighteen, sir. Just pray she'll wake up and see that man for what he is."

Dolly wanted to explain to this man how impossible that was. Tiny was joyful, but so naive. She took things on their face and held them there always. She had never asked about made-up things because she never questioned them. Once, she found her Christmas presents in the back of Dolly's closet. She was staring right at the pink plastic sled she had asked for after seeing it at the mall, and all she said was, "Oh!" Quickly, Dolly said, "Sometimes he has to drop off presents ahead of time, if he's in the neighborhood." Her daughter kept smiling, and responded with, "I know that, Mom." Though, of course, she didn't know.

Tiny ate the sandwich slowly. She was not starving and this almost disappointed Dolly. She took small bites and chewed them for too long before taking another. Dolly could hear her daughter swallow. The hole in her daughter's tooth showed itself only once or twice while she ate and Dolly thought maybe this was why it was taking so long. Tiny had to be careful because her teeth were rotting.

The phone rang again, but the air in the room had changed and as if watching cracking glass Dolly was braced for the break in silence, this time. She grabbed the phone off the hook in the middle of the second ring, but instead of saying "hello," she just watched her daughter's face. The person on the other end was quiet. Dolly heard them part their lips and push them back together and swallow. Then they hung up.

"Mom?" Tiny asked, softly.

"Yes, baby?"

"He's so angry."

"Did he do something to you?"

"He wouldn't," Tiny said, but she said it to herself. She looked at the red skin she'd scratched away at her thumb and Dolly could tell her daughter wasn't breathing.

"Am I different now?" Tiny asked.

"Of course not," Dolly said, lying again.

"He loves us all, even those children—it just had to be."

The front door swung open and shut inside of a second and both women held their breath.

Don said, "Someone just standing in the middle of the road out there, high as a goddam kite, wouldn't move when I got close and I almost had to drive up on the grass getting around them."

He came into the kitchen and Dolly couldn't see his face, but she could hear the way his body went when he saw his daughter at the table.

"Tiny," he said.

"Ruth," Dolly said. "Please."

Don swallowed and then squared his shoulders.

"Sure. Ruth."

"Hi, Dad."

"Hi."

"Come sit down, Don."

"Are you home, now?" Don asked.

"For now," Tiny said.

He came to the table, to the chair next to his daughter, and he pulled it out so he was sitting in the middle of the kitchen, far away from both of them.

"When you're done here, are you going back there?"

"Don, we don't need to figure this out yet," Dolly said.

"No. I can't." When Tiny said it, something caught in her throat and there was a break in her voice. Don ran his hand down his face and then put his hands on his knees as he got up. He was getting older and Dolly hadn't noticed. She wondered if it was a shock to Tiny, but her daughter wasn't watching.

"Well, then, we won't talk about it in this house. When you're here, you won't talk about it. Understand me?"

Tiny stared at him, almost glaring, before she nodded.

"Good. I'm sure your mother told you, everything's as it was in your room."

"Yes," Tiny said. "Thank you. I'm tired, do you mind if I go to bed, Mother?"

"Do whatever you like," Don said.

"Are you sure you don't want to talk more?" Dolly asked.

"She said she's tired."

"Don, Jesus Christ." Dolly whipped around and narrowed her eyes at him.

Don opened his mouth and then shut it.

"Now, do you want to tell me something, Ruth?" Dolly asked.

Tiny stood and shook her head.

"I'm tired, is it all right if I just go to bed?"

"Sure. Maybe tomorrow we can call the dentist, too, yeah?" Don asked.

There was a moment where it seemed as if her daughter wanted to jump out of her own skin, and Dolly desperately wanted to keep her all together.

"That's fine, baby. Okay," Dolly said.

Tiny left and Dolly heard her room door shut softly. She had never shut it like that, before. She was reckless with the way she would close it, always too excited, and she moved part of the frame out of place over time. That part was still off. Alone in the kitchen, Dolly went over to the sink to wash her daughter's dishes for the first time in two years. She scrubbed them with her hands instead of the sponge, touching all the parts her daughter touched. Outside the kitchen window, she saw someone walking slowly up the sidewalk, past their house. She did not know them. She turned her back to the window and leaned against the sink. She was waiting for the phone to ring—she felt it coming through the hairs on her arms. She rushed to it, snatching it off the hook and then letting it drop on the floor. It twisted around like a snake on the tile and when she heard the dial tone beeping, she shut off the lights and walked down the hallway into her own bedroom. Don was awake in the dark, she could tell, but she didn't speak to him. She took off her clothes and crawled into bed, keeping a distance of inches of cold sheets between them. After a while of listening for movement from her daughter's room on the other side of the wall, and hearing nothing but the silence that had been there before, her body relaxed and she drifted off to sleep.

It was still dark when she woke up, and she had the sense that she had just been having a very vivid dream, but she couldn't remember it. She was about to turn over and put her arm around her husband when she saw a shadow on the wall next to her bed. It shifted slightly, but didn't get bigger or smaller, just swayed. She watched it for a little while until she couldn't bare it anymore and shut her eyes. She shut them tightly, hoping her daughter couldn't see her face from where she stood in the doorway. Dolly breathed slow and shallow, trying to listen for her daughter's breath, but she couldn't hear it. Maybe, her daughter wasn't there at all, but Dolly didn't want to know. She kept her eyes closed and did not sleep well.

REBECCA TURKEWITZ

Sarah Lane's School for Girls

FROM *Bayou Magazine*

I HAVE TOLD this story many times, but I have always told the simple version, which is to say I have always told it wrong. The version that I tell is this: When I was a sophomore in high school, the dean's sixteen-year-old son fell through the ice and drowned in the lake near campus. I tell people about the wave of morbid excitement that rippled through the hallways of our dormitories. I tell people that the event had a profound effect on me even though I'd only spoken to John a handful of times, and I let people draw their own conclusions as to why that might be. Maybe people assume it was an early eye-opening experience that proved death can be brutal and doesn't always spare the young. Maybe they interpret it as a quiet woman's desire to relive melodrama or nostalgia for the peculiar comfort one feels after a communal tragedy. All of the above is true, but it doesn't do the story justice. Although I always hope it will, telling the sound-bite version doesn't make me feel any better or get me closer to the answers I want. If nothing else, after all these years I'd like to finally get the story right.

I attended Sarah Lane's, an all-girls boarding school in Vermont. The buildings were mostly Georgian Revival, a solemn red brick with side gables and neat rows of windows. A high stone wall surrounded the campus on three sides, with woods on the fourth, and beyond that, a lake. Though the gates were always left open, we rarely left campus. Howland, Vermont, didn't have much to offer us except for a video rental store, an ice cream shop, and teenage boys we never had the guts to talk to anyway. We did our work and were mostly polite to our teachers, and we had enough fun living with one another instead of our parents that we didn't complain much, even in the oppressive stillness of the long Vermont winters.

I wound up at Sarah Lane's on a scholarship that the school put in place to smooth over tensions with the locals. My guidance counselor had told my mother I was a likely candidate, and for the rest of eighth grade Mom insisted on helping me finish science projects and essays. She was a night nurse, and my father was an electrician whom she had never married, and her daughter would be going to school with the children of politicians and lawyers. It was 1994 and the Clintons had just entered Chelsea at Sidwell Friends. My mother joked that we were following suit. I was worried that the other girls would recognize me as an outsider right away, so I spent my freshman year watching and listening, keeping my head down. I only visited my parents on holidays, even though they both lived less than twenty minutes down the road. At the start of my second year, I realized that I'd overcorrected and blended in too well. Everyone liked me well enough, but only because I kept my mouth shut and didn't take sides. The thrill of being at a new school and the fear of failure that had kept me sharp started to wear away. By December I was crawling out of my skin, desperate for a break from the monotony. Then John disappeared and shook us all out of our routines.

Most of the girls at Sarah Lane's barely knew John, but we were intensely curious about him. He was a junior at Howland High, the town's public school. We'd watch him eating dinner at the faculty table in the dining hall with his father, whose dark hair and broad shoulders he'd inherited. Occasionally he'd catch us staring at him and flash a crooked smile. Giggling, we'd turn away before his father noticed. We were all terrified of Dean Anderson, whose mission in life was to scare teenage girls into becoming serious, respectable women. The dean was enormous, with sunken eyes and a close-lipped smile that never seemed genuine. His right leg dragged behind him slightly when he walked, which gave his movements an air of deliberateness and added to the impression that every move he made was calculated. Dean Anderson's wife had died when John was a baby, and we shuddered when we talked about John trapped alone in the dean's house with only his austere father for company.

Susannah Wayland, whose uncle was a policeman in Burlington, was the first to hear about John's disappearance. At the start of geometry, she whispered the news to Missy Davis, who asked Mrs. Conway whether or not it was true. Our teacher reluctantly confirmed the rumor but asked us to keep quiet about it until more information became available. By third period, it seemed like every girl at the school had heard about the dean's missing son. In chemistry, I tried to catch the eye of my roommate, Nicky, and was surprised to find that she was still and silent, staring down at her notebook. I'd seen Nicky alone with John several times, but whenever I asked her about it, she skirted the subject with an abruptness that only increased my curiosity.

Nicky had been my roommate since freshman year, and after a week of living together she'd anointed me her best friend. She always gave off the impression of barely contained energy, even in the dead of winter when the rest of us were tired, beat-down, and settled into our routines. She snuck off campus on mysterious trips and never got caught. She had a secret stash of cigarettes that replenished itself without explanation. She spoke to our teachers with a boldness that would've gotten most of us suspended, but for Nicky there never seemed to be any consequences. At least part of Nicky's immunity came from the fact that her family was the type of wealthy I'd thought only existed on television shows or in countries with noble bloodlines. But Nicky was a force in her own right, impossible to oppose.

Nicky was also our resident authority on everything grotesque. Friday evenings, she occasionally gathered us at the stone fireplace in the student lounge and regaled us with urban legends that thrilled us and left us unable to sleep. So when the rumors about John escalated and we began to talk about death instead of disappearance, everyone wanted to bring their theories and questions to Nicky.

Late that afternoon there was a meeting in our dorm room to discuss what we'd heard. Eight of the girls from our hall squeezed together on the rug in between Nicky's bed and my own. Outside our window thick streaks of snow were falling. John and his father had been seen walking into the woods before dinner on Tuesday—two days ago—and only the dean had returned home. The dean had called the police after John missed dinner. In the early hours of Wednesday morning, a search party found John's blue parka hanging on a tree branch next to the lake. About twelve feet away from the bank there was a large hole in the ice. And that was all we knew.

Every girl had her own theory, and we were divided. The less imaginative girls suggested it had been a terrible accident; John, in his recklessness, had tested his luck on the ice and fallen in. Sarah Johnston was the first to mention suicide. She pointed out that only a fool would have believed the ice was safe this early in what had been an unseasonably warm winter. Laura Parks leaned in close to the center of the circle and whispered that with a father like Dean Anderson, suicide might make sense. I suggested that it was possible John wasn't dead. What if he'd staged his disappearance? Why would he leave his parka hanging there like some morbid place marker if it was just an accident? Swayed by this romantic possibility, several girls changed allegiances. Our debate continued as dusk fell, and then night. We talked through dinner and study hall, distributing granola bars and care-package cookies instead of trudging to the dining hall.

It was almost ten when Nicky finally spoke up. "You're all wrong," she said, and the group grew silent. Our room was dark now; only my small desk lamp shone in the corner. Nicky's eyes darted across our faces, and her mussed blond hair reflected the lamplight. "It was murder." Just then Ms. Tiggs, our dorm monitor, burst into our room, eliciting shrieks that peeled into laughter. She shooed everyone out, muttering about how we shouldn't be enjoying ourselves when tragedy had struck so close to home. She glared at Nicky but did not admonish her.

As we prepared for bed I asked Nicky if she really believed what she'd said.

"It couldn't be suicide, and I don't think he would run away either. He wasn't reckless. He was stupidly safe. He would've known not to go on the ice."

"Be honest with me, Nicky," I said, studying her. "Were you and John dating?"

"We were lovers," Nicky said, as if this was the first time I'd asked, as if she would have always answered so frankly, as if this was a normal sentence for a sixteen-year-old girl to utter.

"But who would hurt him?" I asked. "Why would anyone want him dead?"

Nicky made a funny sound like a giggle. I realized she was crying. I stood near her awkwardly, hoping she'd give a sign of what she expected from me. I rested my hand on her shoulder, feeling the bounce of her sobs.

When I woke the next morning Nicky was already dressed, applying mascara in front of our full-length mirror.

"We're going to investigate," Nicky said, somehow sensing that I was awake.

"Investigate what?"

"John's disappearance."

"That's not our job," I said.

"Really, Emily? John's missing. Who cares whose job it is?" Nicky locked eyes with me in the mirror without turning around.

"But where would we even begin?"

"I think his father killed him."

I laughed. "You have to be kidding."

"John told me stories. Dean Anderson's as terrible as a person can be. He used to hit John. I saw the bruises. No one knew because the dean always hit him where his clothes would cover it. He'd wince sometimes when I touched him."

I couldn't believe it, but I also didn't understand why Nicky would make the story up.

She sat down on the edge of my bed. "If you think I'd lie about this, then you don't know me at all."

"I believe you. But you have to admit it's a pretty wild theory."

"That's why we're going to investigate." Then she laid out her plan. During the all-school meeting, we would sneak out to the lake. It was almost a mile away, and I wondered what would happen if we got caught rooting around the place John had last been seen.

Nicky hopped off my bed and went back to the mirror. "Get dressed," she said, and I didn't ask any more questions.

School meeting usually consisted of announcements about clubs and weekend trips, but that Friday the meeting began with a speech from the police chief. We were told to cooperate if anyone asked us questions, show sympathy to the dean, and support one another. As he spoke, Nicky fidgeted, pumping her leg so hard I could feel the vibrations in my own seat. John's body still hadn't been recovered, the chief said. Tripping over his words, he explained that John's body could have drifted to any part of the lake. The hole was already beginning to ice over again. He implored anyone who had information about the incident to come forward. Every part of me was burning to tell the chief what I knew; I would've felt the urge to help him even if I didn't have pressing information to share. That was just how I was then—how I probably still am. Nicky put her lips against my ear and hissed, "Let's go."

She pulled me from my seat and put her arm over my shoulder, angling me toward her, as if I was crying. The other girls, bored with the chief's rambling speech, watched enviously as Nicky led me down the aisle. Once we were outside Nicky reached out and zipped up my coat. It was an uncharacteristically tender gesture, almost maternal. I followed her to the edge of the woods. The sky was already growing dim and a steady snow had started to fall. A walking path snaked through the woods to the lake, but the snow had rendered the path nearly unrecognizable.

"Are you going to tell the police that you and John were dating?" I asked as we wound through the trees.

"They'd just tell Dean Anderson. And I don't want to answer all their stupid questions."

"Don't you think you need to tell them what you know?"

"Things aren't that simple, obviously."

I didn't want to admit that I couldn't understand why it wasn't simple, so I let the matter drop. My snow-covered hair stuck in clumps to my face and water dripped through the collar of my coat. After a while I said, "The dean is a lot bigger than John."

"So you think he would have fallen through the ice too."

"Yes."

"I already thought about that. He could have held John under the water and then swam back, climbing onto the thicker ice by the edge. But probably he killed John in some other way, and made the hole himself, then left the jacket for the police to find. John wouldn't have drowned otherwise. It's not like he couldn't swim."

"What if he hit his head or something? Or got hypothermia. I read somewhere that it only takes a few minutes."

"You've already made up your mind," Nicky said.

"Haven't you?"

She shook her head, the ice in her hair knocking together. "I think either the dean killed him or he ran away. Maybe he's just lying low somewhere, waiting until the police go away, so he can contact me."

I stared at the back of Nicky's legs as we hurried forward, trying to keep my balance and avoid missteps. The snow had turned into icy rain, and I could barely see. The trees twisted and swayed around us. Everything seemed to be moving. I looked down and discovered that my right hand had been cut and was bleeding. My clothes stuck to my body. I yelled for Nicky to slow down. She turned to face me and said something I couldn't hear. A streak of mascara stained one cheek, and her face was pallid from the cold. She darted away, and I stumbled, losing sight of her.

I wondered if I'd be able to follow my footprints all the way back to campus or if they'd been erased by the storm. I knew Nicky would be furious with me if I turned around. I pushed on, until suddenly the white plain of the lake spread before me. It was smaller than I remembered. Ripped police tape dangled from a nearby tree. I imagined Dean Anderson, lumbering through the dark pines.

There was a rustling to my right, and only a dozen or so yards away there was a body hunched over by a tree, clawing at the snow. I screamed. The figure rose and turned to me, and before I could flee, I saw it was Nicky. She was smiling and holding a small wooden box in her hand.

"It's John's. He wouldn't have left it if he'd run away. Or there'd be a note for me."

"We came all the way out here for that tiny box?" I tried to curl and uncurl my frozen toes.

"I didn't know what we'd find," Nicky said.

"We need to get back to the dorms right now. It's late. They're going to notice we're gone. We're going to get into so much trouble."

"That's not going to happen."

"Not to you, maybe. Not everyone's so lucky."

Nicky gestured toward the lake. "You call this lucky?"

"I'm serious," I said. "If we get caught, I could lose my scholarship. We need to go now."

We ran, stumbling through the snow, the entire way home. I never looked back, terrified that I'd see someone chasing us. I don't know what I was expecting—a menacing stranger, the lumbering dean, or John's bloated corpse. Even after we'd finally fled the woods, I still felt that there was something sinister at our heels.

*

Back in our room, wrapped in my comforter and rubbing the feeling back into my feet, I demanded that Nicky show me what was in the box. She took out a few sheets of folded paper: poems and notes written in a meticulous hand. But she never lingered long enough on any of them for me to read more than a few words. We changed quickly, and Nicky helped me wash and bandage the gash on my hand. Then we rushed to make an appearance in the dining hall. The other girls kept asking us where we'd been and why we were flushed. "We don't feel well," Nicky told them. "We had to rest."

Sarah Rodriguez gave us the update on everything we'd missed. Other girls now suspected Dean Anderson, and someone had posited the theory that John and Mrs. Mullen, a young English teacher, had been having an affair. When Nicky left the table to get tea, the other girls asked me if she'd said anything about John. I said she was taking his disappearance pretty hard.

"Some girls are starting to talk about her," Laura Parks said, her eyes wide and innocent.

"What're they saying?"

"That they've seen her with John. That she's always leaving campus, and—"

Nicky returned with an extra cup of tea for me, and we all studied our food.

"I hope you're not coming down with anything, Nicky," Laura said. "Especially so close to midterms."

"How can you possibly think about midterms right now?" Nicky shook her head. "A person has disappeared and is maybe dead. It's ridiculous to worry about exams."

The rest of us sheepishly agreed with her, but we knew that the drama of John's disappearance wasn't going to stop the gears of Sarah Lane's from turning for long. Our commitments were waiting, and we of the never-missed deadlines, of the always prepared, would be ready to meet them.

The next day, while Nicky was in her cello lesson, I turned our room upside down. John's box was tucked inside a dirty shirt in her hamper. The box held songs and poems written in meticulous handwriting, packed inside two layers of Ziploc bags. So there was some echo of his father's deliberateness in John. Many of the poems were dedicated to or about Nicky, and most were a little angsty and brooding, but there was nothing about abuse or his dad.

That evening I confronted her. "You've got to give me a better reason not to go to the police."

"They wouldn't believe me," she said.

"Maybe that's because you're wrong."

"Dean Anderson is a lonely, perverse man, and I know that he did it. I feel that he did it. He acts so calm and put-together all the time, but there's a reason everyone tiptoes around him."

"What if they ask me how you knew John? I'm not going to lie to the police."

"Are you threatening me?"

"Of course not. But you're asking a lot. If you really think the dean is involved, we have an obligation to say something."

"What about our obligation to figure out the truth? To make sure there's justice for John."

"You're not thinking clearly, Nicky."

"If the dean ever found out we accused him, he'd try to have us expelled."

The prospect of returning to my mother's house a failure, surrendering the promise of a Sarah Lane's future, was impossible to consider. "Okay. I'll keep quiet about it. For now."

"I knew that's all it would take to convince you, Emily," Nicky said. "I just had to get you thinking about yourself."

"I've done so much for you. I nearly froze to death yesterday," I said.

"John probably did freeze to death!"

"Lower your voice," I hissed. People could probably hear Nicky through the thin walls. If the girls were talking about her, they might be talking about me too. The realization made me nervous, but it was also exhilarating.

"Listen. John and I were at the lake last week and I walked onto it—just a few feet in," Nicky said. "It was completely solid at the edges. But John wouldn't even take one step onto the ice and begged me to come back to land."

"You need to tell someone this."

"I'm telling you."

"That's not enough. This is a big deal."

"He loved me," Nicky said, her eyes filling with tears. When I reached out to her, she gripped my hand. "We need to go to John's house."

"What are we going to find there that the police haven't already uncovered?"

"There might be something. John wrote everything down." She put her arms around my neck and held me. "Please," she said. "You're my best friend. I don't trust anyone but you."

Nicky planned our next trip more carefully to ensure that our absence wouldn't be noticed. I was to go through the week like nothing was wrong and arrange for us to have lunch at my mother's house on Sunday.

That Wednesday, as I was leaving my English class, I ran into the dean. I smiled and edged past him, but he asked if I had a moment to talk. I hadn't had a full conversation with Dean Anderson since my first semester at the school. I moved to the side of the hallway, but he said it would be better if we went to his office. He led me out of Hartley Hall and across the snowy lawn.

In his office, he motioned for me to sit. The room was uncomfortably warm; an old steam radiator ticked in the corner. He took a long time to settle down, pulling off his leather gloves and laying them carefully on the desk, unwinding his scarf and hanging it with his jacket on an ornate coatrack. He eased into his chair with a pained expression. "The leg gets worse with the cold," he explained. His eyes were circled by purple shadows, and there was a small red cut under his chin where he must have nicked himself shaving. I wouldn't have trusted a display of dishevelment from a man like Dean Anderson, but these small signs of grief seemed genuine and moving.

"I'm sure you want to know why I asked you in here," the dean said. "And I'm not going to keep you in agony. I wanted to check in with you about your roommate, Nicky."

I nodded and tried to remain as impassive as possible.

"She must be going through a very difficult time right now. I know how close she and John were and how devastated she is, though she isn't showing it. The last time I spoke with her, she mentioned that you'd been helping her and keeping her company through this ordeal."

"I'm doing what I can," I said. Nicky hadn't mentioned any check-ins with the dean, or that the dean knew about her and John.

"That's good," the dean said. "That's what's important—that Nicky is taken care of. Perhaps she should go home for a little while, or begin seeing a counselor."

I shook my head. "I think she's very upset, but she's coping."

"Good. She's not exactly fragile, is she?" The dean paused. "Emily, I need you to tell me the truth. I hope that you understand the gravity of the situation. My son is missing. I'm not accusing Nicky of lying, but Nicky is under a lot of stress right now, so she might not be in the best place to be . . . forthcoming."

"I'm not sure what you're asking."

"Has Nicky said anything to you about what she believes may have happened to John?"

I forced myself to count to three and looked up to my right. "I really can't think of anything. She wishes she knew what happened."

"John might have said something to her in private."

"About what?" A knot had formed in my throat.

The dean suddenly pushed his chair back from the desk so it screeched against the floor. "You're doing extraordinarily well here, Emily. You don't take this place for granted. You realize what an opportunity you've been given and you take advantage of it."

"Thank you, sir."

"Does it surprise you that my background is much more similar to yours than it is to Nicky's? You're here entirely because you are smart and you earned a spot. Not many of the other girls can claim that. You also, I imagine, have a little more perspective."

I nodded.

"So you know what the stakes are. Can you tell me what Nicky told the police?"

"She didn't talk to the police," I said. "I mean, I don't think she did. None of the other girls know about her and John, at least not for sure, if that's what you're asking."

"I didn't think you girls kept many secrets from one another. I guess she's always held herself a little apart." The dean glanced at his watch and then turned to look at the windows, which were foggy with condensation. "It's nice that she found a friend like you, especially with everything she's been going through, on top of missing John."

I didn't want to take the bait, but I couldn't resist. "What other things?"

The dean snapped his eyes away from the window and studied me. He let out a long, exaggerated breath, as if I was forcing information from him. "I assume you already know that Nicky is pregnant."

After a long pause, I said, "That's not true. It's ridiculous."

"Not ridiculous," the dean said. "Sad, perhaps. John told me several days before he went missing."

"Do the police know?"

"I haven't told them. If Nicky wants to, that's her decision. I don't see that it would change much, except the way people think of my son."

"Nicky doesn't think he ran away," I said. "Or that he drowned on purpose."

"You will understand when I say I take small comfort in that."

"But if John was afraid of what might happen—or didn't want to be a dad? Maybe he did run."

"I raised John better than that," the dean said. "You may go, Emily. If you think of anything, I hope that you'll come to me right away. My door is always open to you."

I nodded and got up. I needed air. "What if Nicky needs help?" I asked. "With the baby?"

"I don't think that Nicky's family requires assistance from anyone."

As much as I wanted to flee the room, there was one more question that had been bothering me. "Why do you think John left his coat on the tree?"

The dean shrugged. "We'd walked almost a mile. I'd taken my jacket off too." His answer sapped all the magic and promise from the detail, which I'd hoped would be the key to the mystery. I regretted asking.

On Sunday morning, my mother picked us up in her twelve-year-old hatchback, her too-red hair pulled into a tight knot. She talked the whole way home, telling me about my uncle's messy divorce and her best friend's new job. She asked me questions about my classes and the quality of the dining hall food. I must have answered, though I have no memory of what I said. I was worried about what Nicky would make of my childhood home, a duplex in a row of houses that were nearly identical. I was afraid Nicky would be appalled at the place's size and shabbiness. Or maybe the house wasn't run-down enough, and it would belie my image as the resilient scholarship kid, climbing out of squalor.

When we arrived, Nicky took in the living room's faded rug, the chunky Dollar Store candles on the mantle, and the yellowed curtains and declared the place "cozy." As we sat on the overstuffed sofa and sipped Diet Cokes, I was surprised by how easily Nicky and my mother fell into conversation. Nicky asked my mom about the stack of library books on the coffee table, about growing up in Vermont, about her Christmas plans. I couldn't understand how Nicky was so calm, considering the risk we'd be taking in just a few hours.

After Nicky told my mother about the new wing of the school library, my mother confessed how much she would have loved Sarah Lane's. Nicky asked where my mother had gone to college. I hoped Mom would give Nicky the short version, but Nicky got the full explanation. My mother, valedictorian of her high school, was the first in her family to attend college. She'd started at the University of Vermont, in the honors college, but had become pregnant with me the summer after her sophomore year. She'd left the university and gone for her nursing degree at a community college while we lived with my grandparents.

"Were you scared when you found out you were pregnant?" Nicky asked her.

My mom considered. "I must have been. But mostly I remember being so angry. At myself, of course." She looked at me, but I couldn't read her expression. I wonder, now, whether this is the closest I've ever come to an explanation of why my mother decided to keep me. She wasn't religious or conservative, but she had high expectations for herself, and perhaps felt she deserved to face the consequences of not meeting them.

After a lunch of chili and grilled cheese sandwiches, my mom drove us back to school. She put her hand on my arm and waited for Nicky to climb out of the car before asking, in a low voice, "Why'd you really want to come home?"

"I was homesick," I said.

"Are you in trouble?" Mom asked. "You can tell me if you are." I swore I wasn't.

"This is the best place for you," Mom said. "Don't mess it up."

"I really miss you," I said, surprising us both.

She hugged me, and I climbed out of the car.

After Mom was out of sight, I wanted only to return to my dorm and curl up in bed with whatever book I was supposed to be reading for English class. But Nicky was already ushering me forward, informing me that we only had an hour before the dean came back from his after-church errands. I didn't know what to say as we made our way to his house. Something felt different between us. Nicky filled the silence.

"You know, the dean's limp isn't real. John told me the leg was injured in a car accident, but it healed. The dean didn't stop limping because he liked the affectation."

"That can't be true."

"Why are you still defending him? This is how he gets away with everything. You think because he's a dean, he's too respectable. No one wants to break the Sarah Lane's spell."

"What do you mean?"

"You know. The myth that this place is perfect, that it's better than everywhere else."

"It is better," I said.

Nicky sighed, and her breath made a cloud in the cold. "I guess you really believe that."

The back door was unlocked when we arrived, as Nicky had said it would be. The house was small but stately, with vines hugging the brick and thick-paned bay windows. Inside, there was a stale, damp scent I normally associated with basements. We were silent as we crept upstairs, as if the house might collapse on us at the slightest noise.

John's room was in complete disorder. Clothes and books on the floor, lights knocked over, sheets in a clump at the foot of the bed. Nicky picked up a Walkman and turned it over in her hands, looking more like an archaeologist exhuming ancient artifacts than a detective gathering evidence. She sat down on John's bed and put her head in her hands. She stayed like that until the silence made me squirm.

"I know," I said finally. "About the baby."

Nicky lifted her eyes to me and then narrowed them.

"The dean knows too," I said. "John told him."

"And then the dean told you?"

"He wanted to find out if I knew anything. I told him I didn't."

"This changes everything. That's his motive. He has a horrible temper, and if John finally told him . . ." Nicky began to rock back and forth. "How could you hide that from me?"

"You hid a pregnancy from me. You hid a relationship from me."

"I wanted to tell you."

"I would have helped you if you'd trusted me."

Nicky shook her head. "You don't understand. I'm starting to think you'll never understand. You always do whatever's expected of you, as if that's the only option."

"I don't have other options. Not everyone gets to make mistakes and stay on top. I shouldn't even be here right now."

"Then why did you come?" Nicky asked.

I had no answer.

Nicky pulled a folded piece of paper from her pocket and held it out to me. It was a letter from John—short and focused, unlike his moody, abstract song lyrics. In it, he said he couldn't understand how she was considering keeping the baby. He insisted he loved her. He'd loved her their whole relationship and loved her now and would love her no matter what happened. But his father would be furious when he found out. Nicky pointed to a sentence, underlined twice: "He'll kill me."

"Now do you believe me?" she asked.

"Nicky, this," I said, shaking the letter, "is evidence. We need to give it to the police."

"You're not on my side anymore," Nicky said. "If you ever were." She stood up and kicked at the mess on the floor. She ripped the blanket off John's bed. I tried to quiet her, but she scrambled back onto John's mattress and screamed into his pillow. In the presence of her fury, I only felt embarrassed.

The sound of tires outside finally quieted her. We listened for a moment, then raced to the hall. We could've made it. We could have run through the front door and been free, but we stood, paralyzed, until it was too late. We heard the slow twist of the door handle. Nicky took one step toward the stairs before spinning around and nearly knocking me over. We stumbled back into John's room. A door slammed; keys clinked onto a table. Nicky threw open the window. A burst of cold air blew her hair away from her face. She swung her legs up and climbed on the ledge.

"Don't," I hissed. But she'd already jumped. The footsteps downstairs stopped. I ran into John's closet, hiding myself behind the clothes. There was a baseball bat leaning against the back wall. I picked it up.

"John?" the dean called weakly. I heard his footsteps pounding up the stairs. A man with his limp could never move like that. Just before he rounded the corner I slipped out of the closet and opened the bedroom door.

I thought that if I surprised the dean I'd be able to see in an instant what he knew, whether he'd witnessed the accident or even caused it. But his face revealed nothing. He recovered his composure before I could even speak, pushing past me into John's room.

"Nicky!" he roared.

"She's not here," I said.

"Where is she?" He opened the closet.

"This was my idea."

He turned to me, chest heaving. "Don't lie to me, Emily. You are not in a position to lie."

I still had the note Nicky had shown me balled in my fist. I smoothed it out and handed it to him. "Nicky showed this to me last night, and I thought you should have it. I was going to leave it for you, anonymously. I don't know what I was thinking, coming upstairs. I was just curious."

The dean read the note. The paper shook in his hand. "This is a serious violation. You won't be coming back from this, I'm afraid. You must know that."

I put one hand on the doorframe. My mother's chili rose to the back of my throat and burned.

"Maybe," the dean said, folding the note, "if you tell me where Nicky is and admit that she brought you here, I could help. If you tell the truth, the repercussions won't be as severe."

"Okay," I said. "This was Nicky's idea. I don't know why she wanted to come, I swear. But she left, a while ago. I came back alone." I tried to think about what a real Sarah Lane's girl would say to shake herself free of consequences. "I wonder," I said, and then stopped because my mouth was so dry I needed several tries to swallow. "I wonder if my being here might look pretty bad for you too. I mean. That I knew how to get inside your house? That we were here alone, together?"

"You're not very good at threats," the dean said. "If that's what that was."

"I gave you the letter from John," I said. "Please."

We watched each other until I could hardly bear the silence.

The dean nodded. "Get out."

"Thank you," I said, close to tears. "I'm so sorry. Thank you."

"You are done playing detective, Emily. There will be no more chances."

I turned and fled down the stairs and out into the street, taking in big gulps of the fresh cold air. When I reached an intersection, I stopped to get my breath and heard footsteps crunching across the snowmelt. I whipped around and saw Nicky running toward me. She had been waiting for me all that time.

We didn't talk until we were back in our room. I leaned against the door, my heart racing. Nicky clutched her right hand to her chest.

"What happened?" she demanded. "How did you get out without the dean seeing?"

"I didn't," I said. "He found me." I told her the excuse I'd invented and about my ill-formed threat. I thought Nicky would be impressed.

"You gave him the letter?" she said. "My letter?"

"I had to give him something. He was going to throw me out of school. You still don't get it—I can't just shake consequences off with one call home to Daddy. I didn't have a choice."

"God. That's just like you. Of course you had a choice. That letter was our proof. And it wasn't yours to give."

"You almost ruined my life and now you're angry at me?"

"You're proud of yourself, aren't you? For weaseling your way out of trouble. He's going to destroy that letter or use it in the wrong way—twist it around into something it's not. You're a coward. You think that Sarah Lane's will somehow make you matter, or make you matter more than everyone else. But it won't. You're a small person, carving yourself off from everything that might make you less small."

"You're a hypocrite. You would've given in too." As soon as I said it, I knew I was wrong. Nicky navigated the world by her own set of inscrutable rules; she didn't compromise.

Nicky climbed into bed, still holding her wrist. Days later, when she finally went to see the nurse, we learned she'd sprained it in the fall from the window. Soon after, we found out the baby hadn't survived.

Nicky and I never told the police about the pregnancy or the dean's knowledge of it. In retrospect it seems bizarre and almost wicked that we withheld so much information, not only about the pregnancy but also about Nicky and John's entire relationship. The mystery of John's death was never solved. His body, or what was left of it, was found in April when the ice thawed enough for a proper search. For months I kept myself awake at night, imagining that John's ghost would return, furious that I hadn't told his story. I continued to speculate, always considering some new perverse explanation. Maybe, once John was alone, egged on by Nicky's accusation that he was too tame, he stepped onto the ice. When the spiderweb of cracks spread underneath his feet, he would have realized it was too late. Still, he'd have turned to the shore and taken one long stride toward his hanging parka before sinking, forever, into the slime of the lake. Or, perhaps, he was trying to escape the heavy future that suddenly loomed before him, in the only way his adolescent mind could see how. And I suppose it's not impossible that Nicky was right to blame the dean.

Soon, all the girls knew about her pregnancy, although they never confirmed whom the father was. Nicky kept John's secret, just as the dean suspected she would. The girls' envy quickly turned to pity; Nicky's brashness—her unapologetic rule breaking—became an object of ridicule instead of admiration. Nicky was pregnant again by the time I was a junior in college at Wellesley. Once I'd elbowed my way in, I never left the small, protected world of academia. I finished third in my class and, after graduate work at Harvard, secured a job as an American studies professor at Emerson. Nicky and I fell, mostly, out of touch.

The last time I spoke with her I was a senior in college, up late one Friday night working on my thesis. Nicky called, frantic and sobbing, demanding to know why I hadn't gone to the police. Why hadn't I told the truth? Her voice dripped with anger. From the way her words ran together, I could tell she'd been drinking.

"He's still out there, Emily. He's still there."

"Who is? John?"

"Dean Anderson. He never got what he deserved. That bastard. That complete and utter bastard. He took everything from me."

On the other end of the line, I heard a loud knocking and a man's muffled voice.

"It was just an accident, Nicky," I said with more confidence than I felt.

"You are so full of shit." Nicky paused for such a long time that I thought she'd hung up. "No, it's not that at all. You're empty. You never felt anything. You just knew things. You knew that they would never discover the truth, and you knew that I was going to lose everything. I thought you might have had the courage to be on my side."

"I was on your side." I paused to think about it, to remember. "I was."

"If that helps you sleep, you can believe it."

Nicky hung up before I could respond. The air in my dorm room seemed to be buzzing with electrical charge. Nicky had not lost her dramatic flair or her ability to leave me with fresh doubt, dread, and excitement. I put away my books and went to the window to watch girls stumbling back from parties, happy and comfortable in each other's company.

I think I understand now why we didn't go to the police. My world, my new and superior world, couldn't have remained intact if the dean was hiding such a hideous secret. And Nicky needed the dean, the embodiment of all that had not protected her, to be guilty. So we kept silent, tolerating a mystery that allowed both of us to go on living in the worlds we had constructed for ourselves.

I still dream about John. In my dreams, Nicky and I weave through a snowy forest, with trees that writhe and thrash on every side of us. Although he never speaks, sometimes the dean is there, slinking through the shadows at the edges of my vision. We reach the lake, and John is waiting. He hangs up his blue parka and turns. Nicky runs to stop him, but he pushes her aside. John dances onto the ice, and Nicky follows him. The ice begins to split and groan beneath their weight. The dean appears at my side while I watch, and I feel his enormous hand on my shoulder. Then the ice cracks open with a noise like thunder. Nicky lunges to save John, but he casually sidesteps the fissure, sending her into the water. When she surfaces and reaches out to me for help, I find that I am frozen, and I cannot move.

LISA UNGER

Unknown Caller

FROM *We Could Be Heroes,* Amazon Originals

I.

The call comes in just as my shift is about to end.

It's been a slow night and I've already packed up my things, getting ready to go. If I don't answer, the call will bounce to Espo, my supervisor, who is by far the best among us here at the Crisis Center. He's calm, steady, soothing, his voice like a warm blanket wrapped around you. He's been doing this a long time. Most people burn out, move on to other, less intense work. But he's still here.

Even though some folks from the next shift are already arriving, sitting down in their cubicles, donning their headsets, I don't even consider not answering. That's why I'm here. The only reason. To answer when someone makes the last call she might ever make.

I click the flashing green button on the phone in front of me, put my headset back on. A number appears on the ID screen right away. Sometimes the caller's name is listed there as well, but not tonight. Just Unknown Caller.

"Hey," I answer. Keep it light, keep it casual, like I'm hearing from an old friend. "You've reached the Crisis Hotline." I offer the standard statement about confidentiality. Then, "This is Charlie. I'm listening."

There's a pause, and I wonder if the caller hung up already. Or if it's one of our regulars, gearing up to put me through my paces. Our incel, after another failed Match.com date; he usually asks for me, but he'll take one of the other young women on duty in a pinch. The vet with PTSD, who has bouts of insomnia; that call usually goes to Bruce, who specializes in counseling veterans. The elderly lady who calls when her cat doesn't come in right away at night. She knows us all by name.

"Hi, Charlie."

A young voice, deep. Male, I think, but you can never be certain, and you should never assume. That's one of the first things Espo taught me. Assume nothing. Be a blank slate for every call.

"Who's this?"

I glance at Espo, whose large, round-shouldered form fills his chair in the glass-walled supervisor's office, and I wish I could take the words back. But he's not listening to my call; he's probably tied up with Darren, who's still training. Darren's sitting in another cubicle on the far side of the room. I can hear the low tones of his voice.

What can I call you? or *Who am I speaking with tonight?* That's what Espo would have said.

Who's this? or *What's your name?* Those are confrontational, put pressure on the caller, who is obviously under enough pressure. Sometimes people don't want to give their names, and that's okay.

Another long pause; I sink into it. *Learn to wait. Patience saves lives.* More Espo-isms, as we like to call them here.

"I'm no one," the unknown caller finally says.

I try to put a smile in my voice. People can hear kindness; it has a tone and timbre. So do judgment, fear, panic, anger.

"I can't call you *that*, can I?"

Another pause.

I listen to breath every night. It tells you so much—ragged, shallow, faint, sobbing, waning. His is none of these. His is slow and measured. In the background, I hear music, low and tinny. Something I almost recognize, but I can't quite hear it well enough to pin it down.

"It's okay," I say when he doesn't answer. "You don't have to give your name. We can just talk."

Here's the thing.

Some people just want to die.

They have their reasons. Grief. A lifetime battle with depression. A terminal diagnosis. And those folks? You can't stop them. Every cop will tell you that there are suicide-hotline phones at the top of most high bridges. Those who really want to die—they park their car, run, and leap. They pull the trigger, double-check the noose, take all the pills, and they walk through that doorway and don't look back. They don't pick up the phone, because they don't want to be talked out of it.

But the people who linger on the edge, looking down, the people who pick up the phone and reach out for help? Most of the time, you can talk them down. They are looking for a way back to the light.

If they've called—Espo taught me—you *can* reach them. They want to take the hand you're offering; they want to be drawn out of the darkness. Much of the time.

"So, how are you?" I say into the sound of his breathing.

Another stupid question. But sometimes it's enough. Because that's a question that gets asked a lot in life, but people rarely wait for the real answer. It's more like a greeting, and we're expected to answer quickly—*Fine! Great! Howaboutyou?*—and move on.

"I called a suicide hotline," he says flatly. "How do you *think* I am?"

"Good point," I say lightly. "So, what's on your mind?"

More breathing, growing deeper. I'm pretty sure he's going to hang up. I'm sweating a little, feeling uncomfortable, nervous, like I'm fucking it up. I measure my own breath. Wait. Finally, he speaks again.

"Have you ever lost anyone?" he asks.

"Yes," I answer truthfully.

"Does it ever go away? The pain."

I draw in a deep breath, release it. "It changes. You find ways to live with it. Your life grows around it."

I sense his surprise at the honesty. Maybe he was expecting the usual pat answer, a time-heals-all-wounds or we-learn-to-let-go-and-move-on platitude. But that's not my way.

"Who did you lose?" he asks.

You decide how much to give, Espo says. *Don't get out in front of a drowning man; he'll take you right down with him.*

Meaning don't give so much that you're the one who will need the suicide hotline one day.

"My best friend."

She was more than that, really, but that's too much, too deep.

"How did she die?"

I think about lying—car wreck, I could reasonably say. But the truth has a tone and a timbre too.

"She killed herself." The words still stick in my throat. "I wish I had been there for her the way I can be here for you."

More breathing, measured, deep. Then, "Is that why you're there, answering desperate calls in the middle of the night?"

"That's part of it. Sure."

I know I've lost control of the call because he's asking all the questions.

"But you didn't call to talk about me, did you?"

"What if I did?"

The music I heard in the background comes up a bit in volume. And then I recognize it, and it makes my heart start to thud, and I'm shuttled back there, listening to the car engine gunning and the sound of her screaming. The rain. The horrible crunch of metal and shattering glass.

"Who is this?" I whisper.

But the line goes dead.

You're allowed to call back, so I do. But the phone just rings and rings, and no one picks up, and it doesn't go to voicemail. I sit and stare at the phone, my heart an engine.

"What happened?"

Espo's voice is in my ear, and I look up to see him watching me, concern furrowing his brow. He pushes back his thick black glasses. He has a wild ring of curls around a bald scalp, like a clown. It's a look that shouldn't work, but it does.

"Caller hung up," I say.

"Did you try back?"

"No answer."

I'm still there, triggered and sandbagged by memories. My hands shake, and I clasp them together.

"Did he say he was going to hurt himself or someone else? Should I contact emergency services?"

"He didn't say that, no."

Espo issues a sigh. "Maybe he'll call again."

I linger, watch the phone for a while longer, still hearing that song.

"Go home and get some rest. Big day tomorrow," Espo says over my headset. He's watching me through the glass wall of his office, gives me a smile and motions toward the door.

I wave, but sit a moment longer and wait, willing the unknown caller to ring me back. But he doesn't, and finally I just go home, still shaken.

2.

The next day, I stand on the small stage at city hall, along with Espo. Steve Esposito is his full name. Jane Martinez, founder and president of the Crisis Center, stands to my right, grasping my hand, while the mayor gives her speech about our lifesaving work.

Espo is sweating, his big belly straining against what looks to be a new plaid shirt, the creases from where it was folded in the package still visible, like he didn't bother to iron it or didn't know he was supposed to. Jane, on my other side, is straight backed in her signature black suit. There's a glittering red heart pin on the lapel, the logo for the Crisis Center. She's perfectly coifed, as always, thick hair styled loose and natural, and her nails are a shiny blood red. She gives off a kind of energy—passion, presence, efficiency. It's electric.

We're here because a couple of months ago, I took a call from the mayor's daughter.

Her call came in late, after midnight, and I was the only one on duty.

"Hey, this is Charlie. I'm listening."

"I need a reason," she said, her voice soft, sad. Very young.

"A reason . . . ," I prompted. It's a technique. To let a sentence dangle and hope the caller picks up the thread.

"Like, *why*? Why should I stay?"

"That's a really good question," I offered. "What can I call you?"

This is always a difficult moment, the place you most often lose them. When you name yourself, you take responsibility for the call you've made. You admit, in a way, that you don't really want to die.

She hesitated. Then, "Zoey."

"Zoey, I'm Charlie."

"Hi, Charlie."

"Do you want to tell me what's going on?"

"I don't know," she said, voice heavy with sadness, words slightly slurred.

"Have you taken anything tonight? Been drinking?"

"My mother. Everyone thinks she's so perfect, so in control. Do you know she has a medicine cabinet filled with bottles of pills? Everything from Ativan, Oxy, you name it. I took some of her Vicodin."

"How many, Zoey?"

"I don't know. The bottle is empty now."

"Okay," I said easily. "Talk to me."

I typed a message to Espo: We need emergency services. Possible overdose.

"There's this girl," she said. "I see her on my social media feeds, in the newspaper. I see the way other people see her. She's beautiful; she's smart. She runs track, and she's the captain of her team, headed to nationals. She'll graduate from high school next year, and she'll go to a good college. Anywhere she wants, probably. Her boyfriend is hot. *Anyone* would want to be her."

"You envy her."

"Yes," she said, releasing a sob. "I want to be that girl on the screen. So badly. But I'm not. I can never be."

"We can never be someone else." I kept my voice light. "We can only be who we are. And it's enough, more than enough."

"That's the thing," she said, voice growing softer. I strained to hear. "Who I am, truly am inside. It's not enough—not enough for my parents, my friends. It's not even enough for me."

Even though I was listening to Zoey, I heard that other voice in every call, desperate, frantic. *I thought you were my friend. I thought you loved me. You knew me, the real me that I never show to anyone else. Where are you?* Every call is my chance to be there.

"What *would* be enough?" I asked Zoey.

She issued a heavy sigh but didn't answer.

Espo hits me back: We were able to get an address. Paramedics on the way. Try to keep the caller on the line.

"Zoey, are you with me?"

"I'm here." But I could tell she was fading.

"Because I promise you, the girl you see on that screen is not the real person. She has all the same doubts and fears that you do. Chances are she doesn't see herself as perfect. Just like you, she only sees her flaws."

Sometimes when you get through, there's a moment of silence, when your words land just right. But then she laughed weakly.

"I know," she said. "Because that girl is me. I *am* the girl on the screen. And still—I'm nothing like her. She's perfect. And I'm—broken inside."

I should have seen that coming. I chose my words carefully.

"That's everyone these days, Zoey. We broadcast one version of ourselves, cropped and filtered and out there for consumption. But the real person is hidden behind that."

"Hidden and alone," she said. "No one wants the real me. They want *that* girl, the perfect one, the one who never loses, who always looks just right, the one who's always smiling. If they could see me now, they'd hate me."

I strained to listen, hoping to hear the approach of sirens, and kept talking.

"You're wrong. We're all flawed and broken in some way. That's what makes us unique, special. Imperfection makes us who we are, because it's real. You're enough, Zoey. I promise."

"You don't even know me."

"I do. In this moment, I know you better than anyone. Because you revealed yourself to me."

She issued a deep, long sigh and then went quiet. Her breath stuttered, and then I heard the phone drop.

"Zoey."

Then in the background, the sirens, finally.

"Zoey?" I said again. I wanted to crawl through the phone and put my arms around her.

"You're enough. You're more than enough. I promise." I hoped she could hear, even if she couldn't respond.

That's what I would have told my friend, if *she* had called and reached the me that I am today, the one who has accepted all my many flaws and broken places, and hers. I could have said those words to her. I am only shattered pieces now, glued together with hard-won wisdom. I'm a better person than I was when she needed me and I couldn't be there. I hope.

I stayed on the line until I heard the paramedics enter the room, a woman's voice crying in the background. *Oh my god, Zoey. Zoey, please, baby, wake up.* I heard all the notes of love and fear and despair. Zoey was loved. She just couldn't see it.

Later, we heard that she'd made it.

I slept well that night. Espo always says: *You can't save them all. But when you do, that's a good day.*

*

Now, on stage, it's Zoey's turn to speak.

"In my darkest moment of despair," Zoey says after her mother introduces her, "I reached out and found a hand waiting for me."

She turns to look at me, and I'm struck by the dewy quality of her skin, her bright-green eyes. She wears no makeup, her dark hair pulled back from her face. There's a light shining from within her, something bright and mesmerizing.

"The last thing I remember hearing before fading away was: *You're enough. More than enough. I promise.* I didn't believe that before. I am starting to believe it now."

She turns to look at me and extends a hand.

Oh, no. I didn't plan to say anything.

But Espo nudges me forward, and I join Zoey at the front of the stage. The audience applauds. Her hand is warm in mine, and mine is sweaty. Standing close, I smell the clean scent of her shampoo. Out in the audience, packed with reporters, all eyes are on me, lots of smiling faces. Because this is a feel-good moment. A moment to celebrate that—sometimes—things turn out okay.

"This woman, Charlie Kroft, was the voice on the other end of the phone. The words she spoke to me that night not only saved my life, but changed it."

Technically, I didn't save her life. Not really. That was the paramedics who gave her Narcan and then rushed her to the hospital, where the waiting ER staff pumped her stomach.

All I did was answer the phone.

"I was lost," she goes on. "I had disappeared behind a fake version of myself, thinking that my avatar was the only thing about me that people could ever love. Since recovering, I have changed all my feeds and I am challenging girls everywhere to do the same."

More applause, camera flashes.

"No more cropping or filtering, no more staged photos, or arched-back bikini poses, no more pretending you're having fun when you're not so that other people are jealous. Stop using the face-altering filters, making your eyes bigger, your skin clearer, your face thinner."

She pauses again. Then, "Let me see your bad hair days, that zit you got right before prom, your muffin top. And then show me your accomplishments—your art, your poetry, your science experiments, the equation you solved after failing a hundred times, your volunteer work at the shelter. Because it's what you *do with your life* that matters. It's not about how you look. Because you don't have to be perfect. No one is. You are enough. You are more than enough. And it's time to get real."

Now there is wild applause from the audience, people getting to their feet.

"I've been able to raise $20,000 for the Crisis Center."

An assistant holds one of those ridiculously big checks from the fundraising campaign Zoey ran on her new Instagram page, @therealzoey. Zoey hands it to Jane, and they stand with it for a moment, smiling, letting everyone take pictures.

More applause, and then Zoey goes on. "This small group of employees and volunteers are standing on the front lines of despair. When you call, they answer, they usher you back into the light if you let them. They are heroes."

And then I'm alone at the podium with all eyes on me, phones and cameras held up recording.

"I'm no hero," I say softly, my voice wobbling with nerves. "It was the paramedics who arrived at the scene and the ER staff that saved Zoey's life. They are the real, everyday heroes whose role in our society is often undervalued. When the worst thing happens, you pick up a phone and this group of strangers comes to save your life. They do it every day, without fail, without question. Without press conferences like this one."

Behind me, Jane clears her throat.

"The Crisis Center can, however, be the first line of defense against self-harm. When you're in a place of despair, when you don't know where to turn, when you think you might hurt yourself or someone else—call us first. Dial 211. We can help. We can talk; we can offer services. We are a voice in the darkness, a hand before the fall."

I am distracted for a moment by a hooded figure standing in the shadows at the back of the room. He is taller than the people around him, black jeans, black hoodie over a New Order T-shirt. I can't see his face, just a flop of brown hair over his eyes. His energy is familiar, unsettling. Who is he?

Another nudging cough from Jane snaps me back.

"I'm so glad I could be there for Zoey. But if it hadn't been me, it would have been one of our other team members—cops, EMTs, psychologists, counselors, employees, and volunteers who devote their lives to just being there on your worst day. If you're in trouble, we can help. Call us. Thank you."

More applause. Zoey and the mayor both pose with Jane and the check. Then Zoey embraces me on the stage.

"Thank you," she whispers. "The things you said. They changed me."

I return her hug and tell her she's welcome and that I'm so glad I was there for her. And then she's surrounded by reporters.

She thinks I'm a hero, and maybe here, right now, to Zoey, I am. But this is just a penance. The work I do to make up for all the things I didn't do to save the girl who needed me most. The things I did to hurt her.

I look out into the audience again, and he's still there. I can feel him staring from the darkness of his hood. I return his gaze, until he turns abruptly and leaves the room. Then Jane has her arm around me, pulling me toward the mayor, who embraces me and thanks me tearfully for saving her daughter's life.

"This has been a wake-up call for our whole family," she tells me. I force myself to focus on the mayor, forget about the hooded figure. "I thought she knew how much we loved her. Not what she does, just who she is."

"She knew she was loved," I tell the mayor. "On some level she *did*, or she wouldn't have called."

The mayor nods, wipes at her eyes. "Thank you for that. That helps some with the guilt."

I know all about guilt. She wears it around her shoulders like a cloak. I know how heavy it is. I think of the medicine cabinet full of pills that Zoey raided.

Afterward, Jane, Espo, and I go for burgers and a beer.

"Good work, kid," says Espo, as we slide into a booth. "On the call and today."

"You're an excellent speaker, and you've done a great job with all the interviews. It's been a nice awareness raiser for the hotline," says Jane, sipping from her pilsner. "Zoey wants to know if you'll do a couple of events with her, to raise more money for the Crisis Center."

I don't see how I can refuse.

"Okay," I say. "Sure."

They raise their glasses to me.

The bar is overwarm, and I'm still a little amped up from the press conference. When the jukebox changes tracks, an old U2 song I know too well starts to play. It never fails to give me chills. It's the same song my unknown caller played. The same one my friend was listening to when she died. Who knows what that song means to me? No one. Just a coincidence, I tell myself.

"To the hero," says Espo, who's saved more lives in his years on this job than anyone can count. I notice how Jane's and Espo's hands touch and I think, not for the first time, that there might be something going on between them—which is a little funny because she's so pressed and polished, and he's so, well, not. It would be like Wonder Woman dating Oscar the Grouch.

"I'm not the hero here," I say, raising my glass to Jane. She's the hero. She's the one who took her personal tragedy and turned it into a crusade to help others in their deepest moment of despair. If not for her, there would be no local Crisis Center.

"That's what heroes always say," she counters.

One of the weird things about insisting that you're not a hero: no one ever believes you.

3.

I pull up to school in the old junker my father gave me for my birthday. He was so proud of it, and I should be grateful, but the upholstery smells like somebody had been chain-smoking with the windows closed for years, and it rattles like the rusty toolbox Dad carries around the house fixing all the many broken things. I pull to a stop at the edge of the parking lot, far from the new cars that the other kids drive, and breathe through my daily dread.

The sky is a steely gray, with golden fingers of light breaking through the cloud cover. I stare at the view, momentarily distracted, wondering how I could draw that, what blend of light and shadows could make that feel real on the page. Finally, when I know I'll be late if I wait any longer, I drag my bag out of the back seat and walk toward the big metal doors, shuffle in with the rest of the school hustling to make it before the bell rings.

In English class, I shift into my seat and take out my tattered copy of The Great Gatsby *and my notebook.*

Laughter. It always startles me. Her laughter especially.

I look up to see Lanie and her new friends gathered by the door. Shiny hair and bodies toned from cheerleading, glossy lips and perfect skin. I smooth down my frizzy mass of dark curls, straighten my denim jacket. It looked cool at home, but in the harsh light of the fluorescents, it looks shabby and cheap.

I watch them a moment, aware of the heft of my own lumpy form, the spattering of acne on my chin.

She catches me watching, gives a wave. "Hey, Chloe!" she calls. It's sickly sweet.

"Hi, Lanie."

The other two stare, brows wrinkling at me, like I'm a strange forest creature they can't quite place. They are so secure in their beauty, in the knowledge that all eyes are on them always. When I look away, they whisper and laugh. Lanie too. Not nasty, not mean like the other two. Lanie looks at me with pity. Which is way worse.

"Chloe." Ms. Harding stands beside me, holding my essay. I can see the A-plus emblazoned in bold red on the cover page. "Your essay about the symbolism of the color green in The Great Gatsby *was one of the finest I have read."*

She says it loud enough that other students turn to look. Lanie and her mean-girl group do a kind of collective eye roll thing. They are C students at best. Lanie still calls me late at night for help with chem or trig, to read aloud the essay she can't quite finish so I can dictate a conclusion. I'm not sure it's that they're stupid. It's just that they care more about their Instagram feeds, their boyfriends, and that the cheer team is going to some national competition next month than they care about their grades.

"Thank you, Ms. Harding," I say, keeping my voice low. When I meet her eyes, she looks at me kindly; then her gaze drifts over to Lanie's group.

"Take your seats, girls," she says sternly.

Then she leans in a little closer to me.

"You're special, Chloe," she whispers. "Sensitive, artistic, talented. Don't forget that. High school doesn't last forever."

She, too, has frizzy hair and thick glasses. Her cardigan, as Lanie would say, is "tragic," pilled and oversize, hiding a tatty floral dress. For her, it seems, high school has lasted forever; she's still here.

"Thanks, Ms. Harding," I say, and she gives my hand a pat. She passes out the other essays, and there is a chorus of groans, whispered comments, complaints.

I am a ghost in this place, drifting through the halls, attending my classes, eating my lunch with the math-club kids, all geeks like me. But they seem okay with their place in the high school ecosystem; at least they have each other. I don't feel like a part of their group, either, even though they're kind and funny and they welcome me. The only place I ever felt like I belonged was with Lanie. But that was forever ago.

The day, like every other day, is a slog, and finally it's time to go home. I get into my old beater and wait for some of the other kids to drive off—the boys in their big pickup trucks barreling through the parking lot without looking, the girls in their pretty sports cars. I watch Lanie get into the brand-new Jeep Izzy got for her sweet sixteen. I watched her social media story—a big party with a DJ, towers of balloons, cascades of flowers, and all her friends. Clips of them all dancing, then a walk outside where the bright-blue Jeep was waiting with a big bow on its roof. Lots of squealing and a big hug for her father.

"Stay off that stuff," my mother warns me. "It's not real life. It's just not true. There are so many more layers to people than what you see on the surface."

But it is true. It's the only truth.

For my sweet sixteen, we picked my grandmother up from the nursing home and had dinner at a pizza parlor. My family loves me. I'm grateful. I am. I posted about the big cake with sparklers the waiter carried out, and how the whole restaurant sang "Happy Birthday," and my little brother sang the loudest. I got three likes. Lanie commented: "Happy birthday, girl! Tell your mom I miss her."

You miss her? *I wanted to write.* We live less than a mile apart. Every single summer day, we met by the old oak tree on the road between our houses. You used to sleep at my place twice a week at least. We roamed the neighborhood on our bikes for years, climbed trees, waded through the creek, and looked for frogs under the rocks. You were my best friend. Where did you go?

But, as I always do, I just liked her comment and said nothing. Because what can you say when someone takes their friendship away? Even though it feels like someone took the stars out of the sky, you can't call the friendship police and make them give it back. You can't call an ambulance to take you to the heartbreak hospital even though you feel like that's where you belong.

If someone doesn't want to be your friend, Chloe, *my mom said on one of the many nights I lay on my bed crying,* there's nothing you can do. And it's her loss. She'll never find a friend like you.

How could she do this to Chloe? *I heard my mom whisper later to my dad.* I should call her mother.

Stay out of it, Beth. This is life. She needs to learn how to handle it, make other friends. She's too sensitive.

This is life. *That's what my dad always says about everything wrong, unfair, hateful, frightening, like that's it. There's nothing else to it and nothing to be done.*

I pull up to the house, tires crunching on the gravel drive, and like every day, my little brother, Sean, and our old lab, Bartley, come running out the creaky screen door to greet me, letting it crash behind them. Sean body slams me as I get out of the car, Bartley running circles around us until I stop to greet him too. And then we all go inside, where my mom has made grilled cheese sandwiches, and Sean talks and talks about his day, his friends, his teachers, how he killed in flag football. He's only in first grade, but it already seems like things come more easily to him than they did for me. I remember crying a lot as a little kid, clinging to my mom when she tried to drop me off. But not Sean. "And I was like bam, and he was like oooof, and Coach said I was superfast." Sean makes my mom and me laugh with his dramatic reenactments of his grand adventures.

And in that space, listening to him, watching my mom smile, I'm okay. I giggle and feel at home in my body. I'm safe.

In my room, though, when I get online and scroll and scroll through the images of everyone else, all the people who are better than me, who have more than me, who are on vacation, or getting a puppy, or having a picnic in the park with a new boyfriend, or posing in a bikini by the pool and looking like a model. What I see online is nothing like what I see in the mirror, nothing like my life where my parents work too hard and don't always make ends meet, where we can't go away even for the beach weekends we used to have because of how much it costs to take care of my grandmother now, where my only friend has ghosted me, and I've never kissed a boy. And the scrolling never ends. It goes on and on and on into oblivion.

The only relief I get, the only other safe space I've found, is a site called the Dark Doorway.

You don't have to suffer, *it promises.* There is a way out.

Sometimes I spend hours there, reading about the misery and heartbreak of others, and how they deal with it. The betrayed. The lonely. The incels. The abused. Those of us who don't fit in, who are just not good at life. You don't just have to white-knuckle your way through your days, *the site asserts,* putting up with injustices until you die. There are ways to take back your power, and if all else fails, there's the Dark Doorway.

I stay up late reading stories of revenge, vigilantism. A girl humiliates her tormentor online; a boy finds the man who raped his sister and beats him bloody, leaving him in a wheelchair for life. Maybe it's fiction; maybe it's true. But what gives me the most comfort are the goodbye threads of those who've decided they can't go on.

Your life belongs to you, *the site claims.* You can decide when it ends.

4.

It's a slow night, and I'm glad for it. When it's quiet I imagine a blanket of peace dropped over the town, everyone sleeping soundly, having pleasant dreams. Matty's here, too, dozing in his cubicle. He's already put in a shift at his EMT job before coming here. He has his ghosts too. I can tell. He usually startles awake as soon as he drifts off, looks momentarily terrified by what he's seen behind his own eyelids. He's a retired marine who served two violent tours in Iraq; now he drives an ambulance. The things he's seen, he says, he can't unsee. He doesn't sleep much, so he might as well spend his time patching up the broken people he can find, helping those who make that call in the night.

Midnight to eight, those are the hours of my watch, he repeats again and again like a mantra.

"Shit," he says, flailing awake.

"You okay?"

"Never better." He rubs his eyes, takes a swig of his big coffee. He tracks a hand over his crew cut, bicep bulging against his tight blue polo shirt, still wearing his EMT uniform.

The phone rings, and he glances over at me with tired eyes.

"I'll get it," I say.

"Great. I'm gonna hit the head."

He is the king of too much information.

Unknown Caller. Same number from last night. I put on my headset quickly.

"Hi, it's Charlie. I'm listening."

"Hi, Charlie." The voice, for some reason, gives me chills. It's raspy, but maybe familiar? "I saw you on the news. I loved the speech you gave about heroes. Nice."

I clear my throat. "You hung up on me yesterday. How are you feeling tonight?" I ask, keeping the focus on him. "I never did get your name."

"I told you. I'm no one."

I scribble down the number, though it will be recorded in the system. "What do you want to talk about tonight? You said you lost someone."

"I didn't say that. I asked if *you* had."

"Did you, though? Lose someone?"

There's a pause; I hear him breathing. I'm listening, too, for background noise—the music I heard during the first call. I've since convinced myself it was a coincidence, or I was just mistaken.

"Yes," he says, and I hear the heavy pitch of sadness.

"I'm sorry," I say.

I am at her grave in the rain, watching helplessly as they lower her into the ground. There are so many flowers, a forest of pink roses. Her mother's face is a mask of grief, glassy eyed, lips parted as if in a silent wail. She's being held up, it seems, only by her husband's arm around her shoulder; her knees keep buckling. The little brother is still and pale, leaning against his father's leg.

"The pain," he says. "It only seems to get worse, not better."

"It *does* get better," I say.

"You said it changed." His voice is cold as a razor's edge.

"It does. And you go on living, and life grows over the pain. There can be joy again, love, good times."

He pushes out a mirthless laugh.

"But not always, right? Sometimes the pain gets darker, deeper. It was my fault, so maybe I don't deserve all that."

This is where it gets tricky because here is where I want to say that it's a choice. You choose to move on and live, do what good you can, have a life. Or you choose another path. But sometimes that advice sounds like a confrontation, or even an accusation.

"Do you know about the Dark Doorway?" he asks before I have a chance to speak again, and the question startles me.

We all know about that website.

Jane is on a crusade to have it taken down. So far no luck, though she has testified in front of Congress, made an appeal to the FBI about its danger to those dealing with suicidal depression. The IP address keeps changing. No one knows who's responsible for it, who is hosting it. The best guess is that it lives on a server overseas, someplace untraceable. Meanwhile, over five hundred people a month log on to leave goodbye threads, ask advice on different ways to commit suicide, and get encouragement to do so. There's also a revenge-and-vigilante forum about getting even with people who wronged you before taking your own life.

This is a disease, raged Jane during her testimony. *Preying on the most emotionally vulnerable, encouraging violence and self-harm.*

It's still up there, more visitors every month.

"The website that shows you ways to die?" I ask.

"Or get revenge."

My heart is thudding, and suddenly I feel a little lash of anger. "This line is for people looking for help. Do you need help?"

I look around to see if Matty has come back. He hasn't. Espo is off today. I'm the supervisor, so there's no one to reprimand me for losing my cool.

"We all need a little help sometimes, don't we?" His voice has taken on that edge again.

I breathe, regain my equilibrium. Or try to.

"Will you let me help you?" I say, surprised at how desperate I sound.

"They called you a hero," he says. "Do you think you're a hero?"

"Far from it."

That tinny music starts to play again in the background, and I strain to listen. Bono croons about how the heart is a bloom, grows up from the stony ground.

But then the line goes dead again, and I am left with my thumping heart and sandpaper throat.

"What happened?" asks Matty, coming back.

"Caller hung up. Ringing back."

But the call just rings and rings.

"Can't save 'em all," says Matty. It sounds more sad than cold.

I stare at the number scribbled on the scrap of paper, then open another window on my screen to find the reverse directory, a service we pay for. If it's a cell phone, I won't find out exactly where the call's coming from, but I can at least find the address of the owner of the phone. I type in the number, and it's a street I recognize. My whole body is tingling.

Then I sit, hoping he'll call back, while also hoping that's the last I'll hear from my unknown caller. Silence for a while; then the phone rings again. Matty grabs it first.

"Hey, this is Matty. I'm listening."

I steal a glance at the call log—there's a name this time, a different number.

"Hey, Amber," he says. "I hear that. Parenting can be hard. So overwhelming, right? Tell me what's going on."

The phone rings again, and I pick up. A girl who's being bullied. A boy who's afraid his father will hurt his mother. A man who thinks his neighbors are Russian spies. The night winds on; I field the calls. I listen, talk it through, call emergency services twice, send social services once.

Finally, my shift ends and I go home.

5.

Zoey thinks we're friends now. We've spoken at three high schools, been interviewed for the local morning show, done another interview with the local newspaper. She hugs me a lot, and she's always bringing me some little gift—a bag of candy, a friendship bracelet, tiny stuffed animals.

"Charlie's my hero," she never fails to say. "If she hadn't answered my call that night, I don't know what would have happened to me."

"If it hadn't been me, it would have been one of the other people at the Crisis Center," I respond when she does. "It's what we all do, try to be a lifeline for those in need."

"What led you to do this kind of work?" the reporters always ask.

"I lost someone once. There was no one there for her when she needed it most."

"Who was it?"

"I don't like to use her name. Her family has suffered enough."

And it was my fault, I don't add. I didn't kill her, but I might as well have. I think they call it depraved indifference. When you had the means and opportunity to help but simply stood by and did nothing.

Today, we're talking at the posh private school Zoey will graduate from in the spring. She has already been accepted at Princeton, and she's planning to attend in the fall. Since her suicide attempt and the epiphany that perfection is not within reach, her Instagram following has tripled. I heard her mother is getting her an agent; there's talk of a book deal.

I'm worried that she's just traded one brand of attention seeking for another. Now she's perfect at being imperfect. She bites her cuticles; sometimes they're so raw they bleed.

Looking out into the audience, I see that things haven't changed since my private school days. You have the rich, gorgeous mean girls with their long nails and silky hair, the brains sporting glasses and looking awkward in their own skin, the alternative crowd with tattoos and dyed hair, dressed all in black. The loners, hiding on the edges.

Zoey gives her talk, ending with the words she says saved her: "You're enough. You're more than enough. I promise."

And there are tears, and sneers, and whispers, and nodding heads. Some will hear her; some won't.

We field questions from students, from teachers. I do my bit about the Crisis Center, how we're there if you're thinking about hurting yourself, or if you're not safe at home, how if you know of someone else who is in trouble, you can reach out.

As I'm speaking, I see the hooded figure again. He lingers near the back in the dark of the auditorium. I squint in his direction. He's tall and lean, slouching. I can't see his face, but I can feel the energy of his stare.

As I step away from the podium, my phone vibrates. I surreptitiously steal a glance at the text.

> Unknown Caller: Do you ever get tired of pretending to be a good person?

My gaze snaps up in time to see the hooded figure slip back toward the exit, leave through the rectangle of light that forms when he opens the door.

As the applause rings out and a crowd of admirers gathers around Zoey, I move quickly from the stage, excusing myself, and head out of the auditorium. I exit in time to see the heavy metal doors at the end of the hall slam shut.

Are all high schools the same through eternity? Same floors, lockers, lights, smells? I could be back at my high school as my footfalls echo off the walls.

Outside, the air is growing cold in the late afternoon; a thick cloud cover threatens rain. The trees whisper around me in the breeze.

A black Charger roars from the parking lot. I try to read the license plate, but it's too far away.

Who was that? I watch the car disappear, the rumble of its engine fading.

Maybe it's no one. Just some kid cutting early. Not my unknown caller, who apparently has my cell phone number now.

No one.

And, yes, I do get tired of it. Pretending to be a good person. It's fucking exhausting.

6.

It's late, and I'm up doing a chem assignment I should have started days ago. I've been spending too much time watching all the feeds of the popular girls, the sad threads of the wronged on the Dark Doorway, endless reels of puppies and kittens, scrolling through all the bad news of the world.

When my phone rings, I practically jump out of my skin. No one ever calls me. Lanie's name and a picture of us at the beach years ago come up on my screen. Maybe, just once, I shouldn't answer, let her struggle with math or English or whatever she's calling about. But I'm a loser, so I pick up.

"Hey," I say.

"Hey, Chloe," she says. "What are you doing?"

"Chem homework." Embarrassing, but true.

"It's Friday night."

"Yeah, but it's due Monday."

She breathes out a laugh. "Are your parents sleeping?"

I heard the television go off a while ago. "Yeah, probably. Why?"

We both know that once my parents are asleep, they're hard to wake up. My dad sleeps with a CPAP machine, and my mom wears earplugs and an eye mask.

"Brad's having a party. Want to go?"

I'm not an idiot. I know she's calling because she needs a ride. Those friends of hers probably left her in the lurch. Because she's not quite one of them, is she? She's just a little less pretty. Her parents aren't rich like theirs are. She's just hanging on to her place in that group, and she knows it.

"It's late," I say. "It's probably over."

"Girl, no," she says in that mischievous tone that's almost like a dare. "It's just getting started."

There's a clattering at my window. When I push back the curtains, Lanie's on my lawn.

"Come on, Chloe. Live a little," she says, still on my phone.

"I don't have anything to wear."

"Let me up. I'll find something."

Bartley follows me to the door, but doesn't bark. Lanie is an old friend, and he wags his tail happily as she pets him and gives him a kiss on the snout. I give him some treats, and he trundles off back to his place beside Sean, who's a deep sleeper like my parents.

In my room, Lanie sifts through my closet and, as if by magic, pulls out a pair of skinny jeans and a flowery top I'd forgotten I even had. My daily I-don't-care uniform is leggings, a variety of oversize hoodies, and Converse high-tops. Lanie is sharp in a pair of black jeans, a clingy gray knit top, and thigh-high boots. Her long golden hair spools over a slender exposed shoulder.

I change in the bathroom, annoyed at myself for being so happy she's here, for abandoning my chemistry homework. I fix my hair into a twist, even try a little makeup. Maybe I look okay.

"Wow," she says when I come out. "You look great."

"What happened to your friends?" I ask.

She looks away. "They blew me off."

I want to say, I would never do that to you. *But instead I just say,* "That sucks. I'm sorry."

"There aren't many friends like you, Chloe."

She only calls or comes over when she wants something—a ride, help with homework. I know that. And I let her do it, every time. Because we've been friends since before I can remember. Maybe you're still friends with people even after they hurt you, even if they keep hurting you. Because there's something there. Something true and deep that stays even when it aches.

We sneak out without incident and drift my old rattler down to the end of the drive without starting the engine or turning on the lights until we hit the street.

I would have been grateful to have my own car when I was your age, *my dad told me.* Not many kids get their own car. *Except that it seems like everyone at my school gets a car for their sixteenth birthday— shiny new ones. I'm there on merit scholarship; the exorbitant tuition paid in full. My parents wouldn't be able to send me there if not.*

I am grateful. I am.

"So," says Lanie, as we drive to Brad's. I know the way. Brad's mom *and mine used to be friends; I used to play in his sandbox. He's never been a nice kid. Once he pushed me off the slide ladder on my swing set. Our moms stopped being friends after that.*

"I heard that JJ has a crush on you."

I push out a breath. "Doubtful."

"No, really," she says, nudging me. "He thinks you're cute."

"Isn't he going out with Sloane?" Sloane is gorgeous. You don't go from bombshell to geek. Even I know that. Doesn't matter that we've lived less than a mile apart and known each other since kindergarten and I've been in love with him for almost as long.

Lanie shakes her glossy hair. "They broke up. She's with Racer now."

Racer. What a stupid name. And he's a total tool.

Even so, JJ has never even looked in my direction. Not even when we were little. It was Lanie whose hand he always tried to hold. Now he's a lacrosse captain, but smart. Cute. Soooo cute. I follow him on social and like all his posts. He doesn't follow me back. No, I'm not in the same universe as JJ.

I say as much, and Lanie makes a clicking noise with her tongue. "Chloe, you always sell yourself short."

We pull up in front of Brad's, and the street is lined with cars, all the windows in the big house lit up, music pouring out the open front door. Wow. How have the neighbors not called the police? I'm nervous suddenly. My parents would kill me if they knew I was here. Maybe I'll just drop Lanie off and go.

"No way," she says when I suggest it. "Come with me."

We find a spot away from the other cars and park. We're both embarrassed by my car, though neither of us says so.

The party, as promised, is wild, and nowhere near ending. We push our way inside, and there they are, Lanie's friends, all gathered in a little clique by the pool outside, visible through the sliding glass doors. There are people lounging, swimming, talking, making out, smoking dope, drinking. I'm invisible. I feel myself disappearing. Even though I haven't been here in years, I see the pool all the time on Brad's Instagram, which is just him, usually shirtless—in various poses that expose his toned, tanned body; his floppy sandy-blond hair—sporting a variety of board shorts and sneakers. He's trying to be an influencer and has some ridiculous number of followers, like thousands.

"Hey, you made it," says Sloane to Lanie when we walk outside, voice high and tight.

"Uh, you were supposed to give me a ride?"

"Was I?" She's so fake. Big eyes, fiery red hair, huge tits, her back in a permanent arch pressing them out into the world. "Oh my god, girl. I'm such a flake. My bad."

"You're here now," says Izzy. She's less slutty, more sly. Hair jet, eyes blue, thinner than the others. Maybe a shade too thin, if there is such a thing. "That's what matters."

Lanie looks back at me. "I came with Chloe."

"Oh," says Izzy, looking at me like something she'd scrape off her shoe. "Hi, Chloe."

"Hey," I say. Awkward.

Actually, though? I wind up having a good time. There are lots of people here. Not just the jocks and the popular kids, but some of the geeks and punks too. My peeps. I wind up talking, drinking just a little. I know better, but just to seem like I'm cool. Even Brad is nice to me.

"Hey, Chloe. How's your mom? She made the best chocolate chip cookies."

The night winds on, and I almost forget I snuck out of the house. It's after one when my phone rings.

Oh, shit. It's my mom.

"Don't answer," says Lanie, wide eyed. She didn't ditch me totally on arrival, as I suspected she would. She checked in with me now and then, leaving the cool group to come slum with the weirdos, where she seems happier and more relaxed.

"I gotta answer. Hi, Mom."

"Oh my god. Did you sneak out?" Her voice is low, whispering so as not to wake my father, I suppose.

"Uh," I say, stupidly. "I guess?"

"You get home right this second, miss. Have you been drinking?"

"No," I lie.

"Then get home right now. Right now, Chloe."

"Okay."

I hang up and look at Lanie. "I should go. Do you have a ride home?"

"Look," she says. "JJ is watching you."

I follow her gaze, and sure enough, he's watching from the upstairs balcony. He gives a little wave, but it's not for me. It's for Lanie. He's looking at her. Obviously. He's been watching her, lovesick since we needed help opening our juice boxes.

"Stay," she says. "You're already in trouble. Might as well have a good time."

"Come with me," I say, moving toward the door. "Nothing good happens after midnight, right?"

"Who knows?" she says with that mischievous grin. "Maybe all the good things only happen after midnight."

"How will you get home?"

"I'll find a ride," she says. "Don't worry about me."

She's staring up at JJ, and he's looking back at her. Of course she's not leaving with me. She gives me a hug, whispering, "You're the best friend I've ever had."

I leave alone, running down the street to my car, and drive carefully home.

Oh, wow, did I ever get in trouble. Yelled at, grounded, dishes for a week. It was totally worth it.

7.

I catch Espo and Jane making out in the unisex bathroom. "Oh my god," I say, backing out. "I'm so sorry." I stand in the hallway, my face burning.

"No, Charlie," says Jane, coming out. She smooths down her skirt, runs manicured fingers through her thick black hair. "I'm sorry. That was—inappropriate. We can discuss this if you feel violated or triggered in any way."

"It's cool," I say.

Espo comes out, cleaning off his glasses, cheeks pink. "That was our bad, Charlie."

"Really," I say. "I'm happy for you. Be happy."

Jane smiles and gives me a hug. "Now what's this I hear about a recurring caller?"

"I listened to the logs," says Espo. "Sounds to me like he was messing with you."

"Yeah," I say. "I don't know."

I don't tell him about the hooded figure at my talks, or about the text. That would be a whole thing. Besides, I don't know who I saw. Or if it was even the same person. But Espo is looking at me, squinty with concern. "Let me know if you need an assist. If he calls again tonight."

"Will do."

"Some people take advantage of the crisis line, use it to cause trouble or get attention," he goes on. "Our resources are limited. We can't have people abusing our staff."

But the night is quiet. And the hours unspool with glacial slowness, time seeming to stop around 1 a.m. Espo dozes off, and the phone stays dark. It's unusual for a Tuesday. Weekends are always the slowest, but on Monday and Tuesday, despair seems to be at its apex.

I open the website I haven't visited in a while.

The Dark Doorway.

It's kind of like the opposite of the Crisis Center. When you call our hotline, we try to walk you away from the edge and into the light. When you log on to the Dark Doorway, the people lurking there have different advice. On the Dark Doorway, the people who have committed suicide or acts of revenge are considered the heroes. There's a page dedicated to them and their stories. The "Our Heroes" page is an endless scroll of goodbye threads, news articles about successful attempts, detailed accounts of how and why, final acts of revenge, gory accounts of murder-suicides left by "observers," people tapped to tell the story when there's no one left to tell it.

I have a login and a password. New ones. When it's slow here, I log on and try to be a guiding light in the chaos. I have been kicked off about five times. Jane is on there, too, sometimes. I occasionally bump into her in the suicide chats. I can always tell it's her because she's not subtle.

Suicide is not an answer. There's more to your life than this moment of despair. Call us at 211.

There's a path back from trauma into the light. Call us at 211 if you want to live and be well again.

Hurting people doesn't make us hurt any less. It's a never-ending cycle of pain. Please call us for better ideas on how to be well again at 211. There's always someone to answer your call.

Jane lost her son to suicide. On a night when she was traveling for work, he reached out for her, and she was on a plane home. He was gone before she landed and heard his message. All this is just her way of trying to keep another mother from knowing her pain. Her zeal and passion drive the whole mission of the Crisis Center. But the high frequency of her message can scare people away sometimes. It also draws hatred and fire from the trolls who linger on the Dark Doorway, taking delight in pushing the unstable into terrible acts of violence against themselves and others. They rage and rail at her, find her email and send daily death threats via our website.

I'm not as direct as Jane. I lurk in the shadows of the chat rooms and wait. I like the "Partners" page, where people seek others to help them end their lives, or to go out together. My theory is that if you're looking for help, maybe you're really looking for an alternative, a friend.

I click around a while, give some advice to a young woman named Starr who's seeking a partner for a Thelma-and-Louise-style exit. She intends to kill the man who raped her and left her for dead in a park, then got off and is still out there. Then, when he's dead, she plans to "drive off a cliff somewhere." A fiery exit from the hell of this unjust life.

We think that hurting others will make the pain go away.
But it won't. There are other ways.

Like what?

Trauma is a head trip; there are people who can help you
get past it.

**Therapy? Been there. Done that. Still can't sleep at night.
Meanwhile he's still out there, loving life.**

It takes time. That's the hard part, but there's light
ahead. Joy again. Love.

Fuck you. Get off this forum. You don't belong here.

My friend committed suicide, and it destroyed her whole
family. If only she knew how many people loved her.

**I'm reporting you.
There are so many other ways to feel better.**

Then the familiar message from the admin: Your access to this site has been revoked.

And I'm shunted back to the home page. *Come with me if you want to die*, it reads.

I am creating another login and password when the phone lights up.

Unknown Caller and his now familiar number.

"Hi, it's Charlie. I'm listening."

"Hi, Charlie."

I glance over at Espo, who is tilted back in his chair, head lolling to one side. He's snoring like a caricature of someone snoring, breath sawing rhythmically.

"Hello again. What can I call you?" I ask, trying to keep my voice light.

"I'm no one."

I feel a little lash of anger, undercut by fear. Who is this? What does he want?

"Was that you in the auditorium?" I ask.

There's a moment of quiet while I listen to him breathe. "What do you think?"

"How did you get my cell number?"

"You're not hard to find."

"Look," I say. "This line is for people who need help."

"I saw you on the Dark Doorway. That was you, right? Charlie-angel333?"

I don't respond.

"Do you believe that?" he goes on into the silence. "That there's light ahead. Joy again. Love."

I feel a twist of pain, of sadness. "I do," I say, my voice wobbling, betraying me.

"You're a liar, *Charlie.*"

Espo is still snoring.

"Who is this?" I whisper.

But the line goes dead.

8.

I float through the weekend, even as I do the dishes every night, and listen to my dad's epic poem about responsibility and honesty. I even post some pictures on my Instagram, a selfie with Lanie, one with some of the math nerds trying to look cool, and get tagged in some photos from the party too.

The party. Everyone is talking about it.

The police came a while after I left. But Lanie's posts from before they arrived looked epic. Bikini clad in the pool, drink in hand, posing with her friends. She didn't post the one of us together. But that's okay. Izzy and

Sloane blew her off and were clearly trying to shut her out, and I was there for her. She must see that. I keep hearing what she said: There aren't many friends like you, Chloe.

Maybe this will be when things go back to the way they were. But she never calls over the weekend. She doesn't answer any of my texts.

On Monday morning, I find Lanie at her locker. She's alone, which is a rare thing.

"Hey," I say, sliding up beside her.

"Oh, hey, girl. Thanks for the ride this weekend."

She looks fresh and dewy in an oversize red T-shirt and torn-at-the-knees skinny jeans.

"Yeah, thanks for inviting me. I had fun. Want to go to the movies this weekend?"

She's about to respond when JJ comes up behind her, buff and floppy haired, making my heart thunder. For a second, I think he's here to talk to me. But then he drops an arm around Lanie's shoulders, and she looks up at him with stars in her eyes.

"Hey, babe," he says. "Hey, Chloe."

It's like in slow motion as their lips touch. And her eyes meet mine with some expression that's pity and victory and shame. It cuts deep. She knows I've been in love with him since kindergarten. I stare, stupid, dumbfounded.

"Can I let you know?" she asks. "About the movies?"

All I can do is nod, feeling all my happiness from the weekend shrivel into a hard little ball in the pit of my stomach.

She's a user, Chloe. She used you to get what she wanted. *That's what my mom said this weekend, and I screamed at her, telling her that she didn't know what she was talking about and asking her why she hated it when I was happy. I slammed the door in her face, and later I heard her crying.*

I'm still standing there when the bell rings, and I'm late for class, and Mr. Rand doesn't say anything but gives me a look as I take my seat.

The rumors fly. Lanie stole JJ from Sloane; they slept together while Sloane was skiing with her parents. Lanie and JJ are together now. But Sloane is trying to get Lanie kicked off the cheerleading team. Lanie is saying that Sloane hasn't been the same since her knee injury and she's holding the team back. I stumble on Sloane crying in the bathroom, and I almost feel sorry for her until she snaps at me, What are you looking at, troll?

I go to the nurse and tell her I have my period and bad cramps. She calls my mother, who says I can come home. As I drive home, I think about how one girl on the Dark Doorway planned to drive her car into Quarry Lake. She left a long thread saying goodbye to the people she loved and telling off all the assholes who hurt her. And then nothing. I googled "girl drives into quarry lake," but I never found anything. Did she die? Or did she just go on living but was too embarrassed to come back on the Dark Doorway forum and say she chickened out? Or does she linger on the chat boards like I do, just reading, still trying to screw up the courage to put an end to it all?

My parents are both working, and Sean's still in school. The house is empty except for Bartley, and this would be the perfect time. I feel a floating sense of peace. There's so much advice there on how to die; I know exactly what to do, how to do it.

I get on the Dark Doorway and start my goodbye thread.

9.

When my shift ends, I plug the scribbled address into my navigation computer and start to drive, following its directions.

Sunrise is just a couple of hours away, and they say it's always darkest before the dawn. It seems like that tonight—the sky starless, moonless, the light from the streetlamps faint and grainy. I drive through the quiet streets and finally wind out of town, taking the twisting road that curves through the thick woods.

I've lived in this town all my life. I thought I would leave one day and have a glamorous life doing—something, anything. I was never sure what. Something artistic. But life happens, and this place has a way of wrapping around you like a clinging vine, and so do the consequences of your actions, and your inactions.

I shouldn't be doing this, tracking down my unknown caller. It's a big no-no. Is he a lost soul, crying for help? A troll looking for trouble or attention, like Espo said? A predator looking for a victim? Anyway, this work. You can't take it personally. That's one of the first things Espo and Jane taught me in training: You are the life preserver, the line dropped down the well. You can only put yourself out there, offer to help. The person in crisis must do the reaching back and the holding on. It's up to them to do all the work. You're just the light to guide the way out.

But my unknown caller. I feel a pull to him, like he's the one holding the rope and I'm the one grabbing for it. But it's not a lifeline. It's a lure with a hook on the end, and I'm as helpless as a fish in a pond.

The road winds on, and the night seems to grow darker.

Finally, I come to a tilted mailbox by the side of the road.

"You have arrived at your destination," the navigation computer announces.

I pause before making the turn onto the drive, my engine running. I think about calling Espo, but I know he'd tell me to come back right this second and report the caller to the police and leave it at that.

But I know this place. This address.

So, finally, I make the turn.

10.

So I guess the truth is I'm a coward. Which is just another thing to be depressed about. The only way out of the day-to-day misery of my shitty life is too terrifying a prospect. Even with all the encouragement from people on the Dark Doorway, when the time came to drive my car into the big oak at the end of our rural road, I just couldn't do it.

I never even made it out of my driveway. I just sat there, stuck in some petrified limbo. Then my mom came home early from work, worried about me, and she made me some hot chocolate, and I cried and cried with my head in her lap. And I felt better.

That JJ is a bad kid anyway, *my mom said.* I wouldn't let you go out with him even if he was smart enough to ask you. And Lanie, well, she's lost her way, I think. When she calls next time, don't answer.

My mom, she always knows what to say. Her voice is powerful and true. And all those voices on the Dark Doorway faded.

It's the hero's journey into the unknown.

You can do it.

This world is not good enough for you.

No one ever said: What about your mom?

And then Bartley and I walked to get Sean from the bus stop, and we took the long way back, stopping at the dairy farm up the road and getting a homemade ice cream from Mrs. Miller. That ice cream tasted so sweet, and the air was fresh, and the sun was warm. Sean and Bartley romped around, tumbling and getting grass stains on Sean's shirt. Finally, we walked home with Sean chattering endlessly about his teacher, Miss Apple, who he loves.

At dinner, my dad looked sad because Grandma is not doing well, and the bills are piling up, and his job at the tire factory is a bear. But then he said, Well, even though things aren't good out there, at least they are in here. *Meaning at home, with all of us. And I guess he's right. Not perfect, not Instagrammable, not enviable, maybe. But good.*

I stay up late doing my honors calculus, which seems like it was invented to give you a migraine. I promised myself I'd stay off the Dark Doorway, and I wonder how many other people wrote goodbye threads and then chickened out. But after my parents' light goes off, I log on again. The despair there is a kind of quicksand, pulling you under.

I start to think about it again.

Then my phone begins to ping and vibrate.

> Omg!
> Have you seen this?
> Lanie is such a slut.
> Can you believe she would do this?

Bubbles keep popping up on my screen.
??? I type into the math-geek group chat.

> Check your email.

I log on to my web mail and see it right away.

> To: Morris High School Families
> From: Unknown
> Subject line: Lanie Freedman is a whore

I hesitate, but then of course I click on it.
There she is, her long golden hair flowing. She's naked, sitting astride someone whose face can't be seen on camera.
She moans, tilting her head back.
Oh, *I think, confused at first.* What are you doing, Lanie?
It's the full sex act, Lanie caught on camera bouncing and holding her breasts, crying out in pleasure. It's erotic, revolting, mesmerizing.
Oh, JJ, ohmygod.

He can be heard too. But it's her that you see, only her. She obviously has no idea she's being filmed. My heart breaks into a million little pieces and flutters into my stomach. I feel sick. I wish I could crawl through the screen and cover her up. I'm angry at her—How could she do this? Angry for her—Who would do this to her?

I imagine this in everyone's email, on everyone's phones. How quickly people will upload it to other places, put it on their social media feeds, upload it to those revenge porn sites. It will be out there, everywhere, forever.

I go to call her.

But then I don't.

I can hear my mom's words, that Lanie used me to get what she wanted. I can see the way she looked after she kissed JJ in front of me.

And later that night, when she calls me, once, twice, three times, I don't answer. Just lie awake thinking about her, that look on her face, how she told me JJ liked me when he obviously never did. I realize that our friendship has been like death by a thousand cuts. I've bled out. There's nothing left.

The next day, it's a total shit show at school, parents storming the place, and an assembly called to try to get someone to come forward and identify the perpetrator. A cybersecurity expert is brought in to warn kids about the dangers of exposing themselves online. He tells us Lanie is underage and this is a federal crime.

Everyone knows it was Sloane, who now seems to be back together with JJ. The two of them linger in the back, in the pack of cool kids, beautiful and apathetic. Sloane's smile is wicked, victorious. JJ drapes his muscular arm around her shoulders. The team goes to nationals this Friday. Lanie isn't in school at all.

He never even liked me, *she texted me last night when I didn't answer her calls.*

It was Sloane's idea to see if I would sleep with him, I guess.
They set up a camera in his room.
I didn't know.
My life is over.

The text bubbles came in one after another.

I know you're there. Please answer.

But I didn't answer.

11.

The house is how I remember it. Small and dark, buried behind overgrown shrubbery, surrounded by towering trees—oak, pine, maple. It looks abandoned, windows fogged and eaves sagging. The gravel beneath my tires crunches as I bring the car to a stop, surprised to see a light glowing from inside, a faint orange flicker.

The engine knocks and cools as I sit, waiting.

What am I doing here? This is a breach of protocol, a foolish action that has put me in danger, risking my job and the ethics of the center. Common sense takes over, and I start the car again, put it in reverse.

I am about to pull out when the front door opens and a hooded figure steps out onto the porch.

It's so eerie, so spooky, that for a second I feel like I might be dreaming.

He moves closer to the car, and instead of driving away as anyone would, I am frozen. Waiting to see the face of the unknown caller.

12.

The week winds on, and the furor dies down a bit. Lanie still hasn't come back to school, and she has stopped calling me.

A pall has settled over everything, and the world seems grayer and more miserable than ever.

I log on to the Dark Doorway almost every night now, reading the tales of revenge, the goodbye threads, the chats about ways to die. Apparently, there's a meat preservative that's easy to obtain. It's the most popular method for ending your life, or so they say on the site.

I am starting to wonder who these anonymous people are— tigercatmouse24 and mordor18 and kailowren69. When I walk through the hallways at school, I stare at faces, wondering if any of the people I know are part of the anonymous chorus urging others to end their lives.

On Thursday I stay late to get extra help in calculus, because even though I still sort of want to die, I know my parents will kill me if my grades start to slide. Afterward, as I head to my car in the waning light, there's someone standing there, waiting for me. He's leaning against my car and stands up straight as I approach.

JJ.

I can't even look at him, only seeing Lanie on top of him, a porn star with golden hair and moaning lips.

"Hey," he says, dark hair flopping in front of his heavily lashed eyes. He pushes it aside, but it flops right back.

The sky is bruised by dusk, clouds drifting. The football field is lit, Coach blowing his whistle, yelling at the practicing team. The cheerleaders are gone, off to the national competition without Lanie.

"Have you talked to Lanie?" he asks.

I shake my head.

"How could you do that to her?" I ask.

He blows out a breath, looks away. "She wanted it. She wanted me to film her."

I shake my head. "No."

"She did, so she could send it to Sloane. So Sloane would know that Lanie and me were together and break up with me."

I don't say anything. That's not what Lanie said, and how am I supposed to know what or who to believe? Anyway, why do I care?

"Anyway, what do you care?" he says, echoing my thoughts.

"She's my friend."

"I hope you have better friends than that," he snaps. "You should hear what she says behind your back."

My shoulders hike. "What? What does she say?"

"She tells everyone that you used to suck your thumb, that your family is broke, that all she has to do is call and you run right back to her, do whatever she asks."

Each thing he says is like a punch to the gut. All of it true. I feel sick with the betrayal, my stomach clenching.

He must see how much he hurt me, hangs his head. "I'm sorry."

"What do you want, JJ?"

"I just—I just wanted to know if she was okay."

We stare at each other a moment, and I see it—in the deep lines etched in his brow, in the tightness of his mouth. He cares about her, maybe even loves her. That hurts more than all the rest of it.

"She won't return my calls," he says.

"Who sent the video to Sloane?" I ask.

He shrugs. "She did, I guess. That was the plan."

Grunting and shouting carries from the field; the sky grows darker, a stiff wind picking up.

"If you talk to her," he says, "will you have her call me?"

I don't answer him, look down at my trashed sneakers.

Finally, he steps aside. I get in my car and drive away, look back to see him walking toward his own car, head bowed, shoulders hunched, a line drawing of despair against the gloaming.

It's late when I log on to the Dark Doorway again.

I scroll through the various pages—more misery and anger, depression, angst. I am about to click off when I see a name I recognize.

LalaKitty17.

LalaKitty has been Lanie's screen name since we were kids playing Animal Jam.

It's a goodbye thread.

I start reading. Her dad is sick, and she got kicked off the cheerleading team. How she made love to her boyfriend, and he took a video without her knowing. That it was a setup, arranged by a girl she thought was her friend, but who just wanted to get her kicked off the team. The video, it's everywhere now. A friend saw it on Pornhub, and it had over twenty thousand views and counting. Her parents called the police, but there's nothing they can do. Even if she changes schools, she knows it will follow her everywhere. She'll never get into college now. And she's been terrible to the only true friend she ever had, and now she has no one. Her mother can't even look at her, and her father doesn't have much time left. His final days will be consumed by the awful thing she's done. Then she apologizes to her mother, her father, her little brother, who's Sean's age.

Finally, she apologizes to me. Chloe, you were a true friend. And I abandoned you. Treated you badly. Used you. I never deserved you even when we were little. I'm sorry. I love you.

The chorus has already started, all the people encouraging her to end her life.

> Be brave, girl. The end is a release.
> You sound like a horrible person, and the world will be better
> off without you.
> You're a hero for walking into the unknown.

The phone is in my hand.

But I don't call.

I don't chime in with the other trolls, but I don't speak up either.

I can't stop thinking about her telling all those mean girls private things about me, how she used me and knew she was doing it, bragged about it.

I could have called her, or her parents. I could have called the police.
But I didn't. And when she called me a little while later, I didn't answer.

That night, as I was tossing in my bed, Lanie stole her parents' car. Later,
police would learn that her blood alcohol was twice the legal limit. She
drove the car to the bottom of the road that separated our houses. Then she
drove the pickup at eighty miles an hour into the oak tree, dying on impact,
just as the chorus on the Dark Doorway promised.

The next day I finally listened to her messages, each more desperate than
the last, until the final one:

I thought you were my friend. Why won't you answer me?

Her voice was taut with misery and despair.

Then all I heard was the engine revving, Lanie screaming in rage or in
fear or both, the music blaring, Bono singing about how you're on the road,
but you've got no destination. And then a terrible crash, crunching metal,
shattering glass, and then nothing.

13.

The figure approaches, and even though I'm afraid, shaking, I put
the car in park and climb out. I see the light break over the hori-
zon, and the tall, broad form is just a shadow, a wraith moving
toward me.

When he's upon me, he takes down his hood. A gasp escapes
my throat; I never thought I'd see him again. The world we inhabited as children is as far away as the moon, even though it's
just a few miles from where I live my life now, just a few short
years ago.

His eyes are sunken, stubble darkening his jaw. His clothes hang
off him, shoulders slouched as if he's carrying a huge weight. I remember his light, his beauty, the glint of intelligence and mischief
I thought I saw in him. But now he's a hollowed-out version of the
person he used to be.

We both are.

"How do you live with it, Chloe?" JJ asks, his voice edged with
anger and sadness.

JJ, my childhood crush. Chloe, the person I used to be.

I shed her like dead skin, using my middle name, Charlene,
Charlie for short, to move forward in my life after Lanie killed

herself exactly the same way I had intended to kill myself. Did she read my goodbye thread? Is that where she got the idea? I'll never know. Could I have saved her? Could I have talked her out of it if I had answered her calls? I think so. But I didn't do that.

I had to kill Chloe to survive the pain of losing Lanie, of my failure.

"I made a choice."

I saw what Lanie's suicide did to her whole family. Her mother died of a heart attack a year later; her father killed himself. Her brother is in jail for drug dealing. I promised myself that I would live. No matter how painful it was to do that.

"What kind of choice?"

That's when I see it. The gun in his hand. It's flat and black, full of menace.

"The choice to live, to use my life to do better, to spend my days repenting by helping others the best I can."

I didn't go to college, though everyone expected me to. When I turned eighteen and graduated from high school, I trained to be an EMT and spent the next few years driving an ambulance around, rushing from accidents to scenes of domestic violence to elderly folks dead in their beds. Then I met Jane when she came to make first responders aware of the Crisis Center.

I saw something in you, she told me later. *The knowledge. Of life and all its pain, the decision to stick around and do better. That's what heroism is, you know? It's not goodness. It's not bravery. Not just. It's the courage to keep fighting, keep trying to be a light in the darkness even when you've failed at that already.*

I've been working for her ever since. Now I'm taking classes toward my degree at the community college and hoping to become a family therapist. My parents wanted more for me, but they're supportive of my path. Sean is a star student, about to graduate with honors. He'll do great things, no doubt.

JJ is crying, big tears falling from his eyes, shoulders shaking. Does he still live here, in the house where he grew up, just a short distance from my childhood home? It looks run down and deserted, but he's still here. He's remained, frozen in this place, in his grief. It happens.

"I can't make that choice. I have no right," he says. The gun is down by his side. "It was me. I did set up that camera for Sloane. Lanie didn't know."

This does not surprise me. I never knew the truth, but I suspected. Lanie wasn't always a good friend, but I could never quite believe she'd do that to Sloane, herself, or anyone.

"We were kids, JJ," I say. "All of us. You couldn't have known it would end in Lanie killing herself."

He wipes at his eyes with his free hand, looks away.

"Don't forgive me," he says. "I don't deserve it."

"It's all any of us deserve."

I think I've reached him, see his shoulders soften. But then he lifts the gun to his temple.

"That's not true," he says. His voice is high pitched and full of rage. "Sloane—she doesn't even care. She went on with her life. You know she's married now, some rich guy?"

Yes, I follow Sloane on Instagram. She's as gorgeous as ever, a wellness influencer, married to a hedge fund–manager husband, with two toddlers every bit as gorgeous as she is. They live in a huge house not far from where we all grew up. If her feed is to be believed, her life is perfect, not a single shadow cast by what she did to Lanie.

"I asked her about it," he says, weeping now. "Sloane said that *she* didn't kill Lanie. Lanie killed Lanie. All she did was leave the bait—me. *Lanie* was the one who slept with her best friend's boyfriend. Lanie chose to die. She deserved what she got."

I close my eyes against the pain of all these memories.

"Do you forgive Sloane too?" he yells when I don't answer.

It's hard to explain forgiveness to people in the throes of pain, clinging to the way things are supposed to be, should have been. Forgiveness is not saying that certain deeds are acceptable or forgotten. Forgiveness is an acknowledgment that we are all deeply flawed, and some of us make terrible mistakes or do horrible things. But to cling to rage, hatred, or grief, to rail against what is or has been, is to kill yourself again and again, rob yourself of what life you have left, what good you can still do.

I forgive Sloane and JJ. I forgive Lanie.

I still work on forgiving myself—that's harder. Jane says that it comes in time. A kind of peace, a certain brand of happiness with sadness stitched in like a slub in the fabric of your life.

"I forgive us all," I say. "What else is there to do now?"

His hand shakes, the gun wobbling.

I calculate—Can I rush him? No, too risky.

"My life," he says. "I've done nothing. I have no one. I am no one."

So it *was* a cry for help, those calls. Not just a way to torture me by playing the song he must have known Lanie loved. It could be that he didn't know it was our favorite song, or maybe she told him that about me too. Or he was just listening to it as a way to feel closer to her, as he reached out for the only person he thought might be in as much pain as he was.

"JJ," I say. "If you end it now, you never have a chance to do better. To *be* better. Every time I talk someone through a crisis in their life, I save Lanie. Sloane—she's right, in a way. Lanie made her choice. But you and I? We can make a different one."

Very faintly in the distance, I hear the approach of sirens. I bet Espo listened to the logs and then tracked the Crisis Center car I'm driving.

JJ hears them too. This is the moment when he'll choose.

We lock eyes, the gun still quaking in his hand, his shoulders still heaving.

Finally, he drops to his knees, folds onto the ground, the gun dropping harmlessly to the grass. I feel a rush of relief and move to him quickly, kicking the gun away, then helping him to his feet.

He falls into me, and we hold on to each other, as the sirens close in.

14.

Zoey and I are still on the circuit, speaking at schools and doing press interviews. But I've started talking about Lanie more because I realize that I've been hiding that dark part of myself. I thought I had killed Chloe, but that lost and awkward teen has been raging inside me all these years, wanting only to finally be forgiven.

I stand at a podium in a big public school out of town.

I see all the kids—the popular ones, the brains, the jocks, the punks, the burnouts. They are not who they will become. This moment, teenage life, it feels like the whole universe, but it's only a millisecond.

"When you compare your messy three-dimensional life to the filtered and curated two-dimensional version of everyone else you see on social media, you're not getting the whole picture. Real life is what happens *between* those posts. And you only know the version people show you on Instagram. It's a fiction. And I guarantee every single one of those perfect people you see out there is feeling as lost and insecure as you are."

Zoey joins me.

"Charlie is my hero," she says. "She taught me that I am enough—flawed, broken, bad hair day, late for school, zit on my chin, blew my chemistry exam. That's everyone. No one's perfect, and no one *needs to be.*"

"Call us at the Crisis Center if you need to talk, if you're thinking about harming yourself or someone else. Close down your social media feeds, and go out and feel the sun on your skin, play with your dog, listen to the birds."

I find myself thinking about JJ, how we took a walk in the park yesterday and talked about Lanie. How the sun was shining and the leaves whispering. And how there was a new kind of peace in that moment for both of us.

"You'll find true happiness in the smallest things."

There are some tears, some sneers, some whispered smart-ass comments. Some nodding smiles.

Do they hear us? I hope so.

In the back of the room, I see her. Lanie.

She's as bright and as beautiful as she ever was, washed in golden light. My friend.

Even though she hurt me, and I abandoned her in her hour of need, and she's gone now, the silvery, bright love of our childhood friendship never died.

It lives. Apart from us. Despite us.

Holler, Child

FROM *Holler, Child: Stories*

PART OF ME glad my son in here and ain't out there where Don
Earl can get ahold of him. Part of me scared cause I ain't never
seen this wildness in his eyes. He always been the most beautiful
boy in the world. Skin like dark chocolate and eyes like honey.
Even when he was five, he was a grown man ready to take care of
his momma. My baby always been something special.

But tonight, for the first time ever, I think he look just like the
man that took half my sight. Eyeballs bloodshot. Look like somebody done scratched red lines in them with they fingernails, and
his face got welts coming up all over.

I sat at the dining table looking at the front door for hours fore
he come busting through it like some kind of storm. Sat there
all that time with my lips wrapped around a Thunderbird bottle,
telling myself this was gone be easy cause I know my baby. Now he
here, I don't know how to say what I'm posed to. What I told my
friend Brooks I was gone say.

She called me at work just hours earlier. Told me to hurry to
her house cause Don Earl wanted to see me and was real upset.
I told Brooks she must be out her mind, thinking I can leave
work like that. The university dining hall busiest at lunchtime
and leaving the serving line liable to lose me my job. But I went
soon as the rush was over and found her and Don Earl waiting
on me. Brooks eyes was wet and Don Earl's was too. That there
scared me to death cause I know how dangerous the work out
there at Don Earl's place can get. He got a junkyard slash hogpen.
Little place where he scrap old cars and raise hogs. Sometimes

Quinten work with Don Earl. It's always plenty for him to do out there.

When I saw them—my friendgirl and that grown man sitting there crying like that—I knew something had happened to my baby out there at Don Earl's place. Turned out, though, they accusing him. And they accusing him wrong. Now Don Earl and a whole bunch of other mens out looking for him. Want to hurt him. Make him pay for something he never could've did. I told them to least let the law handle it. Prove my baby innocent. They want they own kind of justice, though. They want him dead in a hard, ugly way.

"Whole lot of people out there looking for you, son," I say when I see he just gone stand there at the front door like a fool. Look like he want to go back out but know he can't. He don't want to come in either, though. Look like he stuck between good and bad or heaven and hell or something. He trying not to look at me, but that's kind of hard to do, cause the living room and the dining room the same room. He walked right in to me staring at him, trying to see his face. I just need to hear it from him, cause I know my baby ain't done nothing.

"You do what they say, Quinten?" I come on out and ask him. I ain't got to be scared of what his answer gone be. I know him. He ain't nothing like what made him. Nothing like that.

Don Earl girl always flirting with my baby. Call herself having a little crush on him. She ain't but thirteen. Really too young to know any better. My heart go out to her. She remind me of me, and that's what got me tore up in two. I want to be mad at her for letting her crush on my son get him blamed, but I know what it's like to crush on somebody you ain't got no business crushing on.

It ain't never mattered to me that Quinten come from the worst night of my life. Last time any man ever touched me with hisself or with his fist. Quinten daddy was the Sunday school teacher at Right Way Church of Christ. Forced hisself in me. Knowed I was saving myself for marriage. He the one taught me that was the right thing to do—to save myself. And then he took it from me. Beat me good and called me a tease. Beat my right eye out my head that night. Been wearing a patch ever since then. Folks look at me like I'm weak cause I just got one eye, but Quinten don't judge his momma by that.

When he was little, he used to bring his fingers to my face and rest them soft on the patch. Used to beg to see the empty socket. I used to close my other eye and let him explore my face till he was tired. Let him ask all the questions he wanted to, and I'd make up pretty lies for answers. He used to cry when I told him bout how I lost my eye on a fishing hook. Hated fishing and hooks cause he loved me so much. It's been just us. Me and my baby. He growed up early to protect me—to help me raise him up to be a man.

"Quinten," I say. "Talk to me. Tell Momma. What happened out there, baby?"

He don't say nothing at first. Just look at me real hard. He look like he want to say something to me, but then he shake his head like he trying to turn something loose on the inside. "Momma, you got all these lights on? Ain't nobody here but you. You running up the bill." He put his hand on the light switch next to him.

And I think maybe he right. It ain't all the way dark outside, and we do try to keep the lights off most of the time. And him thinking about the lights—conserving and managing our bills—being the man of me, give me some kind of comfort. I member when he was seven, and I was having a hard time finding a day job. He'd stay home all by hisself—all through the night—and didn't never tell his teachers at school. He was a good boy. A real good boy. Always done tried to be the man of me. Look after me. Called hisself my husband when he was five. I told him nawh. He can't never be that, but he can always be the little man of me. He the one come to me bout working with Don Earl last year. The lights was off cause my check don't always cover all the bills. He had just made the eighth-grade basketball team, but when he walked in the house and found me sitting at the table by candlelight, he give it up. His eyes was bright that night. He was holding his basketball in the loop of his arm and his backpack was on his shoulders. He walked in the house and flipped the light switch, and, when ain't nothing happen, his eyes scanned the dark room for me. I was just sitting there at the dining room table, watching him. I ain't know what to say.

He found me and the candle and let the ball fall to the floor. "Lights off again, Momma?" he asked. And I couldn't give him nothing but a sigh.

"Momma," he called, moving close to the table.

"I'm trying, baby," I said, and I couldn't control the crying in my voice. I was tired that day. Tired of struggling and not never getting nowhere. I didn't mean to show him that, but I just couldn't help it. "I'm trying to keep it all together, but Jesus . . . Lord, I just don't know sometimes."

Quinten dropped his bag, fell to his knees, and rested his head on my lap. "Don't cry, Momma," he said in a grown-man voice. "Mr. Don Earl say he can use my help whenever I got the time. We gone be all right. I promise we gone be all right." And I believed him, so I let him give up basketball to be the man of the house.

It made me proud cause everybody thought he was gone be so troubled when he was little. Took him a while to catch on in school, and he acted out sometimes. But when his teachers sent us to the doctor, and the doctor gave us the medicine for his attention problem, he was better. He was good.

Now, I just deal with the same stuff anybody else with a fifteen-year-old boy deal with. Teachers call and say he can be disrespectful sometimes, and he got caught stealing from the mall a few times. Quinten try to nickel-and-dime drugs, but I think it's just a phase. Boys gone be boys, and I'm pretty sure all this gone pass. He a good kid. Even with all that boy stuff, he still a good kid.

I move away from the table and bump it with my hip. The Thunderbird bottle wobble a little bit, but it don't fall. Me and Quinten look at it. He probably thinking bout the past. How Thunderbird was with us every night. I want to explain to him that I ain't drinking again, I just needed something to chase the demons away, but I can't. I ain't never told Quinten bout his daddy. Ain't never want him to carry them demons. Ain't want to curse him with knowing. So, for a long while, Thunderbird carried the demons for us.

I move closer to where he standing. "Don't you turn that light off, Quinten. Don't you touch it," I say, and I sound like I'm gone whup him or something, even though I ain't never did it. Ain't never put my hands on him, not even a light spanking.

His hand slide off the wall, but his eyes drop to the ground. "Quinten. Look at me, baby," I say real soft, trying to plead with him. "You a good boy. You always been a good boy. Look at your momma and talk to me."

*

The Sunday school teacher who raped me knew the Bible like he wrote it. He loved the Old Testament, the law. I loved that— that he stood for something. He taught me that ain't nothing change on the cross—not the laws anyway. He was thirty and I wasn't but seventeen, so I loved him to myself. I ain't tell nobody, not even God.

His name was Kenneth Gray Ross, and I thought he was beautiful. He was tall with chestnut skin, and his smile was soft and sweet as buttermilk cake. When he talked bout Jesus, I saw love in his eyes, and I wanted him to be my life. But I knew he was too old for me, so I kept my dreams to myself. It was just a crush. But when he invited me to the house he shared with his momma to help plan his Sunday school lesson, I lied to my momma—told her I was going to the library—and I went to him.

Quinten tall just like Kenneth Gray. Handsome like him too. He lift his head up and look at me, and his eyes ain't wild no more. They sad and scared and confused. I want to go and wrap him up in my arms like I used to do when he was little, but he rub his whole hand across his face and start talking.

"I love her, Momma. And she wanted me. She was just scared. Thought her daddy was gone be mad. I would've stopped if she really wanted me to, Momma. But I wanted her and she wanted me too."

He go quiet and I do too. I want to understand what he saying. Make sense of it in a way that I can report back to Brooks and Don Earl. Me and Quinten ain't never talked about sex, but he my son, so I know he know better than to do what they saying he done. I got to make them know what.

I nod my head. "So y'all decided together? She said yes all the way?" I ask.

He nod his head and say, "She wanted to. I know she did."

I smile cause I know my son, and then I ask one last time just for the confirmation. "So she said yes? You heard her say it?"

His face look confused. He don't shake his head and he don't nod it.

I feel my hands go to shaking. My nerves acting up. "Nod your head, Quinten. She said yes. You mean to nod, baby. You confused, cause everybody know a shake mean no and a nod mean yes."

He nod his head, like I got it, and I feel relieved. Then he start talking. "You got to understand. This ain't our first time fooling around, Momma. We always . . ." He let his words go and sigh. "Man, she wanted me. We was kissing and stuff and it just led—"

I block his voice out my ears, and I'm in Kenneth Gray place again. He telling me about how pretty my eyes is and putting his hands on my titties, and I'm liking it, and then I'm remembering what the Word say and I'm convicted cause it's wrong, and I'm slapping Kenneth Gray hands away and saying no, and he telling me to stop playing. He getting mad with me and beating me in my face with his fists. He gritting his teeth and saying, *I know you like it.* I'm screaming and crying and he tugging at my panties, trying to rip them off. And I'm trying to figure out how all his love turned to this. I'm trying to figure out what that mean.

And when I can hear Quinten again, I know.

He say, "She wanted me, Momma. I know when somebody want—"

I shake my head. "You ain't do *that,* Quinten," I whisper. "Not that. You ain't telling me you did *that,*" I whisper again. Cause I don't want to hear it. I don't want to know it. There got to be some type of explanation. Some type of way for him to still be who he always been.

He drop his eyes to the floor again, and I think about what made him.

I flirted with Kenneth Gray just like Don Earl girl been at Quinten. Was being fast and grown and wound up where I wound up. God come for us in the strangest ways. I lied to my momma face that day. Told her I was going to the library and put on fresh panties cause I knew what was in my heart. Kenneth Gray knew my heart too.

I shake my head and put my palms together, letting my index fingers fall against my lips. I start backing up, moving back toward the table. "Nuh-uh," I say. "You a good boy. You my son." I pat my chest with my open hand. "I raised you to do right things. I ain't raise you like *that.*"

His eyes still on the ground and that's fine by me. I don't want to see his face no more. I don't want to see what I know there.

I shake my head. I'm trying to understand all this, but processing it is hard. Quinten stayed on my breast till he was almost four. Would ask for it—just point to my blouse and ask for it anywhere. I nurtured him till he was old enough to stop on his own. I wanted to give him as much of me as his spirit needed to cancel out Kenneth

Gray. He didn't never once bite me. Was always so gentle. Didn't never just go for my breasts neither. Fore he could talk, he would point at my chest with a question in his eyes. After he could make sentences, he always asked like a gentleman. Always waited for a yes fore he moved in close to my body.

I nod my head and ask, "She said yes, not no, Quinten? That girl said yes?" I point my finger at him and say, "Say it right now. Say she said yes."

He don't say nothing. Just keep looking at the ground.

My face is hot and I feel tears behind my eye. "Nuh-uh." I take a few steps toward him, till I'm so close I know he feel my breathing on him. "Not my son. My son wait for yes."

He lift up his head, and his eyes look so lost and so young that I want him to look down again. His hand go to his face and he feeling at the scratches and the welts and I can see his hand start shaking and his mouth start trembling. That's when I see something pass through him. It's like a spirit, like the truth or something holy. Silent tears start rolling down his face and I know he know too.

He shake his head. "She didn't say yes," he whisper and then put his hands up in a surrender. "But I swear she wanted me, Momma. She liked it. She did. I—"

I slap him so hard my hand sting, and I shake it to get rid of the burn. And I feel all the pain on his face inside of me, but I don't look away or back down. "Don't say that!" I holler. "You can't say that," I say, softer. "You can't be that kind of person. You good. You kind. You you, Quinten. You mine." I'm talking fast and loud in his face. I can feel spit spraying from me and my mouth going dry. And then I just stop. Close my mouth so hard I'm scared I done broke my teeth.

I start stepping back again. Away from Quinten. Away from Kenneth Gray. I keep moving back until I touch the table and he look at me with his hand on his face and his eyes almost closed into slits.

When Kenneth Gray ripped inside of me that day, I went silent. My mouth was open but wasn't nothing coming out. I was scared my scream was stuck in my throat. I wanted to keep telling him no. I wanted to keep fighting, but I just lay there, with blood dripping down my face, looking dead in his eyes, through the one I could still see with, while he pounded hisself in and out of me. I kept telling myself to holler. *Holler, child.* But wouldn't nothing come out me. He was saying something. Maybe talking sexy to me. I can't remember. All I could hear was the sound of his body clapping against mine.

When Kenneth Gray was done with me that day, when he had got what he needed out of me, he yelled in my face, told me, "Get out." He was still on top of me when he said it. Still inside of me even. "Get out, you tease," he said and just put his whole hand over my face and pushed it to the side. And then he pressed his palm down on the side of my face and lifted his body off mine. "Nobody gone believe you if you tell them it was me. Nobody, you little whore," he said.

And I knew fore I left him cussing me that day that I wasn't never gone tell nobody it was Kenneth Gray that hurt me. I knew fore I left him that I ain't want nobody to know. But when I stepped out the front door of the house, his momma was coming up the walkway, carrying a bag of groceries. If I hadn't been standing there holding my eye, trying to stop the blood from pouring down my face, if my clothes hadn't been tore up and hanging off my body, if I hadn't been sniffing snot, tears, and blood, I guess she could've thought I was just some fast-tail gal leaving her house, leaving her son. But the way she stopped walking and her eyes widened, the way her mouth opened slack and she dropped her bag of groceries, I knew she knew what her son had done. So I just ran. Ran until I was far from that house, ran until Kenneth Gray and his momma was far behind me.

I lied and said a stranger attacked me on my way home from the library. Kenneth Gray momma ain't never come out bout what she saw. She ain't come forward at church a few weeks later when the pastor called for prayer over the pulpit bout my situation. Kenneth Gray ain't come to church with her no more after that, ain't teach Sunday school no more after that, and his momma ain't never even look in my direction. I was relieved when she stood up one Sunday many months later and asked for prayer for her son. When she said he was moving to Reno with her brother. That they had found him work there. I knew I'd never see him again and I was glad about that. I didn't never want nobody to find out it was him. I ain't want to be embarrassed—to be judged for being fast. Didn't want all the bad parts of what I did to come out.

And I ain't never imagined that I was raising somebody that would hear the nos and ignore them. That would hear the pain and hold hell in his eyes. I ain't never imagined that I was raising somebody that was gone make me look at the nos and wish to make them yeses.

But when I look up at him, it's Quinten, not Kenneth Gray. He still holding his hand on his cheek and now he sniffing like he used to when I'd get onto him when he was a little boy. I can tell it's gone be one of them cries that stay with him for a while. One of them where even at dinner he sniffling, even through his smile. He the baby I rocked to sleep at night and nothing I do can shake that from my mind.

I shift my weight and my hips hit the table and make it shake. That cause the Thunderbird bottle to wobble fore it roll off the table and make a thud on the carpet.

We both look down at the bottle and I imagine we having the same thought.

"Momma, I didn't mean to hurt her. I just thought . . ." he say and start crying like a baby.

He sound like he five again, trying to be strong and help me carry groceries across the field to our projects. He sound like he used to when one of the brown paper bags would tear up, and he was scared he was gone get in trouble for breaking my bottle of Thunderbird.

I shake my head and close my eye and think about when he was little and asked me who his daddy was. He smiled and said, "I'm glad you stayed, Momma," when I told him his daddy had run off and left us. I ain't never want him to know he come from something so ugly. He deserved to come from love, so I told him he did. Told him me and his daddy loved each other, but sometimes love run its course and you have to let it go.

Quinten was so sweet and precious, and his smile was so perfect. I never thought about him when I was telling them stories about love running its course. He was tiny and needed me so much. I think about his honey eyes when he volunteered to be Don Earl slave and how I needed him to be just that. I feel like with what I know, I should be able to let him go. I should turn him over to Don Earl the way I should've turned Kenneth Gray over. I think about going to the front door and opening it. Bout screaming, "He here. He here. Come get him. My son in here."

But I can't stop seeing his tiny body carrying our groceries. I can't stop hearing him call me Momma. I can't stop seeing his question mark eyes when he wanted my breasts. I can't stop seeing none of his little life inside my head.

I catch all my good memories of my baby and hold them until I open my eye again. Then I push myself away from the table and stand up straight and call out my child's name.

He try to pull hisself together, but he can't stop crying. Can't stop saying sorry over and over again.

"Pull yourself together, boy," I say through gritted teeth.

He wipe his eyes and try to stop crying. He heaving and it look like he struggling to breathe. I want to go to him. Be a comfort to him, like he done been to me so many times, but I got to make him know the way things is.

I point to the door he walked in through and say so low it's a whisper, "You gone say shit like that—say that girl ain't say yes—you get your ass on out of here."

He look back at the door, but he don't leave.

"Come here," I say, pointing to the floor in front of me.

He step slow and careful toward me till he almost right up in my face. I can tell he afraid. More afraid of me than he done ever had a reason to be.

I shake my head and open my arms to him and let him fold hisself into me. He start crying again and I can feel the wet of him on my shoulder.

"Shh," I say. "It's all right, baby. Momma here." I sigh and say, "Just don't never let me hear you say that, kay?" I peel him away from me and look up at him. Make sure he can see the tears in my eye. See how much this hurt me. I nod my head and sniff before saying, "She wanted you. You hear me? It was her idea. She said yes. She took your clothes off. She said yes all the way. You hear me?" I say.

I wipe away the tears from his face and he pull away from my touch.

He shake his head and say, "But Momma, I—"

Fore I got time to think about it, I slap him, and when his face turn from the one slap, I use my other hand to slap the other side, and then I ball up my fists and close my eyes. "Listen to me," I say through gritted teeth. "Listen," I repeat.

This time he don't cry. His mouth is closed, but I can tell he clinching his teeth cause the side of his jaw is twitching a little bit. I want to be gentle with him and promise him we'll get through this, but now ain't the time for that. I got to give him what he need.

I clutch his shoulders and shake them a little before I whisper, "Listen."

And I know I got his attention. He looking down at me with confusion and anger, or maybe it's fear in his eyes. And I'm looking up at him with all the words to keep him safe.

Contributors' Notes

Other Distinguished Mystery and
Suspense of 2023

Contributors' Notes

Megan Abbott is the Edgar Award–winning author of eleven crime novels, including *You Will Know Me, Give Me Your Hand,* and the *New York Times* bestseller *The Turnout,* the winner of the *Los Angeles Times* Book Prize. *Dare Me,* the series she adapted from her own novel, is streaming on Netflix. Her latest novel, *Beware the Woman,* is now in paperback.

• Joyce Carol Oates, the editor of the anthology, approached me about writing a story of "body horror." I was inspired by the real-life case of a so-called "murder house" in the Los Angeles area that's always haunted me—both the original crime and (even more so) the way the house itself seemed to have an enduring power. Many houses where crimes have occurred get saddled with the idea of a curse, but this house in particular remained a vital, living presence for decades, a place you might dare visit, peeking in its windows, but only at great risk, as if the house's evil were contagious. The story became a way to explore the way we project ourselves—our own anxieties, fears, shame, and guilt—onto these cursed places, giving them perpetual life, granting them endless power.

Frankie Y. Bailey is a professor in the School of Criminal Justice at the University at Albany. Her areas of research, writing, and teaching are crime history and crime and mass media/popular color. She has written two books about crime fiction, *Out of the Woodpile* (1991), about Black characters in crime fiction, and *African American Mystery Writers* (2009), examining the contributions of Black writers to the evolution of the genre. Bailey has been the coeditor of two local histories: one on Danville, Virginia, her hometown and the inspiration for "Gallagher" in her Lizzie Stuart series; and the other on Albany, New York, the real-life setting fictionalized in her Hannah McCabe series. She has also been the coeditor (with Steven Chermak) of a series of true-crime encyclopedias. Bailey is currently working on a book about gangster films that is a historical thriller set in 1939. She is also working on a book about dress, appearance, and criminal justice. Bailey is a past executive vice president of Mystery Writers of America and a past president of Sisters in Crime—National.

• When I was invited to contribute to *School of Hard Knox*, I decided I wanted to write a story set in the post–World War II era. Family life and the relationships of married couples after the war is a topic that I've been interested in for some time. I've been analyzing the depiction of marriage and family life in crime films of the 1940s and '50s. The "matter of trust" came to me as I was thinking about young wives and mothers during this era. Jo Radcliffe, the protagonist through whose eyes I tell a portion of the story, made her debut in *Ellery Queen's Mystery Magazine* in "The Singapore Sling Affair" (November/December 2017). That was followed by "Nighthawks," a story in *Midnight Hour* (2021), an anthology of crime fiction by writers of color edited by Abby L. Vandiver. Those two stories and the story in this book are set in Eudora, New York. Eudora is a fictional place, but it was inspired by real-life upstate New York villages. Jo is a former Army nurse, and she has come back to the house that her late great-aunt left her. The secret she mentions in this story is one that she discovered about her mother.

Barrett Bowlin is the author of the story collection, *Ghosts Caught on Film.* His essays and short fiction appear in places like *TriQuarterly, Barrelhouse, Ninth Letter, Waxwing, Salt Hill, Bayou,* and *The Saturday Evening Post,* and he's the winner of both the James Knudsen Prize for Fiction and the Bridge Eight Fiction Prize. An Arkansas expatriate, he now lives and teaches and rides trains in Massachusetts. News and links to his stories, essays, and articles can be found at barrettbowlin.com.

• Just north of the small city where I grew up in Arkansas, there was a highway interchange system that made a border of concrete around a few acres of land. That patch of green next to the highway was dense with trees, and, growing up, I always wondered if someone could live in there. Years later, I thought it might be fun to populate the space with bones and fruit trees and a feral child, and to make him a local boogeyman. I'm pretty sure this is how most of my stories come together, then: as piles of old images and memories, waiting to be stitched together like body parts, and for the right amperage to make them sit up and lurch forward.

Alyssa Cole is a *New York Times* and *USA Today* bestselling author of romance novels, thrillers, sci-fi, and more. Her debut thriller *When No One Is Watching* won the 2021 Edgar Award for Best Paperback Original, the Strand Critics Award for Best Debut, and is one of *Time*'s 100 Best Mystery and Thriller Books of All Time. She currently lives in France, and in her free time she can be found collecting cool rocks, walking in the woods (despite the objections of her overactive imagination), or watching k-dramas with her husband and their menagerie of pets.

• I held out on joining TikTok for a long time, but pandemic bore-dom and isolation eventually wore me down. One thing that intrigued me was the concept of "story time," where people share interesting, and often embellished, stories from their personal lives with an audience of total strangers. Another aspect that captured my interest was the rise of the "manosphere" and the platforming of misogynistic men in new and frightening ways.

I decided to tell the story of what happens when a young woman's viral "story time" reaches the wrong audience, using snippets of various social media platforms and emails instead of a character POV. By telling the story through technology that connects strangers, I hoped to show how social media can be used to amplify and coordinate harassment, but also how it can be harnessed to build community and protect others.

Tananarive Due (tah-nah-nah-REEVE doo) is an award-winning author who teaches Black Horror and Afrofuturism at UCLA.

A leading voice in Black speculative fiction for more than twenty years, Due has won an American Book Award, an NAACP Image Award, and a British Fantasy Award, and her writing has been included in best-of-the-year anthologies. Her books include *The Reformatory* (winner of a *Los Angeles Times* Book Prize and a *New York Times* Notable Book), *The Wishing Pool and Other Stories, Ghost Summer: Stories, My Soul to Keep,* and *The Good House.* She and her late mother, civil rights activist Patricia Stephens Due, coauthored *Freedom in the Family: A Mother-Daughter Memoir of the Fight for Civil Rights.*

She was an executive producer on Shudder's groundbreaking documen-tary *Horror Noire: A History of Black Horror.* She and her husband/collabora-tor, Steven Barnes, wrote "A Small Town" for Season 2 of Jordan Peele's *The Twilight Zone* on Paramount Plus, and two segments of Shudder's anthology film *Horror Noire.* They also cowrote their Black Horror graphic novel *The Keeper,* illustrated by Marco Finnegan. Due and Barnes cohost a podcast, "Lifewriting: Write for Your Life!" She and her husband live with their son, Jason.

• I published my second short story collection in 2023, *The Wishing Pool and Other Stories.* Most of the stories were reprints, but my editor asked me to write two new stories. After a busy year of deadlines for other anthol-ogies, I was running dry on story ideas, but I kept circling back to a strange fungus that had surprised me in the shower. Where had it come from? How had it grown so fast? I gnawed over the mysterious fungus creatively for weeks and decided to pair the phenomenon with a troubled protagonist hiding from her own complicity in breaking her daughter's arm. If a desperate character on the road encountered this fungus, what might it mean to her?

Since I'm primarily a horror writer, of course I wanted my fungus to have a supernatural connection as a message from another realm about a horrible event in the past. But all of my horror is character driven, so the most important piece was my protagonist's journey of introspection even as she begins to uncover clues that something very bad happened to another child in the Rumpus Room. Her search for clues about the potential death of a stranger mirrors her own inner search for accountability in what happened to her own daughter.

Abby Geni is the author of *The Last Animal, The Lightkeepers, The Wildlands,* and *The Body Farm.* Her books have been translated into seven languages and have won the Barnes & Noble Discover Award and the Chicago Review of Books Award, among other honors. Her short stories have won the Glimmer Train Fiction Open and the Chautauqua Prize and have been published or reprinted in *The Missouri Review, Epoch, New Stories from the Midwest,* and many other journals. Geni is a faculty member at StoryStudio Chicago and frequent visiting associate professor of Fiction at the University of Iowa Writers' Workshop. Her website is www.abbygeni.com.

• This story was a collision. Some stories are organic things, growing from one seed into a single theme. Others are delicately woven out of related threads. "The Body Farm" was made in the fiery crash of a dozen disconnected ideas. I was thinking about fairy tales, the metamorphic glory of insects, "The Cask of Amontillado," the limits (both logistical and logical) of law enforcement when it comes to stalking, a class I once took on child psychology, *And Then There Were None,* human decomposition research laboratories and the scientists who choose to work there, and a few personal obsessions I won't name. In theory, these things don't make sense together. But sometimes writing happens that way—the impact of ideas, an alchemical reaction, and the fusion of a new story.

Nils Gilbertson is a writer and attorney. He has lived in California, Washington, DC, and now resides in Texas with his wife, son, and German shorthaired pointer. Nils's short fiction has appeared in *Ellery Queen's Mystery Magazine, Rock and a Hard Place, Mystery Magazine, Guilty Crime Story Magazine, Cowboy Jamboree,* and others. His work has also appeared in a variety of anthologies, including *Prohibition Peepers, Mickey Finn: 21st Century Noir, Gone: An Anthology of Crime Stories,* and *More Groovy Gumshoes.* His story "Washed Up" was named a Distinguished Story in *The Best American Mystery and Suspense 2022.* You can find him online at nilsgilbertson.com.

• When esteemed editor Michael Bracken invited me to contribute to *Prohibition Peepers,* an anthology of prohibition-era private eye stories, my first thought was: What do I know about the 1920s? Writing a story set in the distant past seemed like a daunting task. Even after researching the era, I grappled with how to write something authentic—something that wasn't an imitation.

So, I focused on a character. Pat Boyle is a reflective yet ruthless PI who believes that the fight against prohibition is a fight for the human spirit. I then placed this peculiar PI in 1920's Washington, DC, where he is surrounded by warring political factions. From there, the plot materialized and new characters were born.

If you enjoy "Lovely and Useless Things," I encourage you to pick up a copy of the *Prohibition Peepers* anthology. While it was a change of pace to write a story set in the past, I am grateful for the opportunity. A central component of being a writer is exploring other people, other points of view, other worlds. "Lovely and Useless Things" allowed me to do just that.

Jenny, **Diana Gould**'s first feature, was written while she was still in film school. She went on to write features, episodes, pilots, mini-series, and movies for television. She was writer/producer on *Dynasty, Knots Landing, Kay O'Brien,* and *Berrenger's,* the latter of which she also created. She served on the board of the Writers Guild, and founded and was first chairperson of its groundbreaking Women's Committee. Subsequently, she received an MFA in fiction from the Bennington Writers Program. Her first novel, *Coldwater* (Los Angeles: Rare Bird Books, 2013) won the Ben Franklin Award Silver Medal from the Independent Book Publishers Association for Best First Novel and was a finalist for Best Mystery from Foreward Reviews. She's had essays published in *Still, in the City* (Skyhorse, September 11, 2018) and *Hollywood vs. the Author* (Rare Bird Books, A Barnacle Book, November 13, 2018). A graduate of the Community Dharma Leader program at Spirit Rock Meditation Center and of the Buddhist Chaplaincy Training at Sati Center, she was awarded Volunteer of the Year by both Vitas Hospice and the Motion Picture Community Fund. She is a senior teacher at InsightLA, a mindfulness meditation center in Los Angeles.

• Perhaps the fact that my first feature, *Jenny,* was rewritten to its detriment by the director provided the kernel of resentment that led, many years later, to the writing of "*Possessory Credit.*" What better motive for murder than the disparity between the respect, money, and power given to directors over writers? When, as a very young woman inspired by the women's movement, I tried to explain to the Board of the Writers Guild the need for a Women's Committee to combat sexism, a seasoned veteran said, "Writers are the women of the industry." Writers are as replaceable as pencils. It is particularly galling to me that a feature film, which reflects the work of so many artists and craftspeople, can be referred to as "a film by . . ." one person. "*Possessory Credit*" is the *cri du coeur* coming from my thirty-year career as a writer for film and television.

Jordan Harper is the Edgar Award–winning author of *She Rides Shotgun, The Last King of California, Everybody Knows,* and the short story collection *Love and Other Wounds.* He was born and educated in Missouri. He now lives in Los Angeles, where he works as a writer and producer for television.

• As a very personal and very fictionalized story of my teenage life, "My Savage Year" is a story I have been trying to tell in one form or another for decades. It has always felt too large to properly yank out of my skull. When William Boyle asked me to submit a story for the *Southwest Review* noir issue, I took it as a challenge to finally force this thing onto paper. It turns out compressing it down to a short story, leaving so much unsaid, was the key to unlodging it from me. Although the story still haunts me.

Karen Harrington is a freelance writer and author from Texas. Her short work has appeared in *Mystery Tribune, Alfred Hitchcock's Mystery Magazine,* and *Ellery Queen's Mystery Magazine,* where she won the 2021 Ellery Queen Mystery Magazine Readers Choice Award for "Boo Radley College Prep." She also won the 2023 Derringer Award for Flash Fiction. She has authored four novels, including *Sure Signs of Crazy* (Little, Brown), a young adult companion novel to her mystery debut, *Janeology* (Shotgun Honey). She lives in Plano, Texas, with her husband, daughters, and socially awkward dog. Say hello at www.karenharringtonbooks.com.

• First I had the idea of the Remedy Clinic, a place where you could go to solve your problems or disputes in unorthodox ways. With a vision toward creating a book of linked stories, I began writing a series of tales with different characters employing the clinic. The first published story in this series is "Would You Like a Remedy?" which appeared in the March/April 2023 issue of *Alfred Hitchcock's Mystery Magazine.* Then came the idea about author feuds, which I find endlessly compelling. Enter, the sister/author clients of the Remedy Clinic in "The Mysterious Disappearance of Jason Whetstone." I wanted to explore the lengths someone would go to with their need to be right, particularly about a childhood memory. I've always loved Graham Greene's quote "Childhood is a writer's bank balance." To prove Greene's point, I will only add that I recall an absurd ground beef story differently from my siblings. It was a lot of fun to write this short story as an in-depth investigative piece, but the truth is, I originally imagined *Dateline*'s Keith Morrison narrating the story like a true crime podcast. That proved to be a fun way to write the first draft. (Or *was* it?) I'm honored to have it appear in this anthology. My huge thanks and great love to Barb Goffman, the editor of *Reckless in Texas,* where the story first appeared.

Gar Anthony Haywood is the Shamus and Anthony Awards–winning author of fourteen novels and dozens of short stories. His crime fiction includes the Aaron Gunner private eye series and Joe and Dottie Louder-milk mysteries. His short fiction has been included in the *Best American Mystery Stories* anthologies and will also appear in an upcoming story col-lection from Marvel entitled *Captain America: The Shield of Sam Wilson*. His most recent novel, *In Things Unseen*, was published by Slant Books in December 2022 and would be best described as a thriller for fans of non-traditional Christian fiction.

• Lawrence Block always comes up with great themes for his anthologies, so when he invited me to contribute a story to his latest, *Playing Games*, I knew exactly what game I wanted to focus on: Milton Bradley's Mouse Trap. It's an old childhood favorite, colorful and engaging, and the idea of constructing a Rube Goldberg machine as gameplay progresses has always struck me as pure genius. What game could be better suited to a mystery? Will our victim fall into the trap set for him (or her) or not? Will the complex machine built to ensnare our intended victim even work? The only way to find out is to set the cheese out for the mouse and watch what happens . . .

Years back, **Toni LP Kelner**'s editor at Zebra Books said he was editing a Christmas anthology and said, "You write short stories, don't you?" In fact she'd never written a publishable story before, but she faked it well enough that she did indeed appear in that anthology. Since then, she's published more than thirty short stories in various anthologies and mag-azines. In addition to her short work, Kelner is the author of eight Laura Fleming mystery novels and three "Where are they now?" mysteries, and she is a coeditor of seven urban fantasy anthologies. Under her pen name Leigh Perry, she's published six Family Skeleton novels and is working on a seventh. She's won the Agatha Award and an RT BookClub Lifetime Achievement Award, and she has been nominated multiple times for the Anthony, the Macavity, and the Derringer. No matter what you call her, she lives north of Boston with fellow writer Stephen P. Kelner Jr., their two daughters, and an ever-increasing number of books. Forthcoming from Crippen & Landru Publishers is *The Skeleton Rides a Horse and Other Stories*, a collection of short stories by both Kelner and Perry.

• I spend a ludicrous amount of time on the social media platform Reddit reading stories about entitled parents, bridezillas, nosy neighbors, intrusive homeowner associations, obnoxious ex significant others, seat stealers, and so on. Of course, a lot of the posts are complete fiction, but I still feel bad for these people, and I'm particularly sympathetic to women with dreadful mothers-in-law. (Maybe it's because my own mother-in-law is quite wonderful.) As any writer knows, where there are family conflicts, there are stories to be mined, and I started thinking about what it would be like to be stalked by a bad mother-in-law who was trying to take my baby, and how I would defend myself. "Baby Trap" is the result.

Nick Kolakowski is the author of several crime novels, including the recent *Payback is Forever* (Shotgun Honey). His short stories and nonfiction essays have appeared in various anthologies and magazines, including *CrimeReads, Noir City* (the magazine of the Film Noir Foundation), *Mystery Weekly, Mystery Tribune, Rock and a Hard Place*, and more. He lives and writes in New York City.

• I spent the summer of 2020 in a state of blind rage about the state of the world. Between police brutality, COVID, and the election, it felt like everything was coming apart at the seams. I wanted to channel my dark energy into a story, and I thought a tale of a cop ensnared and corrupted amidst a city on fire would be the right vehicle. "Scorpions" tries to tackle a lot of questions I ask myself constantly, but I'm not sure it provides any answers.

Bobby Mathews is a novelist, short story writer, and journalist based in Birmingham, Alabama. He's won several awards and lost even more. His books include the novels *Living the Gimmick* and *Magic City Blues*, and a short story collection, *Negative Tilt*. When Bobby isn't writing, he's probably coaching baseball or napping.

• I always start with character. Cullen is named for infamous Texas outlaw Cullen Baker, and in my mind I pictured the character as a spider hanging above this Old West town—not quite a ghost town, but not quite *not* a ghost town, either. He has the single suit, which he only wears on his birthday, or to his funeral. What happens to him? Why does it happen? I don't outline, so the story really is an exploration of me discovering who this character is and why he holds such sway over his surroundings. Oh, and I have to point out that I was also inspired by the song "The Last Gunfighter" by Guy Clark.

Stanton McCaffery is a writer and nonprofit communications professional from central New Jersey. His short stories have been featured in *Dark Yonder, Mystery Magazine, Guilty, Mystery Tribune, Vautrin, Shotgun Honey*, and more. He has published two novels: *Into the Ocean* and *Neighborhood of Dead Ends*. He is also the cofounder and editor-in-chief of Rock and a Hard Place Press.

• This story was written based on an open call to an anthology that was never published. The anthology asked for stories of death row inmates told from their perspective. I researched the story by watching YouTube videos of interviews with death row inmates. I also channeled some of the experiences I have heard from childhood friends who had difficult relationships with their families and fell on hard times. The thoughts on religion and birds are my own.

Shannon Taft is an attorney from Washington, DC. Her recent short works include "The Codicil" in *Fantastic Detectives,* "Research" in *Hook, Line and Sinker,* "Dead Drop" in *On Spec* magazine, "Race to the Bottom" in *Three Strikes—You're Dead,* and the Derringer Award Finalist for "A Tail of Justice" in *Black Cat Weekly #114.*

• "Monster" began for me with the random thought that most murder mysteries have a corpse who was widely hated in life. With so many people who wanted the victim dead, the challenge for the detective (and the reader) is to discern which character gave in to temptation and did the deed. I wanted to see what it would look like if I turned that on its head and presented a murder victim who was widely loved and had not a single enemy. This led me to ponder many types of love and the forms it takes in our society. In the swirling mix about love of parents, of spouses, of children, and of self, the story snapped into place.

Mary Thorson lives and writes in Milwaukee, Wisconsin. She received her BA in Creative Writing from the University of Wisconsin-Milwaukee and her MFA from Pacific University in Oregon. Her stories have appeared in the *Los Angeles Review, Milwaukee Noir, Worcester Review, Rock and a Hard Place,* and *Tough,* among others. Her work has been nominated for *Best American Short Stories, Best American Mystery,* a Derringer, and a Pushcart Prize. She hangs out with her two feisty daughters, the best husband, and a mid dog named Pam when she isn't teaching high school English, reading, or writing ghost stories. She is represented by Lori Galvin at Aevitas Creative Management. She is currently working on a novel.

• This story was written after I heard about a small religious cult in 1970s rural America. I was fascinated by what happens to the followers after they leave—the ones who aren't dead or in jail. What happens when they go back home? More so, I loved the idea of experiencing a stranger in your own home in the shape of someone you know intimately, like your own daughter. They look like the child you made and raised and loved, but something inside of them has shifted so fundamentally that it's all wrong. They've shed their old skin and what's there now is ugly.

Rebecca Turkewitz is a writer and high school English teacher living in Portland, Maine. She is the author of the story collection *Here in the Night* (2023). Her fiction and humor writing have appeared in *Alaska Quarterly Review, The Normal School, The Masters Review, Chicago Quarterly Review, Electric Literature, The New Yorker's Daily Shouts,* and elsewhere. She holds an MFA in fiction from The Ohio State University.

• The best writing advice I ever received—from my first college creative writing professor—was to write the stories I'd be most excited to read. "Sarah Lane's School for Girls" is a story I'd find it hard to resist as a reader: A boarding school murder mystery? An all-girls dormitory in the middle of the New England woods? The thorny dynamics of a fraught friendship? Set in the '90s? All these elements delight me, and I think I mostly just got out of my own way to write it.

Once I had the setting and the premise and a clear sense of the narrator's voice, I drove toward the questions that were worrying me at the time: How can we trust our memories? How do we build an organizing narrative about our own lives when we are all, to some degree, unreliable narrators? How do the stories we tell ourselves shape the way we move through and understand the world? Why do we want the things that we want?

Lisa Unger is the *New York Times* and international bestselling author of twenty-one novels, including *The New Couple in 5B*. With books published in thirty-three languages and millions of copies sold worldwide, she is regarded as a master of suspense. She has been nominated for, or won, numerous awards including the Strand Critics, Audie, Hammett, Macavity, ITW Thriller, and Goodreads Choice. In 2019, she received two Edgar Award nominations in the same year. Her nonfiction has appeared in the *New York Times, Wall Street Journal, Daily Telegraph,* NPR, and *Travel + Leisure.*

• In "Unknown Caller," I was interested in exploring the concept of heroism, particularly the idea of "everyday heroes" who often go unnoticed. In my area, we are fortunate to have the Crisis Center of Tampa Bay, which offers a lifeline to people struggling to manage any number of challenges. The Crisis Center was kind enough to open their doors to me for research. I was deeply moved by the people who devote their lives to answering when someone calls to say "I need help." What drives people to offer support to a voice on the phone? What makes someone a hero? Like so much in life, the answers are rarely black and white. But those are the questions at the heart of "Unknown Caller."

LaToya Watkins's writing has appeared in *A Public Space, The Sun, McSweeney's, Kenyon Review,* and elsewhere. She has received grants, scholarships, and fellowships from the Camargo Foundation, MacDowell, Yaddo, and Hedgebrook. Her latest book is *Holler, Child: Stories,* which was longlisted for the National Book Award for Fiction.

• The idea for "Holler, Child" came to me while visiting college campuses with my daughters during their last year of high school. At one of the universities, we walked through the dining hall and I saw a woman who inspired the character who later became Quinten's mother. She was unsmiling and moved quickly. As soon as her line was empty, she left. I knew there was a story there.

Other Distinguished Mystery and Suspense of 2023

Zach Swiss
  Something's Happened. *Pembroke*
Scott Von Doviak
  Most Likely to Succeed. *The One Percent*
Joseph S. Walker.
  Off the Shelf. *Mickey Finn*, Vol. 4

Andrew Welsh-Higgins
  Wonder Falls. *Mystery Tribune*
L. A. Wilson Jr.
  Something Blue. *Ellery Queen's Mystery Magazine*, May/June
Paul Yoon
  Valley of the Moon. *The New Yorker*, July 3, 2023

ABOUT

MARINER BOOKS

MARINER BOOKS traces its beginnings to 1832 when William Ticknor cofounded the Old Corner Bookstore in Boston, from which he would run the legendary firm Ticknor and Fields, publisher of Ralph Waldo Emerson, Harriet Beecher Stowe, Nathaniel Hawthorne, and Henry David Thoreau. Following Ticknor's death, Henry Oscar Houghton acquired Ticknor and Fields and, in 1880, formed Houghton Mifflin, which later merged with venerable Harcourt Publishing to form Houghton Mifflin Harcourt. Harper-Collins purchased HMH's trade publishing business in 2021 and reestablished their storied lists and editorial team under the name Mariner Books.

Uniting the legacies of Houghton Mifflin, Harcourt Brace, and Ticknor and Fields, Mariner Books continues one of the great traditions in American bookselling. Our imprints have introduced an incomparable roster of enduring classics, including Hawthorne's *The Scarlet Letter,* Thoreau's *Walden,* Willa Cather's *O Pioneers!,* Virginia Woolf's *To the Lighthouse,* W.E.B. Du Bois's *Black Reconstruction,* J.R.R. Tolkien's *The Lord of the Rings,* Carson McCullers's *The Heart Is a Lonely Hunter,* Ann Petry's *The Narrows,* George Orwell's *Animal Farm* and *Nineteen Eighty-Four,* Rachel Carson's *Silent Spring,* Margaret Walker's *Jubilee,* Italo Calvino's *Invisible Cities,* Alice Walker's *The Color Purple,* Margaret Atwood's *The Handmaid's Tale,* Tim O'Brien's *The Things They Carried,* Philip Roth's *The Plot Against America,* Jhumpa Lahiri's *Interpreter of Maladies,* and many others. Today Mariner Books remains proudly committed to the craft of fine publishing established nearly two centuries ago at the Old Corner Bookstore.

EXPLORE THE REST
OF THE SERIES!